Blood
ON THE
BADGE

D1452749

JOHN GOOD

outskirts
press

I thought I had written a pretty solid crime novel for my first one. Then I shared it with you to review based on your expertise in the world of journalism. After you read it and we met your insight and notes were invaluable. Susy Schultz thank you for your passion and fire and making Blood on The Badge something I've never been prouder of.

CHAPTER 1

Matt O'Neil watched the light mist form on the windshield of his Ford Crown Victoria squad car and was happy the shift was almost over.

It had been the kind of midnight shift all cops hate.

This was a typical March night in the Midwest.

Temperatures were in the mid-thirties and a persistent light rain fell throughout the shift. Light rain was one of a cop's worst enemies.

Against a heavy rain, you had the warmth of the traditional Blauer, long neon raincoat, with hat.

Frigid cold, light weight Under Armour, both for the legs and chest, along with North Face glove liners.

But this type of rain just seemed to slowly seep through your clothes and gave you a shiver every now and then.

The rookie, T.C. Chambers, seemed to be having the biggest problem with the cold and couldn't put enough layers on. Matt figured when you spend most of your life in Berkley, California and you have never seen snow, or been in the Midwest, as T.C. has, it's a whole new experience for you.

In Matt's ten months on the street, with the other rookies, this had easily been the longest and slowest night they had ever gone through.

A couple of minor accidents at the start of the shift and a domestic dispute over on Elm Street involving those wacky Pullmans again, with no one getting pinched. As in the past, old man Pullman came home drunk and began cursing his wife out when she tried to put him to bed. Since Matt was the primary on the call and handled the paperwork, he found when he checked computer-aided dispatch, the neighbors had called in ten of the twelve previous domestics involving the Pullmans, due to all the yelling and swearing coming from 616 Elm Street.

Matt overheard Megan O'Brien talking to Mrs. Pullman and pleading with her to leave Mr. Pullman, but Mrs. Pullman responded with: "Nope, for better or for worse, I still love him deep down and will be there for him until the day we die."

Sgt. Barton had been right again.

Ten guys working the street meant for this kind of night. Every zone covered with five roving cars. Yet, if we were at minimum manpower due to sick leave, training, or vacations, we would be going from call to call and praying for help.

It didn't take long for Matt to realize if he needed the proper answer to a problem, or just good advice, to seek out Sgt. Barton.

Lt. Wayne was the complete opposite and didn't know shit about the street. No one on the shift counted on him for a correct answer.

Matt was sure that every department had their share of Lt. Wayne's.

"Man," Matt thought to himself. He had seen it in the service but thought it would be different in police work. Guys who knew just who to blow to get them up the career ladder. The word in the locker room from Matt's FTO had been just that. Fix a few computer problems, help a couple of big shots out, and next thing you know, you're going places.

In the few kick-ass fights or disturbance calls Matt had responded, Lt. Wayne was always the last to show up—if he even showed up at all. Matt figured part of it was due to Lt. Wayne's size and age. Lt. Wayne couldn't weigh more than 160 pounds and was barely over 5'9".

Just the opposite of Sgt. Barton, in every possible category.

Sgt. Reginald Barton was one of the strongest men Matt had ever met. At 6'2" and guessing an easy 235 pounds, Sgt. Barton was a work-out fiend. Whether at the Lifetime Fitness in Skokie, or after work in the department exercise room, Sgt. Barton could be seen every day doing either cardio or lifting. The word from the veterans on the department had been Sgt Barton got his stripes due to being African American, with the old chief wanting to show the Village Manager, Greenfield had a diversified Police Department.

"Bullshit," Matt found himself blurting out loud. This was a guy who was first on all of the hot calls, didn't panic, never over reacted, and came to work every day ready to get the job done.

Hard to believe Matt and the other rookies Megan, Chris, Ron, T.C., Javier, and Marc had all formed their own opinions about everyone on the shift.

Matt looked out his driver's side window and caught a glimpse of himself in the reflection of Kalom's Pharmacy window and a small smile crossed his face.

Matt looked good in his Greenfield black leather jacket, and he knew he had finally found a home. Only two more months and probation would be over for him and his fellow rookies. They would then be free to solve all of Greenfield's crime problems, without having to worry about being fired.

Yes, the citizens of Greenfield would be in for some major arrests from Matt and his crew.

Well, those arrests would have to wait another day Matt thought as he glanced at his Stauer, Recon Tritium Watch. It showed 0512, and all Matt could think about was a hot cup of decaf coffee and some pecan pancakes, at Denny's with Chris.

Afterwards, they would both check their beats one last time for any signs of damage they might have missed during the shift, refuel their squads, and head in.

Matt knew his wife, Kelly, had reminded him to get some milk from 7-11 on his way home, so he wrote a note to himself and placed it in his right pants pocket.

Tucked under the overhang of Kalom's Pharmacy, Matt's cruiser was out of sight from the public.

The intersection of Greenfield Road at Waukegan Road was only 50 to 60 feet in front of him, and Matt realized this would be a great spot in the future to run radar, or at the very least, get a few red-light violators. With his head tucked slightly back against the headrest, he watched a vehicle slowly go through a red light.

A Ford Bronco, white in color, with some good body damage on the driver's side rear, and a faded White Sox sticker, in the left rear window.

Matt decided the pecan pancakes would take the place of one more red-light violator, on this chilly morning.

"God, it was quiet," he thought.

Between Northbrook and Greenfield, not one officer had been on the radio for over two hours.

"Greenfield 320," Chris Mills called out a traffic stop.

"Go ahead," Greenfield radio dispatcher, Karen Jenkins, answered.

Chris Mills' voice came back on the radio: "Moody and First on a blue Buick, Illinois Registration Victor, Ida, King 23 and no back." Karen Jenkins repeated verbatim Chris Mills' last sentence.

"Shit," Matt said out loud. Lt. Wayne would kill Chris if he was late for Denny's. Matt knew one of the things Lt. Wayne was a stickler for, was punctuality, when it came time to eat.

As Matt slowly closed his eyes and dreamed of hot food, his world was suddenly shattered by a strange, hysterical, voice coming over his Motorola radio. "Help, help, can anyone hear me," yelled a hysterical woman, into the car's microphone. "There's an officer here and he's hurt bad, I think."

"Helllllllp me," she screamed.

Coffee cups and monster energy drink cans, went flying out of squad car windows, for both Northbrook and Greenfield Police cars.

Sgt. Barton was getting out of his unmarked, Dodge Challenger, in the parking lot of the Police Station, when he jumped back in.

Marc Dombrowski, pulled out a wad of money, and threw it on the table at Denny's, as he watched Ron Thomas head out the front door, and run as fast as he could, to his black and white squad car.

T. C. Chambers was at the gas pumps and was half way through filling his squad, as the desperate cries for help came over the shoulder mic of his Motorola radio. Sprays of gasoline filled the pavement, as T.C. pulled the nozzle from the squad and threw it on the ground.

Javier Ortego was home sleeping, since it was his regularly scheduled day off.

He would tell the shift later, at exactly 0515 hours, he was snapped out of his sleep, by the first migraine headache, of his young life.

Dispatcher Eddie Heaviland had just entered the radio room of the Greenfield Police Station, fresh after his breakfast at Dunkin Donuts. He looked at Karen Jenkins and realized something horrible had just happened.

"Northbrook to Greenfield?" Dispatcher Susan Ellis, of the Northbrook Police Department, asked on the Intercom.

"Go Northbrook," Eddie Heaviland answered.

"Our cars 37 and 40 are ready to respond," Ellis said.

Karen answered, "It's on the far eastern part," is all she could get out, before the darkened dispatch center, became filled with the loud beeping noise, of an officer's portable radio emergency ID.

Karen and Eddie quickly glanced at each other, before turning to their respective radio consoles, but both already knew what numbers would be flashing in front of their eyes.

As calmly as she could, with her right hand noticeably shaking, Karen Jenkins pressed her microphone button and stated, "All Greenfield units, Emergency ID for portable radio 320, Officer Mills has been activated, last known location, First and Moody on a traffic stop. Officer Mills are you okay?"

To every Greenfield and Northbrook officer, the sound of silence seemed to hang in the air for a minute, instead of only a few seconds.

"Help me," a soft voice slowly came over everyone's radio, with the same female voice from before, still screaming loudly in the background.

Every Greenfield officer recognized the voice, to be of Chris Mills and sped up a few MPHs faster.

At the sound of the first woman's words on the radio, Matt O Neil's head had sprung off the headrest.

Instinctively, his right hand had shifted the squad car from park to drive and he came flying out of Kalom's Pharmacy parking lot. Fortunately, due to the hour of the day, there was minimal traffic on the street.

Matt figured he was a good two to three minutes away on dry pavement, five or six because of the rain. He slowly mouthed the words to a prayer, as his wailing sirens started to make his head throb.

When Matt finally got close to the intersection of First and Moody Streets, his eyes grew wide as he saw Chris Mills lying flat on his back, almost directly in the middle of the intersection. Matt parked his squad car at a 45-degree angle, next to the right side of Chris' body, in an effort to protect Chris and the scene.

As Matt approached Chris, he could see Chris' left leg bent underneath him at a strange angle. Chris Mills' head was lying in the only puddle of water, on the damp pavement of Moody Street and blood was slowly dripping out of the right corner of his mouth.

Matt yelled, "10-23, send a damn ambulance," over his portable radio, as he sat down on the wet pavement. The sound of multiple sirens filled the air, in the far distance.

Both of their eyes met and Matt tried to hold back the tears, he could feel forming.

"Cold, Matt," Chris mumbled and blood started to ooze from both of his nostrils, as well as his right ear. Matt quickly took off his leather jacket and used it to cover Chris' chest.

Matt was so focused on doing this, when the portable radio spoke just over his head, he nearly jumped out of his skin.

Looking up, Matt could see Officer Megan O'Brien standing behind, but directly over both him and Chris.

"Megan, quick, lift his feet," Matt yelled as he got to his knees supporting Chris' head.

"No Matt," Megan answered, before firmly saying, "You need to wait for the ambulance."

But Matt knew a couple of things.

Chris Mills' injuries looked severe, and even though he was fighting it, Chris was going into shock. Secondly, Matt had lost a couple of men in Afghanistan with lesser injuries, who died only because they didn't get medical attention in time and he wasn't going to let that happen to his buddy. Last, due to the early morning hour, the Greenfield ambulance was still a good 3 to 4 minutes out and every second wasted, could result in Chris Mills living or dying.

For the first time during the entire shift, the light rain ended and thunder filled the skies. A persistent, heavier rain began to fall.

As Matt got to his feet, he placed both of his arms under Chris' shoulders and started to drag him to his squad car. The wet pavement, combined with all of Chris' 260 pounds, with an additional 20 pounds in duty gear, made Matt fall flat on his butt, after only three backward steps.

"Greenfield 327 and all responding units: Greenfield Ambulance 6 just called in reporting they are stopped by a train in the downtown station. Unknown ETA to your location," Karen Jenkins stated in a slightly quivering voice.

As Matt sat there stunned, he was even more surprised to see Megan O'Brien, suddenly come flying toward him and Chris.

Sgt. Barton had slightly pushed Megan out of the way, and without saying a word, had picked up both of Chris Mills' legs.

Matt continued to support Chris' head and shoulders, and in doing so, slowly got to his feet.

In five steps, they had reached the rear door of Matt's squad car.

"Come this way O'Neil," Sgt. Barton commanded. Matt made a 180-degree turn, which placed Sgt. Barton next to the rear passenger door of Matt's squad car.

Sgt. Barton placed both of Chris Mills' legs on the inside of his left forearm and used the side of Matt's squad car for additional support, of Chris' legs. With his right hand, Sgt. Barton quickly swung open the rear passenger door. Sgt. Barton placed both of Chris' legs on the plastic back seat of the car and changed positions with Matt, who proceeded to get into the back seat of the car.

With Matt seated, Sgt. Barton brought the upper half of Chris's body to Matt, until Chris' head was resting in Matt's lap. Sgt. Barton proceeded to close the rear passenger door carefully and Matt leaned his entire body against the door, for additional support.

Sgt. Barton, then ran around the rear of the squad car and got inside, behind the wheel.

Matt had left the engine running, when he first arrived at the scene. Sgt. Barton put the car in drive and the Ford Crown Victoria sped off.

"Greenfield 317," Sgt. Barton yelled into the microphone.

"Greenfield 317 go," Eddie Heaviland responded.

"Call Lutheran Family Center Hospital, and let them know O'Neil and I are coming to their location with Chris Mills, and you can cancel Ambulance 6."

"10-4," Eddie Heaviland responded.

Sgt. Barton was ready to start assigning officers from the shift their new duties, but through the wipers of his squad car, he saw Lt. Wayne pass him in the opposite direction, driving to the accident scene.

Lt. Wayne was traveling at least 5 MPHs under the posted speed limit of 35 and had both hands clasped to the steering wheel.

Sgt. Barton placed the microphone back into its slot, and concentrated on getting Chris Mills to Lutheran Family Center Hospital, as quickly, but safely, as possible. It was now in the hands of Lt. Wayne to handle the accident scene.

Lutheran Family Center Hospital, is located in Park Ridge and for Sgt. Barton to reach it, he would have to get on Dempster Street.

Dempster Street was one of the busiest in the Northwest Suburbs, due to it being adjacent to I-294 and the Hospital, being one of the last Trauma Centers, still open.

At this time of day, Dempster Street would just be starting to get crowded, with tired motorists on their way to work.

Meanwhile, Matt had wedged himself into the rear door pretty well and had Chris' head secured firmly in his lap.

"Matt," Chris said, and a little more blood flowed from both corners of his mouth.

"Shh, don't talk Chris, we're almost there," Matt lied. He reached into his pants pocket and pulled out the only piece of paper he had in there, the note reminding him to bring home milk for Kelly.

Gently, Matt used his right hand to wipe both corners of Chris's mouth, until the note was soaked in blood. When he couldn't use the note anymore, Matt simply dropped it on the floor of the backseat of the squad car, but never moved his hands away from Chris' head.

Matt looked up to see where they were and noticed the lights of a McDonalds. "Chris, we're at Dempster and Milwaukee buddy," Matt said. "C'mon, just hang in there, you can make it."

Matt noticed that Chris was having difficulty breathing, and gently lifted his head, to make it easier.

In the process of doing so, Matt noticed Chris' Glock 22 Gen 4 and Bianchi Holster were gone.

The sheer force of the impact, or a piece of the offending vehicle, had ripped both of these items off the left side of his gun belt.

"Damn," Sgt. Barton blurted out, and again Matt picked his head up to see a flood of red and blue mars lights flashing, at the intersection of Dempster Street and Greenwood Road.

Four, Cook County Sheriff's police cars, had blocked the entire intersection, allowing Sgt. Barton to fly through the intersection and save valuable time.

With the sharpest right turn of the entire trip, Sgt. Barton avoided a parked ambulance and pulled up to a crowd of doctors and nurses, standing at the emergency room doors, of the hospital.

There were so many of them, a couple of the doctors were standing in the rain, which had now slowed to a light drizzle.

"Chris, we made it," Matt yelled, as he turned to look at Chris.

With one final breath, Chris smiled at Matt and slowly turned his head.

"Noooooo," Matt screamed, but the doctors and nurses who would now fight to bring Chris Mills back to life, drowned Matt's cries out.

_____

Within seconds, Chris Mills was on a gurney and being wheeled through the emergency room doors.

Sgt. Barton drove the squad car down to a parking spot reserved for police cars; whose officers would usually come to Lutheran Family Center Hospital, to take initial reports. These reports often varied from sexual assault victims, who had come to the hospital, in a state of shock, not knowing if they even wanted a police officer involved, to parents who had abused their children. These parents often went to a hospital away from where they lived, after the second or third time they abused their kids, in hopes the doctors or nurses would buy their story of how little Mary or Johnny got that black and blue mark on their arm, or that burn on their body.

As Sgt. Barton turned off the squad car, he made a mental note to have a formal letter written by the Greenfield Chief, to the Cook County Sheriff, thanking them for their assistance, in hopefully saving the life of Officer Chris Mills.

Sgt. Barton then came around to the rear door of the squad car and, upon opening it, found Matt still slumped in the back seat, covered in Chris Mills' blood.

"O'Neil, you hurt anywhere?" Sgt. Barton asked.

Matt sat there, stunned at what he had witnessed.

Matt O'Neil was no stranger to death and had seen men and women die before.

But that was in an unannounced war, fought for oil, and they were soldiers.

Soldiers had hoped, but in the back of their minds knew, they could die at any time and in any place, while serving their country.

Hell, five of Matt's men had died going down in a MC-130 Combat Talon, when it hit a mountain top, coming in for a night landing.

This was so different in so many ways.

Critically injured, standing next to a stopped car, at 0500 hours, in tiny Greenfield, Illinois. It just made no sense whatsoever.

Their first instructor, in the firearms retention portion, at the Illinois Law Enforcement Training Center, had said one of their classmates would not be at their 20-year reunion, due to a serious injury or death.

Matt never dreamed in a thousand years, it would be a Greenfield cop, and one of his best friends.

"O'Neil, I'm talking to you," Sgt. Barton barked again.

"No sarge, I'm okay," Matt responded.

"Then let's go," Sgt. Barton said, and escorted Matt O'Neil for the first time in his career, through the emergency room doors, of Lutheran Family Center Hospital.

CHAPTER 2

"**H**oney, it's 9 o'clock, and I need to take you home and get you to bed," Kelly O'Neil says softly to her husband Matt. He nods his head slowly yes, but he cannot manage to get up from Chris Mills' side.

Chief Fitzsimons has just left, and the only three people in the room are Chris Mills, Matt, and Kelly.

Unable to stop himself, Matt O'Neil replays in his mind, for the 30th time this morning, the sight that hit Sgt. Barton and him as they walked through the emergency room doors, roughly three hours earlier.

It wasn't hard to figure where they had taken Chris Mills. Due to the time of day, there were only two other patients in the entire ER.

In the biggest ER, Matt O'Neil had ever been in, a team of doctors and nurses worked feverishly on Chris Mills. When Matt O'Neil and Sgt. Barton got close enough to the table Chris Mills was laying on, neither could see a thing, due to the table being at least two deep, in hospital personnel.

Matt and Sgt. Barton stood there in silence and watched a series of IVs being hooked up to Chris Mills' massive arms.

Matt heard a doctor yell "more light!" Matt followed the light as it moved across the room and flickered off two, black colored, Greenfield Police Department leather jackets, laying in the corner of the room. On the floor next to the jackets, was Chris Mills' duty belt, along with his spit polished 5-11 TAC boots.

Each of these items were so new, the boots didn't even have the traditional crease across the top. Yet, each of these items were covered with the blood of their owner, who was now fighting for his life.

That was the last thing Matt and Sgt. Barton saw, as one of the ER doctors suddenly realized the presence of both Greenfield officers and calmly said to his nearest nurse, "Please close the curtain."

Suddenly, both Greenfield officers were staring at a blue and white hospital curtain.

"Officers, why don't you come with me," a soft voice said. Both officers turned instinctively to find an elderly woman, standing behind them.

"I am the chaplain on duty right now," said Sister Gertrude Agatha, extending both of her hands to Sgt. Barton and Matt.

Standing about 5'3" inches in height and wearing a blue blazer, with grey skirt, very few people would have recognized Sister Gertrude Agatha as a chaplain, until Matt looked carefully and saw the chrome-colored crucifix, she was wearing around her wrinkled neck.

Both Matt and Sgt Barton took a hand of Sister Gertrude Agatha as she slowly led them away from the hospital curtain and down a long corridor, making idle small talk along the way.

After a few minutes, all three found themselves standing in front of a wooden door, with a sign on it reading, "Families Only."

Sister Gertrude Agatha entered the room, followed by Sgt. Barton. Matt O'Neil stood out in the hallway and looked inside. Like a new puppy being brought home for the first time, he scanned the entire room slowly. Inside were two cheap brown wooden couches, a couple of cloth-lined chairs, a lamp stand, with a cheap lamp on it, phone, and a big box of Kleenex tissues.

He was hesitant about going into the room, because he knew what this room was meant for. This was the death notification room.

Matt had seen this room numerous times on every hospital show he and Kelly watched. The fact she's a nurse, coincidentally at this hospital, also played a part in both of them watching religiously.

Matt often bragged to Kelly, he could repeat the doctor's speech, word for word when it was delivered. "Mrs. Smith, Jones, Miller, or whatever the heck the patient's name is, your son, daughter, nephew, husband, was brought in with massive internal injuries. We tried a number of different measures and worked on him, her, but to no avail. I am deeply sorry for your loss," after a few seconds, the doctor would turn and walk away.

Please God Matt thought, do not let me hear that speech today, for Chris Mills.

"Is there anything I can get you gentlemen?" Sister Gertrude Agatha asked.

Sgt. Barton replied, "No."

Matt O'Neil finally entered the room and sat down on one of the couches, while Sgt. Barton sat down on the other.

Sgt. Barton finally ended the silence, which seemed to hang in the air by asking, "Is there any news?" when suddenly, Sister Gertrude Agatha's phone went off in a series of quick, loud beeps.

The look on her face when she read the text message, worried both Matt O'Neil and Sgt. Barton.

"I'm needed somewhere else right now, but I'll be back to you two as soon as I can," said Sister Gertrude Agatha. Quickly she turned and left the room.

It seemed the door had just closed behind her, when a nurse opened it and said, "Officer, they're in here."

Officer T.C. Chambers, of the Greenfield Police Department, walked into the room.

Both Matt O'Neil and Sgt. Barton got to their feet in hopes he had heard something about Chris, or at the very least, could tell them what was going on back at the accident scene.

But before either could say a word, T.C. Chambers asked, "How's Chris doing?"

Matt O Neil's head was bowed and he was silent. Sgt. Barton finally spoke, "It's too early to tell."

After a long and uncomfortable pause among the three of them, Sgt. Barton decided to break the ice.

"T.C., what's going on back at the scene?" he asked.

"Lieutenant Wayne's handling it," T.C. Chambers smiled, which showed off the shiny gold tooth in the upper right front part of his mouth.

Sgt. Barton, Matt O'Neil, and T.C. Chambers each pictured in their minds, Lt. Wayne barking out orders and the sweat pouring off his brow, even though the temperature was only in the midthirties.

"Lieutenant Wayne had Marc and Ron handling traffic control at the scene, until Sergeant Garza and his Traffic Bureau arrived to take over the whole thing, since this is a possible death investigation," said T.C. Chambers. "Joey Grant and Bobby Christensen were doing the initial canvas of the neighborhood. Megan is in the process of bringing Mrs. Loftus to the station so the detectives can interview her. She was the driver of the car Chris stopped before he was hit. On my way over here, I heard Lieutenant Wayne ask on F-2 if the Chief and both Deputy Chiefs have been notified, and Karen told him yes."

"Good," Sgt. Barton replied, and once again a silence fell over the room, as the three of them couldn't think of anything more to say to each other.

Two minutes had gone by before T.C. Chambers said, "I did forget something important. About five minutes before I left the scene to come here, I overheard Lieutenant Wayne trying to interview Mrs. Loftus."

Sgt. Barton and Matt O'Neil both stared at T.C. Chambers, leaning forward on their respective couches with their mouths hanging open, waiting for more information.

"She could barely talk because she was so hysterical," T.C. Chambers continued, "but she did manage to say the vehicle which hit Chris was an old, white, Ford Bronco."

A cold shiver went down Matt O'Neil's back, which he'd never experienced before.

"Yeah, she knew it was a Ford Bronco because her late brother had died in a car accident years ago while driving one. That's also why she was so out of control at the scene," T.C. Chambers finished.

Matt O'Neil sat hunched over on the couch.

Physically, he was at Lutheran Family Center Hospital, but

mentally he was back at Greenfield Road and Waukegan Road, under the canopy of Kalom's Pharmacy.

A cold fog seems to engulf him. Suddenly, Matt O'Neil is back in his squad car. Over and over again, he watches the Ford Bronco drive by him in slow motion.

Nothing unusual about it except for the old, faded White Sox sticker in the rear window. Each time the Bronco gets bigger as it passes directly in front of his squad car.

Each time Matt O'Neil strains to lift his head off the headrest in his squad car to see the driver of the Bronco, but each time he is unsuccessful.

Some kind of force is holding his head down, preventing him from seeing who is behind the wheel of the Bronco, and responsible for badly injuring Chris Mills.

All Matt O'Neil has to do is stop the Bronco, stop the Bronco, stop the Bronco.

"Matt O'Neil, Matt O'Neil," a strong, male voice said above him.

Matt O'Neil looked up to find a small crowd had gathered around him.

Chief Ryan Fitzsimons was standing in front of Matt O'Neil, calling his name.

Sgt. Barton and T.C. Chambers joined Chief Fitzsimons in the crowd.

Matt O'Neil looked at the faces of each of these men, but there were no expressions, just blank stares, looking directly back at him. Matt then saw them and he began to shake.

Dr. Greg Murphy and Sister Gertrude Agatha were standing directly behind Chief Fitzsimons, but Matt never saw them, due to the dwarfing size of the Chief.

Chief Fitzsimons stepped aside and watched as Dr. Murphy approached Matt O'Neil. Dr. Murphy's name is sketched in navy blue on the right side of his lab coat, but something entirely different caught Matt O'Neil's attention.

On the chest of Dr. Murphy's scrubs were numerous red stains, which Matt O'Neil recognized instantly as blood.

For Matt O'Neil is confident, the blood Dr. Greg Murphy is

wearing, was the same blood that once flowed through the body of Chris Mills.

Dr. Murphy took a deep breath, looked straight into Matt O'Neil's brown eyes and began, "Your good friend Christopher Mills, was brought into the hospital with massive internal injuries." Dr. Murphy paused and took a deep breath almost in an effort to get the remainder of what he needed to say, out in its entirety, without having to stop.

Dr. Murphy continued, "Despite numerous efforts to save him," while Matt O'Neil heard the words he was not listening. Instead, Matt O'Neil pictured in his mind Chris Mills healthy and laughing. A laughter that could fill an entire classroom at ILETC, or a navy barracks.

Dr. Murphy concluded with, "I am deeply sorry for your loss," and there's a long and dreaded period of silence from all parties.

Matt O'Neil suddenly felt the strong hands of both Chief Fitzsimons and Sgt. Barton on his sagging shoulders, as they tried to comfort him.

Dr. Murphy abruptly turned and left the room, accompanied by Sister Gertrude Agatha. Unbeknownst to them, Matt O'Neil slowly started to follow them. Matt O'Neil finally caught up with them at the check-in desk of the ER.

Suddenly, every nurse and doctor standing at the desk stopped what they were doing and watched in silence, as Matt O'Neil reached out and touched Dr. Murphy, on the right elbow of his lab coat.

As Dr. Murphy turned, he was startled to see it was Matt who had touched him. Matt saw a look of fear on Dr. Murphy's tired, young face. From the right side of the ER desk, Sister Gertrude Agatha started to walk over, in an effort to step between them.

Before she could get there, Matt O'Neil extended his right hand and said in a soft voice, "Thanks doc for all you did. I'm sure Chris' mom would want me to thank you." Matt continued, "I know all of you tried the best you could to save his life."

Still holding Dr. Murphy's right hand, Matt looked at the doctors and nurses standing by the E.R. desk. Dr. Murphy was speechless, but held onto Matt's hand with a firmness which surprised Matt for a second.

Matt asked in a voice that could only be heard by both Dr. Murphy and Sister Gertrude Agatha, who was now standing next to Dr. Murphy, "Can I see him now?"

Dr. Murphy let go of Matt's hand and replied, "Sure, just come with me." Alone, the two walked slowly in silence.

No cell phones went off, just two men alone with their thoughts, walking side by side, with their reflections shining off the newly waxed hospital floor.

They passed examination stalls with curtains wide open and empty patient carts, until they finally arrived at the end of the hallway, to the first examination room with a door instead of a curtain.

The door was also different, with a piece of blue fabric in its tiny window, preventing anyone from seeing inside the room.

Matt glanced back to see if anyone had followed them, but the hallway was entirely empty.

As Matt turned back toward the door, Dr. Murphy had already started the process of opening it slowly.

There, lying flat on his back on the examination table, was the massive body of Chris Mills. Chris' naked body was covered with a thin, blue sheet

Only Chris' face was visible. Matt noticed a fresh bruise on the right side of Chris' face. Matt was shocked by the lack of blood on Chris' body or the sheet covering him.

When Matt had experienced death before in the service, the victim's body and uniform were often ripped apart by a bullet or IED and usually drenched in blood. This was so clean and surreal, like Chris was only taking a long nap.

Then, the closer Matt got to Chris' body, he started to smell it. The smell of antiseptic and alcohol began to fill Matt's nostrils, to the point where he had trouble breathing.

Matt walked over to the examination table and stood directly next to the right side of Chris' head. Dr. Murphy also walked over and stood next to Matt. Again, the two of them were speechless, as they found themselves staring at Chris Mills' body.

After a minute, Dr. Murphy's cell phone went off. He slowly backed out of the room, leaving Matt alone with Chris' body.

Matt reached out with his right hand to prove to himself once and for all Chris was dead. He placed it directly on his heart. He was shocked by the softness of Chris' chest and slowly pulled the sheet back to his waist.

All over Chris' chest, Matt found fresh stitching and puncture wounds from needles used in an attempt to save his life.

Matt didn't know how long he'd been standing next to Chris' body before Sgt. Barton was standing in the same spot where Dr. Murphy previously stood.

"I didn't really know him, but he seemed like a good kid," Sgt. Barton said.

The word kid, seemed to hang in the air forever. It burned a slight hole in Matt's forehead, as if he'd been hit by a hot arrow.

Slowly, Matt turned and looked directly at Sgt. Barton and said, "He may have been young, but he was years ahead of us all in wisdom and judgment." With anger slowly filling Matt's face he finished by saying, "He saved my life Sarge in the war, but when it came time for me to save his, I couldn't pull it off."

Sgt. Barton had heard the rumors within the department about Chris, T.C., and Matt, being in Special Ops, but he had no idea what branch of service they had been in, or where they had served.

Without saying another word, Sgt. Barton quickly walked across the room and grabbed a wooden chair.

Quickly, he returned, placing it at the back of Matt's legs. With tiredness setting in and the shock of seeing his best friend lying dead in front of him, it didn't take much for Matt to slowly ease his body into the chair. He became seated just below Chris' head.

For the next hour, a steady stream of Greenfield police officers entered the examination room, to pay their respects.

Lt. Wayne was the first and easily the quickest both in and out of the room. Never once during his brief time in the room, did he make eye contact, or say a word to Matt.

Ron Thomas and Marc Dombrowski were next and set the standard for their fellow officers to follow. Both Ron and Marc stood on the opposite side of the examination table, which enabled them to see both Matt and Chris Mills' body, at the same time.

At one point, Matt looked up and saw each of their lips moving in silence, as both Ron and Marc mouthed the words to the Hail Mary.

Upon completing their prayer, Marc took his right hand and slowly hit the left leg of Ron, before returning his hand to the side of his Blauer pants. Exactly five seconds later, both of their right hands shot up and held a rigid salute for 30 seconds, in honor of their fallen friend, Chris Mills.

Before leaving, each stopped briefly and placed their right hand on Matt's shoulder.

All of the visitors were able to hold in their emotions, except Karen Jenkins with Ed Heaviland.

Matt could see each of them had just come from work, because both were still wearing their light blue dispatcher shirts.

Karen Jenkins was in her mid-forties and a very attractive woman with her short, brown hair and navy-blue eyes. Her body was in great shape mainly due to the fact she and her husband Tom, avoided having children and were fitness freaks.

Matt had occasionally seen both of them either running, or roller blading, on the bike trail, in Harms Woods. Plus, their favorite winter sport was cross country skiing.

Karen Jenkins considered all the new probationary officers to be her little ducklings.

Senior officers on the shift kidded Karen about always assigning "the new kids" low-priority calls.

So, it was no surprise for Matt to see Karen start sobbing the minute she entered the examination room. Her crying only became more severe the closer she got to Chris' body.

After only a few minutes, Ed Heaviland saw she was having

trouble breathing, due to her crying. He placed his arm around her shoulders and escorted her out of the room.

Matt continued to sit by Chris, but was never alone for more than a few minutes as an officer or group of officers continued to enter the room.

As these officers were preparing to leave the room, Matt acknowledged them with a mere upward movement of his head.

Matt was caught off guard when Chief Fitzsimons finally entered the room.

Matt got to his feet to show his respect, but the Chief motioned with his right hand and said,» Sit down, Matt. Please sit down," the chief ordered, but Matt continued to stand because it actually felt good to get the blood flowing in his legs again.

As Matt shook Chief Fitzsimons' hand, he was shocked at how big it was and how it totally engulfed his own.

Chief Ryan Patrick Fitzsimons had only been with the Greenfield Police Department for 14 months, but in this little time, he had made his presence known.

The Greenfield Police Department Policy Manual read that officers on duty could carry anything from a 357 revolver up to a 9mm. Chief Fitzsimons put an end to that within the first six months and budgeted for every officer to carry a 40 Caliber Glock on duty.

After seeing the Greenfield squad cars were totally white, with a huge yellow star on each side, Chief Fitzsimons commented to a few officers, "What's it like driving a pizza delivery car?"

It didn't take long before Chief Fitzsimons created a Squad Car Committee, with their main assignment being to outfit the car from slogan, to interior, exterior, and design.

The word in the locker room was the cars colors weren't under consideration and would be the traditional black and white LAPD design Fitzsimons wanted, but everything else for the squad car, was on the table for the committee's consideration.

Chief Fitzsimons was constantly around, commenting, observing, getting officers reactions to certain things and seeing what other changes needed to be made.

He had been a police chief in two previous cities—one in Illinois and one in Wisconsin—and many officers, including Matt, liked that he could bring big city experience to the quiet little town of Greenfield.

The main reason Chief Fitzsimons had been hired, was to facilitate the building of a new police station for the Village of Greenfield. He had built new police stations in each of his two previous chief jobs, and in both cases, had done it under budget. This looked extremely good on his resume and was an attractive plus when he competed for and eventually got the Greenfield police chief job.

Chief Fitzsimons came from a long line of Fitzsimons who, upon arriving in this country, joined up with their Irish countrymen and became police officers. But no one had climbed the ladder, or had been as successful as him.

Matt was amazed at the energy level Chief Fitzsimons possessed because no one ever saw him working out at the department's exercise room.

Yet, with the traditional red hair, Chief Fitzsimons appeared years younger than his real age of 63.

"How are you holding up Matt?" Chief Fitzsimons asked.

"Better Sir," Matt replied. "It's finally sinking in Chris is gone."

"Has Kelly been contacted or can I do that for you?" Chief Fitzsimons asked.

"Officer Chambers told me he was going to take care of it, so I expect her anytime now, Sir," Matt responded.

"Speaking of family, Chris' mom lives in Belvedere, Illinois. I was wondering about notifying her in person," Matt continued.

"Matt, Deputy Chief Gyondski made me aware of this earlier today by phone," Chief Fitzsimons responded.

Chief Fitzsimons continued, "I instructed Lieutenant Wayne to pick one individual from your shift to accompany our social worker, Debra Santiago, and drive to Belvedere and tell Mrs. Mills about her son's death, in person. Which is why you may have noticed Officer O'Brien hasn't been to the hospital yet to pay her respects. She is accompanying Social Worker Santiago and they left about 40 minutes ago, for Belvedere".

Chief Fitzsimons finished by stating, "Mrs. Mills, when it's best for her, will then be driven back to our town and given the option of staying with you and Kelly or at the Marriott Courtyard, whichever she prefers. Is there anything else I can do for you at this time?"

"No Sir, and thank you again for everything you've already done," Matt replied.

Chief Fitzsimons started walking toward the door. Then he stopped and turned around abruptly. With a look of anger on his face, which Matt had never seen before, he approached Matt.

"I will use every officer and every agency available to us to find the person who did this to Officer Chris Mills, so help me God," Chief Fitzsimons said firmly.

Matt nodded his head and softly whispered, "Thank you Sir," as the Chief left the room.

All Matt could think of doing was sitting down and closing his eyes, when his wife Kelly gently shook him awake.

"Matt, Matt," Kelly is shaking him now. "Honey, it's 9 o' clock, I need to take you home and get you to bed," Kelly says.

Slowly, she helps Matt to his feet. When he is fully out of the chair, she throws both of her arms around his neck.

No words are exchanged as Matt leans slightly forward to take some of the strain off of his neck, due to the height difference between himself and his beautiful wife. In a matter of minutes, the front of Matt's bulletproof vest cover, is damp from tears coming from Kelly, as her embrace becomes stronger around Matt's neck.

Slowly, Matt reaches down and gently kisses Kelly's lips, which are quivering slightly.

"I love you sweetheart," Matt says softly into Kelly's right ear.

Kelly proceeds to look up at Matt and can only say in a soft voice, "I will always love you, Officer Matt O'Neil," before placing her head gently into her favorite spot-on Matt's chest, near his left shoulder.

Without moving Kelly's head, Matt guides her slowly out of the room, and down the hallway, before they are finally at the visitors parking area, of the hospital.

Matt starts to feel a cold rain fall on the both of them. He's too exhausted to care and too comfortable, having the love of his life in his arms once more.

At Kelly's silver Honda Accord, he opens the passenger door and Kelly turns to him saying, "Matt, I'm fine now and want to get us home safe, please let me drive."

Without hesitation, Matt hands her the keys, knowing at this point there is no way he's going to win this argument.

Matt gets into the passenger seat and waits patiently for Kelly to turn on the cold Honda.

As Kelly does, a blast of cold air comes out of the closest vent to him, momentarily hitting him in the face and reviving him.

Quickly, he switches the temperatures from defrost to heat on the control panel.

Matt begins to lower his head on the headrest of the passenger seat, waiting for the Honda to warm up, when he's jolted back into reality. Never again will he be able to be in Kelly's car, his car, or in his squad car and place his head on a headrest, without the vision of the Ford Bronco passing in front of him.

Instead, Matt places his head against the passenger side window in hopes the coldness from the rain will keep him awake.

Slowly he feels himself drifting off into a deep sleep with Chief Fitzsimons' stern look and statement playing over and over in his head, "I will use every officer and every agency available to us to find the person who did this to Officer Chris Mills."

CHAPTER 3

C hris Mills' funeral procession is over four miles in length. Greenfield Officers, Afattati and Wilson, lead the procession, on their Harley Davidson, Electric Glide motorcycles.

Since the first documented use of a motorcycle for police work, was by the Evanston Police Department, in 1908, two of their officers ride in this procession.

Slowly, all thirty-four motorcycles drive so each of their bikes cover a front headlight on the black Cadillac hearse, carrying Chris Mills' body.

The sun beats brightly down on them and Wilson looks up into the sky but can't find a cloud anywhere in sight.

The sun's glare seems to dance off every chrome part on their motorcycles and triple polished helmets.

Officer Wilson thinks to himself how fitting it is Chris Mills would slowly die in the rain filled streets of Greenfield, and now he would be buried on the most glorious day Greenfield has seen, on this final day of winter.

It doesn't take long before every sidewalk becomes filled with people of all ages.

Workers come out of the Jiffy Lube at Waukegan and Golf Road to point, and in some cases, just stare at the whole scene.

Saint Mary of the Holy Cross gave all their students a small American Flag, which they hold solemnly as the procession passes them slowly.

On some streets, people stand three deep, just to catch a glimpse of the huge motorcade.

Occasionally, the glare of the sun bounces off a piece of either

Afattati's or Wilson's bikes, or uniform badges and blinds the people on the sidewalk.

Chris Mills' hearse is the second vehicle in the procession.

Some of the younger students of Saint Mary of the Holy Cross turn and yell to their teachers when they realize the flag they're holding, is the same as the one covering Chris Mills' casket.

Harriet Mills rides in the third vehicle, a black-colored, stretch Cadillac limousine.

Matt O'Neil sits directly across from her with his back to the driver of the limousine, who he knows only as Steve.

Seated next to Harriet Mills is her new best friend, Megan O' Brien.

Matt can only stare in awe as Megan sits only inches apart from Mrs Mills, and every few blocks, offers her a kleenex, or drink of Ice Mountain water.

The funeral director filled a small Igloo cooler with Pepsi, Canada Dry Ginger Ale, and water which they conveniently placed on the floor near Megan's left foot.

As promised by Chief Fitzsimons, Megan and the Greenfield Police Department Social Worker, Debra Santiago, used MapQuest and made it to the Belvedere Police Station in record time.

Of course, the fact that Megan was driving a marked Greenfield police car and doing 80 MPH helped.

Megan told Matt and T.C. at Chris' wake, how well Harriet had taken the news her only son was dead.

It was a good thing Megan had driven fast. Kelly told Matt when she first got to Lutheran Family Center Hospital, the day of Chris's' death, both ABC and WGN news crews were already setting up in the parking lot.

It's a well-known fact every major news outlet, in the greater Chicago Metropolitan area, has a police scanner.

Matt knew it would be only a matter of time before the news crews filled in the general public, on what had taken place at the intersection of Moody and First, at 0515 hours that day, in the little North Shore town of Greenfield.

"Thank you, Matt," Harriet says and slowly leans forward in her seat, extending her right hand to him.

"You're welcome Harriet, but honestly, I didn't do anything," Matt replies.

"Nonsense," says Harriet. "Last night's Honor Guard was so beautiful, and a few people who I don't even know told me how impressed they were with your precision and uniforms."

"You're welcome Harriet," Matt replies and he thinks to himself the Honor Guard did kick ass.

After only 9 months on the job, Matt had been asked by Lt. Miler, who was in charge of the Honor Guard to join, due to the retirement of Officer Castellano.

Matt took it as a huge compliment, as neither T.C. or Chris, had been asked at the time.

Even though he took a verbal beating in the locker room from the other Greenfield cops, he wore his Honor Guard uniform with pride.

Hours upon hours of practice had paid off and the whole Honor Guard detail looked sharp last night, especially when it came to changing every half hour, at Chris' coffin.

Lt. Miler had wisely sent out a department-wide e-mail and placed a memo to be read at every shift's roll call, about what the Honor Guard could and couldn't do at the wake.

Since they had been formed as a unit, this would be their first time working at a Greenfield police officer's death.

The biggest thing for other officers, and the general public, would be to have no conversation with any member of the Honor Guard who was standing at Chris' casket.

If only people knew, Matt thinks to himself, how hard it is to stand for a half hour motionless, with your hands behind your back, as you stand either at the head or feet of a fallen officer's casket.

He recalls the day Kale Uniforms representative; Tom Frazianno dropped his Honor Guard uniform off at the Greenfield Police Department.

Matt couldn't wait to get home with it and make sure all of the items were the proper size and see how he looked.

Kelly had unexpectedly come home early from the hospital due to not feeling well.

Upon seeing Matt's, Chevy Camaro in their driveway, she quietly crept into the house through the side door to see if she could sneak up on him.

Instead, Kelly stood in amazement and shock at how good her man looked.

Kelly thought her man looked hot in his Navy Dress uniform the first time she saw him, but this was something different.

The Honor Guard dress pants were navy blue along with the dress jacket, but what made them standout was the grey striping on the outside of each pant leg, along with the matching silver buttons on the dress jacket.

Top that off with white dress gloves, Sam Browne black leather belt, with a black, high ride holster which carried a 9mm Beretta, black dress shoes, and Matt was one bad ass looking dude.

Roughly 35 minutes later, the uniform lay neatly on their bedroom floor, next to her Victoria's Secret bra and white panties, after they had finished a passionate love making session.

Matt is forced to hold back his grin while thinking about that afternoon, in case Harriet or Megan looked at him.

Harriet had no family left in Belvedere, Illinois, and requested Chris's body be buried in Carol Stream, Illinois, alongside her former husband, Henry Mills.

Henry Mills was a truck driver for A+A Freight, out of Appleton, Wisconsin.

The long hours on the road, constant fighting when he was home, excessive drinking and Harriet's loneliness, put a continuous strain on their marriage.

When Chris was four years old, Harriet had enough and filed for divorce, hoping to find another man who could be the father her son deserved.

Henry Mills died on a snowy night, December 10, 1994, when

his semi-trailer started to skid on an icy part of Highway 39, near Portage, Wisconsin.

A normal skid for an experienced driver such as Henry Mills shouldn't have been a problem.

Unfortunately, two major factors contributed heavily to his death.

Instead of just going off the road, Henry's rig went into a ditch and his Peterbilt Cab was turned upside down and crushed in the process.

Wisconsin State Trooper Traffic Reconstructionist were puzzled how an experienced trucker like him, who handled hundreds of skids before, couldn't recover from this one.

Then his logbooks were located in the mess of his cab and revealed he had been driving nonstop for close to 26 hours, in an effort to get home.

Unknown to the troopers, Henry's only son's birthday was December 11th.

In Henry's wallet were two Green Bay Packer tickets against the Chicago Bears, for that Sunday at Soldier Field.

Chris told Matt his mom believed those tickets were going to be his birthday surprise, because Chris had never been to a professional football game and his favorite team was the Green Bay Packers, just like Henry's.

Chris was somehow able to get the two tickets from his father's personal belongings, which Harriet had stored away in her bedroom closet.

Chris carried them proudly in his wallet for the rest of his life.

Life could be stranger than fiction Matt thought to himself.

Both Mills men died in totally different circumstances.

The only thing they had in common was both had the same Packer tickets in their wallets, at the time of their deaths.

"Shit, what's the chances of that?" Matt says softly to himself.

The fourth vehicle in the funeral procession is a black Chevy Malibu filled with Chief Fitzsimons and his command staff.

Detective Mike Untiedt had been chosen to be the driver.

Chief Fitzsimons sits in the front passenger seat across from Untiedt.

Seated directly behind Chief Fitzsimons is his new Deputy Chief of Operations, Andrew Bart.

The new Deputy Chief of Support Services, Frank Gyondski, sits behind Detective Untiedt.

Fitzsimons took little time in shaking up his Command Staff after he had gotten to know his personnel.

The person who took the hardest hit was the infamous Lt. Wayne.

The previous Chief of Greenfield had been Edward Angeli.

A large man in his late sixties, Angeli had been forced to retire when it was discovered he had prostate cancer.

The difference between Angeli and Fitzsimons was like night and day.

Angeli was an easy going, good natured Italian, who never wanted to upset the residents of Greenfield, or a Village Board member.

Fitzsimons was willing to ruffle a few feathers and asked for anything he could get from the Village Manager, or trustees.

Angeli was always for status quo, while Greenfield personnel saw Fitzsimons was eager to make change wherever he thought it could improve the overall department.

Lt. Wayne never stood a chance with the hard-charging Chief Fitzsimons.

It took little time before Chief Fitzsimons could see Lt. Wayne was an Angeli clone.

Chief Fitzsimons had instituted an open-door policy and even rode a few days with some of the veterans on each shift to pick their brains.

The veterans had more than a few ideas about changes, but they were always met with the famous line, "If it's not broken don't fix it," from Lt. Wayne.

Fitzsimons just needed time to find the right person who practiced his Patton-like philosophy of full speed ahead at all times.

Unlike Angeli, who made all promotions without feedback, Fitzsimons asked for department personnel to serve on a committee and give him advice on who his new Deputy Chief should be.

Lt. Bart was the odds-on favorite going into the selection process and with good reason.

Lt. Bart was a cop's cop.

Unlike some of the other Greenfield Police Officers, who only took the job for the pay and the chance to meet women, Lt. Bart had demonstrated he liked making arrests from day one.

In his sixteen and a half years on the job, Lt. Bart had made plenty of arrests with the highlight being a bank robber who had tried to rob the Greenfield State Bank, located on Waukegan Road, during a lunchtime rush in 2011.

Matt's first FTO was a wonderful Irishman named Patrick Carll, who was no longer with the Greenfield Police Department.

Barely meeting the height requirement, Carll's nickname was "Munchkin."

On their first day of riding together, Matt recalled Carll's opening comment. "Matt my boy, if you want to be in high-speed chases, get in big-time shoot-outs, and catch bank robbers, then you need to go be a Chicago Copper.''

Carll continued with his thick Irish accent, "Department policy says we can't get involved in high-speed pursuits, and after the last one, bank robbers don't even dare to try and hit one of our banks. Just about all our banks are located either in shopping centers, or the middle of town, and the belief is robbers' figure if they did a bank job, they could never get out of town, or that damn shopping center, before we grab them."

Matt heard what FTO Carll was saying, but it didn't sink in at the time.

Like every new cop, Matt's head was constantly spinning.

Matt had experienced something similar during his first few days in the Navy and then again when he moved to Special Ops.

This on the other hand, was different in its own peculiar way.

There were no drill instructors in his face telling him how long he had to eat and what time he had to go to sleep.

Instead, he had a 51-year-old, loveable Irishman, standing about 5'7" with a small stomach, gray shiny hair, hearty laugh, and a love for telling cop stories, controlling his future.

Matt wanted to make a good first impression with Carll and make law enforcement his future.

The first step in the process would be to have a successful first year and get off probation.

In order to do just that, Matt would have to keep his mistakes to a minimum.

Consequently, Matt's head seemed ready to burst every day.

Like his laptop at home, he filled his brain with more information and attempted to hit the delete button now and then.

The military used a different alpha system as opposed to most law enforcement agencies.

Matt took a royal beating from Carll and later from the Greenfield veterans, the first time he made a traffic stop and called out the license plate number of the offending vehicle as, "'F' as in Foxtrot, 'B' as in Bravo and 'E' as in Echo," only to learn it was incorrect.

The Ten code and Alpha characters would gradually come in time, and Carll had prepared a cheat sheet to help speed up the process.

Now, all Matt needed to do was learn the damn Greenfield streets.

Over and over, it had been stressed at the Illinois Law Enforcement Training Center, to all of the recruits: "You can't do a God damn thing unless you get there safely, know how to get there, and make sure everyone knows your exact location at all times."

Matt wondered how a town the size of Greenfield, could have two Maple streets and two Main streets.

It was finally in their third week of training, when he felt confident enough in his progress, to bring up the bank robbery situation to Carll.

"Besides," Matt thought, "I can gain a few brownie points with a guy who loves to tell stories and we're basically running out of other things to talk about."

They were having dinner, at a greasy little spoon, in the heart of Greenfield called Carson's, when Matt asked, "Hey Pat, tell me about the Greenfield State Bank robbery of 2011."

Slowly, Carll pushed aside his plate containing the last bit of lasagna and placed his left arm slowly over the back of their booth.

With his right hand still holding his brown-colored coffee cup, Carll began, "It was your typical Saturday before Christmas, filled with a combination of retail thefts and traffic accidents. Everybody was down except for two guys, one being a kid named Edwards, who a year later laterally transferred to Naperville PD and Bart."

"Two weeks before Christmas, to please the retailers, we take two guys out of the detective bureau and have them only patrol the main retail areas, in hopes of preventing some of these freaking retail thefts," Carll said. "So right before noon, a guy named, Bobby Delprino, walks into Greenfield State Bank, over on Waukegan Road and patiently waits in line."

"A little background on Delprino," stated Carll, "Delprino had no contacts with us and for that matter anyone, because he had never committed a crime. Delprino was living the life of leisure, being a commodities broker and living over on Olpine Drive in Indian Lake. He wasn't married, but he was a half-way decent looking guy so he was picking up broads left and right. Plus, he's getting all he can handle, if you know what I mean," Carll smiled broadly.

"Problem is one of these named Lunisia Tonesky, turns out to be an addict and before you know it, she has Delprino hooked as well," continued Carll. "Turns out, it's the age-old story: boy meets girl, boy likes what girl is providing in the bedroom, so boy will do anything at any time to keep girl."

"Yeah but," Matt interrupted, "he's got an eight hundred-thousand-dollar home and a high paying job, he needs to rob a bank?"

"Matt my boy," Carll responded, "In Greenfield, like most of the North Shore, image is everything," Carll then continued. "He had two mortgages on the house, his credit cards were tapped out and his Mom's giving him shit about Tonesky not being the type to give her good Italian babies. So Delprino has his back to the wall so to speak. But we found a picture of Tonesky on Facebook. Sweeeeeeeet Jesus my boy, what a body and looks to kill. Tall with long legs that never stop, blonde hair, blue eyes," Carll stopped and smiled broadly, thinking about Tonesky. "I tell you she looked like a young Christine......, I can't think of her last name," Carll said.

Matt watched as Carll got so into telling the story he pushed his coffee cup aside, leaned forward in the booth for emphasis and continued.

"When it's Delprino's turn he pushes the traditional note across the counter to the teller. It said, 'Give me all of your money, or I'm going to blow your fucking brains out." Then, he follows it up by opening his black, North Face ski parka, revealing the wooden grip on a Colt Python, 357 Magnum.

"Sound like the perfect plan Matt?" Carll asked.

Matt simply nodded his head and replied, "Yes."

Suddenly Carll's right hand slapped the table with such force, all of the plates moved and other patrons stopped and stared for a minute.

"Wrong, Wrong, Wrong," Carll responded and he went on explaining. "Unknown to Delprino, Patrolman Bart was working the beat next to the Greenfield State Bank that day. Bart made a habit of driving through every bank parking lot to look for any suspicious cars, when time allowed for it during the shift."

"The robbery goes down and the bank manager called it in instead of the bank teller since the bank teller was so scared, she couldn't hit the button to let us know there was a bank robbery in progress. The bank manager was also able to give us a description of Delprino's car—a dark brown, Buick Regal."

"What about the registration?" Matt asked.

Matt was surprised just how engrossed in the story he had become.

"Only the first letter of the plate, which was a 'B,'" Carll responded. "Karen Jenkins was on her game again that day and got the information out to both Edwards and Bart in just over a minute, after Delprino left the bank."

"So," Matt countered, "Bart got there before Edwards did and he grabs Delprino?"

"Naw," Carll replied, "Bart told the press later he figured Delprino would go south on Waukegan Road so he started heading in that direction. But he had a huge advantage over Edwards, who was assigned to go to the bank as the primary officer."

"What was the advantage?" Matt asked.

"Bart had driven through the bank parking lot about ten minutes earlier, just checking things out, when he found Delprino's car tucked away in a rear alley running. Bart figured something was up and wanted to sit on it like a good cop should," Carll replied.

"But as luck would have it, Bart got assigned to a personal injury traffic accident, just down the street from the Greenfield State Bank and had to respond," Carll said.

"What the fuck Pat," Matt said. "How did he wind up catching Delprino, if he's got the accident?"

"Easy Matt my boy," Carll answered. "Bart gets to where the cars are supposed to be and the caller, in their excitement, confused the address for Greenfield, when in reality, it was in Northbrook. So, Bart goes 10-23, then 10-24, coding it 7Q and then the bank robbery comes out.

Then, like I said earlier, he heads south on Waukegan Road and at Golf Road he pulls into the Audi dealer on the corner and waits."

"Less than two minutes later, here comes Delprino in the Buick. When traffic allows, Bart pulls behind him. Seeing the first letter on the license plate is 'B,' he feels he has his bank robber," Carll said. "There was only a slight glitch to the traffic stop," Carll added for suspense.

"What happened?" Matt asked.

"In his report, Bart states he is waiting for back-up from our guys to make a felony stop on Delprino. Instead, here comes a Morton Grove copper who is monitoring our frequency. Bart was worried about getting into a shootout on Waukegan Road and a possible crossfire situation involving the Morton Grove cop, so he quickly turned the overheads on and stopped Delprino's car," Carll suddenly started chuckling as he continued. "The minute Bart hit the overheads, Delprino stops, opens his car door and ends it," Carll finished.

"Why was that so funny Pat?" Matt asked.

"Because when I got there, I thought Bart had killed Delprino," Carll replied.

"What the hell?" is all Matt could respond and found himself sitting in the booth, with his mouth wide open.

"Yup," Carll said, "I pull up and Bart has his gun out and trained on Delprino, who happens to be lying face down in the snow and slush on Waukegan Road, spread eagle, not moving, with a big red splotch underneath him."

"Let me guess," Matt says, "dye pack from the bank?"

"Yeah," Carll answered. "But in the heat of the moment and with neither Bart or Delprino moving, I got caught up in the action and it looked for a second like real blood," Carll answered. He let out the loudest laugh Matt got out of him the entire FTO period they were together.

A laugh so loud, it causes Matt and even a few of the restaurant patrons to start laughing.

"Something funny Matt?" Megan asks.

With that comment burning in his ears, Matt looks up to find both Megan and Mrs. Mills staring straight at him, both with puzzled looks on their respective faces.

"Sorry Mrs. Mills," Matt replies. "I was just thinking of a funny story involving Chris while we were together in the service."

Suddenly Harriet Mills' frown turns into a broad smile and she replies, "Matt, that's how I would want Christopher remembered." Slowly, tears begin to run down her cheeks.

Matt next looks at Megan, who still has a puzzled look on her young, freckled face.

She shakes her head once, before she turns and comforts Mrs. Mills.

Matt also turns his head to the right and is close enough to the side window of the limousine, his face almost touches the glass.

It's only then he realizes what his years on this earth have become.

Riding in a car, a bus, a Humvee, a helicopter, and now a limousine, going somewhere and not knowing what to expect.

Riding in a car with his mom, Colleen O'Neil, off to kindergarten, for his first day of school at St. Constance, in Chicago.

Riding in a darkened bus as quarterback and captain of the Gordon Tech Rams, as they travel to Gately Stadium, for his first game against their arch rival, Weber High School.

Riding with his unit on their first mission together, in a darkened helicopter, to meet and kill an unfamiliar enemy.

Now, riding in a limousine to a funeral and then to a cemetery, to bury a friend which was closer to him than his five brothers.

Yes, Matt thinks to himself, he's always been the passenger.

He aimlessly stares out the window, not even registering what's directly in front of him.

CHAPTER 4

The last car in the funeral procession is a Gilles Police car. Seated alone in the backseat is Officer Kurt Thompson, who obtained permission to go to the funeral, by telling his Chief, he had gone to the Illinois Law Enforcement Training Center with Chris Mills and the other Greenfield rookies and felt a special bond with them.

He couldn't believe his Chief bought the story.

Kurt grins ever so slightly, recalling how sincere he acted that day.

Hell, he didn't even go to Chris Mills' wake, using the excuse the veterans from Gilles Police Department should go, while he worked the street.

Kurt hated those Greenfield pricks in every possible way.

While he hated to see Chris Mills dead, he had little use for Mills and the rest of the Greenfield police recruits.

The way they carried themselves at ILETC, was like they owned the place.

"Fuck all of them," he thought.

Now, he stares out the window of the black and white Dodge Charger, with a huge Village of Gilles emblem on each side of it.

Kurt looks at some of the faces in the crowds lining the streets.

"What a freaking sick carnival this is," he says only to himself.

He recalls the Ringling Bros. and Barnum & Bailey Circus coming to Rosemont every year, when he was a little kid.

He would sit on his father's shoulders and point at the different animals as they were paraded from their carriers or crates and made a slow march to their new home for their weekend performances, at the Rosemont Horizon.

Slowly, the animals moved as if they were tranquilized and walking to their deaths.

"What is the difference with those animals and today? "Kurt thinks.

In both cases, people stood on the sidewalk with their mouths hanging open, pointing and not even sure what they were pointing at.

In both cases, there were flashing lights, sirens or bells which alerted the public of something big heading their way, which they shouldn't miss.

Finally, like the animals, the participants in the funeral procession move slowly in a straight line, not even sure where they were going.

Unlike the circus performers, an occasional animal would turn towards the noise of the crowd in an attempt to acknowledge it.

Today, not one officer in the funeral procession, whether they were on a motorcycle or riding in a squad car, acknowledged the crowd.

For each of these officers is thinking the same, exact thing, "Thank God it's not me lying inside that coffin."

"Do you guys ever think about dying?" This was the most common question besides "Who gives you guys the best discounts?" Kurt had experienced since graduating from ILETC.

"Of course, we think about it," he would tell his Southern Illinois University buddies, over a Budweiser or Miller Lite at Chewers, in Gilles.

How couldn't you when every day you came to work, opened up your locker, put on a Kevlar level II bulletproof vest, along with a 40 caliber Glock and enough ammo to take on the Chinese Army?

When over 40% of the classes at ILETC, centered on trusting no one, shoot to kill, and protect your damn weapon rookie.

Each of those instructor's voices still echoed in Kurt's head.

"We don't think about it every day or we would go nuts," he would respond, before moving on to another subject.

Kurt didn't care about his college friends right now, or even his fellow police officers in the same squad car with him.

All Kurt wanted more than anything, was to be in the second car of the funeral procession, seated next to, Megan O'Brien.

Whether holding her hand, or rubbing her back, Kurt knew Megan needed comforting, the type only he could provide.

Since they had graduated from ILETC, they had never gone this long without communicating with each other.

But with the death of Chris Mills, Megan going to Belvedere to get Mrs. Mills and then attending the wake, it had been over 72 hours since they had any contact between the two of them.

This definitely didn't sit well with Kurt.

Even the few text messages he had sent Megan hadn't been returned.

A smile slowly starts to cross Kurt's face as he recalls all the ways he had tried to gain her attention and win her heart during their time at ILETC.

The instruction and training left little time for partying and most cadets were in bed early, due to the fear of missing their two-mile run at 0630 hours.

It didn't dawn on Kurt why every time they ran, Ron Thomas would fall in directly behind Megan.

He assumed it was the Greenfield guys protecting their own, until one day Thomas was late and Kurt got in behind her.

Then he saw what Thomas had been looking at every time.

No one could fill out a pair of navy-blue gym shorts the way Megan could.

By far, she was the most beautiful cadet in the ILETC and for that matter, one of the most beautiful women he had ever seen.

With her glowing red hair, blue eyes and cute freckles, she had the face of a teenager yet the body of a fully mature, hot looking woman.

When she wasn't in gym clothes, or sweats, for defensive tactics classes, she always dressed prim and proper with never a button open to reveal too much.

The running only seemed to accentuate her beauty.

During the run, Kurt couldn't take his eyes off her ass.

Yet, when they finished the run and he tried to talk to her, Matt O'Neil stepped in front of him to give her a bottle of water.

Before long, the remainder of the Greenfield Cadets followed, shielding her from the other cadets.

That was Kurt's only time to talk to her for what seemed like an eternity.

Meal time was hopeless as well because she always sat with her fellow Greenfield Cadets and her roommate, Cynthia Mallory, from the Peoria Police Department.

Of all the roommate pairings at ILETC, Megan O'Brien and Cynthia Mallory were easily the strangest.

Megan barely spoke and when she did, it seemed to be in a soft, monotone voice.

Cynthia's voice seemed to echo off any wall of the building the cadets were in.

Megan made both men's and, in some cases, women's heads turn when she walked by them.

At 5'8" and weighing about 160 pounds, Cynthia would never be confused with any Hollywood starlet.

But many of the cadets took an instant liking to her, with her beautiful dark tan, continuous smile and enthusiasm.

The fact Cynthia was one of the best shots at ILETC, made all of the cadets like her even more.

For Cynthia, like every other woman police officer, whether they were driving a squad car in Chicago, New York, or Houston, needed every advantage they could get.

"Child rearing and making an occasional hot meal, that's all women cops are damn good for," Tommy Thompson would say.

Tommy Thompson had been a police officer in Barkin, Wisconsin, for close to 30 years and eventually rose to the rank of Chief, before retiring.

Kurt would sit for hours listening to the "war stories" about police work, his Uncle Tommy would share with him at the conclusion of a relative's birthday party, Thanksgiving, or Christmas family get-togethers.

Uncle Tommy would often wait until his wife Edith, had left the room and it was just Kurt and maybe Kurt's father John, before the insults would start flying.

"When the shit hits the fan, do you really want a woman or a guy?" Uncle Tommy would often say.

"Not to mention, I didn't have one guy who volunteered to work with a woman. Every guy knew his wife wouldn't't be too crazy about him working with some chick and heaven forbid you get home late from your shift, the old lady is thinking you're banging your partner somewhere, instead of coming home. Who needs that kind of headache?" Uncle Tommy would always finish up and hit himself with his right hand, on top of his forehead.

Kurt didn't know what to think just yet.

At that time, all he was trying to do was get through ILETC and make his family proud.

Kurt actually felt sorry for Megan.

If it wasn't a cadet from another department trying to get to first base with her, then it was an instructor also giving it their best shot.

When she looked for a little quiet time, one of the guys from her own stinking department was hitting on her.

The worst of the entire ILETC class, had to be Ron Thomas, who was unmerciful.

Whether it be on a break, during classroom time, or even during their three daily meals in the cafeteria, Ron Thomas would find any excuse to try and win favors with Megan.

But the minute things got a little carried away, Matt O'Neil would step in and end it.

Sometimes with a simple, mean glare or, if things were really starting to get out of hand, a single, loud "Hey," would often do the trick.

All of the cadets believed Megan and Matt had nothing going on.

"Or did they?" Kurt often wondered.

Kurt couldn't quite figure out Matt O'Neil.

Matt was different than all of the other cadets at The Illinois Law Enforcement Training Center, but Kurt didn't know why.

It couldn't be the military thing since four other cadets, including Chris Mills and T.C. Chambers from Greenfield, also were former military.

Like Megan, Matt was the only other cadet to have never stepped foot inside a Champaign bar, since all of them had arrived at ILETC.

"Was it his age?" Kurt thought.

Matt O'Neil was the oldest cadet at the ILETC by two years and five months and he certainly was the most driven, due to his constant hours of individual study and devotion to his wife Kelly.

When Kurt walked by O'Neil's room, he was either studying, on the phone, texting, or e-mailing his wife.

Kurt had seen a picture of Kelly, which Matt had on his desk at ILETC and she truly was stunning.

Kurt knew the minute he saw the picture, she looked like someone he knew.

But for some reason, he just couldn't place her.

Then, one day he was channel surfing in his room after an especially boring Criminal Law class, when he came upon the movie, "The Wolf of Wall Street," featuring a new female star.

"That's her!" Kurt caught himself yelling out loud.

He quickly looked around and was thankful his roommate, Carl Eckert, was in the shower and didn't hear him. The female lead in the movie, could have been Kelly O'Neil's twin sister.

"Shit," he thought. "I can't even imagine waking up next to that every morning.

But was it all just a hoax?"

Now, Kurt thought Megan only cared about him, but he only thought this briefly while they we're training together.

He remembered fondly the exact day, time and the crazy events leading up to her proving her love to him.

Wednesday evening and exactly forty hours before graduation.

The ILETC realized years ago the day before graduation would be a complete waste of time.

Consequently, a couple of first aid classes in the afternoon and a walk through of the graduation ceremony, was all which was planned for the day.

The day before, every recruit had passed the range qualification and scored enough on the written tests in the past months, to be certified by the State of Illinois, as a police officer.

The authorities at ILETC knew every cadet realized this situation as well. Since a number of cadets had been told, by fellow officers from their respective departments, who had previously come to ILETC.

On the first day of attending class, every cadet was given eight hours of time off to be used for sick leave, or a non-specific emergency.

The cadets were told these eight hours could be used at any time while enrolled in the program.

Not one cadet in the program had used their respective eight hours.

Every cadet had saved the time for the next morning, because they knew what would be happening that evening.

The time had come to celebrate in style.

After graduation many of these cadets wouldn't see their fellow classmates for some time, if ever again.

The celebration began, and it seemed like every recruit except for, Megan and Matt joined Kurt, at P.J.'s Sports Bar on Des Plaines Avenue, in Champaign.

Kurt had never seen so many plasma televisions, or pool tables, in one sports bar.

The waitresses wore short, dark blue and orange shorts and an orange University of Illinois t-shirt, cut off at the navel, with "Fighting Illini," written across the front of them.

Kurt's head started to spin from a combination of beer and yelling from the adjoining Greenfield table.

"Sweet Jesus," he said out loud, "those guys can drink and drink some more."

He remembered thinking he couldn't believe some of the

Greenfield guys could still be standing after consuming beer after beer after beer. But even he was shocked at how grab ass their table became with any female who walked by.

Kurt caught himself glancing at the door where a couple of security guards stood as bouncers. For some unknown reason, they seemed intimidated by the size and actions of both Chris Mills and T.C. Chambers.

Kurt was no prude, but even he thought the Greenfield guys were out of line with their actions and believed the Greenfield Cadets thought they could get away with anything they wanted.

Just when Kurt thought it couldn't get any worse, it did.

The cutest waitress by far, working at P.J.'s Sports Bar, was Jody Lopez.

A striking, tall brunette, Jody Lopez, unlike the other waitresses, had made a few cuts to her orange Illinois t-shirt to show off her God-given natural assets.

Combine the t-shirt with her orange and blue gym shorts, which were a bit shorter than all of the other waitresses, and every male customer in the establishment couldn't take their eyes off her.

Especially, when she walked by their table, or purposely bent over to pick up an empty beer mug, or bill from a table.

Jody Lopez enjoyed the attention she was getting and she was getting plenty of it.

Unfortunately, she had the Greenfield table as one of her assigned tables.

As she had passed out the 6th round of drinks to them, she walked by Ron Thomas, as she was returning to the bar.

Without the slightest hesitation, Ron turned slightly, while still talking to Javier Ortego, and grabbed Jody Lopez's ass, with his left hand.

Upon seeing what Ron had just done, Javier let out the biggest drunken induced yell of his entire 22-year-old life.

A yell so loud, anyone in close proximity to the Greenfield table, had to stop and look.

A yell so loud, it actually startled a couple of people at another table, in Jody Lopez's assigned area.

This table, had walked in relatively unnoticed, due to everyone else in the bar watching the actions of the Greenfield table.

For this table was made up of six members, of the Fighting Illini's, varsity football team.

One of the six, was Stefan "The Rock" Joshua, who happened to be the starting middle linebacker on the team.

Stefan "The Rock" Joshua had led the Big Ten in two significant categories last year.

Those categories were tackled for losses and personal fouls for unnecessary roughness.

At 6'3" weighing 243 pounds, Joshua had earned the nickname "The Rock" due to transforming his body with an aggressive, off season conditioning program.

When he reported for summer camp with his teammates, Joshua had gained an impressive 17 pounds and lowered his body fat to 2%.

The one thing Stefan "The Rock" Joshua hadn't been able to lower was his temper.

It seemed like the slightest thing could set him off—holding by an offensive lineman, someone treating his pit-bull badly, or someone other than himself touching his girlfriend, Jody Lopez.

He never took his eyes off of her the entire time he was inside P.J.'s Sports Bar.

Joshua didn't need Javier Ortego's yell to realize Ron Thomas had grabbed his girlfriend's ass, because he'd witnessed it himself.

The only thing his tablemates heard him say was, "Shit," as he headed to the Greenfield table.

Joshua came around the adjoining table, just behind Ron Thomas, like an unsuspecting quarterback.

Poor Ron never had a chance.

With one, swift left forearm shot, Ron suddenly found himself knocked off his chair and onto the floor, with an angry, young male yelling, "Get up motherfucker!"

Suddenly, pandemonium broke out inside P.J.'s Sports Bar.

Without hesitation, T.C. Chambers and Chris Mills each grabbed an arm of Stefan "The Rock" Joshua and started to twist it behind his back.

T.C. seemed to be better at this than Chris, until T.C. found a screaming Jody Lopez on his back with her arms wrapped around his neck and her fingers trying to poke his eyes out.

Kurt had seen enough and ran for the back door with Cynthia Mallory close behind him yelling, "Hurry up. Hurry up."

Once safely outside, both Kurt and Cynthia stopped and turned, walking slowly towards a lower-level window of P.J.'s Sports Bar.

Each peered in the window like two kids looking inside a window at Macy's on State Street, in Chicago at Christmas time.

With their eyes aglow in amazement, they couldn't believe what each was witnessing.

The five remaining members of the University of Illinois football team were no longer seated and were rushing towards the Greenfield table.

Each of the five had a look on their faces like they had just come out of the Memorial Football Stadium tunnel after hearing their head coach chew their respective asses out at half time.

The security guards finally made their way toward the Greenfield table and one of them was trying to get Jody Lopez off the back of T.C. Chambers.

The other security guard was trying to calm down Joshua, but was having a hard time doing so.

A table of six cadets from ILETC, figured it was time to use some of their extensive training and were also headed toward the fight.

Seeing this, fellow waitresses and college students felt for the first-time, law enforcement had gained a far superior edge in manpower and headed toward the Greenfield table.

No one knew who threw the first Miller Lite bottle, but it easily went nose first through one of the 60-inch plasma television sets, located next to the bar.

Just as all parties were about to meet, the sound of sirens filled the air.

Both Kurt and Cynthia turned to see two Champaign, Ford Crown Victoria black and white squad cars, enter the alley they were standing in.

Blue and red lights from the squad cars mars lights bounced off the glass windows of each building the squad cars passed.

Without hesitation, Kurt reached out and grabbed Cynthia's left hand as they ran down the alley, in the opposite direction of the squad cars.

As they ran, two things amazed Kurt Thompson.

First, after drinking practically non-stop for four hours, the ease at which he was able to run.

The months of early morning ILETC runs, were finally starting to pay some dividends.

Second, the ability of Cynthia Mallory, to run almost stride for stride with him.

Twice, Kurt remembered looking over his right shoulder and each time there was Cynthia, barely breaking a sweat.

As they ran, the alley was coming to an end.

As fate would have it, ending at Alley Street.

When they both reached the end of the alley, as if previously rehearsed, each split in opposite directions.

Cynthia turned right, running back toward the business section of Champaign.

Kurt turned left and continued running westbound on Alley Street, toward the University of Illinois campus.

He just kept running and running, passing Memorial Stadium.

Before long, he was climbing the stairs and fell into his bed at Bromley Hall, clothes and all.

Kurt awoke on Thursday morning, with the worst hangover, in his young life.

As he headed for the bathroom, he stumbled and tripped over his New Balance 529's, which he had kicked off in the early morning rush to get to bed.

Upon reaching the bathroom, he opened the mirrored medicine cabinet and grabbed his best friend for the past three months since being here, Advil.

Throwing four tablets into his mouth, he quickly downed them with a warm, half empty bottle of red Gatorade, which for some unknown reason, was left sitting on the bathroom counter.

Looking into the bathroom mirror he was pleased with the reflection.

A couple of bloodshot eyes were the only damage, from one of the craziest nights of his life.

Wow, he backed up for a minute to get a total look at his upper body and he was impressed with it also.

Yes, ILETC had been very good to him·

It helped turn an average, former college student's body, into a firm, fighting machine with a couple of actual biceps and flat stomach.

Walking from the bathroom, Kurt passed Carl Eckert's perfectly made bed and a small smile crossed his face.

"Well, well, Eckert got laid last night, the lucky SOB," Kurt said to himself· " Fellow cadet or University of Illinois student?" he wondered as he began straightening out his own bed·

"Has to be a college student, otherwise where would he sleep?" Kurt thought, as he finished tucking his pillow underneath the comforter.

Glancing at the clock radio seated next to Eckert's bed, Kurt saw 0950 hours and breathed a sigh of relief, as he realized he had just slept the longest since being at ILETC and still had time to get breakfast in the cafeteria.

A quick shower, a clean pair of khakis, combined with the traditional ILETC shirt, navy blue short sleeve, button down polo, with the name Thompson over his right breast and he soon found himself in line for food in Bromley Hall's cafeteria.

The excessive drinking, length of time since his last meal and mere fact he had one hour before the first aid class, allowed him to load his plate and tray with French toast, scrambled eggs with bacon and two steaming cups of coffee.

Finding his traditional seat near the milk dispenser, gave him an excellent view of the entire cafeteria.

With eagerness, he sat alone, as he had done from day one, since eating his first meal here.

Oblivious to the noise around him, Kurt waited for the Greenfield group to make their appearance and to see what kind of injuries they had sustained in their altercation, at P.J.'s Sports Bar.

He didn't have long to wait.

After finishing one of the steaming cups of coffee, Kurt looked up to see Chris Mills enter the cafeteria, followed by the remainder of the Greenfield Cadets.

Each of the Greenfield Cadets seemed to have gotten their ass kicked, to put it bluntly.

Both Ron Thomas and Marc Dombrowski had bruises on their faces which appeared to be relatively fresh.

Javier Ortego seemed to be wincing as he walked and why was Chris Mills wearing sunglasses?

But things seemed different in a couple of other ways.

Not one of the Greenfield group was talking to each other, after they had gathered their food and found a long table to sit at.

Each of them seemed to be in their own separate world.

Where the hell was Matt and, more importantly Megan, since they weren't with the rest of the Greenfield group?

Kurt was so enthralled in watching the Greenfield group, he never heard the person standing next to him, until she asked gently, "Mind if I sit down?"

He recognized the voice immediately, even though he'd heard it only a couple of times in training classes.

In one quick move he found himself standing and turning until he was face to face and only inches apart from Megan O'Brien.

"Sorry if I startled you," she said and quickly backed up a few steps.

For a full five seconds he couldn't answer her.

Up close, she was even more beautiful than Kurt had thought.

Her blue eyes seemed to be even bluer and more glistening in the cafeteria lighting.

But he soon realized this wasn't the same Megan he'd been watching and dreaming about at night since day one at ILETC.

For the first time, she was wearing makeup.

Nothing too drastic, but a slight bit of eye shadow and rouge on her cheeks.

When the shock of her standing in front of him wore off, he smelled perfume coming from her.

He recognized the scent as being White Shoulders, because a former girlfriend couldn't go without it.

Also, for the first time Kurt could recall, all three buttons on her blue polo shirt were undone.

Due to his height advantage, he found himself looking slightly down at her and was startled to see scratch marks on the base of her neck, which looked fresh.

Megan must have noticed for she asked, "Do you mind if I join you for breakfast?"

But this time in a slightly louder and firmer voice.

Kurt recalled how caught off guard he was by the question.

"No, no, I mean yes, of course," he found himself stammering as he pulled out the chair seated next to his.

Instead, Megan ignored the chair and carrying her tray, slowly walked around the table, until she found the chair directly across from his, and sat down.

When he sat down and pulled his chair in, the first of his problems that morning started.

Blame it on the coffee, the excessive amount of alcohol from the night before, or sitting across from the most beautiful woman he had ever met, but Kurt began to sweat.

First, it was both of his palms.

But in a matter of minutes, he could feel it in his armpits.

The harder he tried to fight it, the worst it became.

Then, Kurt did something terribly foolish.

He took his gaze off Megan's beautiful face, as she stopped her conversation, to drink her hot tea and he looked over her head to find what seemed like 10,000 eyes staring at him.

His sweating problem only became drastically worse.

The entire Greenfield table was giving him death stares, with T.C. Chambers, Chris Mills and Ron Thomas turned around in their chairs, glaring at him.

One whole bead of sweat traveled from the small of his back, down into his Hanes underwear.

Glancing quickly to his left and then to his right, he realized every cadet and instructor were looking directly at him, with a wide range of emotions.

Some cadets were smiling, while others had their mouths hanging open.

Over in the corner, sitting with Cynthia Mallory, was his roommate Carl Eckert, who gave him a thumbs up with both hands.

"Cynthia Mallory and Carl Eckert together?" Kurt wondered.

Seeing them together brought a smile to his face, and the sweating stopped.

Kurt recalled how easily the conversation flowed for the 25 minutes they sat across the table from each other.

Megan did most of the talking, in her soft voice, on a wide variety of topics all pertaining to, or related to their three months at ILETC.

Favorite instructor, worst instructor, and best defensive tactic move, were some of the things he recalled them talking about, until she looked at her watch and said, "Oh my gosh, I have to get to class."

"I? Why not we?" Kurt thought.

As she stood up, he did so as well, grabbing his sweat shirt and throwing it over his shoulder.

With his right hand, he picked up his tray, her tray with his left hand and headed for the conveyor belt to deliver both trays.

As he walked towards the conveyor belt, with Megan behind him, Kurt's second set of problems awaited him.

Almost on cue, the entire Greenfield table got up in unison, as he neared their table to get to the conveyor belt.

Kurt's sweating problem started up again.

As he and Megan neared the Greenfield table, a voice yelled out from the north exit door to the cafeteria.

The yell was so loud, it momentarily stunned him.

"Sit down Greenfield," and it seemed like every person still left in the cafeteria, was now looking at Matt O'Neil, who was standing with his arms folded across his chest, in the cafeteria doorway.

Slowly, each of the Greenfield cadets began to sit down, grumbling to themselves and shaking their throbbing, hangover induced heads.

Without hesitation, Kurt rushed to the conveyor belt and placed the trays on it.

Then, he walked directly towards the north cafeteria door.

As he passed his new savior, Kurt said, "Thanks Matt," and kept on walking, until he was safely outside Bromley Hall.

Kurt stopped to put on his grey, SIU sweatshirt.

While in the process of pulling it over his head, he said, "You better put something on Megan."

After pulling the sweatshirt down and slightly straightening out the hood, he looked around.

Megan O'Brien was suddenly gone.

Kurt found himself in a state of shock and confusion.

Making a complete 360-degree turn, in an effort to find Megan, he proceeded to knock down a small, female Asian, University of Illinois student, who was hurrying to class.

From the ground, this student looked up at the towering Kurt Thompson standing over her.

The student began shaking, with a combination of fear and anger spreading over her young face.

"What the hell you doing, asshole?" she screamed at Kurt.

"I'm really sorry," is all Kurt could say, while extending his right hand to grab hers and lift her up off the ground.

"Thank you jerk," she responded and quickly walked away.

Occasionally glancing over her right shoulder, the student looked to reassure herself Kurt wasn't following her, after she swore at him.

In only a few minutes, Kurt found himself standing at the front door of Thompson Hall, which housed the classrooms, for the ILETC cadets.

Suddenly, a thousand different thoughts raced through his head.

"Do I say anything to her if she's in there?"

"Do I play tough guy and just ignore her and see what happens next?"

"If she smiles at me what should I do?"

The sweating problem started all over again.

As he was preparing to enter Thompson Hall, Kurt felt a shove on the top of his shoulders that moved him to the left.

He straightened himself and watched each of the Greenfield Cadets, led by T.C. Chambers, pass him with their left hand out and middle finger extended, except for Matt O'Neil, who wasn't with them.

"Enough," is all Kurt could mumble to himself.

"Months of putting up with their shit is over," he thought as he felt his face turning red.

His anger grew as he slowly climbed the Thompson Hall stairs, to his second-floor classroom.

With each step, he grew angrier and he realized two things.

He had never been this mad in his entire life.

Secondly, he was actually fearful for the first Greenfield Cadet he would encounter.

Without hesitation, he entered the classroom and the first Greenfield Cadet he saw was Megan O'Brien, sitting in her assigned seat alphabetically.

Seated on Megan's right sat Chris Mills and on her left, where he had sat from a day one, Matt O'Neil.

Kurt couldn't help but stare at her as he climbed the stadium type seating.

All he could remember was she never looked up.

Matt and Megan had their heads down in their American Red Cross manuals.

The exact second he sat down, Instructor Dan Mcaullie, from the American Red Cross, started his lecture, leaving little time for Kurt to ponder the situation.

If Kurt wanted to even think about it, his chance went out the window as Dan Mcaullie called upon him first, with a question about the signs and symptoms of a heart attack.

He spent the next three hours, with breaks included, switching his attention from Dan Mcaullie, to Megan.

"Turn around and look at me Megan, please give me some type of sign this morning meant something," he found himself thinking over and over.

She never turned around the entire class.

Even during the skills section of the training program, when there was some free time, Megan failed to look at him.

Instead, whenever time allowed, she would wander out of the classroom, or huddle in the corner with her roommate, Cynthia Mallory, and no one else.

Graduation practice was even worse.

The entire cadet class marched over to Assembly Hall, where they spent the next hour, going over how the graduation procedure would go the following morning.

Upon completing the practice, they broke up into small groups and filed out of Assembly Hall, anxious to get back to their dorm rooms for either a quick nap before dinner, or to start the process of packing for their trips home.

Each cadet knew tomorrow would go by quickly, and not one of them was willing to spend an extra minute here.

Kurt had given up and had no idea where or with whom Megan had left Assembly Hall.

Instead, the idea of a nap before dinner seemed like a great idea.

Whatever energy he had at the start of the day was completely gone.

When Kurt reached his room in Bromley Hall, he almost got knocked over by Carl Eckert, running out the door.

"Have someone waiting for me roomie," is all Eckert blurted out, as he headed for the stairs.

"Good riddance," Kurt said quietly to himself as he entered their now vacant room.

Kurt had planned to make at least one friend while he was at ILETC.

Instead, he hadn't made a single friend the entire time.

Not one person from this cadet class would he ever bother to call or even text on a midnight shift when he was totally bored out of his mind and fighting to stay awake. Even his roommate Carl Eckert, had little if any use for Kurt.

But trying to fall asleep was the predicament he was in right now.

Carefully he reached over from his bed and set his alarm for 1730 hours, which would enable him to get about an hour nap, a quick dinner and still have time to pack and watch the end of the Cubs vs. Pirates game.

It seemed like he had been asleep for only a few minutes, when the loudest thunder he had ever heard filled the sky and seemed to land right outside Bromley Hall.

The thunder ended and a steady downpour of rain began.

"Just fucking great," he said out loud as he rolled over and tried to fall back asleep, pulling a pillow over his head.

After a period of six to seven minutes, he seemed to have found sleep only to be awoken this time by a gentle knocking on his door.

"Jesus," he blurted out as he walked slowly to the door yelling, "Eckert, where's your God damn key?"

Kurt timed it perfectly as he got the word, "key," out and ripped open the door to find a rain-drenched Megan standing in front of him, shivering.

"Meg," was all he was able to say before she quickly used the index finger on her right hand and put it up to his lips to quiet him.

She then used her left hand to gently push Kurt back inside his dorm room.

Not a word was spoken between the two of them for the next 25 minutes.

Once inside his dorm room, Megan used both of her hands to pull his white Hanes t-shirt over his head.

She threw the shirt over her shoulder as she continued pushing him backward toward his bed.

Kurt was not going to be out done and proceeded to pull her polo shirt, which was soaking wet, over her head and toss it on the floor.

Once they reached the foot of his bed, they both stopped.

With their arms around each other, Kurt started to reach behind Megan to undo her white bra and momentarily stopped, surprised for a second.

Megan was helping speed up matters by kicking off her Nike gym shoes and unbuttoning her wet blue jeans.

With her bra undone, he lowered his head and began kissing two of the most perfect breasts he had ever seen.

Slowly, he used both of his hands, to slip off her baby blue panties.

Once done, he started to reach for the only item either one of them was still wearing—his Converse gym shorts.

But he stopped, because Megan was taking them off him instead.

When finished, she gave him a gentle push, causing him to fall slowly backward onto his bed.

Slowly and carefully, Megan joined him by getting on top of him in his bed and gently began kissing the right side of his neck and then his right ear lobe area.

Kurt was amazed at how quickly he was able to get an erection.

This also didn't go unnoticed by Megan, who took her left hand to slowly guide his penis into her.

Kurt was no virgin and every rumor at ILETC, about Megan being one, seemed false by her actions in his dorm room that evening.

The way she slowly moved her hips in a circular fashion, only enhanced the sheer pleasure of the moment, for both of them.

As Megan climaxed, her head slowly went backwards and she gently moaned.

Once finished, Megan slowly slid off Kurt and positioned herself, on the left side of his body.

Carefully she put her head on the left side of his chest and neck.

Then, she placed her left hand across his chest and turned inward, cuddling up with him by putting her other hand underneath the pillow, his head laid on.

After five to six minutes of laying still, Kurt finally moved his head slightly to the left to give Megan a slow, soft kiss and was amused to find her already asleep and gently snoring.

Kurt's sexual experiences in his life had been short, but he'd never encountered anyone who snored so slowly and smoothly after sex and it brought a huge smile to his face.

Before he knew it, Kurt also fell asleep.

The loud chirping of his alarm clock, along with the numbers 5:30 flashing in red inside his darkened dorm room, snapped Kurt out of his nap.

Quickly he turned to his right and in one smooth motion while using his right hand, moved the switch turning off his alarm

When finished and while still in bed, he turned to his left saying in the process "Megan it's time to wake up".

Kurt Thompson though found himself all alone, in an empty bed.

Jumping out of bed, he rushed to his dorm room door, to find it in the locked position, from the inside.

With his left hand he felt his chest and realized he was still wearing his Hanes, white colored tee shirt, along with his Converse gym shorts.

Then reality quickly set in for him.

It had only been a dream and Megan O'Brien had never stepped foot in his dorm room.

Remembering that night brought a huge grin to his face and the start of a slight erection in his uniform pants.

In a flash, Kurt Thompson suddenly found himself sliding off the black, rubber back seat, of the Gilles Police Car and onto its hardened floor.

"Thompson you okay?" asked Mike Antonio, who was driving the Gilles squad car.

While still laying crunched up on the car floor, Kurt asked, "Yeah, what the fuck just happened?"

"Shit, some freaking woman lost control of her German Shepard and the stupid pet ran out into the street. The Skokie guy stopped from hitting it, but then got rear-ended by a Chicago squad, which caused all of us to hit our fucking brakes. Sorry kid," Antonio finishes.

"Yes, a freaking sick carnival," is all Kurt can think to himself, unaware in coming months, he would be one of the main acts.

CHAPTER 5

I t had been five days since officer Chris Mills' death.

Yet those five days, like today's funeral service, seemed like a blur to Matt O'Neil.

During those days, the sight of the Ford Bronco going through the red light, never seemed to leave Matt.

A license plate character, a number, or a description of the driver, could make all the difference in the world, and he knew it.

But as hard as he tried, he couldn't think of anything different, about the damn vehicle, or its driver.

Matt's focus now was on giving Harriet, the proper burial of her son, which both she and Chris deserved.

The funeral mass was held at Our Lady of Faith Church, in Greenfield.

In Matt O'Neil's life, he had never seen a church like Our Lady of Faith and he prayed, he would never have to visit it under these circumstances, ever again.

Built in 1907 and serving only 18 families at the time, Our Lady of Faith Church was majestic, both on its interior, as well as its exterior.

Visitors and parishioners entered the church through six large, white, wooden doors, which were overshadowed by four white, Roman style columns.

Once inside, the church housed a majestic main altar, with seating located on three sides of it.

Our Lady of Faith was one of the first of its kind to have the traditional clock tower steeple on its roof, which could be seen from miles around.

With the death of Chris Mills, it would also have the distinction of being remembered as the first church in the history of the Greenfield Police Department, to be used for a line of duty death.

Remarkably, in their 98-year existence, no other Greenfield Police Officer had been killed on duty, before Chris Mills' passing.

Matt remembered being somewhat surprised when his FTO Pat Carll mentioned it during a shift they had worked, only a few months prior.

The citizens of Greenfield had shown great respect with the passing of Chris Mills, in a number of different ways.

A makeshift memorial had been set up on the corner of Moody and First Streets.

The memorial had a number of different flower arrangements, a gold frame containing a picture of Jesus Christ, a mixture of different size candles and five small, American flags, stuck in the ground.

The public had also dropped off a number of cakes and desserts at the Greenfield Police Department.

Finally, most members of the Greenfield force were surprised by the number of Greenfield citizens who had never met or knew Chris Mills in any way, but still waited patiently to view his body and pay their respects, at Donnelly Funeral Home.

Chris Mills' death would require the entire Greenfield Police Department, both sworn and non-sworn, to attend his funeral.

Consequently, this would put into action, a plan every police department in the world had buried in a file cabinet, or on a bookshelf and hoped they would never have to use.

The day when no one in their town, city, or village, would be available to police their citizens.

Although the chance of this happening was slim (for example, if a terrorist attack or labor disagreement occurred), every police department needed to plan for it.

Today was a new day and every citizen of Greenfield, while possibly still sad about the death of Chris Mills, expected police protection as they went about their daily activities, left the village to go to work, or watched as their children boarded a bus to go to school.

The responsibility of providing this protection, fell on the shoulders of Deputy Chief Andrew Bart.

Within 90 minutes of Chris Mills' death, Deputy Chief Bart was back at the Greenfield Police Station, after visiting Chris Mills' accident scene.

Even though both deputy chief's duties were completely different from each other, they shared a common goal.

The goal being, Chris Mills' funeral would function smoothly and without any glitches.

Each deputy chief knew this task would be in addition to their regular duties and would require the possibility of 14-hour days. But they also knew when they were promoted to their positions of deputy chief, the death of one of their own was a possibility.

During the course of the next 96 hours, Deputy Chief Bart used a combination of phone calls, texts, and e-mails, to accomplish this task.

Starting exactly at 0900 hours and ending at 1400 hours on the day of Chris Mills' funeral, Wilmette Police Department would provide police services to the east side of Greenfield.

Northfield Police Department would do the same, for the north side of Greenfield.

Gilles Police Department would cover the south side of Greenfield.

Finally, Northbrook Police Department would cover the west side of Greenfield.

Each of these towns would be supported by the Cook County Sheriff's Police, who would supply two patrol units and a K-9 unit, to rove throughout Greenfield.

Next, Deputy Chief Bart's attention focused on meeting with the supervisor of the Traffic Bureau, Sgt. Humberto Garza.

Through the use of Garza's personnel and motorcycles, they had the significant task of closing down intersections, for the funeral procession.

Of major concern to both Sgt. Garza and Deputy Chief Bart was the exact length of the funeral procession, which no one could predict.

Deputy Chief Gyondski had put out the traditional LEADS message for the death of Chris Mills and the address of the Donnelly Funeral Home.

But few, if any, police departments responded to these messages. Instead, they chose to send one officer and squad car if they had enough personnel working the day of the funeral, as a show of respect for their fallen brother or sister officer.

Fortunately, every officer attending the funeral had a place to park their vehicle and a short walk to the church with Our Lady of Faith's massive parking lot and three commuter train parking lots only a few blocks away.

Choosing to go with a safe timetable of 35 minutes for the funeral procession to travel safely through each intersection, the plan should work.

Unfortunately, Deputy Chief Bart was a believer in Murphy's Law.

To help guarantee the plan would work, he picked two of the newest Greenfield Officers, Ron Thomas and Marc Dombrowski, to supplement the Traffic Bureau in closing down intersections.

Finally, add to the mix, the review of daily activity logs, with a 0900-daily briefing, on Chris Mills' death investigation. Attending these briefings were Chief Fitzsimons, Deputy Chief Gyondski, and the head of the Criminal Investigations Unit, for the Greenfield Police Department, Lt. Dan Alderman.

Deputy Chief Gyondski's tasks were less complex and mainly boiled down to informing the Chicagoland media of Chris Mills' death, as well as keeping the news media informed of the ongoing death investigation and working on any logistics for his funeral.

Deputy Chief Gyondski's task started at Lutheran Family Center Hospital.

When Chief Fitzsimons stopped and returned to talk to Officer Matt O'Neil, Deputy Chief Gyondski continued walking toward what was awaiting him.

D.C. Gyondski wore a number of different hats for the Greenfield Police Department.

His biggest assignment, being the project manager for the construction of the new Greenfield Police Station.

A task so monumental, the new facility would set the village back, $22 million.

Yet, due to the size of the police department and the relative lack of serious crime, Chief Fitzsimons decided Deputy Chief Gyondski would also assume the role of Public Information Officer, for the police department.

Fortunately, this had required a small amount of work in the past, but today would be different.

In roughly twelve minutes, Deputy Chief Gyondski found himself standing in the first-floor hallway, just west of the main entrance to Lutheran Family Center Hospital, before a set of closed doors.

He passed this room on numerous occasions while visiting ill friends at the hospital and prayed he would never have to use this room in his present position.

He took two deep breaths and exhaled slowly through his mouth, in an effort to calm his nerves. Satisfied he had done so, he entered the huge multi-purpose room, which had become the center for the Chicago media, due to the rain and cold.

As he approached the podium, he stepped onto the platform it rested on and into a series of bright lights.

He saw reporters on cell phones and a series of cameras, all pointed towards him.

An eerie hush fell over the crew of reporters, some of whom still held their cell phones next to their ears.

In a clear, yet firm voice he spoke into a sea of microphones. "Ladies and gentlemen of the press, if you're ready I have prepared a statement for you. After reading it, I will try to answer any questions you may have."

"Sir, could you please give us two more minutes to set up, since we just got here due to morning rush hour traffic," said a reporter.

Deputy Chief Gyondski recognized the reporter as Alexa Stmomum from the Fox Station in Chicago and calmly answered, "Sure."

As if an alarm clock had gone off, it seemed like every television reporter in the room turned to their camera man for last minute instructions and preparation.

As Deputy Chief Gyondski waited patiently, his Motorola cell phone went off, indicating he had a new text message.

While still looking out at the reporters, he carefully removed the cell phone from its case to see the following message from Chief Fitzsimons: "Where the hell are you?"

Before he could reply, both doors to the room opened violently.

Chief Fitzsimons entered the room, walking directly towards the podium.

Deputy Chief Gyondski had seen this look on Chief Fitzsimons' face only once before, at a command staff meeting, and without hesitation, he stepped away from the podium and microphones.

Chief Fitzsimons stepped in front of the microphones, paused for a moment to collect himself, and then began.

"Good morning, I am Chief Ryan Fitzsimons, of the Greenfield Police Department and it is with great sadness that I need to announce the death of one of our own. I needed to get confirmation the family of the officer had been notified before I addressed you and that assignment has been completed."

"At roughly 5:25 AM today, Officer Christopher Mills, a rookie officer on our police department, was brought to this hospital, with severe internal and external injuries. Despite the heroic work of the emergency room staff, Officer Mills was unable to overcome his injuries and was pronounced dead at 6:00 AM."

Upon the word dead, coming out of Chief Fitzsimons' mouth, two reporters actually gasped.

To let everyone, catch their breath, he paused for a moment before continuing. "Officer Mills—besides being an excellent officer—was also a highly decorated veteran, who served this country proudly in the war in Afghanistan. Officer Mills is survived by his mother, Harriet Mills and funeral arrangements are pending. Our thoughts and prayers go out to Harriet and the Mills family."

Chief Fitzsimons continued, "Officer Mills was critically injured while conducting a traffic stop. The driver of the vehicle which struck Officer Mills is currently still at large. It should be obvious to all of you, we are only in the initial stages of our death investigation. I have very little information that I can divulge to you at this time."

Leaning forward and looking directly into the cameras of both WBBM and ABC 7 News, he stated, "I wish to inform you, earlier today I had a brief telephone conversation with the Cook County State's Attorney, who offered her condolences to the Mills family, as well as the services of her office."

Pausing for the longest time since he had begun speaking and firmly grasping the podium with both of his massive, freckled hands, Chief Fitzsimons' face began turning beet-red as he stated, "The Cook County State's Attorney confirmed for me if you impede our death investigation in any way, by supplying us with false information, or failing to disclose information, she will bring Felony Obstruction of Justice charges against you. I will have my Deputy Chief of Support Services, Frank Gyondski, put a special telephone number on our department website. He will also be sending out a press release, with a telephone number for anyone with information regarding this investigation to call. In the initial press release, there will also be an updated biography on Officer Christopher Mills and we will be sending another press release, when we have finalized funeral plans for Officer Mills."

"We will not, let me repeat, we will not be holding press conferences in the future, just for the sake of holding a press conference. My personnel's time is very valuable at a time like this. When we have something of substance, you will be notified in advance and you should have adequate time to get to our police department, or the Cook County State's Attorney's office, located at the Second District Courthouse, 5600 Old Orchard Rd. Skokie."

"In closing, my main concern presently is getting my police department healed from today's tragedy, comforting the Mills family and obviously apprehending the person responsible for the death of Officer Mills." Chief Fitzsimons paused for a brief second to catch his breath. Then, with his voice cracking for the first time since he took the podium, he finished his speech with, "Officer Mills' death will stay with all of us for some time. His death, I assure you, will not be in vain. Thank you and no questions at this time."

Upon finishing his speech, Chief Fitzsimons turned to the right and briskly walked out of the conference room.

Reporter Julian Youmans, from WGN News, yelled out, "Chief, can you give us more information on the suspect's car?"

Chief Fitzsimons never turned to acknowledge Youmans and never stopped to glance at the stunned press group.

Deputy Chief Gyondski followed, walking slightly behind him.

With his head down and continuing to stay behind Chief Fitzsimons, they walked separately through the revolving doors and into the rain, passing patients, doctors and nurses coming into Lutheran Family Center Hospital.

Not a word was said between them.

Each of them was deep in thought, as to what their first task would be, once they got back to the police station.

In a matter of minutes, Deputy Chief Gyondski was standing next to his silver Chevy Malibu, covered with raindrops, which had formed on different parts of the vehicle.

Upon entering his car, he turned the heat switch to high, even though he knew it would take a minute or so to kick in, due to the temperature outside.

As he was raising his right hand to switch the gear shifter from park to reverse, he heard a loud knocking sound on his driver's side window and turned to find Chief Fitzsimons standing outside his driver's side door.

Deputy Chief Gyondski started to lower the window, but before it was completely down, Chief Fitzsimons had already placed most of his head inside the vehicle.

"What the hell were you thinking back there Frank?" Chief Fitzsimons barked.

Deputy Chief Gyondski found his face only inches from Chief Fitzsimons' face and could literally feel Chief Fitzsimons' breath.

"Last time I checked, I was still the God Damn Police Chief of the Greenfield Police Department, isn't that correct?"

"Yes," was all he could utter, before Chief Fitzsimons continued.

"Then, what in God's name were you thinking holding a press conference without first running it by me?"

Deputy Chief Gyondski knew better than to respond to the Chief's comments.

Instead, he waited for the next volley from Chief Fitzsimons.

"You weren't my guy Frank," Chief Fitzsimons yelled. "You were Angeli's guy, and he spoke very highly of you before he retired. That, combined with your solid educational background, is the reason you're my Deputy Chief of Support Services and Project Manager for the new police station. But if you pull another fuckin' stunt like you did today to show me up, you will be a sergeant working on the graveyard shift!" Fitzsimons yelled.

"Anything going out to the press on this one gets run by me first Frank," Chief Fitzsimons roared.

Pausing for a few seconds to catch his breath, Chief Fitzsimons finished up with one word, "Understood?"

"Yes Sir," is all Deputy Chief Gyondski could say, as Chief Fitzsimons' head left the window of the vehicle.

Deputy Chief Gyondski watched as Chief Fitzsimons quickly walked two parking spaces over to his black, Chevy Malibu, entered it and slammed the driver's side door, before pulling out and leaving the Lutheran Family Center Hospital parking lot, at a high rate of speed.

Deputy Chief Gyondski found himself sitting motionless, for a good five minutes.

Finally, the air coming out of his car vents turned to heat.

Yet, Deputy Chief Gyondski didn't need the heat from the vehicle's engine to keep him warm, for he was burning up inside the car, from his own anger.

Slowly, he gripped the steering wheel with both hands, as tightly as he could and squeezed until his hands ached.

He continued squeezing the steering wheel and could still

see Chief Fitzsimons' face in his mind, as he tried to squeeze the steering wheel even harder.

In all of Deputy Chief Gyondski's 44 years on earth, no one had ever spoken to him with that tone of voice.

Not a teacher, his parents, grandparents, or his dad's brother, Stanley.

"Jesus H. Christ," Deputy Chief Gyondski screamed, in an effort to relieve some of the stress, which had built up inside of him.

Finally, he moved the gear shifter to reverse and slowly backed his vehicle out of its parking spot, heading toward the police station. As he drove, D.C. Gyondski pondered his next move.

One part of him wanted so desperately to walk into Chief Fitzsimons' office and tell him what he really thought of him. What a cocky son of a bitch, Greenfield Police Chief, Ryan Patrick Fitzsimons was and so full of himself.

Granted, Deputy Chief Gyondski was Chief Angeli's hand-picked candidate for the Deputy Chief of Support Services, but very few people had known the real Chief Angeli, the way he had.

A large, good-hearted Italian, with a hearty laugh and a firm handshake, Chief Angeli may not have been the ideal police chief from a financial perspective, but no one could top his people skills, or his love for the members of the Greenfield Police Department.

But Chief Fitzsimons had done some significant work in the short time he took over the Greenfield Police Department.

Morale, Deputy Chief Gyondski thought, seemed to be improving and why shouldn›t it, with these guys getting a new police station in roughly 14 months.

But did the Village of Greenfield really need a new police station to the extent they were building this one?

By the time he pulled into his parking spot, with a number two painted in yellow on the ground, Deputy Chief Gyondski made up his mind as to what his next move would be—keep his mouth shut for now.

No good could come from taking on Fitzsimons now, during a

time when the Greenfield Police Department was going through its greatest tragedy.

Confident with his decision, he opened his driver's side door.

He looked down to avoid stepping into one of the numerous puddles which had formed in the pothole-filled parking lot with the heavy rain, when his cell phone began ringing.

Looking carefully at the number on the front display, he was surprised it had taken this long for the caller to finally contact him.

"Hello," he calmly said to the caller in a firm voice.

"I watched the press conference Frank," the male voice replied.

Before Deputy Chief Gyondski could respond, the male caller continued. "He made a total ass out of you in front of every person in that room and whoever watched it on television."

"There was nothing I could," was all Deputy Chief Gyondski could yell into the phone, before the caller cut him off.

"Hey, hey, Frankie, take it easy. You've got a ton of shit on your freaking plate, and I didn't mean to bust your stones like that," the caller yelled back, in a deep Italian accent.

Both people remained silent, as each gathered their thoughts. After roughly half a minute, the caller continued.

"Fitzsimons was never our pick from the start and you know, from me telling you numerous times, all of the trustees except Waite, wanted you buddy."

"But that prick of a Village Manager McMartin, wanted Fitzsimons so bad and presented such a strong argument for him, we couldn't overrule him. Plus, we never had a clue McMartin would screw us by going to Tennessee, three months after Fitzsimons was hired, Mother Fucker," the caller finished.

"Shit, listen to me. We're turning into fucking Chicago," the caller said.

With Deputy Chief Gyondski still not talking, the caller sensed he needed to say something, anything, to get him out of his funk.

"Frank, we know he has a bad temper. Shit, I asked him a question at a budget meeting earlier this year, and he started to lose it, with his famous vein sticking out the right side of his head," the caller said.

"Yeah, I've seen it," was all Deputy Chief Gyondski could mumble in a soft tone.

Sensing for the first time he had Deputy Chief Gyondski back in his corner, the caller responded, "Frank, you know he's going to fuck it up with the temper, so just sit tight and kick ass on the new station. Before you know it, Fitzsimons steps on his dick and you're back in business. You've got more education and experience than Bart, correct?"

"Of course, I do," Deputy Chief Gyondski answered, in a firm and convincing voice.

"Good, good," the caller said.

"Hey Frankie, I have to go but before I do, my thoughts and prayers on the loss of Mills. Didn't know much about him and only saw him at his swearing in ceremony, with the rest of the recruits, but seems like impressive credentials and an all-around good guy," the caller said.

"He was," Deputy Chief Gyondski responded, before hearing the phone line go dead.

Placing his phone back in his carrying case, Deputy Chief Gyondski found himself still seated in his car, staring at the east side of the Greenfield Police Station.

What the caller said seemed to make perfectly good sense to him.

He was relieved to hear someone else had recognized Chief Ryan Patrick Fitzsimons for what he truly was—a big, Irish bully, who used his position and size to push people around.

Unfortunately, like so often in life, waiting for the reward would be the hardest part.

After two to three minutes, the sun finally broke through the grey, overcast sky, for the first time all day.

The sunlight reflected off the windows of the Greenfield Police Department and through the front windshield of his Chevy Malibu.

The sunlight seemed to snap him out of the final stages of his funk, and he proceeded to open the driver's side door of his car.

Stepping from the car and closing the door confidently, he walked assertively for the first time all day into the sunlight, towards the Greenfield Police Station.

Deputy Chief Gyondski knew he had a shot of someday becoming Chief of the Greenfield Police Department, but for now he had a funeral to plan.

CHAPTER 6

Megan O'Brien sat on a black, metal folding chair at the gravesite, with nothing but time on her hands.

As she watched in front of her, people of all ages and occupations, moved all around her.

Each of them had been instructed where to go by D.C.Gyondski, depending on what their connection had been with Officer Chris Mills.

All Greenfield personnel, whether they were sworn or non-sworn, would stand directly across from where Harriet Mills and Megan were seated.

Any other law enforcement person attending, would stand to the right, or near the head of Chris Mills coffin.

Finally, all dignitaries or any other person who had a reason for attending, would stand directly behind Megan and Harriet.

Harriet Mills sat on Megan's immediate right and seemed to have finally composed herself.

Megan glanced over at Harriet, who was in awe at the sheer number of people who had come to pay their respects, at her son's funeral.

Slowly, Megan brought her right hand up to her neck area, which wasn't covered by her blue uniform dress shirt and tie.

Using both her index and middle fingers, she slowly moved them around her entire neck in an attempt to find the scratch marks, she had suffered, a number of months ago.

The Kiehl's skin cream her mother Sara had recommended, had done the trick and healed the physical marks in record time.

Megan had worried she might never recover from the incident.

The physical suffering and wear and tear on her body, from all of the medicine her family doctor in Stoughton, Wisconsin had prescribed for her, gave her headaches, as well as occasional vomiting.

Some of the mood swings she was sure were caused both by the medicine, as well as the incident. But she had no solid explanation for the constant nightmares, as well as the crying spells she would experience at a moment's notice.

She had been assured by her therapist, Dr. Jill Dybus, this was all to be expected and unfortunately there was no time period when she could expect these issues would suddenly end.

"Each victim is obviously different on how they handle the aftermath of the incident based on so many different variables," Megan remembered Dr. Dybus saying, after one of their early therapy sessions.

Slowly Megan turned her head to the right to see what Harriet was doing, but instead found her mother Sara O' Brien, seated in Mrs. Mills chair.

"God, I miss you mom", Megan said softly to herself as the vison of her mother dissipated and Harriet Mills reappeared in the chair she had occupied, since arriving at the gravesite.

Calling her mother back in Wisconsin, on the night of the incident, only added more stress to the entire situation, for Megan.

For a good twenty minutes, Megan had paced in her dorm room, trying to find the right words to at least start the conversation, explaining to her mother what had just taken place.

It was no use and Megan finally realized she was just going to have to tell her the truth.

Megan was sure the time of her phone call played a small part in the problem, but she was only able to get one sentence out, before her mother knew something horrific had occurred to her daughter.

A mother's intuition, on the actions of their children, is a powerful tool to possess.

There was no use in stopping now and without being too graphic, Megan explained to her mother the details.

Megan realized her mother would be arriving for her graduation ceremony in roughly 36 hours, but this event had taken on a whole new meaning after tonight.

It took all of Megan's willpower to tell her mother not to come to Champaign, Illinois and be a part of what was supposed to be the biggest day of her life.

Fortunately, her mother understood when Megan told her she would be coming home to Stoughton, Wisconsin, and be with her, sorting this entire mess out, after the graduation ceremony.

Megan was just starting to relax, when she felt a pair of strong hands, suddenly on her shoulders.

Megan opened her mouth to scream with all of her might, but nothing came out today.

The same way nothing had the night of the incident.

CHAPTER 7

Megan O' Brien didn't need to turn around to figure out who's hands were on her shoulders.

In a stern voice, but without yelling she said, "Kurt take your hands off me now."

Without hesitation, Kurt Thompson's hands were off her shoulders and apparently startled by the tone of her voice, took a small step backwards into two other mourners.

Megan O'Brien slightly tilted her head back and proceeded to take such a deep breath, it caused Harriet Mills to take her eyes off the Greenfield Police Department Honor Guard carrying her son's coffin and look questionably at her.

If Megan could have screamed out loud and gotten away with it, she would have.

Instead, she just continued taking deep breaths, in an attempt to calm her nerves, which were rattled to say the least.

Even though his hands had only been on her shoulders and nowhere near her neck, Megan still felt suffocated.

"Megan my dear are you going to be okay?" Mrs. Mills asked her and went as far as to put her left hand on Megan's right forearm.

"Yes," Megan answered before continuing "Mrs. Mills, apparently Chris's death is finally sinking in and I'm so sorry for my outburst."

Gently, Harriet Mills tapped Megan's right forearm saying "I totally understand dear," before she turned her attention back to the gravesite.

"I'm going to kill this fucking Kurt Thompson, "Megan said softly to herself, so no one else could hear her.

Granted, since their graduation from the Illinois Law Enforcement Training Center, she had acknowledged most of Kurt's text messages and spoken to him on the phone a couple of times, when he had telephoned her.

Megan admitted it was confusing as hell to her why she was doing all of this.

Megan never found him to be attractive, from the first time she saw him.

He was definitely full of himself, the few times she actually heard him speak at all to their fellow classmates, who apparently had no use for him.

Something just seemed different with him and she based her opinion on a couple of significant facts.

He was a loner in every sense of the word.

Everyone attending ILETC, had made a new friend or two, who they would share a meal or at least a cup of coffee with, sometime during their training in Champaign.

Kurt Thompson was the exception to the rule and Megan believed he hadn't made one friend their entire time there.

Breakfast, lunch, or dinner, he ate alone, which was strange by itself, but what made matters even stranger, it didn't seem to faze him.

Now to be fair, he was the only cadet to come to ILETC, by himself.

Every police department had sent a minimum of two cadets to ILETC, with the Naperville Police Department sending eight, and all of them seeming to be great people.

Secondly, Megan would watch him in the cafeteria and the way he looked at other cadets who passed his table, gave her the creeps.

The way a wolf sits and stalks its prey, was the image Megan couldn't get out of her mind watching Kurt Thompson.

He would slowly turn his head in the direction the cadet was heading and just stare at them until they were out of sight.

The entire time Kurt Thompson would have this weird grin, or smirk on his face, would force Megan to look away in disgust.

Megan was fascinated with all aspects of people and what made them tick.

Thus, her minor at Western Illinois University, was psychology and she had even brought two textbooks with her to ILETC, in case she needed to analyze any of her classmates.

Megan was still putting together her profile of Kurt Thompson, but felt confident he suffered at the minimum, from Anti-Social Spectrum Disorder, or the old name for it, Asperger's.

Which was why it was so critical for Megan to see how Kurt would do in two different training scenarios while at ILETC, Crisis Intervention Training and the age-old Defensive Tactics.

With the Village of Gilles bordering the southwest side of Greenfield, Megan felt chances were pretty good she may have to interact with Kurt on some type of serious felony call, once they graduated and started their law enforcement careers.

Social skills, decision making skills, communication and of course how he would handle his temperament, would all be on display during both of these training scenarios.

Kurt Thompson was horrific in both of these.

Megan had to admit, for a large man he moved effortlessly and you could tell had some type of athletic background.

This was about the only positive Megan could give him.

In the defensive tactic's scenarios, Kurt seemed more interested in arresting the suspect and often antagonizing them as well.

Consequently, an additional charge of resisting arrest would be added on.

Kurt displayed no empathy during the Crisis Intervention Training scenarios, much to the dismay of both the actors playing the victims and the course instructors as well.

Since these scenarios were videotaped and shown in class the next day, his failures and critiques brought more than a few catcalls and whistles from fellow cadets, while viewing them.

Megan had no idea why, but T.C. Chambers and Chris Mills in particular seemed to have the most fun teasing Kurt about his mistakes.

Needless to say, he didn't take the criticism well at all from the actors, instructors and especially Greenfield cadets.

Chief Fitzsimons spoke slowly and passionately kneeling in front of Harriet Mills holding the tightly folded United States flag in both of his massive hands.

Megan O'Brien quickly snapped out of her daydreaming.

Unfortunately, she had a slight problem hearing what Chief Fitzsimons was saying but didn't want to be too obvious by leaning forward to hear him.

Instead, she stayed glued to her seat and continued looking straight ahead at a sea of Greenfield personnel, all of who seemed to be looking back at her.

Even though she was probably 60 to 70 feet away from these people, in her mind Megan somehow could hear what each of them was thinking "Why didn't you tell someone in authority?"

CHAPTER 8

Matt O'Neil stands at the rear of the hearse carrying Chris Mills' body, and waits patiently.

Lt. Miler and the five other members of the Greenfield Police Department Honor Guard, stand alone on a gravel road, away from the rest of the Greenfield Police Personnel.

In groups of two or three, they watch as a wide variety of attendees, ranging from law enforcement personnel, the Greenfield Village Manager, Village Trustees, and the entire Command Staff of the Greenfield Fire Department, make their way to Chris Mills' gravesite.

Due to the sheer number of officers attending and the limited parking, a few officers were forced to park nearly a quarter mile away.

Fortunately, they can walk through the cemetery, in a serpentine fashion, as a shortcut to the gravesite.

Matt knew there would be police personnel from the surrounding states, including Indiana, Michigan and Wisconsin, but he never expected to see representatives from as far away as New York City.

He is starting to realize the brotherhood of police officers wasn't limited to the tiny Greenfield Police Department, or even the State of Illinois, but instead stretched across the United States of America.

When an officer died in the line of duty, every police officer and their family, shared in the pain and suffering of the deceased officer's family, in some small way.

Chief Fitzsimons finally arrives with Deputy Chief Bart and they walk directly to the front roll of where his Greenfield personnel are standing. Chief Fitzsimons winds up standing in the middle of the front row of his personnel.

Both of his deputy chiefs will eventually be standing on each side of him, followed by the remainder of his supervisors. The rest of the Greenfield Police Department personnel, will fall in behind this front row.

Directly across from the Greenfield Police Department personnel, were two black colored folding chairs, which had been placed there by employees of Our Lady of Saints Cemetery.

There wasn't any doubt in Matt's mind who would occupy these chairs, once the service started.

Matt is so focused on these two chairs and the numerous police officers passing him, he doesn't notice two people who come up behind him.

"How you doing Matt?" Startled, Matt turns around quickly and finds himself standing face to face with Carl Eckert, whose right hand is fully extended for a handshake.

Matt uses his right hand to shake Eckert's hand.

With his left hand, he pulls Eckert into him for a hug. During the hug, he suddenly realizes they aren't alone, as Cynthia Mallory stands next to his right side.

Letting go of Eckert's hand, Matt places his free right hand around Cynthia's shoulders.

Now, both of his arms are over the respective shoulders of Eckert and Mallory.

Not a word is spoken amongst the three of them for a good minute.

Finally, Matt removes his arms from both Eckert and Mallory's shoulders and in the process, takes a step back, so he can talk to both of them at the same time.

Eckert is the first to speak and asks, "How you holding up?"

"Pretty good," is all Matt can mumble, as he looks at Cynthia Mallory, who has a stream of tears flowing down her cheeks.

"The rest of the Greenfield Police Department?" Eckert asks.

"All pretty well, but really the only two who knew him were T.C. Chambers and myself," Matt responds, this time in a clear and firm voice.

Suddenly, a large group of police officers, from a wide variety of police departments, start to walk by the three of them.

Carl Eckert realizes this really isn't the time or place for a conversation with a stressed-out Matt.

Carl takes his left hand and places it on Cynthia's right bicep. With his right hand he slaps Matt on his right shoulder saying, "Matt, we're going to get going." Carl then leads Cynthia to the gravesite, with the next group of arriving officers.

Once Matt is sure Eckert can't hear him, the words, "he's something," slowly comes out of his mouth, as he lowers his head and looks into the back window, of the black Cadillac hearse.

"Thank God," Matt says softly, while still looking at Chris Mills' coffin. "Man Chris, I thought I was going to get a hernia, getting you inside the church," Matt whispered, so no one else could hear him.

Matt couldn't believe how heavy Chris's coffin was, and he thought for sure he wasn't going to get him up the seemingly endless set of front steps, at Our Lady of Faith Church.

With people still arriving at the gravesite, Matt uses the time to reflect on the church service for Chris.

Upon placing the coffin in front of the altar, the Honor Guard moved to the second set of pews, with each Honor Guard member entering their pew, depending on what side of the coffin they were on.

Upon entering his pew and sitting down, Matt found himself sitting directly behind Mrs. Mills, who sat in between Megan on her left and Chief Fitzsimons on her right.

For some reason, the entire 90-minute mass seemed to fly by to Matt.

Every song, every prayer, seemed to roll quickly on, which pleased Matt, because the stress of the past 96 hours, was starting to catch up to him.

Matt was also impressed one of his own was saying the mass.

Speaking with a thick Irish brogue, Father Tom Doyle, was doing the best he could, under a stressful situation.

Father Doyle was in his late sixties and dressed in the traditional green vestment, with flowing grey hair. "If this was a movie," Matt thought with a slight smile on his face, "Father Doyle had his role down perfectly."

Matt realized he hadn't smiled in close to a week.

Chief Fitzsimons and the Village President, handled the two scripture readings, after both Matt and T.C. Chambers turned down the offer to do them.

While there was some shuffling in the pews when the Village President did his reading, you could hear a pin drop, when Chief Fitzsimons approached the lectern to do his.

Even from where Matt O'Neil was sitting, every police officer seemed to sit up a bit straighter in their pews and more than a few of them could be seen fixing their clip-on ties, to make sure they were straight.

The Village President did his reading, as if he was reading the ingredients from his favorite cereal box.

Chief Fitzsimons did his reading with sincerity and placed the right emphasis where it was needed, while slowly reading Psalm 10.

As he was leaving the lectern and returning to his front row pew, Chief Fitzsimons suddenly stopped to straighten out the American Flag, on Chris Mills' coffin.

Finished, he slowly raised his right hand and saluted Chris Mills for a good five seconds, before returning to his pew.

More prayers were then exchanged from the huge crowd gathered inside Our Lady of Faith Church.

Matt was surprised to see both Lt. Wayne and Sgt. Barton bringing the communion gifts up to Father Doyle, who was standing with three altar boys.

Each of the altar boys were dressed in their traditional red Cossacks, with a white, cloth outer garment.

Each of the altar servers, who Matt estimated ranged from 5th to 7th grade, had wide-eyed, glassy looks on their faces, similar to the first time they sat on Santa Claus' lap at Sears. Little did they realize they were part of something so big and prestigious, which would remain a part of their lives forever.

Finally, it was time for Holy Communion to be given out.

After receiving it, Matt returned to his pew and slowly lowered himself onto the kneeler.

He closed his eyes and touched both of his hands to his forehead. He prayed, "Lord, I've asked you for so little in my life, but this time you have to help me. Please, please, heavenly Father, allow me to see the driver's face in the Bronco, or at least one or two numbers of the license plate. That's all I'm asking for. I'm asking not only for me, but for the Mills family, so they can have some closure with all of this, Amen."

He opened his eyes and crossed himself, before pushing himself backward off the roller and into his seat.

Matt O'Neil turned his head slightly to the right and watched as an endless stream of people walked up the center aisle, in two lines, to take Holy Communion.

Father Doyle stood on the right side, just below the altar, with another priest standing on the left side of the altar.

The last two Greenfield personnel to take Holy Communion, were Karen Jenkins, followed by Eddie Heaviland.

There wasn't any doubt among Greenfield personnel, as to whom on their police department had taken the death of Chris Mills, the hardest.

This person being Karen Jenkins, who wisely had passed on attending the wake and hadn't been able to work, since Chris Mills' death.

Even now, as the entire Greenfield Police Department watched her walk shakily, they could tell Eddie Heaviland was just waiting for her to collapse.

As Karen stood next to the coffin, she suddenly turned to her right, bent down, and kissed an area of the coffin, not covered by the American Flag.

Her actions caused Harriet Mills to start to cry and for some unknown reason, Megan began to cry also.

Upon receiving her Holy Communion, Karen Jenkins walked back to her pew.

But seeing the two other women crying, she decided to join them in crying as well. With tears flowing and her feet shuffling like a 99-year-old woman, she slowly made her way back to her pew.

Matt and the rest of the attendees, some who had never even met Karen Jenkins, let out a collective sigh of relief, upon seeing her enter and finally sit down in her pew.

Confident, she was in good hands, Matt turned his whole body back towards the main altar and was stunned to see who was standing next in line, to receive Holy Communion, from Father Doyle.

Dressed immaculately, in a beautiful but proper black dress, Kelly reached slowly out with both hands to receive the communion wafer.

For some peculiar reason, Matt felt these five days, had been harder on their relationship, than when he was serving his country, in Special Ops.

When he was in country, they both knew when he should return and counted the days until they would be in each other's arms.

But this situation was so different.

Matt would be the first to admit he hadn't been himself these past five days and couldn't even justify to himself why.

He found himself leaning forward in his pew, to watch his beautiful wife.

After receiving her Holy Communion, Kelly gently put the wafer on her tongue and crossed herself slowly with her right hand.

Walking slowly back to her pew and having passed Matt's pew, she gave a quick smile to her husband and continued walking.

Matt felt a combination of love and slight embarrassment over the smile and put his head down to hide his own smile and blushing face. "You are one lucky Irishman," Matt said to himself, so quietly, no one else in the pew could hear him.

Upon raising his head, Matt's huge grin quickly left him.

Matt watched as Father Doyle put the wafer, in Kurt Thompson's hands.

As he watched, Kurt Thompson never lowered his head as he walked back toward his pew.

The minute he walked past Chief Fitzsimons in the first pew, he made direct eye contact with Matt and raised his left hand to his waist.

Boldly, Kurt shot out the middle finger on his left hand and mouthed the words, "Fuck you," to a stunned Matt, who could feel the hairs on the back of his neck starting to stand up.

Matt closed his eyes briefly to fight the urge to get out of his pew, confront Kurt Thompson and ask him one simple question, "Have you lost your fucking mind?"

"O'Neil you ready?" Lt. Miler asked.

Matt opens his eyes to a stunned Greenfield Police Department Honor Guard, who are now standing in a semi-circle, at the rear of Chris's hearse, with each one of them having a puzzled look on their faces.

Matt takes a step toward the group and puts on his white Honor Guard gloves, which he can't recall taking off since arriving at the cemetery.

Just as he is about to reach the circle of his fellow members, he feels a slap across the middle of his shoulders. He turns his head in time to find a smirking Kurt Thompson walking past him, accompanied by two other Gilles Police Officers.

"O'Neil, focus," Lt. Miler says to him in a firm voice.

Matt O'Neil knows he has already pissed off a man who had been very good to him, since he joined the Greenfield Police Department.

With two additional steps, Matt is standing in his designated position, second from Chris Mills' head, on the right side of the coffin.

As Matt and his fellow Greenfield Honor Guard members watch, a representative from Donnelly Funeral Home opens the rear door of the hearse and starts to pull Chris Mills' coffin out.

With the coffin being on rollers, it doesn't take much effort to easily get it out of the hearse.

As the coffin passes each member of the Honor Guard, they grab a rail of the coffin and pass it on to the member standing next to them.

In less than a minute, the coffin is completely out of the hearse and in the hands of each member of the Greenfield Honor Guard, except for Lt. Miler.

The Honor Guard members such as Matt, who is standing on the right side of the coffin, grab hold of the coffin with their right hand.

Conversely, the Honor Guard members, who are standing on the left side of the coffin, grab hold of it with their left hands.

Lt. Miler watches as each member of his Honor Guard, gather themselves in a different way, with their remaining free hands.

A couple of member's finishes straightening their clip-on ties, while the remaining members check the member standing in front of them, to make sure their hat is straight.

Upon believing each of his personnel are done, Lt. Miler steps in front of them, which results in him standing at the head, of Chris Mills' coffin.

"Anyone have any last questions?" Lt. Miler asks.

Not one of them says a word.

"Good," Lt. Miler answers.

"Remember, slow, half-speed steps. Just take your time," guides Lt. Miler. "There may be a few holes in the lawn so be careful. Finally, when we get to the flag folding part, make the flag as tight as possible before it's handed off to me.

"Gentlemen, it's go time. Let's make Chris Mills' family proud," finishes Lt. Miler.

With that he takes one step back, pauses for about ten seconds, turns so he's now facing the crowd, and then yells as loud as he can, "Honor Guard, attention."

Matt O'Neil is impressed. Lt. Miler's yell is so authoritative, it makes the entire Greenfield Police Department snap to attention.

After another period of roughly ten seconds, Lt. Miler gives his next command of the day. "Honor Guard, commence."

With that, all six members of the Honor Guard, carrying Chris Mills' coffin, take their first steps forward.

For the members on the left side of the coffin, this means leading with their right foot. Thus, for the members on the right side of the coffin, this means taking their first step with their left foot.

Slowly and meticulously, the Honor Guard makes their way to the gravesite.

Matt can't believe a crowd this big, can be so still and quiet.

Out of his right eye, Matt knows they are getting close, when he sees Mrs. Mills and Officer O'Brien seated in their folding chairs, across from where Chris Mills' coffin will be placed.

Upon arriving at the gravesite, each member of the Honor Guard slowly places the coffin down on silver rails.

Next, all six of them turn, so they are looking directly at the officer who had carried the coffin to the gravesite, on the opposite side from them.

Each Honor Guard member stares straight ahead, hands at their sides, in a clenched-fist position.

Out of the corner of Matt's left eye, while still looking straight ahead, he observes a sudden movement from the area directly behind Harriet Mills, which had been a motionless sea of black, only moments before.

Suddenly, a figure emerges from this crowd.

When the figure gets closer to the coffin, Matt realizes it's Father Doyle.

Dressed in black, except for his white collar and a beautiful purple stole, Father Doyle stops next to Lt. Miler and opens a black, worn bible, which he holds in his left hand.

As loud as possible, yet without screaming, Father Doyle begins, "Heavenly Father, we are gathered here today to say our final goodbye to Officer Christopher Mills, beloved son of Harriet and Henry Mills. For Father, Christopher Mills is a young man who died..." With the word died, Matt's focus is drawn away from the words of Father Doyle.

Again, Matt looks directly to the area, where Father Doyle had just come from.

As he looks on in amazement, people are stepping aside and moving from where they were previously standing, to let a figure move in front of them.

All of them act like someone dropped a mouse on the ground and they are trying not to step on it.

Finally, after roughly twenty to thirty seconds, the movement stops and a figure finally emerges from the pack and winds up taking the same spot Father Doyle had vacated only a few minutes earlier.

Matt actually has to blink, even though there isn't any sunlight shining on his face, to guarantee he isn't seeing things.

"Kurt Thompson," Matt mumbles to himself and he watches as Kurt takes both of his hands and places them on the shoulders of Megan O'Brien, who he is now standing directly behind.

Every Honor Guard member, except for Matt, says the word, "Amen," loudly at the end of Father Doyle's prayer.

Matt's focus is now where it needs to be, on Christopher Mills' coffin.

Lt. Miler takes two steps, so he's standing at the head of the coffin.

Softly, he says the word, "Begin," so only the Honor Guard members can hear him. A word each of the Honor Guard members had been trained to mean to start with the American flag folding part of the ceremony.

Lt. Miler and the other five members of the Honor Guard, out of the corners of their eyes are now looking at the foot of the coffin, where Officer Joe Curtis is standing.

Officer Curtis takes the portion of the American flag directly in front of him and folds it into the tightest triangle, while the remaining members of the Honor Guard hold the flag tight.

This triangle and the remainder of the flag is then handed directly to the Honor Guard member who is standing directly across from them, on the other side of Chris Mills' coffin.

Slowly and meticulously, the flag continues to be folded.

Matt is very impressed with the thoroughness the Honor Guard is taking with this process.

He'd done this in the service before, but the Greenfield Honor Guard was not to be out done.

Once the flag is in a perfect, tight triangle, the flag is handed to Lt. Miler.

Upon receiving this flag, Lt. Miler makes a 180-degree turn and takes three steps forward, to a waiting Chief Fitzsimons.

Lt. Miler proceeds to salute Chief Fitzsimons, who upon returning Lt. Miler's salute, is handed the flag.

As the entire audience watches in complete silence, Chief Fitzsimons walks directly to where Harriet Mills is sitting.

Stopping directly in front of her, Chief Fitzsimons bends over slightly and says a few words that only Harriet Mills and now Megan O'Brien, who has been pulled closer by Mrs. Mills, will ever know.

When finished, Chief Fitzsimons hands Harriet the flag, which only minutes ago had covered her son's coffin.

Taking three steps back, Chief Fitzsimons slowly begins to raise his right hand, to salute Harriet Mills, when he hears Deputy Chief Gyondski scream at the top of his lungs, "Attention."

With this, every law enforcement member in attendance, raises his or her right hand quickly, in a formal salute.

As Matt salutes, he feels slight tears running down his face and he quickly blinks twice, in an effort to rid himself of them.

He remains in place with his fellow Honor Guard members, as someone on the far-left side of the audience plays *Taps,* on a bugle that rings out through the cemetery.

Matt is so caught up in the moment, he never sees the U.S. Navy Honor Guard, who have been in place a quarter mile north of the gravesite, watching the entire ceremony.

At the conclusion of *Taps*, the rounds from the U.S Navy Honor Guard M1 Carbines, ring out in unison.

Matt is thrust back in time, to a distant land where history was being made and he was proudly a part of it.

CHAPTER 9

Things have gone way too smoothly, for Senior Chief Petty Officer Matt O'Neil and his Navy Seal Team One.

Sure, everyone seemed to know and talk about Navy Seal Team Six, but his unit had some of the best soldiers, he ever had the privilege to command.

As he rode in the middle of the unit, on his white stallion, two thoughts continued to play in Matt's head.

First, he never dreamed he could be this hot.

Matt's Corpsman kept encouraging the entire unit to constantly keep drinking water or Gatorade to fight the heat, which was estimated to be about 115 degrees during the day and only a low of 90 degrees, at night.

Contributing to the problem was his MP5N, plus the 100 rounds of ammo he carried for it. Matt also had four magazines, of Smith & Wesson 9 mm, 40 grain hollow point ammo, for his Sig Sauer P226, strapped just above his right knee, beneath his burka.

Then, you throw on a Condor bulletproof vest and you have a real issue.

The Camelback, Military Specs model, Matt was carrying on his back, helped immensely.

Thank God his Commander had purchased one for everybody in the unit, because Matt didn't even want to think of the condition his guys would be in without them.

Yet, there was no escaping the sun, which seemed to constantly be hanging directly over them and continuously beating down on them.

Matt realized, in his relatively young life, whenever he entered a new phase of it, intense heat and sun always played a major role.

Named starting quarterback, his senior year at Gordon Tech, he had two-a-day summer practices. Try wearing a football helmet, shoulder pads, hip pads and doing 90 minutes of running and hitting, in the August heat of Chicago.

Which was a walk in the park compared to Bud/S notorious "Hell Week", when Matt attempted to become a Navy Seal.

Five and a half days of continuous physical activity, meant to increase both your physical, as well as mental toughness.

Matt ran close to 200 miles that week in combat boots, with the majority of it being on San Clemente Island.

Matt crawled through mud in the middle of the night, helped to hoist and haul a log that weighed the same as a telephone pole, barely slept and found an inner strength and determination, he didn't know existed.

140 candidates started Bud/S training with him.

By the time Matt finished, only 29 were still in his class.

ILETC morning runs.

Even though the staff at the Illinois law Enforcement Training Center had deliberately scheduled the runs for the early morning hours, no one had bothered to tell the sun.

Of the sixty days the entire class ran, 58 of them were cloudless.

This allowed the sun to have its way with any runner not up to the task at hand, on the black-topped farm roads, of Champaign, Illinois.

The only two days the class ran in the rain, was such a pleasure.

The entire group laughed and giggled, like first graders on recess, during their entire run.

"Focus Matt," he said to himself, as he stopped daydreaming about his earlier life.

To make matters worse, the desert sand only seemed to reflect the sun upward into the faces of the entire squad, when they needed to dismount from their horses.

"Thank you, Kelly," Matt said softly, as he took off his Oakley SI Ballistic Frame sunglasses, that the love of his life had surprised him with on his last birthday. These sunglasses had shielded his eyes from both the sun and desert sand and were a godsend.

The entire unit came to a stop to let their horse's rest.

Matt jumped off his horse, raising his MP5N in the process and sliding the safety on the weapon to the firing position.

Quickly, his feet began to sink into the hot, desert sand.

Instantly, he looked down at his tan-colored, Rocky Desert Vented Boots.

As he watched, his boots seemed to disappear, as the sand engulfed them completely and tiny ants attempted to get inside of the boots.

Matt was only able to get the word "Fuck," out of his mouth, before he realized what was happening.

"You're turning into a cissy Matt," he said quietly to himself and was comfortable no one in the unit had heard the comment.

For Matt was suddenly jolted back to his senses, when he realized any of the 2,753 people who had perished in the September 11, 2001 attacks in New York City, would gladly trade places with him in a heartbeat.

Heat wasn't even an issue that day, as opposed to the fires they faced in both Twin Towers.

Like everyone else in the nation, Matt O'Neil looked up at a small, Sony model television, mounted on a wall, in the north corner of his classroom, at St. Constance.

One of the teachers, seated in the classroom, said out loud what others were thinking, "A terrorist attack on our country from within our country?"

With their mouths wide open, they watched as business men and women launched themselves out of the boardroom windows, of the Twin Towers.

Each of those individuals knew they were falling to their deaths, but had no choice, due to the flames filling their conference rooms, or business offices.

More than a few of his fellow classmates, who watched with Matt, looked on in disbelief, with their mouths wide open. Some classmates shook their heads in disgust. A few put their heads down on their desks closing their eyes and a couple of them began crying, which forced their teacher, Ms. Geri Sullivan to quickly turn the television off and lead them in prayer.

Due to this incident, Matt became fascinated with terrorism.

He did a research paper on the subject, for his Social Studies class, at Gordon Tech.

On February 26, 1993, six Islamic Extremists, headed by Ramzi Yousef, parked a Ryder rental van in the parking garage, underneath the North Tower, of the World Trade Center.

When the van exploded, it left a crater over 500-feet deep, in the middle of the garage, killing six and injuring close to a thousand people.

On April 19, 1995, Timothy McVeigh parked a rental truck, full of explosive-grade ammonium nitrate fertilizer, in front of the Alfred P. Murrah Federal Building, in Oklahoma City, Oklahoma. The resulting explosion killed a total of 168 men, women, and children and wounded hundreds more.

Two days after the bombing, Matt O'Neil couldn't get the picture of the Oklahoma City fireman, holding a baby in his arms, whose head was covered in blood, out of his thoughts.

Senior Chief Petty Officer Matt O'Neil and his unit were flown into Afghanistan on September 21st, 2013 with their goal of going on kill and capture missions and working with C.I.A. operatives, on occasion.

If they were to come in contact with Taliban fighters, then as their company Commander Steve Bucklin said to them, "Inflict as much pain and death on those motherfuckers, their Allah won't recognize them when he sees all of them in hell."

As he and the remainder of the unit, remounted their horses and started riding, the second thought occurred to Matt O'Neil.

Like an old western staring John Wayne, Matt was on a horse, dressed like an Arab, looking for bad guys to kill in the desert.

Matt's unit was not unique for their attire, or for riding horses in fighting the Taliban.

In his brilliant book, *Horse Soldiers*, Author Doug Stanton depicted the actions of a small group of Special Forces soldiers, who secretly entered Afghanistan shortly after 9/11 and rode horses, as they fought the Taliban.

Matt regained his focus from the heat and turned to see how members of the unit were doing.

Thirty days before the unit's departure from their home base of Coronado, California, two new members were assigned to the team.

Staff Sergeant, T.C. Chambers, U.S.A.F, would serve as the Unit's Combat Controller and Petty Officer Chris Mills, would serve as the Unit's Explosive Ordinance Disposal Technician.

Matt and the Unit's Commander, Lt. Joel Detloft, had some concerns on how the new additions would do when the proverbial "shit hit the fan," but they knew that day and their answers, would come soon enough.

Lt. Joel Detloft had spent the past 30 days, putting his Navy Seal Team One, through every possible training scenario he could imagine, in an effort to indoctrinate them on how he wanted things done.

To not burn his warriors out, a few days were spent running and lifting, to get them in their best physical shape, so they could handle anything thrown at them in the future.

Matt had complete faith and trust in Lt. Joel Detloft for good reason.

Standing at exactly 6'2" and weighing 205 pounds, Lt. Joel Detloft was a freak of nature. Lt. Joel Detloft was called, "The Machine," due to a rigorous workout routine of both weights and cardio, combined with being a health nut. He managed to maintain a physique that was admired by his troops and swooned at by any female nurses he came in contact with.

But his physical appearance wasn't the only thing his personnel admired about him. Lt. Joel Detloft came from a family of Fighting Detloft's, whom had both served their country and different branches of the military as well.

Grandfather Sam Detloft was at what he called the, "Island of Hell," which in reality was Iwo Jima.

Legend has it, he was at the peak of Mt. Suribachi, when the American Flag was raised, but wasn't part of the flag-raising team. He was the fortunate Detloft, in the fact he was able to come home physically intact.

Sadly, he was scarred for life mentally, by what he and his fellow Marines had witnessed at Iwo Jima.

When asked about it at family get-togethers, he refused to talk about it and, in some cases, would even break down in tears.

Sam Detloft died of a heart attack, in 1998.

Lt. Joel Detloft's father, Frank Detloft, served with the 173rd Airborne, or "Sky Soldiers", as they are also known. Frank Detloft rose to the rank of Captain, but was killed in action on November 4th, 1967, at the Battle of Dak To.

Lt. Joel Detloft never got to meet his father, because his mother Margaret, became pregnant with Joel, only days before Frank Detloft was deployed to Vietnam, in 1967.

As he rode in the front of the unit today, Lt Joel Detloft knew he had great shoes to fill in keeping the Detloft legacy growing.

He had started filling this legacy by attending the U.S. Naval Academy, where he rose to the position of Class President.

Upon graduation, he left with leadership, fitness, and academic achievements on his resume.

Most of Lt. Joel Detloft's military career was currently classified.

He received a Purple Heart for a gunshot wound to his right hand, as well as a Bronze Star for bravery, during a Special Ops mission, which only a few people with, as the saying goes, "higher pay ranks and more medals" knew about.

Yet, his demeanor was one of quiet confidence, which Senior Chief Petty Officer Matt O' Neil noticed, seemed to fill every man in the unit with additional confidence.

In addition to filling his men with confidence, they were easily the best trained and equipped Navy Seal Unit currently deployed.

Anything he could do for his men to help them handle the environment better, or provide increased safety, Lt. Detloft did.

Departing from Karshi-Khanabad, home base for the U.S. Special Forces, at 0330 hours to beat the heat, was a Navy Seal Team One composed of, Lt. Joel Detloft, Senior Chief Petty Officer Matt O'Neil, Staff Sergeant T.C. Chambers, Petty Officer Chris Mills, Petty Officer First Class Tom Frederick, Petty Officer Tim Heiser, Petty Officer Ron Cassidy and Afghan interpreter, named Mohammed Jabber.

Each of them would be part of part of, Operation Lion Head.

They would meet up with two CIA agents, who had obtained intelligence on Taliban leader, Mullah Mohammed Zawer's plan to blow up the Afghanistan-Uzbekistan Friendship Bridge.

The CIA agents' role, would be to lead Lt. Detloft's unit, to this location in Termez, Uzbekistan.

Upon arriving, they would kill or capture Zawer, destroy his arms cache and eliminate any guards they encountered.

Matt was uncomfortable with the plan, but couldn't put his finger on exactly why.

Perhaps it was the role of the CIA agents, but this wouldn't be the first time working with men and women of this agency in country and they never had a problem before.

By starting early in the morning, it allowed Lt. Detloft and his team additional time for surveillance, along with a view of Zawer's camp, which satellite photos couldn't supply.

But would they have enough time?

Mohammed Jabber could be making Senior Chief Petty Officer Matt O'Neil uncomfortable, because the team, more or less, had him assigned to them, without any say, or time to do any background work on him.

Lt. Detloft was in the lead, roughly two klicks from Zawer's camp, when he suddenly raised his right hand in the air, bringing his stead and the remainder of the unit to a sudden halt.

As the entire unit looked down from the top of a ridge, while still mounted on their horses, they heard the sound of sporadic gunfire and explosions and could see black smoke coming from the village.

Turning his body in a 45-degree manner, Lt. Detloft pointed at Staff Sergeant T.C. Chambers, who was in the rear of the unit and yelled "Chambers get on the horn and call C.I.A agent Medina for me".

Unknown to Lt. Detloft, the village was under siege from a rival faction.

With his head still turned and right hand away from his MP5N, Lieutenant Detloft had no chance to see the actions of Mohammed Jabber.

Quickly, Mohammed had positioned his horse, roughly two feet to the right of Lt. Detloft's horse.

In one quick motion, Mohammed Jabber raised his right hand, which contained a blue steel Walther PPK380, and pointed the weapon at the only part of Lt. Detloft's unprotected upper body—his face.

Mohammed Jabber then yelled, in an earth-shattering voice, "ALLAHU AKBAR"!

He emptied the entire Walther PPK 380 clip into the right side of Lt. Detloft's face, with two of the rounds going into his right eye.

As Lt. Detloft's body fell to the ground and rolled once to the right, Mohammed Jabber's body quickly joined it.

Senior Chief Petty Officer Matt O'Neil's three rounds, from his Sig Sauer, had made a hole the size of a quarter, in the middle of Jabber's forehead.

Without hesitation, Senior Chief Petty Officer Matt O'Neil was off his horse in a matter of seconds.

Bending down, he grabbed the Walther PPK 380 out of Mohammed Jabber's right hand.

Next, he checked Mohammed Jabber's carotid artery on his neck, finding no pulse.

The rest of the unit stayed mounted on their horses, preparing for an ambush.

Taking six steps to the left, Matt straddled Lt. Detloft's body.

Looking down, it was almost like Lt. Detloft had two different faces.

He felt the right side of Lt. Detloft's bloody and disfigured neck, praying for a pulse, but knowing it would be in vain.

He was correct and not finding one, knew Lt. Joel Detloft was dead.

Quickly he lowered his right arm and carefully removed his seal skinz extreme glove from his right hand, in an effort not to get Lt. Detloft's blood on himself.

With the index finger on his clean, right hand, he closed Lt. Detloft's left eye, which was still open.

Then Matt made the sign of the cross over Lt. Detloft's face, with this hand.

Taking one step back, so he stood at Lt. Joel Detloft's feet, Senior Chief Petty Officer Matt O'Neil snapped off a quick salute to his dead boss.

Taking small steps, he slowly walked, with Lt. Detloft's blood still dripping off his left gloved hand, toward Mohammed Jabber's body and in the process, placed his glove back on his right hand.

A rage seemed to fill him, more and more, with every step he took, as he got closer and closer to Jabber's body.

With every step, his glove-covered hands became clenched and his breathing shorter.

For roughly two minutes ago, Senior Chief Petty Officer Matt O'Neil, lost not only his boss, but also his best friend in the Navy.

He stopped, when he had reached the left side of Jabber's body.

Mohammed Jabber was lying flat on his back, with his head tilted to the left. A steady flow of blood came from Jabber's head wound and it flowed into the desert sand, forming a puddle.

In a move totally uncharacteristic, Matt brought his right leg as far back behind his body as he could, while balancing his entire body on his left leg. With all the force he could muster, he kicked Mohamed Jabber in the chest.

On the second kick, Matt heard the sound of ribs breaking.

A mixture of blood, saliva and sweat flew from Jabber's body, due to the force of his kicks.

Loud enough so his men could hear him, Senior Chief Petty Officer Matt O'Neil, said to the dead Jabber, "Enjoy hell, asshole".

Upon finishing, he pointed at Staff Sergeant T.C.Chambers and yelled "Get me a medevac as well as"......"

The word "as" would be the last word to come out of his mouth, as an RPG landed roughly 20 feet east, of his location.

Killed instantly from the blast were Petty Officer First Class Tom Frederick, Petty Officer Tim Heiser and Petty Officer Ron Cassidy, along with their horses and the horse of Senior Chief Petty Officer Matt O'Neil.

Matt was thrown into the air from the blast and upon hitting the ground, knocked unconscious, with a piece of the RPG, lodged in his left thigh.

It took him 57 days to find out what really happened next with his unit and specifically, himself on a ridge located two klicks, from the village they were attempting to raid.

Part of the delay involved being flown almost 8 hours, after being injured, to Ramstein, Germany, home of the United States Air Force Headquarters, in Europe.

Due to his possible head injury and concerns about brain trauma, he was flown on a specially outfitted cargo plane.

Upon arriving at Ramstein, Germany, Matt was transported by ambulance to Landstuhl, Germany where American soldiers wounded in Afghanistan have surgery.

Matt's surgery was a complete success, with no signs of any brain injury.

Six days later, he was flown back to Bethesda Maryland, home of Walter Reed National Medical Center, for physical therapy.

Matt focused on two things the entire time in physical therapy. The love of his life Kelly and seeing the report which had been filed on his October 25th, 2013 mission.

After completing his physical therapy and finally getting signed off by a doctor as being ready for active duty, Matt headed directly to his home base.

Trying to steal gold from Fort Knox would have been easier, than seeing the report on his unit's mission.

Being a classified mission, with the use of CIA agents, appeared to be the main issue.

Using every contact, he ever made during his military career was to no avail.

Tired of running into a brick wall, Matt decided it was time to switch to Plan B, which consisted of making a couple of phone calls and being completely honest with his new Commander Dan Munn.

Matt carefully laid out his reasoning for Commander Munn, who listened intently and even nodded his head in agreement twice during the presentation.

Plan B worked to perfection, and Matt scratched his head wondering why he had spent so much time with Plan A.

Now it was time to execute the second part of this plan.

At exactly 0530 hours the next day, Matt found himself on a U.S. Marine Corps, H 53 "Sea Stallion," headed to Camp Pendleton, home of the 15th Marine Expeditionary Unit.

Commander Munn had informed him, Staff Sergeant Chambers, along with a member of Navy Seal Team Two, Senior Chief Petty Officer Don Hohs, had been temporarily assigned to monitor the 15th Marine Expeditionary Unit for a three-day period, while the Marines conducted a new urban warfare program.

The purpose was to see if the Navy Seal Units, along with combat controllers, could use anything the Marines were doing.

With no worries about being shot down, or personnel to supervise, Matt strapped himself in securely, falling into a deep sleep instantly after take off.

He had never experienced this feeling before and was so relaxed, he woke himself up once during the flight due to his own snoring. The whole trip was a total of 54 miles, so Matt had just experienced the best nap of his life.

When the H 53 touched down, the jolt of the landing awoke him.

He was shocked at how refreshed he felt, for so early in the morning.

Upon arriving at Camp Pendleton, Matt gave his credentials to one of the Marine guards working the front gate.

If looks could kill, Matt O'Neil would be dead.

Apparently, this Marine had no use for Navy Seals or navy personnel of any kind on the grounds of his facility. He slowly scrutinized Matt's paperwork word for word before finally allowing him entry.

Matt headed directly to where he was confident, he would find T.C. Chambers—the mess hall.

Matt didn't have long to wait, before he crossed paths as T.C. Chambers was coming out of the motor pool, alone for some reason.

It wasn't his uniform which gave T.C. Chambers away, but instead, his gold tooth smile.

After the customary salutes, T.C. gave Matt a bear hug so hard, it momentarily took the wind out of him.

"You hungry Boss?" T.C. Chambers asked.

"Starving," Matt replied with a huge smile on his face.

"Seems like I haven't eaten in a couple of days, due to tracking your ugly ass down, buddy," Matt said grinning from ear to ear.

"Really?" T.C. Chambers followed this up with a laugh, which could be heard all around them.

Their five-minute walk to the mess hall was mostly filled with idle chatter. The main theme of the conversation centered on Matt's injuries.

T.C.'s main questions centered on who did the surgery, what was rehab like, and are you fully recovered?

By the time Matt had answered all of T.C.'s questions, they were walking through the front door of Camp Pendleton's enormous mess hall.

Located in the middle of the base, Matt was amazed at both the size of it and how new it was.

Commissioned only seven months to the day Matt O'Neil and T.C. Chambers entered it, the mess hall's maximum capacity was 525 people and it contained every new feature to move troops through the chow line quickly.

After both grabbed a silver, metal food tray, Matt allowed T.C. to take the lead, as they gathered food throughout the cafeteria.

Considering the crowds, the food lines flowed smoothly.

Matt filled his tray with plates of scrambled eggs, bacon, wheat toast, melon, one glass of OJ and two cups of steaming, black coffee.

Taking a seat toward the rear of the mess hall, Matt felt a sense of discomfort, which he didn't understand for a moment, until it finally hit him.

"Hell, I've never been in a mess hall without a weapon on," he realized as he looked around.

Ever since being in uniform from day one of his military career, a weapon had gone with the uniform, until today.

Fortunately, as Matt continued looking around, he realized he wasn't the only soldier unarmed and he started feeling slightly better.

His apprehensions quickly faded as he dug into a big plate of scrambled eggs and bacon. T.C., sitting directly across from him, was throwing down a big hunk of a syrup-covered waffle.

Matt couldn't believe how hungry he was.

Strange, he thought to himself, how a simple plate of scrambled eggs with bacon could taste so different, depending on the cook adding their own different sauce or spice·

Due to being in the military, both T.C. and Matt ate quickly and silently.

Occasionally, they would look around the cafeteria, but to the shock of non-military personnel in the mess hall, each of them ate at record speed.

Kelly and her parents would often look at Matt in amazement when he was home on leave and visiting for dinner. Matt would often be done eating and finishing up his beverage, while they were just finishing their soup or salad.

On occasion, he would catch them staring at him and all he could do was raise his hands, smile, and say "What?" as they looked on.

When you're on a limited time schedule, or have to man a post after your meal, the time factor for eating, often goes out the window.

Matt was surprised by both Kelly's father and his own dad's

reaction to this, considering both of them were still working for the Chicago Fire Department and he was sure had rushed through a few meals in their careers.

Upon finishing his breakfast, he looked over at T.C. and could see he still had a few pieces of cut-up waffle and sausage patty on his plate.

Matt watched in stunned silence as T.C. reached across the table and pulled a small bottle of A-1 steak sauce from a holder. Suddenly, other members of the table looked on as he poured at least one third of the bottle's contents on his remaining sausage patty.

Matt could feel his right knee starting to shake up and down as if he was having a seizure. He had picked up this new habit a few months prior to his injury.

Matt wasn't worried about it because he knew it was simply a sign of nervousness, impatience, or both. Right now, it was impatience kicking in big time.

Matt wanted desperately for T.C. to finish his breakfast.

Matt was like a little kid on his birthday. The child who can't wait to see if the present they asked for, was there.

Matt's present was to quiz T.C. and find out what the hell happened, which almost got him killed, on a ridge in Afghanistan.

With his right leg out of control, Matt couldn't take it anymore and he stood up.

With his coffee cup in his right hand, he walked over to the beverage area of the mess hall and refilled his cup.

Sipping it slowly, Matt noticed that even though the food may be different at military installations, the coffee never changed.

Always hot, Matt thought, and stronger than some soldiers he had been accustomed to in the past.

Matt looked directly at where he had been sitting, and saw T.C. had finished his breakfast and was wiping his mouth with a paper napkin.

Matt walked back toward the table when, in reality, he wanted to sprint back.

Upon arriving, he sat in the same spot where he had been before, directly across from T.C. Chambers.

Before Matt could say a word, T.C. started. "I'm not going to waste time asking you about your breakfast because that isn't important to you right now is it?"

Before Matt could mumble a word, T.C. continued. "Boss, you came here to find out what the hell happened after you almost got that sweet ass of yours blown off, isn't that correct?"

All Matt could do was nod his head slowly up and down once, as T.C. started talking again. "The shit really hit the fan quickly, after Cassidy, Frederick and Heiser bought the farm and you went flying through the air like Superman".

"Knock off the, boss shit and tell me more," Matt responded.

"Okay" T.C. said and after picking up his coffee cup with his right hand, continued speaking. "Well, instinctively Mills and I dismounted and shot both of our horses for cover. Thank God we did, since those crazy Arab motherfuckers came at us like dogs after a fresh bone."

Luckily, Medina from the CIA had been on the horn asking for a Quick Reaction Team, as he and his partner were watching from a different ridge the entire time.

"Even then," T.C. continued, "someone upstairs, really, likes us."

Matt watched as T.C. had quit talking and was pointing upward, with an index finger on his left hand.

"How so?" Matt asked.

"If the QRF had responded from our base, we wouldn't have survived. Luckily, they were already in the area due to being at Temerz Airport for some reason," T.C. Chambers said.

"Not to mention each QRF are made up of a combination of Special Ops and 10th Mountain Division personnel, and those cats know how to kick ass and take names later," T.C. continued. "Shit Boss, they were firing from the AH 64 Apaches, as they were coming into the LZ."

"You said choppers, so there was more than one," Matt clarified.

"Hell yes," T.C. said loudly in a high-pitched voice. The table in front of him turned around to see what was going on.

After the table had turned back around, T.C. continued.

"The Quick Reaction Team's Apaches, combined with an AC130 gunship, were providing air and ground support for the 66th Rescue Squadron, which was based out of shit, I must be getting old because I'm not sure where they were based out of, but that was the helicopter and crew we loaded your sorry, shot-up ass on."

Matt shook his head slowly side to side as T.C. took a big sip of coffee, before putting his coffee cup down and leaning forward.

"Of course, you do owe a debt of gratitude to Chris Mills, who I forgot to mention, saved your life twice that day," T.C. mentioned rather casually, with a slight grin on his face.

"Whaaaaaaaaaat?" was all Matt could mutter, as T.C. went on.

"Boss, I said a few minutes ago we were up to our ass in shit, when Cassidy and Frederick died and just Mills and I were taking them on. After all was done, they counted 37 dead Allah-praying motherfuckers and no, we never fixed bayonets, but the sheer number of them matched with the fire power they brought," T.C. paused reflecting on that day. "Thank God they couldn't shoot straight to save their asses," he stopped.

Matt's patience was wearing thin, and T.C. sensed it, so he quickly continued.

"At one point, one of them tried a different approach to attacking Mills and I, after seeing his comrades get mowed down, after coming at us straight over the ridge. He came at us at a 25-degree angle and actually got within 10 to 12 feet with his AK47 raised directly at your body. I never saw him quite frankly, because my line of fire was straight on and then everything to the left of it," T.C. Chambers stated.

"But Mills sure did and was able to somehow center tap the motherfucker, even at that weird angle. Then, all I heard was Mills yelling at me for some suppression fire. As I turned to do so, he crawled out and grabbed you by your belt and dragged you back behind the horses and our position. Sure, as shit, not more than a minute later one of the assholes laid down a whole stream of AK47 fire right where your body had been. You wouldn't be sitting across from me today with your right leg out of control, if it wasn't for Mills moving you back behind us."

"You said he saved my life twice?" was all Matt could mumble, which was barely audible to T.C. due to Matt speaking in a low tone, with his head hanging down.

"All I know is a piece of the RPG, was in your thigh and causing you to slowly bleed out. Mills somehow, with all the shit which was happening, was able to clamp it and keep you from dying."

"You okay, Boss?"

With no response from Matt, T.C. asked him again, "Boss, are you okay?"

With his right leg shaking as never before, Matt looked up to see T.C. standing alone, at the head of Chris Mills' coffin, as other attendees at the cemetery, were walking to their cars.

"Yeah, yeah, good, thanks for asking," Matt responded as he started to walk towards where T.C. was standing.

When Matt reached the head of Chris Mills' coffin, he lowered his head and kissed it for a couple of seconds.

While his head was still close to the coffin, he said softly, "Thank You," before standing up.

Walking quickly to their Greenfield Crown Victoria squad car, not a word was said between T.C. and Matt, as each was alone with their thoughts.

Each, in their separate ways, was thinking the same thing, the driver of the white, Ford Bronco would never make it alive to a court of law.

They would see to it.

CHAPTER 10

S gt. Humberto Garza takes the last puff of his Marlboro and tilts his head straight back, as he watches the smoke evaporate into the early morning darkness.

"Beautiful," he says out loud, as he looks up at the stars, which seemed to cover the entire dark blue sky.

It had been way, way, too long, he realizes, since he had laid on a blanket, with his wife, Juanita, and looked at the moon and the stars.

A constant problem of being married to a cop and he was confused as to why any woman would want to be.

It seemed like there was never enough vacation time.

If you were assigned to any specialized units in a police agency, call-outs or incidents, could cut even more into your time off.

Garza can still remember missing his son's fourth birthday party, due to a call-out on a fatal crash, involving two cars, drag racing down Lake Avenue, in Greenfield.

Finishing the last drain of coffee, from his small Styrofoam cup, he put the cigarette butt inside the cup and dropped it into a grey colored, plastic garbage can, located near the main employee entrance, to the Greenfield Police Department.

Walking back inside the police station, he finds himself inside his office, in two minutes.

As head of the Greenfield Police Department's Traffic Bureau for the past six years, the past month had easily been the hardest, of his 19-year career in law enforcement.

Chris Mills' death was still unsolved, much to the frustration of everyone involved with the ongoing investigation.

Chief Fitzsimons had been a man of his word and manpower, as well as overtime, had both been used freely, in an attempt to find both the Ford Bronco and its driver.

Checking his office phone for messages, Garza finds no voicemails, for the first time in 18 days.

Getting out of his chair, he walks out of his office toward a small, crowded, conference room shared by both the Traffic Bureau and Social Worker, Debra Santiago.

On a large brown table, the entire accident scene of Chris Mills' death, is laid out in front of him.

Pictures, drawings, accident reports, a copy of the Cook County Medical Examiner's report, on the death, and supplemental reports, all stared up at him.

For easily the 100th time since Mills died, Garza found himself looking at the documents on the table.

Sitting down in one of the four chairs situated around the table, he replays that dreadful morning over in his head, once again.

The one thing Garza wants, besides catching Chris Mills' killer, is to make sure everything had been done correctly, by his personnel in the investigation.

No way, Garza thinks to himself, could he or any of his personnel make a mistake, which would cost a guilty conviction and set the killer free.

With his right hand, he picks up three color pictures, of the driver's side door on Chris Mills' squad car, studying them.

Quickly he's brought back to that fatal morning.

By 0625 hours, Garza and all of his Traffic Bureau personnel, had arrived at the intersection of Moody and First Streets.

Thirty minutes earlier, when some of the craziness had slowed down, Karen Jenkins had been able to put out an MCAT call-out, resulting in police officers responding to the accident scene from Mount Prospect, Northbrook, Wheeling, Evanston and Lincolnwood Police Departments.

Each of these officers would bring with them a specialty needed either in photography, evidence collection, or accident reconstruction.

Upon completing their work and combining it with the other officers' work, they would give Chief Fitzsimons and hopefully a jury someday, an accurate picture of what occurred at this intersection, less than two hours earlier.

As soon as Sgt. Garza emerged from his completely black, slick-topped, Ford Crown Victoria, Lt. Wayne headed his way.

Sgt. Garza actually had to bite his lip, because the more Sgt. Garza saw of Lt. Wayne, the more he reminded him of the character named Newman, from the old *Seinfeld* show on television.

With the way he yelled out things, instead of talking normally, his physical features, puffy face and curly hair, Sgt. Garza quickly thought to himself, "Here comes Newman."

With a full head of steam and sweat pouring off his red, swollen face, Lt. Wayne stopped directly in front of him.

Sgt. Garza raised his right hand and placed his index finger against his lips. This universal signal for quiet, actually stopped Lt. Wayne from talking.

Then Sgt. Garza tilted his head toward the shoulder mic of his portable radio, which was attached to his left shoulder.

Using his call sign, Sgt. Garza spoke firmly with a hint of Spanish accent, attempting to calm the first emergency he faced.

"Greenfield 316," he said into his shoulder mic.

"Go ahead, 316," Dispatcher Susie Patz answered.

Sgt. Garza found himself caught off guard, figuring that either Dispatcher Karen Jenkins or Eddie Heaviland would be answering him.

Instead, Garza would be dealing with Patz, who would make this tragedy somewhat more bearable.

Susie Patz was easily one of the best dispatchers on the Greenfield Police Department.

Standing all of 5'2" in height, with strawberry blonde curly hair and without an ounce of fat, due to daily bike riding, made her the complete package.

Considering she was in her middle 50s and had overcome some severe health issues, made her even more remarkable.

But beauty wasn't Patz's only asset.

With most dispatchers, if you ran a 10-27, you only got back the basic information. This wasn't the case with Susie Patz.

With her dispatching, you always got all the driver's information back, a check on any warrants for this individual, as well as any criminal history this person may have.

"Greenfield, our staging area will be the Immanuel Methodist Church, for any incoming units, Red's Towing Service, the press, et cetera," Sgt. Garza said.

"10-4, Immanuel Methodist Church," Patz answered.

"With its huge parking lot and this not being a weekend, that's a great choice," Lt. Wayne answered.

"Give me just one more minute Boss," Sgt. Garza responded.

In that minute, he proceeded to send out a text message, including the address of Immanuel Methodist Church, to responding MCAT units.

Upon finishing the text, Sgt. Garza put his department-issued Motorola phone back in the right coat pocket of his blue, Blauer, Greenfield Police Department jacket.

"Any word on Chris Mills?" Lt. Wayne asked.

"Nothing," Sgt. Garza replied, slowly shaking his head from side to side.

Lt. Wayne watched as Sgt. Garza stuck the upper part of his body back through the open window of the driver's door, of his squad car. With his right hand, he pushed a round, blue button, located in the middle of his car's dashboard.

Instantly, the trunk of his car kicked open and red and blue lights located on the interior bars of the trunk activated.

Walking to the trunk of his car, Sgt. Garza reached into it and pulled out a portable, aluminum, four-foot high, folding table.

Walking with the table, he passed Lt. Wayne and started opening the table directly in front of his squad car.

"Lieutenant Wayne can you do me a favor?" Sgt. Garza asked, while still working on the table.

"Sure Sarge, what do you need?" Lt. Wayne answered.

"There should be a clear, plastic container in the trunk of my squad car, can you please pull it out and bring it to me?"

"Not a problem, Sarge," Lt. Wayne said and then walked to the rear of Sgt. Garza's vehicle, bent over and pulled the container out.

Although the container weighed no more than 30 pounds, Lt. Wayne seemed to have trouble carrying it the few feet to Sgt. Garza.

Once Lt. Wayne got next to Sgt. Garza with the container, he dropped it at Sgt. Garza's feet, instead of putting the container down gently.

"Thanks," Sgt. Garza responded, with a noticeable sarcastic tone in his voice.

Lt. Wayne watched as Sgt. Garza ripped off the lid from the container, revealing its contents to be a box of red-colored police tape, a box of yellow-colored police tape, a small duffle bag containing a black manual, three yellow-colored extension cords, and different colored cans of spray paint.

Turning to his left, Sgt. Garza saw two of his traffic personnel, Steve Cowens and Jennifer Smythe, unloading equipment from their Greenfield squad cars, which were lined up one behind the other on First Street.

"Steve, Jennifer," Garza yelled to them and motioned with his right hand for them to join Lt. Wayne and himself.

As both officers walked toward him, Sgt. Garza looked at two of his finest officers who were totally different, in every possible way.

Steve Cowens was not only Sgt. Garza's senior Traffic Officer, but with 31 ½ years on the job, he was one of the elder officers, on the Greenfield Police Department.

A tall, stocky Irish Man, Cowens was still able to carry out his duties and added valuable insight to the other Traffic Bureau officers, as well as to Sgt. Garza, on issues, such as overweight trucks and village parking regulations.

Cowens was fond of telling fellow officers, "I've seen it all, I've done it all, but I really don't know it all."

For relaxation, Cowens was the only man Sgt. Garza knew, who still smoked a pipe.

An avid fisherman, Cowens talked of retirement and buying some property in Eagle River, Wisconsin with his wife Sue, to enhance his fishing possibilities.

Jennifer Smythe had 14 years on the job, and was one of only six females on the entire Greenfield Police Department.

Where Cowens was tall and stocky, Smythe stood around 5'6" in height and weighed no more than 110 pounds.

Yet, many members of the Greenfield Police Department would choose her, if they needed backup for a bar fight, or heated domestic dispute.

On more than one occasion, Sgt. Garza saw Smythe handcuffing a drunken husband, who was twice her size, and had beaten the shit out of their wife.

Whereas Cowens went fishing, Smythe's relaxation was playing in a number of softball leagues and karate.

As both Smythe and Cowens reached him, Sgt. Garza held up both of his arms, which contained the yellow police tape in his right hand and red police tape in his left hand, which were still in their original boxes.

Not a word was said between the three of them, as Cowens took the yellow tape and Smythe the red.

As both officers turned and started to walk toward the accident scene, Sgt. Garza yelled at Officer Cowens, "Steve, when you're done with that, c'mon back for another assignment."

Raising his right hand and thumb, Cowens indicated he heard Sgt. Garza, as he continued walking with Smythe.

"Sorry Lt. Wayne, for making you wait, but please fill me in, on what I need to know," Sgt. Garza said calmly.

As if a teapot was boiling and the heat was finally turned up, Lt. Wayne exploded, talking as if Sgt. Garza was in the next county, instead of standing in front of him.

To Lt. Wayne's credit, he was able to cover all the essentials, Sgt. Garza needed, on personnel deployment and their activities, in a matter of minutes.

But Lt. Wayne wasn't close to being finished just yet. "Nothing has been moved or even touched come to think of it," Lt. Wayne said, with a bit of doubt in his voice. "Not to mention, you have the benefit of no paramedics being here, dropping shit all over the place," Lt. Wayne said.

"You do know Sergeant Barton took Mills and O'Neil to Lutheran Family Center Hospital, due to the ambulance being trained at the downtown Metra Crossing," Lt. Wayne finished.

"Gutsy move on Barton's part," Sgt. Garza replied.

"I'll say," Lt. Wayne responded.

"Greenfield 316," Sgt. Garza's shoulder mic yelled.

"316 go," Sgt. Garza calmly responded.

"316, call Deputy Chief Bart on his cell phone," Susie Patz advised him.

"10-4," Sgt. Garza responded, while staring directly at Lt. Wayne.

Scrolling through his cell phone, with his right hand, Sgt. Garza was surprised to see this hand start shaking, while attempting to make the phone call.

Finally finding Deputy Chief Bart's name, Sgt. Garza pushed the send button on his phone and waited for Deputy Chief Bart to respond.

"Sergeant Garza?" Deputy Chief Bart asked, upon answering his phone.

"Yes Sir," Garza responded.

No sooner had the word "Sir," come out of Sgt. Garza's mouth, than Deputy Chief Bart responded.

"Fill me in on the situation out there Humberto," Deputy Chief Bart commanded.

"My full MCAT team is here sir and getting set up as we speak. I have both Cowens and Smythe setting up an interior, as well as an exterior, accident scene with police tape," Sgt. Garza stated.

"Hold it a minute," Deputy Chief Bart responded.

"Sir?" Sgt. Garza asked.

"Are you telling me it wasn't done by Lt. Wayne earlier, since he has the same tape in the back of Squad 10?" Deputy Chief Bart asked.

Pausing for a couple of seconds, before answering, Sgt. Garza finally responded with just four words.

"No sir, it wasn't."

"Are you kidding me?" Deputy Chief Bart responded, before continuing.

"Ok, I'll address that with Lt. Wayne later today," Deputy Chief Bart said. "Look Humberto, the Chief is inquiring, as well as Lieutenant Alderman, about why we haven't heard anything about the license plate, on the Ford Bronco? Please, please don't tell me Lieutenant Wayne hasn't viewed it from inside Mills' squad car," Deputy Chief Bart asked.

"Hold on Boss, Lieutenant Wayne is standing right here, so let me check with him," Sgt. Garza responded.

Looking directly at Lt. Wayne, who hadn't moved the entire time, Sgt. Garza asked, "Deputy Chief Bart wants to know if you've been in Mills' squad car and viewed the video, so that we can obtain a license plate number on the Bronco," Sgt. Garza asked.

In a sound that was barely audible and with him visibly shaking, Lt. Wayne meekly said, "No I haven't."

"No Boss, he hasn't," Sgt. Garza said.

Sgt. Garza wasn't sure if Deputy Chief Bart had heard him and was going to say his response again, since Bart said nothing for a few seconds, before finally responding.

"Humberto?" Deputy Chief Bart asked.

"Go ahead Boss," Sgt. Garza responded.

"There's no easy way to say this, but Officer Mills is dead," Deputy Chief Bart stated.

The word dead, seemed to hang in the air for the longest time.

Upon hearing it, Sgt. Garza realized his responsibilities, had taken on a totally new meaning.

Suddenly, this was no longer a traffic accident scene.

Now, it was a death investigation case, involving one of their own.

Sgt. Garza knew his MCAT team and, most importantly, himself, were the main people who needed to figure out who had killed Officer Chris Mills.

Secondly, he would have to inform all three of his Traffic Bureau personnel, they had lost a fellow officer.

"Where the hell is Officer Matt McCurtain?" Sgt. Garza wondered.

Matt McCurtain was the third member of his Traffic Bureau, whom Sgt. Garza hadn't seen since he first arrived at the scene.

Finally, he knew Officers Cowens and Smythe would be approaching him soon and looked to see where their exact location was.

Sgt. Garza turned and saw they were done with the crime scene tape.

Officer Alvin Lopez, from the Northbrook Police Department, had started a crime scene log, which both Cowens and Smythe were signing.

"Let me tell Lieutenant Wayne, about Officer Mills boss," Sgt. Garza responded.

Turning back to where Wayne had been standing, Sgt. Garza found the spot empty, with no Lt. Wayne around.

Looking off in the distance, Sgt. Garza watched as Lt. Wayne entered Squad 10 and started his car.

With squealing rear tires, which caused every police officer to stop what they were doing and watch, Lt. Wayne left, going southbound on First Street, at a high rate of speed.

Getting back on his cell phone, Sgt. Garza continued. "Boss, I have to be honest with you, Lt. Wayne is gone, and I believe he's probably headed over to your location at the hospital, so I didn't get a chance, to tell him the news," Sgt. Garza said.

"That worthless, motherfucker," Deputy Chief Bart yelled into his phone, so loud, it made Sgt. Garza temporarily move the phone away from his right ear.

"Humberto, I have great faith in you, but after I wrap up a few things over here, I'll be headed over to your location. Yes, it's your crime scene, but I still want to be there, in case anything comes up," Deputy Chief Bart responded.

Before Sgt. Garza could say a word, Deputy Chief Bart continued, "Humberto, what do you need from me?" Deputy Chief Bart asked.

"Boss, nothing I can think of," Sgt. Garza said. "As you know, this is the best MCAT team of all of them and I have complete faith in their work ethic."

"Excellent, excellent, Humberto," Deputy Chief Bart said. "Just so you and your people know, I checked with Patz when I called the station a little while ago, and she tells me you've got rain headed your way that should get to you in roughly an hour. Next, Chief Fitzsimons will be holding a press conference to announce the death of Officer Mills, probably in that same hour, which means you should be up to your ass in curiosity seekers and television film crews, right after the press conference ends," Deputy Chief Bart finished.

"We can handle rain and have done so numerous times boss," Sgt. Garza said. "Now snow's a problem, since it's hard to spray paint the road due to it. Regarding the curiosity seekers and the press, we'll handle it when it becomes an issue."

"Due to this being a death investigation now, Lieutenant Alderman will be contacting you to see what his detectives can do to help your people in any way. I'm under the impression both Detectives Liske and Sutherland are handling the interview of the driver of the Buick, at our police station," Deputy Chief Bart stated.

"Humberto, you're a smart man with a great future here," continued Deputy Chief Bart. "Follow your SOPS, but the sooner you can get me a plate off the Bronco, the sooner I can pass it on to the Chief and the Detective Bureau can go catch the prick that killed Officer Mills, 10-4?"

"Got it," Sgt. Garza replied and he heard a dial tone suddenly on his cell phone, from Deputy Chief Bart hanging up.

Sgt. Garza put his phone back in his jacket pocket, for the second time today.

Suddenly, he found Officers Cowens, Smythe, and McCurtain standing directly in front of him.

Sgt. Garza noticed Officers Smythe and Cowens were holding their police tape boxes, which appeared to be nearly empty.

Smythe asked before Cowens or McCurtain could say it, "Boss, any word on Mills?"

"Yeah, there is guys," Sgt. Garza responded and paused to take a deep breath before continuing.

Looking first at Officer Cowens, then Officer McCurtain, and finally Officer Smythe, Sgt. Garza kept it simple.

"Guys, I'm sorry to tell you this, but Officer Mills couldn't overcome his injuries and he died," Sgt. Garza said.

Upon hearing the news, Officers Smythe and McCurtain immediately put their heads down.

Officer Cowens followed as well, but after he had made the sign of the cross.

Giving each of his officers a moment to reflect, Sgt. Garza also put his head down and said a Hail Mary quietly in Spanish to himself, for Officer Mills.

After completing his prayer, Sgt. Garza looked up and asked Officer Cowens, "Steve, how is Officer Mueller doing, with the videotaping of the scene?"

"I think he has most of the overall work done and did the close up work as well on the driver's car. What's the driver's name? Mrs. Loftus, I think," Officer Cowens said.

"Okay, here's what we're doing next," Sgt. Garza said. "I'm going to sign the crime scene log that Officer Lopez started."

"Steve," Sgt. Garza continued, "I want you to find Officer Mueller and meet me at Officer Mills' squad car, so we can videotape watching the in-car camera. Then, I want you to take custody of Mueller's video tape," Sgt. Garza said.

"10-4," Officer Cowens said and left.

Sgt. Garza spoke to Officer McCurtain next. "Matt, refresh my memory and fill me in on your next assignment, so we're on the same page."

In a loud, confident voice, which appeared to startle Officer Smythe, Officer McCurtain spoke. "Collect and handle any physical evidence at the crime scene after it has been both videotaped and photographed by Officer Mueller. After the assignment is complete, I will help in the handling of the towing of both Officer Mills' squad and the Buick," Officer McCurtain said.

"Very good Matt," Sgt. Garza said calmly and watched as Officer McCurtain walked toward the crime scene.

"Jennifer, what's your next assignment?" Sgt. Garza asked.

"I'll be working with Officer Nolan, from the Wheeling Police Department and we'll be doing the overall measurements for the accident report and reconstruction process," she answered.

After delivering the news to Sgt. Garza, Officer Smythe turned and walked over to where Officer Nolan was standing.

Sgt. Garza followed her, but stopped when he found Officer Lopez standing with the crime scene log.

Not a word was exchanged between the two of them, as Sgt. Garza signed his name, date and time.

Checking the log, Sgt. Garza verified all his MCAT personnel had signed in.

Upon finishing the crime scene log, Sgt. Garza quickly walked towards Chris Mills', Greenfield Squad 7.

Sgt. Garza walked through the middle of his entire MCAT team, while they were doing their assignments, with hardly a word being spoken among them.

Arriving at Mills' squad car, Sgt. Garza checked the entire driver's side door thoroughly, using the small Maglite, he had inside a pocket of his bulletproof vest.

If he could find some damage on the squad car door, it would help in the identification of the Ford Bronco.

If this paint was collected properly by Officer McCurtain, it could prove to be invaluable from a physical evidence point of view.

The Ford plant where the Bronco was built, its year, as well as the dealer where the car was shipped, would all be available just from one, small chip, of white paint.

He found nothing on Officer Mills' driver's side door. Not a nick or even a scratch mark could be seen by the human eye.

"Motherfucker," Sgt. Garza said to himself quietly, so his MCAT Team didn't hear him.

"Motherfucker," Officer Mueller said loud enough to get Sgt. Garza to focus his attention from Officer Mills' squad car door, to Officer Mueller, who was approaching as a light rain began to fall.

"Was hoping we could get this videotaping done before the rain hit, but I guess not," Officer Mueller said with a disgusted tone in his voice.

When Officer Mueller finally got close enough, Sgt. Garza extended his right hand to him and almost had it broken by Officer Mueller's grip.

Sgt. Garza actually winced in pain, which Officer Mueller must have seen, because he quickly released Sgt. Garza's hand.

Sgt. Garza was by no means small, standing roughly 6'0" in height and weighing around 215 pounds. He took pride in his workouts, but admitted to himself on more than one occasion, a one-hour workout at his health club, Planet Fitness, should have taken place, instead of watching soccer on ESPN at home, while downing a couple of cold Modelos.

Sgt. Garza was no match for Officer Howard "Moe" Mueller, who stood close to 6'6" and weighed an easy 240 pounds.

The funny part, Sgt. Garza thought, as he repeatedly kept opening and closing his right hand to get the blood flowing through it, was Officer Mueller probably never worked out a day in his entire life. There was something to be said for being born naturally strong, as opposed to the strength you acquire through weightlifting.

Officer Mueller was second generation law enforcement. Howard Mueller's father, Arthur "Artie" Mueller, recently retired after 35 years of service, with the Arlington Heights Police Department.

Officer Mueller's brother, Michael Mueller, was a 19-year veteran of the Chicago Police Department, with the last 5 years being a homicide detective, working on the west side of Chicago.

More importantly, Michael Mueller was Howard Mueller's twin brother and physically matched him in both looks and strength. It was always a joke they would play on unsuspecting cops' wives, or girlfriends at FOP barbecues, to try and figure out, which Mueller you were actually talking to.

But today was no joke and Officer Mueller's photography work, both taking pictures, as well as videotaping the crime scene, would be critical when this case went to trial.

Drawings and scale recreations of this crime scene, would be fine, but a jury of 12 needed to see, "the real thing", Sgt. Garza and his MCAT team were experiencing right now.

"You ready Moe?" Sgt. Garza asked.

"Bring it Boss," Officer Mueller responded.

With Officer Cowens documenting the time and date in his notepad, and Officer Mueller videotaping, Sgt. Garza got inside Greenfield Squad 7, the car Officer Mills was driving when he was killed.

Sgt. Garza was taken back by the interior's neatness.

The only thing on the front passenger seat, was Mills' 5-11 Tactical Bag, which contained a number of different reports, inside a metal binder, which Sgt. Garza saw in the middle section of the bag. This bag also contained an extra pair of winter gloves, a 2014 copy of the Illinois Vehicle Code, as well as maps of both Greenfield and the entire North Shore.

Finally, Sgt. Garza noticed a Greenfield Village ordinance ticket book, and a small metal box, holding the tickets, Officer Mills was going to issue Mrs. Loftus.

Finally, it was time to get the license plate number of the Bronco.

Turning off the overhead lights for the squad car, caused the video to stop recording.

Nothing that had been said outside of the squad car from the time Officer Mills had been transported to Lutheran Family Center Hospital until now, had been recorded, due to Officer Mills having the recorder for the camera, still in its pouch, on his duty belt.

With his right hand, Sgt. Garza hit the rewind button, on the video camera, and watched as the video seemed to move at a snail's pace.

While waiting for the video to finally stop rewinding, Sgt. Garza felt pressure in the middle of his chest, which he had never experienced before. Turning his head to the left, he took slow, deep breaths, and the pressure started to ease a bit.

Sgt. Garza confirmed Officer Mueller was recording his actions, and Officer Cowens was documenting it, when he saw all of them standing in a half circle, around the driver's side door, of Squad 7.

The pressure started up again, as he witnessed his entire MCAT team, standing behind Officers Cowens and Mueller.

Each of the team members were looking directly at him, knowing what he was doing, and how important it was to their investigation.

Slowly, Sgt. Garza hit the red-colored play button, on the recorder.

For the last time in his shortened life, the words of Officer Chris Mills, came alive.

"Greenfield 320, a traffic stop," Officers Mills said calmly, yet confidently.

As Sgt. Garza watched intently, Officer Mills had activated his overhead emergency lights, which started the video recording of the traffic stop, at the intersection of First and Moody Streets.

Mrs. Loftus brought her Buick to a complete stop and pulled over on First Street and Moody Street.

Officer Mills finished speaking, and is heard on the video, placing the squad car microphone, back into the holder for it.

Officer Mills parked his squad car, as he was properly trained at ILETC. The nose part of his squad car is matched up, with the driver's side rear taillight of the Buick.

His side spotlight is used, and reflects off Mrs. Loftus' Buick, filling the interior of her car with light.

Finally, Officer Mills turned his front wheels all the way to the right, in preparation for the rare situation where his squad car could be rear-ended by another motorist, so his vehicle wouldn't crash into Mrs. Loftus' vehicle.

In the video, Officer Mills is heard getting out of his squad car and taking two or three steps.

The next sound is a loud, "uggh," he makes, as the Ford Bronco strikes him.

Sgt. Garza pulled a small writing pad, from the right pocket, of his bulletproof vest and then a bic pen from a spot on the left side, of this vest, made specifically to hold two, thin pens.

Sgt. Garza is ready to record the license plate number, of the Ford Bronco.

But it is for nothing, as he watched the video in disbelief.

Upon being struck, the video only showed Officer Mills lying in the street, with no Ford Bronco in sight.

Slowly and carefully, Sgt. Garza stopped the video and rewound it again, believing he must have missed something.

Sgt. Garza had missed nothing.

There was no sight of the Ford Bronco, anywhere on the video.

As Sgt. Garza watched in shock, Mrs. Loftus gets out of her Buick.

Upon seeing Officer Mills, she runs to his squad car and picked up the microphone, yelling into it for help.

"Sgt. Garza, how about a cup of coffee?" Chief Fitzsimons asks.

Sgt. Garza is snapped out of his dream, finding Chief Fitzsimons standing in front of him in the conference room, holding Styrofoam cups of coffee, in each of his hands.

Getting out of his chair, Sgt. Garza can only manage to get the words, "Thanks Chief," out, as he takes the cup of coffee the Chief is holding in his right hand, with his own right hand.

Taking a small sip of the coffee, is all Sgt. Garza can manage, because the coffee is extremely hot and bitter.

"How you holding up Humberto?" Chief Fitzsimons asks.

"Fine Chief," Humberto responds, which is a lie and Chief Fitzsimons knows it.

A combination of black and purple bags, are prominent under each of Sgt. Garza's eyes, from lack of sleep.

Radio traffic in the past couple of days, between Sgt. Garza and his Traffic Bureau personnel, has become shorter and rougher, as the stress level of Sgt. Garza, has continued to grow.

"Things good at home Humberto?" Chief Fitzsimons asks.

"Good, good, really the entire family is fine and thanks for asking Boss," Garza answers.

A small pause takes place between the two of them, as they check each other out, before Chief Fitzsimons finally speaks.

"Deputy Chief Bart has been keeping me up to speed on the

investigation, Humberto, and he knows I'm with you right now," says Chief Fitzsimons. "I've never been a big fan of violating the Chain of Command, but this is a different animal to say the least. So, at your leisure, fill me in on what you believe I need to know and tell me anything we haven't done yet to find Officer Mills' killer," Chief Fitzsimons finishes.

"Well, chief you know we completed our part of the accident investigation last Friday," says Sgt. Garza. "Since there's a lack of physical evidence from either the Buick or Officer Mills' squad car, it totally expedited the process and due to the lack of skid marks, we believe the driver of the Ford Bronco, never braked at the scene," Sgt. Garza finishes.

"I'm aware the second canvas done by the detectives, turned up an additional witness besides Mrs. Loftus, Isn't that correct?" Chief Fitzsimons asks

"Correct," Sgt. Garza responds. "A nurse at Redeemer Hospital, by the name of Rebecca Stone."

"Apparently, she was taking her poodle out for its morning business, when the Ford Bronco flew by her at a very high rate of speed. Unfortunately, Ms. Stone didn't have her glasses on and never does when she's walking her dog, so consequently, she was unable to supply our detectives with any additional information on either the driver, or the Ford Bronco," Sgt. Garza says.

"Okay, I can shed some light on this part," Chief Fitzsimons says, as he walks past Sgt. Garza and drops his empty coffee cup into a garbage container, located underneath the table, just past where Sgt. Garza is now seated. "Lieutenant Alderman came up with the idea of hypnotism and earlier today, the detectives took both Ms. Stone and Mrs. Loftus, to the best one I'm aware of, Dr. John Watson, located downtown, on LaSalle Street."

Sgt. Garza finds himself leaning forward in his chair, anxiously awaiting good news, from Chief Fitzsimons.

"Unfortunately, neither one of them could give Dr. Watson any additional information, under hypnosis, about either the driver, or the Ford Bronco."

Sitting back in his chair, Sgt. Garza suddenly finds himself the most relaxed he's ever been, speaking with Chief Fitzsimons. So comfortable in fact, he finds himself raising his right leg off the floor and bending it at a 45-degree angle, so his right ankle, rests on his left leg.

"As you know Chief, we've done a number of checkpoints, at the intersection where Officer Mills died, in hopes of locating the Ford Bronco," says Sgt. Garza. "Obviously, the night after he died, a week after he died, so on and so forth and all of them have turned up nothing. Also, thank you for being at a couple of these check points. It meant a ton I know to my personnel and Officer Mills' shift, who also showed up unexpectedly, offering their assistance, in finding the Ford Bronco," Sgt. Garza finishes.

Chief Fitzsimons is caught off guard by the comment and momentarily he flashes back to the first morning, after Officer Mills' death.

He recalls driving to Greenfield, directly from his condominium, in need of sleep from the hectic day before, but wanting to hear the good news, the Ford Bronco and its driver had been located.

He remembers parking two blocks from the intersection of Moody Street and First Street and walking towards the intersection, on the sidewalk, in both an effort to remain out of sight and hoping the walk, in the morning fresh air, would perk him up.

When he was roughly a half block away from the intersection, he found himself standing behind a huge elm tree, with the widest base, he had ever seen.

For the next hour, he watched the activity of Sgt. Garza and his Traffic Bureau personnel, which turned out to be fruitless, before walking back to his Chevy Malibu.

"Didn't think anyone saw me, since the last thing I wanted to be that morning, to you and your people, was a distraction," Chief Fitzsimons says slowly, while rubbing his chin with his right hand, before continuing. "I'm not sure you're aware Sgt. Garza, but NORTAF has given us two detectives, for the main purpose of reviewing every parking violation, or moving violation ticket, Officer Mills wrote, as well as every arrest he either made, or assisted on in his career. This process will continue for some period of time, along with them looking for any available video from a business, the Ford Bronco traveled past that night," Chief Fitzsimons says and pauses only for a few seconds, before continuing.

"The video from Officer Mills' squad car, has been sent to the FBI crime lab in Washington D.C. for enhancement. Yes, I'm well aware of NASA's capability for enhancing the video and they may be used if we don't get the results we hope for from the FBI," Chief Fitzsimons pauses briefly, before continuing. "Sergeant Garza you happen to be the first to know, an hour ago, I received a telephone call from Bruce Rodman."

"The Secretary of State Police?" Sgt. Garza asks.

"Yes," Chief Fitzsimons answers.

"How will they be able to assist us, Boss?" Sgt. Garza asks.

"Apparently, they have a Police Inquiry Unit," says Chief Fitzsimons. "If you give them any information on the Ford Bronco, ranging from 1995 to present, they can give us a list of all the registered owners for that vehicle here in Illinois. Needless to say, I impressed upon Director Rodman, our appreciation for his help and our need to expedite this matter. Director Rodman assured me this matter will be a high priority with his agency and he may give us one of his people to help, with our investigation," Chief Fitzsimons finished.

Before Sgt. Garza can respond, Chief Fitzsimons bends over at the waist, so that his face is relatively close to Sgt. Garza's face.

"The bottom-line Humberto, as I stated at Lutheran Family Center Hospital, the day Officer Mills died, I will use every agency available to us, to find Officer Mills' killer."

"Any questions Sgt. Garza?" Chief Fitzsimons asks.

"No sir," Sgt. Garza responds, in a mild voice.

The Chief's face is so close to his, he's afraid to say anything louder.

As Chief Fitzsimons straightens up and is finally standing fully erect, he says in a firm voice, "Good, good, Humberto and do me a favor?"

"What's that Sir," Sgt. Garza asks.

"Get some rest. I need you healthy, to work with Director

Rodman's person," Chief Fitzsimons says, as he puts his left hand, on Sgt. Garza's left shoulder.

Chief Fitzsimons then walks quickly out of the office.

Sgt. Garza waits a full minute to guarantee the Chief is gone, before turning around in his chair.

Staying seated, he looks again, for the second time today, at the physical evidence in front of him, lying on the table.

Sitting all alone, near a corner of the table, is an 8 by 10-inch color photo, of Officer Chris Mills.

The picture is taken, at the Greenfield Police Department, after each rookie graduated from, ILETC.

Sgt. Garza smiles for a brief minute, remembering when he had his picture taken years ago, minus the black and grey mustache and slightly puffier face, he now possesses.

He takes the picture with his left hand and studies it for a few minutes.

He's taken back by the youthful appearance, of Officer Christopher Mills.

The picture looks nothing like the thirty-five, which are sitting in a Greenfield Police Department case file, on the other corner of the table.

For those thirty-five pictures, are Officer Christopher Mills' autopsy photos.

Pictures of him scarred and naked, taken from every angle, on a steel table, right before, during and after his autopsy, which was performed by the head Cook County Chief Medical Examiner.

Sgt. Garza suddenly stands up, while still holding, Officer Chris Mills graduation picture.

"We'll get him Chris, trust me son, it's just a matter of time, but we will," he says.

With that, Sgt. Garza places this picture back at the same spot, it once occupied on the table.

He then walks out of the office and turns the light off in the process, as he leaves for a cigarette and a new strategy, for finding Officer Christopher Mills' killer.

CHAPTER 11

Matt O'Neil drives most of the way in silence, occasionally turning on WBBM News radio 780, to catch the traffic report and any late breaking news.

He also likes the soothing sound of Felicia Middlebrooks voice, every weekday morning.

Traffic is light, except for a small bit of congestion near Madison, Wisconsin.

Matt believes this is caused by the University of Wisconsin being located here.

He is so caught up in the moment, he didn't realize the significance of Belvedere, Illinois which he passed earlier today.

"Damnit," he found himself screaming out loud, in the unmarked, Greenfield squad car.

The fact he's actually screaming over his forgetfulness, bothers him.

Belvedere is the home of Harriett Mills, who Matt hadn't telephoned since the funeral.

On the front passenger seat next to him, Matt O'Neil opens a black-colored binder, with an official Greenfield Police Department emblem, engraved on the front of it.

While keeping his eyes on the road, he reaches up to the driver's side visor. Moving his right hand around for a few seconds, he finds what he's looking for.

He pulls the pen down and puts the cap of it between his teeth. While his teeth are keeping pressure on the pen's cap, he's able to pull the remaining part of the pen out, with his left hand. Next, he flips open the binder and writes in big, bold letters across the first sheet of paper: Call Mrs. Mills tomorrow.

It's exactly two months, to the day, Officer Chris Mills had been killed.

Things were not going well, in a number of ways, for Matt O'Neil.

The main issue being, Chris Mills' killer is still unknown, despite the work of numerous law enforcement agencies and their countless personnel.

The fact the killer hadn't been caught yet, didn't sit well with the members of the Greenfield Police Department and especially Matt O'Neil.

Even without Chris Mills' killer being apprehended, Matt O'Neil was comfortable knowing it wasn't from a lack of effort from himself, or members of the Greenfield Police Department.

A week after Chris Mills died, his entire shift, except for Lt. Wayne, assisted on the checkpoint at First and Moody Streets, joining Sgt. Garza's, Traffic Bureau Personnel.

Every time word came down there was going to be a checkpoint, Matt O'Neil and members of his shift, came in, hoping this would be the morning, the Ford Bronco would make the mistake of driving past them.

But even this wasn't good enough, for Matt O'Neil or T.C. Chambers.

Each of them took turns coming in early on Thursday mornings, because this was the day of the week, when Officer Christopher Mills, had been killed.

They would come in on their own time, in plain clothes, as opposed to uniform and use their own personal vehicles.

For exactly one hour, they would sit in the vicinity of, First and Moody Streets.

Both Matt and T.C. were troubled, as to why Chris's squad car camera, hadn't picked up the Ford Bronco, after it had struck him.

Frequent discussion by the shift, at the completion of daily roll calls, came to the conclusion the driver was either shaving, eating, drinking coffee, putting on makeup, or the obvious one of talking on their cell phone.

Every officer on Matt O'Neil's squad, had seen each of these traffic violations, on a regular basis.

Upon hitting Officer Chris Mills, the driver of the Ford Bronco, certainly pulled the steering wheel hard to the left and went down Moody Ave, avoiding the squad car camera.

All of these extra hours of coming in early, had been done for nothing and the lack of sleep, was catching up to Matt.

Fortunately, he was starting to realize it.

Matt was leading his shift in every category, but the arrests meant increased court time.

The Greenfield Police Department, in 2016, was still using the antiquated, eight-hour shift and rotation every month schedule.

This worked great for Matt, if he needed to go to court, when he was on days, or afternoons.

Midnight shift was the absolute killer.

There were days, with a 1330-hour court call, for both his Traffic, Misdemeanor, and Felony cases, which resulted in him getting, only 3 to 4 hours of sleep.

Matt also assisted in backing up other officers on traffic stops, which occasionally led to additional DUI arrests, with even more court time.

If he witnessed the field sobriety portion of the arrest, or any incriminating statements made by the arrestee, Matt would be subpoenaed by the States Attorney's Office and have to testify on those officers' court calls.

Unfortunately, a number of these officers had different court times than Matt, which resulted in even less sleep.

Matt O'Neil was no stranger when it came to not getting enough sleep, from his days with the Navy Seals.

The longest Matt O›Neil had ever been awake, were two and a half days in Afghanistan, when his forward operating base, Camp Bulldog, had been attacked by the Al Qadir leader, Mohammed Zir Lafar.

Matt was convinced, the few grey hairs he currently had, were a result of this attack.

Morning, noon and night, his Navy Seals, fought alongside the troops stationed there, in an effort not to get over run, but mainly just to survive.

Due to death and injuries, Senior Chief Petty Officer, Matt O'Neil, found himself to be the highest-ranking officer, still alive at this outpost.

Checking on his men, moving personnel around, and finally, helping to move the dead and wounded, required Matt to be on his feet for 52 straight hours.

Camp Bulldog was saved, but at an extremely high price.

Nine American soldiers and two North Alliance soldiers, made the ultimate sacrifice, dying while defending it.

But life was so different for Matt back then.

With the Navy Seals, he was constantly on edge and doing something all the time, which kept his adrenaline flowing and him constantly awake.

"Hell, the thought of an AK-47 round, or a knife piercing your skull, is enough motivation for anyone to stay awake," he thought.

Matt O'Neil soon found police work, to be a totally different animal.

Summer time compared to wintertime, was like the difference between night and day.

Summer time, with kids off from school, meant constant activity, throughout all three shifts.

Matt's norcom radio was buzzing with assigned calls, traffic stops, and loud parties, or at the very least, an occasional disturbance, at a McDonald's or Burger King.

Meal times were often questionable and changed on the fly, due to the constant activity.

Midnight shift meant driving around the entire night, with the window rolled down and wind hitting him in the face. He often took calls as late as 0530 hours, especially on the weekends.

Seven days a week, from June through August, it was nonstop action.

His eight hours shift, often flew by in a flash.

As a rookie, he went home and couldn't wait to tell Kelly, or anyone else, about what he had just seen or participated in.

He couldn't wait to get back at it, the very next day, because it was so fresh, exciting and occasionally head scratching.

Like the time Matt was coming in for breakfast, around 0445

hours, on a beautiful July morning and suddenly passed three 13-year-old kids, riding their bicycles, east on Lake Avenue.

Turning his squad car around, he stopped and asked them what they were doing.

Their answer was simple and to the point, "Riding down to Foster Avenue beach Officer, to watch the sunrise."

Forty-five minutes later, all three had been reunited with their parents.

Matt smiled, while putting the last line of his report, into his squad car computer.

Wintertime, was just the opposite and a pain in the ass.

The kids were back in school and once it really got cold towards Thanksgiving, crime and calls for service, started to slow down.

Once the snow started to fall, by December and through February, radio traffic seemed to come to a complete halt, after 2230 hours.

Then he faced the arduous task, of trying to stay awake.

After working an eight-hour shift, Matt spent most of one day in court, for a D.U.I trial. Arriving home, he tried unsuccessfully to take a nap, since Kelly had left the residence, in an effort to eliminate any noise issues.

Two telephone calls, on their home phone, spaced an hour apart, blew up any possibility of getting his nap in.

Returning to work, for his 8-hour midnight shift, Matt did something, he thought he would never do.

He texted T.C. at 0330 hours, and they met at the rear of the Greenfield Golf Course parking lot, each in their respective squad cars.

Matt slept soundly for30 minutes, while T.C. stayed awake.

Vowing to never have to take this chance again, Matt set out to find a product, or two, he could take during his shift, to stay awake.

His first choice being the obvious one, coffee, but the more he drank, the harder it was for him to fall asleep, at the end of his shift.

Next, were different forms of energy drinks, but Matt soon found himself a bit jittery, roughly 20 minutes after taking them.

Finally, he went with a mixture of coffee and water to start the shift, or a can of coke starting the shift and then only water, with constant movement, every 20 minutes.

Matt would get out of his car, no matter what the weather was doing and perform some simple calisthenics.

Thank goodness for days off, when he could grab some sleep.

Matt's record was 12 straight hours of continuous, undisturbed sleep.

Matt woke up reenergized and feeling like a new man.

He gave Kelly a huge hug, as she crawled into bed and snuggled up next to him, for the remainder of the afternoon.

Granted, Kelly was enjoying the extra income, which was helping to pay off bills and furnishing their ranch-style, Morton Grove home.

Also, Matt had started to hear rumors, from other shifts, about him.

He came in one day, to find a piece of white athletic tape, on his locker.

On the tape, someone had written the words, "Golden Boy," in black marker.

Matt was ambitious and hard driving, but he had stabbed no one in the back, always took the calls in his beat and been respectful to everyone.

It would take more than snide remarks and notes on his locker, to slow him down.

Matt dreamed as far back as ILETC, of someday driving an unmarked detective car.

He just didn't think it would happen so quickly, or in this fashion.

Quickly, seemed to be the key word in all of this and in so many different ways.

Earlier today, he received the news from Chief Fitzsimons personally, who had removed him from roll call.

Changing out of his uniform, he put on a pair of old Levi 501 blue jeans, a Chicago Bears hooded blue sweatshirt and a pair of beat up, grey, New Balance 940 running shoes.

Loosening the wide brown belt on his blue jeans, he slipped his nickel-coated, 45 Caliber Colt Commander on it gingerly.

Situated nicely, in its black-colored Desantis holster, the 45 was firm against his right hip, when he finally tightened his belt.

Pausing for a minute, he thought, "What the heck?" and again opened his brown belt buckle, to attach a brown leather clip, which contained two magazines, both held 13 rounds of Winchester, 120 grain, 45 Hollow Points ammo, on to the left side of the belt.

Finally, Matt took his duty badge off his blue, nylon, duty jacket.

While still holding this badge, he bent down to look for a box he had stashed, in the bottom of his locker.

After a minute of looking, he found the box. It had been covered by a plastic bag, he had put in his locker, only two weeks earlier.

This plastic bag contained two bath towels, extra socks, white-colored Hanes underwear, two bars of Dial soap and one white handkerchief. All of these items were spares, in case of accidents, or sudden sickness.

Opening up the box, he quickly found what he was looking for at its top. Pulling it out of the box, he stopped and stared at it, never figuring he would have to use it so early in his career.

A black-colored, round badge case holder, to which he attached his Greenfield badge.

Because the badge case holder had a clip on the back of it, he could attach it to the front part of his leather belt, directly to the right of his Colt Commander.

Looking at the brown, worn bench in front of his locker, he grabbed his portable radio off it and for some unknown reason, placed it in his black, 5.11 travel bag. Matt O'Neil checked the bag thoroughly, to make sure it had everything he needed.

While still focused on this bag, he didn't see the somber looking, Javier Ortego, leaning on a locker, next to Matt's locker, until he looked up.

"Dude, you look like a detective," Javier Ortego said to him.

Matt responded, "Nope, just needed to change into plain clothes, to get this assignment done."

"Need anything before you go?" Javier Ortego asked.

"Nope, should be all set, but thanks man," Matt said. "We're still on for racquetball, in a few weeks, at the Leaning Tower Y"?

"You know it bro, and see if you can finally win a game from me this time, old man. Hey, when you get back, try getting some sleep, because you look awful, Dude," Javier responded, as he left the locker room, chuckling out loud.

Whether Officer Ortego knew it or not, he had just given Matt a present, which he so desperately needed. A laugh, which Matt couldn't remember, the last time he had one.

Locking his locker, Matt put his key ring in the right front pocket of his blue jeans and walked out of the men's locker room, into the lunchroom hallway.

Immediately, he ran into Sgt. Barton and Deputy Chief Bart talking.

"You all set O'Neil"? Deputy Chief Bart asked.

"Yes Sir," Matt responded, with a firm voice.

The three of them stood in the shape of a triangle, with Deputy Chief Bart standing adjacent to the lunchroom door and Sgt. Barton and Matt standing against a wall.

"Here are the keys to 921," Deputy Chief Bart said.

With his right hand he gave Matt a set of car keys, which Matt immediately put in the left front pocket of his blue jeans.

"Thanks Boss," Matt answered and then quickly said, "Deputy Chief Bart, could you please do me a favor and thank Chief Fitzsimons."

"Not a problem O'Neil," Deputy Chief Bart responded.

"I want you to take this," and he reached inside an accordion style manila folder he was holding and pulled out a Greenfield Police Department, Motorola phone.

"I snatched this out of Support Services, since Deputy Chief Gyondski told me they had a spare. You know how to use this one, correct?" Deputy Chief Bart asked.

"Yes Sir," Matt answered. "Sergeant Barton has allowed me to use his occasionally, on follow-up phone calls to the on-duty States Attorney, or to Social Worker Santiago, for domestic battery cases."

"Great, great," Deputy Chief Bart said, before continuing. "No sense using your own phone, especially since you're going all the way to Wisconsin. Do us one favor and call me when you know something and I'll forward it to the Chief," Deputy Chief Bart finished.

"Yes Sir," Matt responded and started to walk past Sgt. Barton, when Deputy Chief Bart suddenly reached out with his left hand and grabbed Matt's left arm, stopping him in his tracks.

"One last thing O'Neil," Deputy Chief Bart said.

"Sir?" was all Matt could say, as he was totally caught off guard.

"It's been brought to the Chief's and my attention, a few members of CAVE, are still carrying on behind the scenes, regarding Officer Mills death and the actions of Sgt. Barton that morning," Deputy Chief Bart stated.

Matt O'Neil quickly glanced at Sgt. Barton, who was expressionless and then back to Deputy Chief Bart before mumbling, "Cave Sir?"

"Yup, CAVE is the acronym I came up with for them, because it represents them so well. Complain about virtually everything," Deputy Chief Bart said. "They believe Sergeant Barton violated policy, by transporting Officer Mills in a squad car, instead of waiting for the ambulance. I can tell you both, the Chief is furious about this and will be putting out a strongly worded memo, commenting on the rumors and innuendoes regarding the incident."

Deputy Chief Bart then finished, "I thought since it involved you and one of your best friends, as well as the fact your shift will be off for the weekend, starting tomorrow, you should know about it now."

Matt O'Neil felt dumbfounded by the entire thing and all he could think of saying was, "Thank you Sir."

Deputy Chief Bart then said, "You should know the Chief reviewed the incident and found no fault with anything Sergeant Barton did that morning."

Matt O'Neil turned and faced Sgt. Barton, who this time, had a slight grin on his face.

No words were exchanged between the two of them, only fist bumps.

After roughly 20 seconds, Sgt. Barton finally spoke for the first time, since running into Matt in the hallway. "Did you take that piece of shit tape off your locker, Officer O'Neil?"

Matt actually found himself blushing, over Sgt. Barton's comment.

As he put his head down for a second, to collect his thoughts, he felt his face turn flush.

"Yes Sir," Matt answered, looking directly at Sgt. Barton, "A couple of days ago, when I first found it."

"Good, no change that to great," Deputy Chief Bart blurted out. "I'm very pleased with the new recruits in general, but specifically you Matt. Your stats are very impressive, as well as your work ethic. Keep doing what you're doing," Deputy Chief Bart said, before suddenly extending his right hand to him.

Matt found himself grabbing it and shaking it firmly, while saying, "Thank you, Sir."

Matt figured it was time to leave, when Deputy Chief Bart let go of his hand and started to walk away from the lunchroom door, with Sgt. Barton.

As Matt headed for the stairs, which would lead him outside, to the parking lot, he realized in the past 30 minutes he had experienced a good laugh and received a huge compliment, from someone he respected.

Matt noticed a little extra kick in his step, as well as a smile suddenly appearing on his face.

He couldn't remember the last time he had a smile on his face, while still on Greenfield Police Department property.

He was snapped back into reality, when his Garman GPS, with a female voice said, "Turn right, one quarter mile, on Sturgeon Bay Road."

Matt recognizes this from his MapQuest print-out, laying on the front passenger seat, as the street for the Door County Morgue.

Pulling the unmarked Chevy into the parking lot, he's surprised to find only one other car in the entire lot. That car being the same exact make, model, and even color, Matt is driving.

"Must be the standard detective car these days," Matt thinks to himself.

Upon getting out of his car, he stretches his upper body, which is stiff from the three-and-a-half-hour car ride.

Looking around the parking lot, he notices the beauty of Door County, Wisconsin. "Stunning," is the only word Matt can think of to describe what he sees. He does a 180-degree turn while still holding his stretch and while turning, feels like he's in a Hemingway novel.

With the Door County Morgue being on a small hill, it allows him to have a panoramic view of the town of Sturgeon Bay.

Looking straight ahead, Matt watches as a wide variety of ships, both commercial, as well as recreational, navigate along the navy-blue waters, of Lake Michigan.

Matt has seen about 1/3 of the USA, due to his military training and while San Diego and Colorado were special, there was something unique, about Wisconsin.

The sights, food and the people, who were so down to earth, made a huge impact on both he and Kelly, whenever they had the opportunity to visit.

When finished stretching, Matt reaches back inside his car and grabs his black-colored, Greenfield notebook, with his right hand.

With his left hand, he grabs the Motorola phone and puts it inside the front pocket, of his Bears sweatshirt.

Entering the Door County Morgue, through a set of spotless glass doors, Matt is surprised by how little the building resembles an actual morgue.

If not for a sign outside in the parking lot, as well as some lettering and a symbol on one of the glass doors, he would have thought he was entering a nursing home instead.

Twice in his short career, Matt had been to 2121 W. Harrison Street, Chicago, home of the Cook County Morgue. The last time being the late summer of 2015, with a five month old, red hair, blue-eyed baby girl named Susan Kohheee, whose parents called, Susie.

One of the first things FTO Carll, had told Matt, when they were in training was, "Never ever get emotionally involved with any of your victims on these calls kid, or you'll turn into a freakin' mess."

Matt acknowledged him at the time and had been really good at abiding by his advice.

Roughly four weeks later, he and Carll were first on the scene of a 10-50 PI, which would turn out to be a fatal accident.

Evidence indicated, a High School senior named Theresa, was killed on her way to school, when she ran a stop sign in her Ford Escape, at the intersection of Harlem Avenue and Robincrest Lane.

Theresa was crushed to death, by a fully loaded garbage truck, which couldn't stop in time, but had the right of way.

Despite Theresa being so young, Matt O'Neil didn't become very emotional about her death.

Maybe it was the fact Sgt. Garza, who was next on the scene, had told Carll and him to block southbound Harlem Avenue, allowing them to leave the gruesome scene quickly.

Or was it because he was so busy, he never got a chance to see Theresa body being removed from her crushed vehicle? Or was it the fact, both he and Carll would learn from Sgt. Garza later, his investigation found Theresa was texting her boyfriend, when she went through the stop sign?

Theresa's death was different somehow than the death of Susie, which he remembered like it was yesterday. Susie's death happened on his third week, of being on his own, without an FTO.

Matt had been ecstatic about coming to work on one of the final days of summer. From looking at the schedule taped to the refrigerator, he knew he would be working his favorite beat of 2-1.

Located on the east side of Greenfield, beat 2-1 consisted of all white-collar, six-figure, income homes, which usually caused very few problems in the morning hours.

Most of these residents would sleep late and then attend mass at Our Lady of Faith Church.

They ended the morning by going out for brunch, with their families.

Matt could get his stats up with a few directed patrols, walk and talks, and a minimum of four traffic stops. But the first sign of trouble occurred right at roll call when Lt. Wayne came in without

Sgt. Barton, who apparently had taken a vacation day for today's shift.

Roll calls for Sunday morning at North Shore Police Departments, usually went about 40 minutes, as opposed to the usual roll call time of 20 minutes, during the week.

Supervisors know Sundays are a time for their personnel to relax, after crazy Friday and Saturday shifts.

It's a time for joke telling, picking on the new guys, and throwing around rumors like when a veteran may retire, whose getting promoted next off the current Sergeant's list and who is dating who.

Unlike Dallas, Los Angles, Boston and other big city police departments, small-sized police departments, usually know everything, about everyone, on their particular force.

Not just on their particular shift, but on the whole damn force.

After getting everyone's lunch times, car assignments and reviewing the daily logs, Lt. Wayne set the record on this particular morning, by doing a complete roll call in a total of nine minutes. Upon finishing roll call, he looked up from his desk, located at the front of the room and barked out, "Everybody on the street now."

Matt was sitting in the very front row of the room, in between T.C. Chambers and Megan O'Brien.

Matt watched as a few of the veterans, such as Evidence Technician Scott Dubbs and Patrolman Johnny Jarecksky, seated in the row adjacent to his, slowly got up out of their chairs, shaking their heads in amazement.

Matt had to admit he had never seen Lt. Wayne yell or act this way before and apparently neither had the veterans.

As the entire shift headed out of the room, Lt. Wayne suddenly barked at Dubbs, who was walking directly in front of his desk, "You got a problem with me, Dubbs?"

"Not at all," Dubbs responded and continued moving, to get away from the wrath of Lt. Wayne.

Not by his own choosing, but Matt was stuck directly behind Dubbs, as they exited the roll call room.

Apparently Dubbs didn't realize it and said softly to himself, "Fire guys don't realize just how good they fucking have it."

Matt knew better and kept his mouth shut, as they continued walking.

For Matt didn't give a shit right now, since he and the other recruits were so new. He wasn't even sure the firemen knew their names.

All Matt wanted and needed, were well trained firefighters and paramedics, who knew how to do their jobs and do it well.

With his very own eyes, Matt had seen what magic the Greenfield Paramedics could perform, when needed.

In two similar cases, they were able to bring victims, who had flatlined, back from the dead.

This was the result Matt was hoping for, as he drove this Sunday morning, to 1327 Deer Path Road, when he was assigned to a Fire Department Assist, for an unresponsive baby.

Since Greenfield Ambulance Six, Truck Six, and the Battalion Chief, had also been assigned to this call, they would have a huge advantage on him, since their Fire Station was only six blocks from 1327 Deer Path Road.

Matt, on the other hand, wasn't even in his beat, when Dispatcher Susie Patz assigned him the call.

Matt and Megan O'Brien had just cleared a residential alarm call, over in beat 1-1.

Since traffic was extremely light due to the time of day, Matt was making good time, as he headed to meet the Greenfield Fire and Ambulance crews.

While stopped at a traffic light on Lake Avenue and Wagner Road, he reached down with his right hand and switched the second radio in his squad off the Gilles Police Department channel, to the Greenfield Fire Department Channel.

He knew he would need up-to-the-minute information, on what was taking place at the scene.

"Ambulance Six, Truck Six and the Battalion Chief are on scene, Greenfield," said a voice Matt didn't recognize.

"10-4," Dispatcher Mike Karp, who was working the Greenfield Fire Band, answered in a short and crisp manner.

With the Greenfield Fire Department already on scene, Matt would get his latest information by monitoring their radio traffic.

While he continued to drive, Matt in his mind played out the proper procedures and order they needed to follow, for dealing with a call of this nature.

If confirmed dead, which of the paramedics checked the body?

Then, which doctor at Glenbrook Hospital, actually pronounced the victim dead and at what time?

Finally, the hardest part of the entire call, would take place, interviewing the family of the victim, who usually would be very emotional over their loss, unless the deceased was an elderly or hospice patient.

Matt would be patient and understanding, but he still needed a detailed explanation as to what exactly happened earlier today for his report.

He would also need every medical issue or problem the deceased had, their doctor and how to go about getting in touch with this doctor, so they could sign the death certificate.

Matt had seen some cops taking notes while interviewing family members.

Others would wait for the interview to be done, before writing a brief synopsis of the interview in their note pad.

Matt was only a couple of blocks from the address when he heard the Fire Department's Battalion Chief, on the scene say, with a hushed tone into his radio, "Are police on the way, Greenfield?"

This time Dispatcher Mike Karp answered with, "Affirmative."

The Battalion Chief's response came back much stronger over the air this time, but was just as short and simple. "10-4".

It was followed by a short pause and then, "Thank You."

"Shit," Matt O'Neil said slowly and calmly to himself, due to hearing the Battalion Chief's radio traffic and realizing this would no longer be a Fire Department Assist, but instead a Death Investigation.

Before Matt could get on his Norcom radio, things took a turn for the worse.

Lt. Wayne got involved in the case.

"Put me on O'Neil's CAD ticket Greenfield," Lt. Wayne yelled into his radio. "I'll be going over there and send an Evidence Technician to the Deer Path Road incident."

"10-4 Greenfield 309," Patz responded, emotionless as always.

"What the Fuck," Matt mumbled to himself, as he was totally confused by Lt. Wayne's actions.

Why the heck would a guy who never responded to anything and let Sgt. Barton do all of the work, pipe up and take such an interest in this call, Matt wondered.

"309 is out on Deer Path Road," Lt. Wayne said with a matter-of-fact tone in his voice.

"10-4, 309" Patz answered.

"374 is with him," Officer Dubbs announced over his radio.

"10-4 374," Patz responded.

Matt turned off Lake Avenue on to Laramie Street, which would lead him directly to the intersection of Deer Path Road.

He was so focused on getting to 1327 Deer Path Road, he didn't see her standing in the shade, in the middle of the intersection of Laramie Street at Deer Path Road, until the very last minute.

There she stood, roughly 75 years old, in her black Adidas work-out clothing, complete with black-colored gym shoes.

A partially smoked cigarette was in her left hand, while she held the leash to her white French poodle, in her right hand.

Both she and her dog had identical pink bows on top of their heads.

The minute she saw Matt's squad car slowing down and approaching her, she began waving both arms over her head, as if she was doing jumping jacks.

She stopped the jumping jacks when she realized she was pulling her poodle off the ground in the process.

Matt drove ever so slow, as he pulled up alongside of her, lowering his car window and being careful not to hit her dog.

"Is there something I need to know about?" she asked with a voice high and squeaky.

If Matt had a can of WD 40, he would have sprayed her entire body with it.

"Excuse me?" was all Matt could say, before she started yelling with a voice so high pitched, he thought his ears were going to start bleeding.

"Over there, over there," she yelled and began pointing in the direction of 1327 Deer Path Road, with the index finger on her left hand.

Matt turned his attention away from her and looked at 1327 Deer Path Road.

All of the Greenfield Fire personnel were entering their vehicles.

"Lady, I really have to go," Matt yelled and drove off.

"Waiiiiiiiiiiit," she yelled, but she was in the distance now.

If Matt O'Neil was surprised by the actions of Lt. Wayne, then he was totally shocked by all of the Greenfield Fire Department Units leaving, before he could interview any of them.

He pulled into the same spot Greenfield Ambulance Six had just vacated, which was directly in front of the residence.

"Greenfield 327 is 10-23," Matt said with a notable sound of doubt in his voice.

"10-4 327 and be advised all Fire Personnel have just cleared your location," Patz said.

"Roger that Greenfield, I'm seeing that as we speak," Matt answered this time, with a bit more confidence in his voice.

Matt got out of his squad car with a green spiral notepad in his left hand.

As he walked around to the front of his squad car, he glanced at the house.

It was a beautiful English Tudor home.

No more than two years old at the most, the owner apparently gave his architect an unlimited budget to work with and the architect ran with it.

There was a beautiful rounded driveway and light-colored brick exterior which gave off a castle effect.

Exquisite landscaping made the home a potential cover for the magazine, *Better Homes and Gardens.*

Matt was blown away by what he was seeing.

"Let's go O'Neil," Lt. Wayne bellowed from the front door of the residence.

Matt O'Neil walked so fast; he didn't think his Magnum Response Two boots even hit the driveway.

When he'd nearly reached the open front door, Lt. Wayne yelled, "Follow me upstairs."

Lt. Wayne started walking up a winding staircase to the second floor of the residence.

Upon finally getting to the open front door of the residence, Matt stepped inside and stood in the front foyer, allowing his eyes to adjust from the sunlight he had just left, to the cool darkness of the first floor.

With his eyes now adjusted, he glanced quickly to his left and saw a beautifully furnished sitting room, complete with long red roses, in a clear vase, on a small table located in the middle of the room.

Then Matt glanced to his right and saw him for the first time.

A rather thin gentleman, balding, in his mid-thirties, dressed in a blue pinstripe dress shirt.

The man was on his cellphone, seated behind the biggest dark brown desk, Matt had ever seen.

His office was complete with walls of old and new novels, neatly tucked away on floor-to-ceiling bookshelves.

But what really caught Matt's attention was instead of paintings covering the walls, pictures of area businesses, such as Abt Appliances and Teddie Kossofs Hair Salon, filled them.

Matt regained his focus on why he was at this home in the first place and walked quickly up the light brown carpeted staircase. When he arrived on the second floor, he found an agitated Lt. Wayne, standing off to his immediate right.

Lt. Wayne was standing outside a small, dimly lit bedroom.

Matt witnessed the flash of a camera going off from inside this room twice.

Matt walked over to Lt. Wayne, while opening his spiral notebook in the process.

Lt. Wayne didn't wait for Matt to be standing directly in front of him, before he began talking a mile a minute.

"The victim's name is Susan Kohheee, DOB is 4/02/15," as Lt. Wayne handed Matt an Illinois Driver's License.

Matt glanced at it quickly, recognizing immediately, it was the same person he had just seen talking on their cellphone downstairs.

Lt. Wayne continued, "Mr. Kohheee got up to check on his daughter roughly 40 minutes ago, walked into this room and saw no signs of life coming from the victim, so he dialed 911."

Lt. Wayne paused due to either being so out of shape he needed to catch his breath, or he wanted to make sure Matt was paying attention.

"Dubbs got here the same time I did and has the name of the paramedics, times, doctor at Glenbrook who pronounced the victim dead and everything you're going to need for the Medical Examiner," Lt. Wayne blurted out. "I excused the Fire Department personnel, upon Mr. Kohheee's request, due to the commotion it was making with the neighbors."

Lt. Wayne took one small step to get closer to Matt, who was writing notes.

Speaking for the first time, Matt asked innocently, "Where's mom?"

"Caught a flight on the company jet out of Chicago Executive Airport at 0630 hours this date, headed for Orlando, Florida for the company annual shareholder's conference, but will be returning home upon getting the news from her husband" Lt. Wayne said.

Lt. Wayne sensed Matt was a bit surprised by his last statement. "O'Neil, apparently you don't know who lives here, do you?"

"No Sir," Matt replied as he put the driver's license into his back right pants pocket.

"Mom is Vice President of Marketing for major tech company and dad downstairs is the President of Greenfield Bank," Lt. Wayne said with a matter-of-fact tone in his voice and stared at Matt O'Neil, waiting for some kind of a response.

Matt gave him nothing and continued writing in his notepad adding the words "Holy shit," which he circled for emphasis.

Lt. Wayne, realizing Matt might not be impressed by his last comment, got close to his face and whispered, "This is fucking big, O'Neil."

Matt looked up from his notes again and, not knowing what to say, looked at Lt. Wayne, who had a puzzled look on his face that expressed, "What aren't you getting here, O'Neil?"

The two of them stared at each other for roughly 20 seconds before Lt. Wayne, apparently unable to take it any longer, leaned in so he was only inches from Matt's face. He whispered, "This will easily be the biggest fuckin' death investigation you'll be primary on kid, so don't fuck it up, you clear?"

"Perfectly Sir," Matt whispered back.

"O'Neil, what do you still need from me?" Lt. Wayne asked.

"I believe I'm pretty much set, since Dubbs will have everything else I need," Matt said with a tone in his voice that he hoped would lighten the apparent stress mode, Lt. Wayne was in right now.

It worked like a charm. "Good, good," Lt. Wayne answered in quick succession and with a bit of calm finally showing in his voice.

Lt. Wayne started to walk past Matt, as he headed for the stairs.

Suddenly, he stopped just after passing Matt, turned and walked back over to him, so they were again standing face to face.

"I forgot one more thing O'Neil," Lt. Wayne said very nonchalantly.

Matt had a puzzled look on his face and couldn't get a word out, before Lt. Wayne was ready to go again.

"If the medical examiner requests the body, I want you to follow the hearse carrying it down to the Cook County Morgue, to guarantee the chain of custody."

This was a new one for Matt, but he knew better than to question any comment or decision Lt. Wayne was making, unless it was against department policy or a criminal act.

Matt's answer was a simple "Yes Sir."

With that, Lt. Wayne was gone.

In his typical, old fashioned style, Lt. Wayne was down the stairs, out the door, and in his squad in record time.

"Thank God," Matt whispered to himself, before taking a moment to review his notes, so he could actually read what he had scribbled down.

Matt then removed the driver's license, from his back pocket.

Slowly and carefully, he began writing all of the information from it into his notepad, so he could return it to the owner, before he left the residence.

With all of the craziness that had just taken place, he prepared himself to enter the bedroom and meet with Evidence Technician Dubbs.

Matt turned his back to the room and took a deep breath. He slowly exhaled the breath, finding himself much more relaxed and better prepared for what he was going to see next.

This was the youngest victim, whose death he would have to investigate so far, in his law enforcement career.

Matt turned back 180 degrees, so he was now directly facing the bedroom entrance, ready to enter and see the entire scene.

Instead, he saw Evidence Technician Dubbs, standing in the middle of the doorway, staring at him.

In Dubbs' right hand, was a Nikon Model, 35 mm camera.

Dubbs' head was titled to the right, with a puzzled look on his face.

"What the fuck are you doing rookie?" Dubbs said slowly.

Matt could feel his face turning beet red from embarrassment and desperately wanted to say something, but didn't know what to say.

"Rook, are you finally done doing circles out here and ready to do some fucking police work, so I can get the hell out of here?" Dubbs asked, with a high tone of sarcasm in his voice.

"Yes," was all Matt could mumble, as he followed Dubbs, inside Susie's bedroom.

As Matt entered, he realized this once was a room filled with love, but now only contained death.

Matt glanced at the rocking chair, countless dressers and shelves, which contained teddy bears, stuffed toys, books, and every creature from the Disney movie, *Frozen*.

Next, he focused on the left-hand side of the room, where a white crib held the precious tiny body of Susie.

Someone had removed her pink-colored one piece and it lay neatly folded, on a changing table, next to the crib.

Susie was lying flat on her belly, head tilted to the left, with her arms stretched out to each side.

A small, white-colored blanket, covered her body, stopping at her head area.

If Matt didn't know better, he would have thought she was sound asleep.

Instead, Susie was dead and her mother was in a private jet, over some unknown state.

Both Dubbs and Matt stood there, alone with their thoughts.

All Matt could think was neither parent would hold this baby again. They wouldn't see her go on her first date, graduate from college, or walk her down the aisle, on her wedding day.

"You okay kid?" Dubbs asked, rather nonchalantly.

"Yeah," Matt lied and answered in an expressionless voice.

"All right then, let's get started," Dubbs replied.

Just then, Matt's phone beeps and he looks down to check it.

There is a text message in capital letters on it from Deputy Chief Bart. It is short and to the point, "ARE YOU AT THE DOOR COUNTY MORGUE YET?"

Matt's text response is just as short, "Yes, and will advise soon."

Matt puts the phone away and continues to walk to the doors, of the Door County Morgue.

He automatically prepares his nose, but does not smell it— formaldehyde.

The smell usually hits him, the minute he crosses the metal set of double doors, at the Cook County Morgue.

After not smelling it, he's shocked by the cleanliness, of the Door County Morgue's, entire lobby area.

"O'Neil, Greenfield Police Department?" A male voice calls out from Matt's, immediate right.

Turning sharply in this direction, Matt finds a middle-aged, white male, wearing the traditional Ivy League student uniform. Khaki pants, white dress shirt, red and blue tie and a navy-blue sports coat.

Walking toward Matt, with his left hand extended, the individual asks, "Greenfield Officer O'Neil?"

"Yes," Matt answers and extends his free left hand awkwardly, to this individual.

"Robert Kenbridge, Detective, Door County Sheriff's Department," the individual says, as he quickly grabs Matt's left hand.

If asked to describe Robert Kenbridge in two words, they would be short and stocky.

Throw in a bad crew cut and that would almost complete the picture of Robert Kenbridge, except for a unique physical feature, a four-inch, deep scar, across the top of his right hand.

Kenbridge sees Matt staring at his hand and instinctively distracts him, by talking about his favorite subject, the Green Bay Packers.

"Bears fan I see," Kenbridge says, while pointing with the index finger on his left hand, at Matt's chest.

"Yeah, a big one," Matt responds.

"Cutler's your best quarterback for sure," Kenbridge comes back with and without even realizing it, Matt finds himself walking down a hallway lined with pictures of scenic Door County, while following Kenbridge.

As they wait for an elevator, which has highly glossed, metallic doors, Kenbridge keeps up the Green Bay Packer talk.

"Although if McCarthy doesn't win a big playoff game in the future, he's going to find himself out of work," Kenbridge says, as they step into the open elevator.

Despite seeing Matt uninterested, Kenbridge continues. "We're so predictable on offense without a running game, it makes me sick. Shit, I think the last great runner we had was Paul Hornung," and Kenbridge let out a laugh so hearty, Matt's afraid it's going to shake the elevator off its cable.

"Paul who?" Matt asks, while stepping off the elevator and into the basement, of the Door County Morgue.

"They used to call him the "Golden Boy" for his reputation, on and off the field, if you know what I mean," Kenbridge says and then gives Matt an easy pat on the back, using his left hand for emphasis.

Matt finds himself so caught up in the conversation about the Packers, he doesn't realize where he is, until he walks through a set of glass doors, into a room which is considerably colder, than both the hallway and elevator combined.

Then the smell is so overpowering, it fills his nostrils, formaldehyde.

The smell floats in the air and is prominent, due to the coldness and overall darkness of the room.

In this room, Detective Kenbridge leaves Matt's side and takes roughly five steps to the right.

In an instant, the room, which had previously been sparsely lit, becomes full of light.

Matt sees them and has a slight problem swallowing, due to the lump in his throat.

Three rows of ten coolers, stainless steel in color, each having their own silver handle.

So massive in size, they take up the entire center wall of the room.

Matt doesn't move, since he isn't sure which of the thirty coolers, contains his reason for being in this room in the first place.

Matt hears a door close behind him, off to his immediate left.

Before he can turn and look in that area, he is again joined by Detective Kenbridge, who stands on his right side.

Suddenly, a new figure walks over and stands on Matt's immediate left.

Matt turns to his left, to check out this new person, who is Matt's height, with brownish hair, but small particles of grey, in the temple area.

This person is wearing a white lab coat, with the name, Dr. Ray Byrne, over the right breast.

Before Matt has an opportunity to introduce himself to Dr. Byrne, Detective Kenbridge asks, "You ready, Officer O'Neil?"

Matt's response is a simple, "Yes."

Matt watches, as Dr. Byrne leaves his side and walks straight ahead, until he stops directly in front of the wall of coolers.

Dr. Byrne pauses for a second, before opening the middle cooler, in the second row.

In one swift motion, he pulls out the metal table inside the cooler, which holds a figure. Dr. Byrne takes two steps and moves to the left-hand side of this table, with his arms now folded behind his back.

Detective Kenbridge then moves, so he is standing on the right side of this table. Matt takes this as his cue, and walks straight ahead, until he is standing next to Detective Kenbridge.

No one says a word, as all three of them, look down at the figure lying on the table in front of them.

Finally, Detective Kenbridge breaks the silence in a room, which for some unknown reason to Matt, has become colder, by more than a few degrees.

"Do you recognize this individual, Officer O'Neil?" Kenbridge asks. "By all means, take as much time as you need."

Matt doesn't need any additional time, for he had prepared himself, on the car ride to Door County, for this moment.

In a calm and clear voice and without hesitation, Matt says one time, "Yes."

Detective Kenbridge responds, "For the record, Officer Matt O'Neil, who is this individual and please speak loudly, since our conversation is being recorded"?"

"There isn't any doubt," Matt responds. "I'm positive this is the body, of my fellow Greenfield Police Officer, Ron Thomas."

CHAPTER 12

Matt O'Neil waits patiently on the telephone, to be connected to Deputy Chief Bart, as Martha Hankels, of the Greenfield Police Department Records Division, pages him over the intercom system.

Matt did this, instead of using his Greenfield Police Department Motorola phone, for two reasons.

Every telephone call coming in to the Greenfield Police Department, like every other Police Department in the United States, is recorded.

Matt wanted this phone call to definitely be recorded, so Deputy Chief Bart would be able to play it back if he missed something, during their conversation and secondly, for the line of communication to be as clear as possible.

Roughly five minutes after finally being left alone by Detective Kenbridge and Coroner Byrne, Matt had texted Deputy Chief Bart.

His text message, like the one earlier, was short and to the point.

The message was all of four words and it read, "It is Thomas, Sir."

Two minutes later, Matt's Motorola phone beeped and he read, for some unknown reason, the text message out loud.

The message was shorter than the one Matt had sent.

In capital letters it read, "CALL ME IMMEDIATELY."

The author of the message being, Deputy Chief Bart.

Now Matt sits alone, in a first-floor office, located in the rear, of the Door County Morgue.

The room had been designated for Public Safety Personnel, a sign on the door said.

Matt is impressed with his surroundings.

The room is relatively small, consisting of a large, brown wooden desk, black leather adjustable chair, phone system and most importantly, a computer with internet access.

In front of the desk, are two, brown-colored, comfortable looking chairs.

To his right and centered perfectly, is another majestic painting, of a huge, white colored, light house, overlooking a bay full of sailboats.

Matt is sure this is of some location, here in Door County, but doesn't know where.

Finally, there is a small sink, with a coffee maker, on the counter, next to the sink. On the countertop is a full set of condiments, for the coffee.

"Very, very, relaxing," Matt comments only to himself, which makes him realize, this is probably the purpose the picture and the calming color the room's light brown walls serve.

He feels terrible about Ron Thomas, but isn't surprised he's dead.

P.J.'s Sports Bar in Champaign, was just one of the endless, drunken escapades, of Thomas's life.

Most Greenfield personnel knew it hadn't stopped, since they graduated from the ILETC.

"Sorry O'Neil," Deputy Chief Bart says, as he gets on the phone and sounds a bit out of breath, "I had another forest fire to put out, just before your phone call came in."

"So Matt, hopefully you've taken some notes and can fill us in on what you learned today," Deputy Chief Bart says.

"Us?" Matt answers, with a confused sound in his voice.

"I'm sitting with Lieutenant Alderman, in my office Matt and we have you on speaker phone.

If for some reason this thing goes south and our detectives need to get involved, Lieutenant Alderman should be in on this from the start," Deputy Chief Bart finishes.

"10-4 Boss," Matt responds and takes a deep breath, realizing for the first time since ILETC, his right palm holding the telephone, was becoming a bit clammy.

Surprisingly, Lt. Alderman speaks, before Deputy Chief Bart does, which catches Matt off guard.

"What method did you guys use, besides visual observation, to identify and verify it's Thomas, O'Neil?"

Before Matt can say a word, Lt. Alderman continues. "I'm assuming since the body was in the water for some time, there had to be some disfiguration of the face and fingerprints would be out of the question, as well."

"Let me back up sir, just a bit, if you don't mind," Matt replies.

"Not at all O'Neil," Lt. Alderman replies, with a somewhat apologetic tone in his voice, which helps to put Matt at ease, for the moment.

But before Matt can say a word, Deputy Chief Bart jumps into the conversation and sounds more than a bit agitated.

"Officer O'Neil, let's start over and take your time to tell us everything. I repeat, tell us every last detail you've learned today about this entire incident. I'll be the one O'Neil, to determine if the information is useful or not, understood?" Deputy Chief Bart finishes with a definite edge in his voice, adding back to Matt's stress.

"Also, Officer O'Neil, when Door County authorities notified us this morning, they told us the body they recovered had been found in the water, so we had some initial information, before we sent you out there," Deputy Chief Bart states.

"Okay Boss," Matt responds and after a short pause, begins.

"Officer Thomas was found on the beach, at Peninsula State Park, by a camper named Robert Fleming, who is a paramedic from Manitowoc, Wisconsin. Fleming told park officers, he was out for an early morning jog, at 0520 hours today. He likes to run in the sand, so the beach at the park, works out great for him. Fleming said he found Ron lying face down and checked him for a pulse. After finding no pulse, he called the park officers, on the cell phone he was carrying. Fleming is currently camping in Peninsula State Park, with his wife, Beth, and four-year-old daughter Tara, which has all been verified by park officers. Fleming was also interviewed by Detective Robert Kenbridge, of the Door County Sheriff's Department, who is the lead investigator on this case," Matt finishes.

"Any criminal history for Fleming?" Deputy Chief Bart asks.

"None Boss," Matt responds quickly and his confidence is growing slightly, as the interview continues.

"Floating in the lake was a canoe, which the authorities here believe Thomas was using shortly before his death," Matt says.

Not hearing anything on the other end of the line, Matt figures things are good and continues talking. "In Thomas's back pocket was his shield, with ID Card, which was the only identification found on him. The only other item found on him, were his car keys, in the right front pocket of his blue jeans."

"His wallet?" Deputy Chief Bart asks.

"Found containing seventy dollars in cash, inside his Toyota 4 Runner, which also contained some of his personal belongings and this vehicle was found in the unlocked position" Matt responds. "The rest of his things were found at his campsite, which is also at Peninsula State Park. It's a fact Ron loved the outdoors, especially hiking and camping. He couldn't tell us enough, about his two trips to the Grand Canyon."

"Still waiting on how he was identified, besides visual," Lt. Alderman says, only this time, with an edge in his voice.

"Fingerprints were used, Lt. Alderman. "The Door County Coroner, Dr. Byrne believes Thomas was only in the water for between 6-7 hours, so they obtained the standard FD258 form he did, when he applied for the position as police officer, with our agency, from D.C. Gyondski this morning". With that being said, Thomas had unique scars, that only a few people knew about,"

Matt stops, knowing this would be unknown to both Deputy Chief Bart and Lt. Alderman.

"Really? Where on his body?" Deputy Chief Bart asks, with a hint of doubt in his voice.

"On the top of his left thumb, he has an old scar that required seven stitches to close," Matt answers in a quiet, calm, monotone voice. "I saw it at the ILETC one night, as we were the last two in the school's cafeteria finishing up dinner."

"The location of the second scar, Officer O'Neil?" Lt. Alderman asks.

"The upper lip, which is why he's had a mustache since he was 19 years old. Claimed it happened to him when he was bit by an aunt's dog, at a birthday party years ago, but if I was a betting man, I would go with a former disgruntled girlfriend," Matt O'Neil finishes.

"All right, all right," Deputy Chief Bart says. "Since we have no doubt its Thomas, how is the Door County Sheriff's office labeling the investigation?" Deputy Chief Bart asks, with an inquisitive tone in his voice.

"Death Investigation," Matt O'Neil answers quickly.

"Good, good," Deputy Chief Bart answers.

For the first time since the three of them had started talking on the phone, there is a long pause between all of them.

Finally, Lt. Alderman speaks with such a soft tone in his voice, Matt has to press the phone closer to his right ear, to hear what he is saying. "I'm assuming no signs of trauma on any part of Thomas's body?"

"Dr. Byrne told me a complete autopsy would be done at 0800 hours tomorrow, but the initial check of the body, by both him and Detective Kenbridge, found no signs of trauma," Matt finishes.

"Good," Deputy Chief Bart says.

"Give me your feelings on Detective Kenbridge, if you can talk freely up there O'Neil," Lt. Alderman asks.

"Seems solid in the little bit that I've had the chance to talk to him. You can tell by the way he carries himself and the haircut, he's former military. I just don't know which branch," Matt takes a small breath, because he wants to keep speaking, before Deputy Chief Bart or Lt. Alderman interrupt him. "I'm not really worried about him, especially with all the physical evidence they've recovered, from both Thomas's vehicle and campsite."

"Explain," Deputy Chief Bart states.

"Inside Thomas's tent and his vehicle, were a total of 12 empty bottles of Coors light. I know for a fact this was his beer of choice, and it had to be bottles, not cans, or he wouldn't drink it. Next, a bottle of Wild Turkey, one unopened in his vehicle, but a second bottle was found in the canoe floating in the lake, with half of the bottle empty," Matt finishes.

"Shit," Lt. Alderman mumbles, before saying, "I never knew Thomas was that big of a drinker."

"Yeah, he could throw them down pretty good," Matt answers.

"Okay, okay, so Thomas throws them down, and then what? Goes out on the lake, at Peninsula State Park, for a rowing contest, in the middle of the night? Really doesn't make much sense to me," Deputy Chief Bart finishes. For the first time since Matt had served under his command, he notes Deputy Chief Bart had a tone of exasperation in his voice.

"You're working off the premise he was alone boss, which was rarely the case with Thomas," Matt answers.

"You seem to have an advantage on both of us, with your knowledge of him. So, give us your take on how you think this whole thing went down," Lt. Alderman says.

Matt doesn't know if Lt. Alderman is being a smart ass, or really wants Matt's theory on Ron's death and figures he has nothing to lose by explaining how he thinks Thomas died.

"Thomas was never without some type of female companionship. Plus, he was a regular up here, with his deceased folks leaving him the little house on Washington Island, so I'm sure he knew a few barmaids and probably invited one to a romantic night at his campsite. He probably brought the booze and she supplied the romance. Sometime during the night, they go out for a little canoe ride and he falls in due to his intoxication. With Thomas being unable to swim, he drowns quickly, and no one hears or sees anything, due to there being no campsites really close to the lake," Matt says.

"She panics, knowing he's a cop and paddles or rows back to shore and then pushed the canoe back out, so it winds up floating in the lake," Lt. Alderman finishes.

"Shit, I was thinking of at least two other scenarios while O'Neil was talking," Deputy Chief Bart answers quickly, but this time confidently, like they finally have something to work with.

"Any security cameras in the park, near the lake?" Deputy Chief Bart asks.

"That's one of the first questions I asked Kenbridge, sorry Detective Kenbridge, when he first briefed me on Thomas's death," Matt answers quickly. "The answer he gave me was 'none' and they've never had an issue until now."

"Shit," Lt. Alderman answers and again the phone line went silent for roughly 15 seconds, as the three of them are deep in thought, as to what to ask or comment about next.

Finally, Deputy Chief Bart breaks the silence with a question. "What was the second question you asked Detective Kenbridge?"

"If a canvas was done of the campers who had campsites near Thomas's Sir," Matt answers calmly.

"I'm assuming Detective Kenbridge said yes?" Deputy Chief Bart asks.

"Affirmative Boss, with negative results," Matt responds and then smiles, since this had been a common response when he was in the military, but surprisingly, rarely used in law enforcement.

"Any idea what Detective Kenbridge has planned next?" Lt. Alderman asks.

"Told me they want to process both Thomas's vehicle and the campsite thoroughly and then go up to Washington Island and check out his house. Going to take their time with this. First, they will have to acquire a search warrant for the house, which Detective Kenbridge doesn't think will be an issue at all," Matt finishes.

"I was thinking they wouldn't need to get a warrant, but Lieutenant Alderman pulled Washington Island up on his iPad and it's still quite a distance from Peninsula State Park, isn't it?" Deputy Chief Bart says.

Not having a clue of the distance between the two locations, Matt answers with the company line, "Yes Sir."

Quickly, Matt responds with, "Peninsula State Park has a few video cameras, at different locations besides the gift shop, such as the golf pro shop, and Detective Kenbridge told me his crew will look for Thomas's vehicle, in all this footage. Basically, they will be trying to put together an idea of how Thomas spent the last 12 hours, before his death."

"Sounds good," Deputy Chief Bart says with a quick, firm response, before continuing, "O'Neil, make sure Detective Kenbridge has our fax number and offer any services we can supply to him."

"Already done Sir," Matt O'Neil replies.

"Good job O'Neil. Now, just get back home safely," Deputy Chief Bart says, before pausing for a few seconds and then saying, "Just so you're not left out in the dark, D.C. Gyondski went through Thomas's death notification file and apparently, he listed an aunt, named Marge Thomas, who lives in Rensslaer, Indiana, as his next of kin and should be notified in case of his death. You don't by chance, know anything about her?"

"No Sir. He never mentioned her, the short time I got to know him."

"Okay, I'll take care of it personally, since it's an actual Death Investigation, instead of turning it over to Deputy Chief Gyondski. Who knows, maybe she'll have some kind of information about Thomas, which could actually help us. Hell, stranger things have happened. Stop in and check with me, when you get back to Greenfield," Deputy Chief Bart says before hanging up the phone, leaving Matt with a continuous ringing in his right ear.

Matt O'Neil leans back in the black leather chair so far; his face is looking directly up at the ceiling.

Blowing out every last bit of air in his lungs, he clasps his hands behind his head, in a manner similar to a person becoming a prisoner, or being arrested.

A wide range of emotions and feelings suddenly fills Matt, as a slight grin appears on his face.

He believes he's made a favorable impression with Lt. Alderman, but more importantly, with Deputy Chief Bart as well. But it seems so confusing to accomplish something, due to another police officer's death.

Matt doesn't have long to ponder the situation, as a combination of a severe headache and a growling stomach, come upon him.

He quickly realizes this is a result of the stress he's been under, combined with a growing hunger.

Plus, the brightness of the fluorescent ceiling lights he's looking directly into, don't help.

As his stomach continues to growl, he realizes other than a bowl of oatmeal he had wolfed down before work with Kelly, he hasn't eaten anything else today and his stomach is crying out to be fed.

Matt tilts his chair forward, until he is sitting normally.

He proceeds to get out of the chair and quickly stands straight up, which only makes his headache worse.

Instinctively, he raises his right hand to the middle of his forehead and begins rubbing in a circular motion, in an attempt to alleviate the pain.

This rubbing does nothing and now his stomach is growling, to the point where the noise is so loud, he is actually embarrassed by it.

Without hesitation, he checks both pockets of his Chicago Bears sweatshirt, to prove to himself he has his Apple iPhone 5 and the Greenfield Police Department's, Motorola flip phone.

Confident he has both of them, Matt grabs his notebook with his left hand and adjusts the pancake holster holding his Colt Commander with his right hand. The holster had unexpectedly slipped slightly to the right on his brown belt, due to all of the sitting and moving around in the chair.

In its present position, the holster and more importantly the weapon, isn't within Matt's immediate reach.

Most police officers know 99% of the time, the perpetrators have the element of surprise, to their advantage.

This means the police officer will always be reacting, to what they are encountering.

Reaction time will consistently be a second, or even two

seconds slower, than the offenders, so the only thing police officers can rely on, is better marksmanship and the ability to fire, while on the move.

Both of these elements, Matt feels, would be to his advantage in any firefight, due to his Navy Seal training.

Matt simply opens his belt buckle and carefully moves the holster, so it's in a position for his right hand to come straight down, and be on the grip of his weapon.

Convinced he has everything in order, Matt turns off the lights, while heading out the door.

He makes an immediate left; confident he knows his way back to the front door of the building.

Roughly 20 to 25 steps later, he makes another left turn and finds himself walking down a long corridor, filled with even more pictures, of majestic scenery.

Every possible Door County scenario fills the hallway, from seagulls, to sailboats, to pictures of the sun setting over a ridge.

Making his first right-hand turn since exiting the office, Matt is still convinced he's headed the correct way.

Suddenly, Matt stops and laughs out loud, after first seeing and then reading, what had been written on a three-by-five card.

This card is scotch-taped onto the famous painting of a grizzly bear standing in a stream. The grizzly bear has its mouth open, in an attempt to catch salmon, which are fighting up stream, with one flying in the air.

Using both yellow and green dry markers, someone had written five words, in such a way, they filled the entire three by five card.

The words are, "CUTLER SUCKS, GO PACK GO," with an arrow on the end of the card, pointed at the grizzly bear in the picture.

Matt realizes two important things.

First, just how much Wisconsin people love their Green Bay Packers.

Matt had first become aware of this on his drive to Door County today.

He noticed the closer he got to Door County itself, how many businesses, such as restaurants, car repair shops, heck even supermarkets, had chosen the colors of the exteriors of their businesses, to be green and gold.

Secondly, just how stupid an idea it was to be wearing a Chicago Bears sweatshirt, in the heartland of Green Bay Packer fans.

Granted, when he grabbed it off his closet shelf this morning, he never dreamed he would be in Door County, Wisconsin later the same day.

It all made sense now, why he got such a strange look from both Dr. Byrne and Detective Kenbridge, when he first met each of them.

Upon shaking his hand, both looked immediately at his sweatshirt, while still holding his hand.

At the time, Matt thought each had a look on their face like he had just farted.

Matt also thought it was more than a bit peculiar, how each had tightened their grip while still holding his hand and he didn't quite realize why, until now.

All of it now made sense to him.

"Huge Packer Backers," Matt says softly to himself.

"Probably season ticket holders, who tailgate their asses off before every home game, in the Lambeau Field parking lot."

"Whatever floats your boat," Matt thinks and he applauded the loyalty they have for their team.

The thought of taking the sweatshirt off does cross his mind for a few seconds, but is quickly dropped at the thought of walking around with his Colt Commander and a few extra clips, exposed to the general public.

"Wait a minute," he thinks, "Wisconsin does have the carry concealed law."

"Nawwwwwwwwwwww," Matt says to himself. "Just leave the damn thing on and chalk the whole experience up as a life lesson."

Matt is correct and the series of lefts and rights down the corridors, put him at the front door, of the Door County Morgue.

Matt pauses for a minute, as he sees himself in the reflection of the Windex-polished, glass double doors.

Roughly two hours earlier, he had entered these same doors, not sure of what was in store for him.

Since then, he'd identified a fellow Greenfield Police Officer's body and had a solid interview with two significant figures, of the Greenfield Police Department.

"Weird shit," Matt says out loud, to no one in particular, as he pushes open the doors with his right hand and starts down the steps, into the parking lot.

As he walks to his car, Matt feels a new sense of urgency.

Blame it on the hunger pains growing in his stomach, or blame it on the stupid Bears sweatshirt, or just blame it on wanting to get home after stopping at the Greenfield Police Department, to give Kelly a great big hug, all Matt knows for sure, he's walking with a quicker pace than he had when he entered this dreaded building.

Also, for some strange reason, the sun seems brighter, than when he entered the morgue.

Matt transfers the Greenfield notebook from his left hand to his right hand.

He uses his free left hand, to pull down the cheap sunglasses, which had never moved from the top of his head, the entire time he had been inside the Door County Morgue.

To combat the sun further, he puts his head down, knowing his car is no more than 10 to 15 steps, directly in front of him.

Matt quickly realizes this is a terrible move.

After no more than two to three steps, the sound of screeching car tires, makes him jump back.

Matt is moving and immediately drops his notebook, while his right hand comes down hard on the thumb release, for his pancake holster.

"Look where the hell you're going asshole," a muffled voice blurts out to him.

The voice is a bit hard to understand because it is coming over the loud speaker of a car.

Matt stops backing up and turns his body into a 45-degree stance, with his right hand now squarely on the blue steel grip, of his Colt Commander.

Matt is flustered and can feel the heat from the car engine, directly in front of him.

But the sun seems to have moved now from being directly on top of him, to bouncing off the front engine compartment of this car, which is newly washed and waxed.

Through squinting eyes, Matt can barely make out the car, which is some type of Ford Mustang and is navy blue in color.

Slowly, the driver's door opens and out steps a Wisconsin State Trooper, whose uniform fits so well, it looks like it had been painted on.

The trooper's look is so pristine, he could have been the cover boy, for any law enforcement magazine.

Closing the driver's side door with his left hand, the trooper takes exactly seven steps forward, putting his Smokey the Bear hat on in the process.

Due to the sun still bouncing off the car into Matt's eyes, it isn't until the trooper speaks, Matt feels comfortable enough to take his right hand off the grip of his gun.

In a firm and loud voice, the trooper says, "Hello O'Neil."

"You're a fucking asshole Dugan," Matt responds and extends his right hand.

Trooper Mark Dugan grabs Matt's right hand and quickly bends it sideways into his chest, which results in both men embracing in a powerful bear hug.

Mark Dugan is an aberration in the world of police work.

The same day Matt O'Neil and his fellow Greenfield Officers were hired, the Lomberdy Police Department hired Mark Dugan.

Thus, all of them were in the same class at the Illinois Law Enforcement Training Center.

Eight days after graduating from ILETC, Mark Dugan came home to his apartment and received the letter in the mail he had been waiting to receive, for over 13 months.

The letter stated he had been accepted by the only Law Enforcement Agency he truly wanted to work for.

Goodbye Village of Lomberdy, Hello Fort McCoy, Wisconsin, home of the Wisconsin State Police Training Academy.

The Village of Lombardery filed a lawsuit, seeking financial reimbursement for training Dugan and the case was still in court.

The State of Wisconsin countersued on a technicality.

Each side was trying to come to some type of resolution, which would make their bosses feel like they won.

Born and raised in Appleton, Wisconsin, Mark Dugan was the only child Steven and Ann Dugan would have, due to complications caused during his birth.

Realizing this, Steven and Ann devoted every minute of their free time to raising young Mark, and he loved it. Mark Dugan also fell in love with all Wisconsin had to offer and took after his father as an avid sportsman.

Life was so good for the three Dugan's, it seemed like they were living a dream.

A dream which soon turned into a nightmare.

On Mark Dugan's 11th birthday, he eagerly awaited his party at school.

But more than anything, he was counting the minutes to the end of the school day, so he could go home and get his real present.

Steven Dugan had promised to take his son, on their first ever deer hunting weekend.

Mark Dugan wasn't the least surprised when Mark Walters, the principal at Mary of The Rosary, came to his classroom and asked him to accompany him to the principal's office. The short trip to the office was filled with idle chatter between the two of them, which suddenly stopped when Walters opened his office door and Mark Dugan found Father O'Malley, the parish pastor and two Appleton Police Officers, standing inside the office.

The only words Mark Dugan would ever remember were, "both of them killed in a car crash." With no other relative living in Wisconsin, Mark Dugan found himself leaving the state he so loved, for a city and state that offered him nothing in comparison, Joliet, Illinois.

Mark Dugan spent the remainder of his childhood living there, with his Aunt Margaret, who had never married.

Making no friends, either male or female, Mark Dugan worked

a couple of odd jobs after school, mainly to help pay some of Aunt Margaret's bills and to kill time.

Barely graduating from Joliet High School, Mark Dugan faced the biggest decision of his life.

Join the Army, or enroll at Joliet Junior College and take a few criminal justice courses, while working part time, at a car dealership, in Joliet.

Joliet Junior College was Mark Dugan's choice.

It took only one course, Police Operations, taught by a retired Will County Sheriff, named John Woodward and Mark Dugan was hooked.

For Dugan was smart enough to realize, whether it be State, Federal, or even Local law enforcement, any of these could give him an opportunity to get back to Wisconsin.

Discover Policing, The Blue Line, Chicago Tribune, Chicago Sun Times, and want ads all became his new best friends, due to Mark Dugan still not having made a single friend in Illinois.

He started working out in his free time at Cardinal Fitness, located in Lockport, to be in the best shape of his life.

He took every test, whether it be for police officer, sheriff, or trooper, just to get his proverbial foot in the door.

The rest as they say is history.

Finally separating himself from Matt, Mark Dugan puts his head down, as he's collecting his thoughts.

Matt looks on patiently, as Mark, in one slow motion, finally raises his head and with his left-hand places it on Matt's right shoulder.

"Sorry about Mills," he says softly, as he looks directly into Matt's sunglasses.

Before Matt can say a word, Mark continues. "I really didn't have much use for Thomas, ever since he started the brawl down at ILETC, in P.J.'s. Come to think of it, I don't remember you being there buddy, were you?"

In a soft voice, Matt answers, "No," and just stares at Dugan.

"O'Neil?" Dugan asks, "Fill me in quickly on what you can

regarding both Death Investigations, before my FTO gets on my ass about reminiscing."

With that, Matt looks around the right side of Dugan, who is still facing him and sees another Wisconsin State Trooper, seated in the front passenger seat, of the Ford Mustang.

"His name is James De Groot. All of the other troopers call him 'Digger,' which I really haven't figured out why yet," Dugan says, while still standing directly in front of Matt and motioning with the thumb of his right hand, back toward the Ford Mustang.

Matt looks on as James 'Digger' De Groot, seems oblivious to what O'Neil and Dugan are doing, instead focusing all his attention on the MDT, mounted between the two bucket seats, in the Ford Mustang.

"You tell me about Detective Kenbridge first," Matt says.

"Former Coast Guard Chief Warrant Officer Two, who never saw any action, due to being stationed in Kauai, Hawaii for his tour," Dugan says.

"Work with him on anything big?" Matt asks, with a noticeable tone of doubt in his voice.

Matt wants to make sure Detective Kenbridge can back up his promise he made earlier, about his team working their asses off, to get to the bottom of Thomas's death.

"Yeah, on my fourth day of riding with FTO De Groot, we had a murder-suicide between a husband, his twin brother and husband's wife, at a rest area, close to here. I think the couple were from your neck of the woods, like South Bert?" Dugan notes.

Dugan continues after pausing long enough to catch his breath. "Kenbridge and his entire team of about 8 people showed up," Dugan says. "I was impressed."

"Why?" Matt asks with a puzzled tone in his voice.

"Husband shot his twin brother, then stabbed his own wife to death 12 times, the autopsy showed. He even slit the family dog's throat."

"Jesussssssssssssssss," is all Matt can mumble, before Dugan starts up again.

"Yeah, then the fucking husband shot himself one time in the mouth, with a Glock Model 23, which we recovered from inside his blood-splattered car. The way Kenbridge and his entire team were able to put the whole series of acts in order, was pretty impressive," Dugan finishes.

"Two minutes for your little police academy reunion," De Groot yells from his seat, with the window of the Mustang rolled all the way down.

"Ongoing investigation with Mills and now Thomas as well," Matt says.

"How the fuck in a few months, with all of these law enforcement agencies working on it, you can't find one old white, Ford Bronco, with a freaking White Sox sticker in the rear window?" Dugan asks highly agitated.

"Yeah, you left out the part about the body damage on the driver's side rear," Matt says in a quiet voice, as fatigue set in.

In his short time on earth, Matt had never wanted to take back something he had said so quickly, after it had left his mouth.

Not in the few fights he had with Kelly, pissing off a commanding officer in the navy, nothing could possibly compare to what he had said to Dugan.

Matt looks straight ahead at Mark Dugan, who has a strange, puzzled look on his face.

Before either of them can say a word, Digger's voice comes bellowing out of the Mustang. "Dugan, times up, Central Dispatch has us backing a Sheriff's Unit on a Tanker accident, roughly six miles from here."

"I never heard about the body damage until now. I'll call you later about it and by all means give my best to Kelly," Dugan says, before walking briskly to the Mustang, getting in behind the wheel, and burning rubber, as they exited the morgue parking lot.

Matt O'Neil stands there with a sense of numbness coming over him.

Suddenly, the white Ford Bronco is going through the red light in Matt's mind, for easily the 500th time and once again, Matt's head and neck can't move from the headrest, of his Ford Cruiser.

There isn't any doubt in Matt's mind, Mark Dugan would be calling him, curious about the new information Matt had accidentally given him, about the Ford Bronco.

For now, Matt has only one thing he can do.

As fast as he can, get the hell out of Wisconsin.

CHAPTER 13

The alarm clock is located on the nightstand, to the immediate left of her head.

Turning her head slightly in this direction, she observes the numbers 5:59 Am in bright red; lit up on the face of the clock.

She quickly reaches out with her left hand and moves the switch on top of the clock to the off position, just as the numbers on the clock show 6:00Am

Kelly rolls straight back on her mattress and lets out a brief sigh of relief, as if she had just diffused an atomic bomb, set to detonate in downtown Chicago.

More importantly, her actions have given Matt some peace and quiet, to complete sleeping, which has been difficult these past months.

Kelly knows catching Chris Mills' killer is Matt's number one priority right now, but she is confused and slightly miffed, as to why it seems to have fallen solely on Matt's shoulders, as opposed to Chief Fitzsimons and the rest of the Greenfield Police Department.

Now with the death of Ron, confirmed yesterday, it was almost like adding a few more bricks to the wall her husband seemed to be carrying on his back.

She and Matt had stayed up to 11:30Pm last night, talking about both Chris and Ron's deaths.

While Kelly had met Chris at their graduation from the Illinois Law Enforcement Training Center, she avoided Ron Thomas at the same ceremony, on the advice of her husband.

Matt had never told Kelly why he wasn't Ron's biggest fan, but just seeing how he acted, whenever Ron stood near her, was all she needed, to form her own opinion.

Yet the brotherhood of police work was all that mattered and the death of "one of their own", even if it was accidental, was still a loss, for all which knew and loved him.

Kelly knew she needed to get up and go to work, but she just looked at Matt and wished she could spend the day with him instead.

It seemed like it had been forever, since the two of them were able to sleep late, in each other's arms. Then go to Kappy's restaurant in Gilles, for their delicious Patrick's Irish Breakfast, return home, and then hop on the bike trail.

Kelly glanced out their bedroom window and with the sun just coming up, knew she was going to be stuck indoors, working all day, and miss a beautiful day.

Slowly and carefully, she slipped out of bed and faced her first, of probably 80 decisions, she would make today.

Shower and take the chance of waking up Matt, or just go with the one she took last night, after returning home from her yoga class?

Allowing her husband, the opportunity to keep sleeping, was the decision she decided upon.

Quickly she slipped out of her normal sleepwear, consisting of an old, grey colored tee shirt of Matt's, from his time at ILETC. The shirt being so big, she could easily have fit another person, her size, inside of it.

For some strange reason, she carefully folded this shirt and placed it on the floor, next to her side of the bed.

She then took off her Resurrection H.S. gym shorts and before placing them on Matt's tee shirt, held them at eye level and just stared at them.

They were the last thing her mother Maureen had purchased for Kelly, before her death.

"Shit, shit," Kelly said softly, but repeatedly to herself, as she realized she was now a good five to six minutes behind schedule.

Fortunately, after her shower last night, she had laid out her clothes to wear to work, where she would change, once she got there.

Upon finishing dressing in a baggy Nike sweat shirt and sweat pants, she reached down and grabbed her Samsung Mobile phone off the floor, next to where she had just grabbed the clothes she had put on.

Kelly practically tiptoed out of their bedroom and gently walked down the stairs leading directly from the second floor, to the first-floor family room.

Immediately, she headed to the kitchen and upon arriving, opened the refrigerator, grabbing her pink colored lunch bag off the top shelf and then closed the refrigerator door in the process.

She opened the Velcro on her lunch bag and peered in, making sure it was complete, before closing the bag again.

Quickly, she grabbed her purse, which had been sitting on the kitchen table and proceeded to place it on her left shoulder.

While holding her lunch bag in her left hand, she grabbed the keys for her Honda Accord with her right hand from a key holder, located next to the side door of the residence.

Going out this side door, she waited until she got to the driver's side door of her car and inserted her key into the lock to open the door, instead of hitting the automatic car door opener on her key chain, avoiding any unnecessary noise.

Kelly put her lunch bag, purse and Samsung phone, on the front passenger seat, next to her and briefly looked for it, but it wasn't there.

It wasn't uncommon for Matt, when their dating had become serious, and they knew they were each other's partner for life, to leave a card, note, flower, for Kelly in her car, as a sign of his love for her.

It meant the world to Kelly and only increased her love for her soldier.

Those items seemed to have vanished in the past few months, and it was affecting Kelly, but she wouldn't say anything to Matt about it for now.

She checked her rear-view mirror for Mrs. Smith, who usually walked Zeus, the biggest German Shepard Kelly had ever seen, every morning at this exact time.

Not seeing either of them, Kelly slowly backed her Honda out of the driveway and in a couple of turns was on Dempster St. headed to her place of employment the past 14 months, Lutheran Family Center Hospital's, Emergency Room.

Kelly, being relatively new, was assigned to the 7:00Pm to 7:00Am shift.

But with a number of nurses going on maternity leave, as well as others on vacation, the hospital was scrambling to fill the day shift rotation and had gone as far as to offer generous overtime, to do so.

Kelly jumped at the opportunity and signed up for a couple of shifts, with today being her first one.

Plus, it would be her first time working normal hours during the day time, to see if this shift was just as crazy as her night time shift.

Kelly now regretted staying up late last night talking about Ron Thomas, due to it cutting severely into her sleep, the night before this shift.

It also was inevitable her day would be crazy, since every other time Kelly had missed her normal sleep, she had to handle everything from fatal accident victims, to gunshot wounds.

Kelly was so focused on her driving; she was oblivious to what radio station she was listening too.

She was wondering how Mrs. Graham was doing, who was brought into the emergency room on the last shift Kelly had worked, with a broken hip she suffered while falling down the basement stairs, of her Park Ridge home.

If her shift was slow, at some point after her lunch break, she would try and get off the floor and sneak up to Mrs. Graham's room and spend a few minutes talking to her.

Every effort Kelly had made to see if Mrs. Graham had a husband, children in her life, had been unsuccessful and Kelly was uncertain as to why she had developed such a fondness for Mrs. Graham.

Sometime this weekend, Kelly also needed to call Moretti's restaurant in Edison Park and check on how her father's 47th birthday party plans were coming.

Being the only child of Seamus and Maureen Walsh had its benefits for sure, but also sucked when it came to planning any kind of family get togethers.

Maureen Walsh died of pancreatic cancer, before Kelly's marriage to Matt.

Kelly missed her mother more and more every day, but even more when family responsibilities were falling on her shoulders.

As if her Honda had a mind of its own, Kelly slowly pulled into the employee parking lot, of Lutheran Family Center Hospital. Quickly, she heads for the employee's entrance door, with her personal belongings in her left hand and key holder in her right hand.

As Matt had taught her, the key to the Honda, as well as house keys, were intertwined between the fingers of this hand.

Although it's roughly 300 feet in distance, from her car to this entrance, Kelly is ready in case someone is hiding in a parked car.

"The benefits of being married to a cop" Kelly thinks to herself.

Yes, Kelly loves her job, because it resembles that of her husband's.

Every day both of them go to work and have no idea what to expect, from the people they will serve.

Often during their shift, they're able in some way, to help someone they came in contact with.

Each of them has been put in stressful situations, which no one would believe if they weren't also in these same occupations.

Kelly shakes her head slightly, remembering some of the sights she witnessed, working her first full moon shift, at this hospital.

On their day off together over dinner and in some rare occasions over breakfast, laughter and looks of shock, filled each other's faces, as they shared what they had just been involved in at work, only a few hours earlier.

Kelly is through the employee entrance and in the women's locker room, changing in front of her locker, all in the span of two minutes.

After changing completely into her blue scrubs, she put all of the clothes she had just taken off, on silver colored metal hooks, inside her locker. She then kicks off her gym shoes, placing them underneath a wooden bench, located in front of her locker.

With her right hand, she pulls out of her locker, her best friend at work from day one, a pair of grey, Nike vapor max shoes.

For the next twelve hours, these shoes would make her feet feel like she was walking on pillows.

From this same locker, Kelly finds her Lutheran Family Center Hospital I.D. Card, she had just used and attaches it to the top of her scrubs, before picking her Samsung phone off the bench.

She slams her locker shut and puts her combination lock on the front of it.

Kelly looks at the face of the phone, which reads 7:02Am

Quickly, she puts her phone in the right front pants pocket of her scrubs and heads for the emergency room. Upon entering, she finds her supervisor, Sally Shattuck, standing at the entrance, waiting for her.

Shattuck's arms are folded across her chest and she stares directly at Kelly.

"Shit," Kelly mumbles only to herself and walks over to Ms. Shattuck, so both are now standing face to face.

"You're late Mrs. O'Neil," Shattuck says, with an icy tone in her voice.

Kelly hated being called "Mrs. O'Neil", because it makes her sound old, but this isn't the time or place to get into it with her boss for the next 12 hours, so she bites her tongue and slowly lowers her head.

"You're correct and I have no excuse for my tardiness today, but I can assure you if we work together in the future, it will never happen again."

"Good and it can't," Shattuck says.

"Also, heart attack patient coming in with an E.T.A. of four minutes and you're assigned to it Kelly," Shattuck says and walks away.

CHAPTER 14

elly immediately walks over to the nearest Purell wall dispenser and places both of her hands at the bottom of it. In a matter of seconds, her hands are filled in white foam.

She looks quickly into room E-7, where on the outside wall of it, this dispenser is located and realizes the room is empty.

Due to the room being empty, Kelly enters it while still rubbing her hands together.

Confident her hands are dry enough, she quickly grabs a pair of purple, size small, latex gloves, out of a box located on the east wall and puts them on. Kelly turns here head and watches as the paramedic crew walks past this room with the gurney.

Kelly believed she had seen every paramedic crew the Park Ridge Fire department had working for them, but these two must be new, since she's never seen either of these guys before.

Finished, with the gloves now on both hands, she comes out of the room and winds up directly behind the gurney, as it makes it way down the emergency room hallway.

The younger of the paramedics is pushing the gurney, while the second one is walking on the right-hand side of the gurney, talking a mile a minute to the primary nurse Kelly has seen before, but only knows her first name as "Taylor".

Kelly admits to herself she's relatively new to this profession, but she's never seen a paramedic talk this fast.

This paramedic keeps telling "Taylor" everything he knows about the patient, as well as what he and his partner have done for the patient in the field, in regards to medicine given.

Taylor just continuously nods her head, acknowledging she's

getting everything this paramedic is telling her, as she writes things down on a small note pad, she's carrying with her.

In thirty seconds, they make a quick left and enter exam room #14.

With the gurney now stationed directly in the middle of the room, Kelly takes her position on the patient's left-hand side, near the patient's waist.

Kelly waits for instruction to transfer her from the Park Ridge paramedic's gurney, on to the Lutheran Family Center Hospital's one, already in the room.

Kelly looks carefully at the woman, who appears to be in her late 80's and lying directly in front of her, when she suddenly realizes something.

"Patient just stopped breathing," Kelly yells out, before reaching for the carotid artery, located on the patient's neck area.

"No pulse, CPR started," Kelly yells, as she quickly puts both of her glove covered hands, squarely between the patient's breasts and begins rapidly giving chest compressions.

Suddenly the room is filled with hospital personnel of all kinds, as both Park Ridge paramedics have a look of shock on their faces, as they slowly back out of the room.

They barely make it out, as the sheer volume of personnel is so great, Kelly is trapped in her present position and forced into the side of the gurney.

Out of the corner of her left eye, Kelly sees one of the doctors dressed in green scrubs, whom she recognizes from working with him before, as Dr. Harry Kim.

Immediately, she feels better knowing she has one of the best working with her right now.

Like a well-trained pit crew, working the Indianapolis 500 race, each of the personnel in exam room #14 goes about their roles, in a valiant effort to save the patient's life.

Stopping only when she hears Dr. Kim yell the word "Clear" Kelly keeps administering chest compressions, occasionally taking turns with another nurse.

Kelly is surprised after 26 minutes, due to the adrenaline rush; she's still feeling strong as well as effective.

Kelly is so involved in this process, she is surprised when a glove covered hand, gently touches her left shoulder, from behind her.

Momentarily startled, Kelly turns around quickly to find Dr. Kim standing directly in front of her.

"Kelly, I called it a couple of minutes ago, but thank you for all you did," Dr. Kim says softly, as he walks away and leaves the room.

Turning her head to the right and then suddenly to the left, Kelly is shocked the only other person in exam room # 14, besides her is "Taylor", who's in the process of shutting off machines.

Slowly, Kelly passes her and steps into the hallway, finding Ms. Shattuck standing just outside exam room number 14.

Only this time Ms. Shattuck has a totally different disposition, with both of her hands at her side and a somewhat sympathetic look on her face.

Kelly walks over to her, but before she can even reach her, Ms. Shattuck asks, "Are you O.K. Kelly?"

Kelly softly says "Yes", but with the adrenaline rush gone and a body in desperate need of caffeine, is shocked just how tired she is.

"Tell you what," Ms. Shattuck says, "take about 10-15 minutes to get yourself some coffee and relax a bit, since its relatively quiet right now."

Kelly doesn't have to be told twice and simply says "thank you" before walking away and throwing her gloves in the first garbage can she comes in contact with.

After grabbing some coffee from a table located behind the nurse's station, she heads directly to the women's locker room, where it seems like she left yesterday, but in reality, it's only been roughly an hour.

Sitting down in front of her locker, but with her back to it, Kelly slowly sips her coffee and eats part of a white chocolate, macadamia nut, Cliff bar she took out of her lunch bag. For some strange reason, due to her earlier being in a rush, was left inside her locker.

She scrolls through her phone, looking for any messages from either Matt or her dad, but finds none.

She is surprised how quickly the coffee and energy bar is taking effect, as her energy level starts to rise.

Kelly realizes she didn't even know the name of the deceased and the personnel in exam room # 14 gave it their best effort, herself included, but the death of a patient is hard to take anytime, but especially your first call of the day.

Somewhat refreshed, Kelly rises and heads back to the Emergency Room, where upon arriving, she heads directly to "the board".

Its located directly across from the nurse's station and contains room numbers, patient's names and their physician's information as well.

Due to the HIPAA law, any kind of patient health issues, are closely guarded, for everyone's protection.

Kelly sees on this board she only has four rooms today; ER 5-9 and a slow smile comes to her, as this same board shows these rooms are currently empty.

"Maybe just maybe being a beautiful sunny day, we won't be too busy," Kelly thinks to herself.

Being relatively new, she doesn't realize you never ever think or say this statement out loud.

She heads to these rooms and checks each of them carefully, guaranteeing they have the medical supplies as well as proper amount of bedding, she may need sometime during this shift.

Satisfied each of them are properly equipped, she heads back to the nurse's station and coffee pot for her second cup of the day.

She never makes it, as Ms. Shattuck stops her in midstride.

Kelly for the first time looks closely at Ms. Shattuck's face and realizes she has the cutest set of dimples she's ever seen on an adult's face, to go with her brown eyes.

"Kelly, the board shows you're currently patient free, as opposed to Nurse Kramer who is jammed to the max on both patients and paperwork, so I was wondering if you could help her out and release her dog bite patient in Exam Room 4," Ms. Shattuck asks?

Kelly feels guilty over being late for her shift and wanting to try and get on Ms. Shattuck's good side, so simply answers "Yes".

"Excellent and thank you," Ms. Shattuck says and hands Kelly the patient in Exam Room 4's discharge paperwork, before walking away.

Before taking another step, Kelly scans the paperwork, making sure she's able to answer any questions the patient, named Lilian Harper, may have for her.

Confident she has everything under control, Kelly is somewhat surprised to see Mrs. Harper is already dressed and seated in a wheelchair.

Kelly is slightly taken back by the blood covered Adidas shoe on her right foot, as well as black workout pants, also slightly covered in blood, near her right ankle area.

Mrs. Harper notices Kelly staring at this area and calmly says "You would think I would know better than to go anywhere near my Rex, when he's eating his breakfast,"

"Rex?" Kelly asks casually.

"My pit bull of course dear," Mrs. Harper answers.

Kelly suddenly feels the urge for her second cup of coffee so she goes through Mrs. Harper's discharge paperwork and since Mrs. Harper has no questions for her, begins to push her wheelchair out of the room. After only a couple of turns they're at the emergency room entrance of the hospital, where they are met by a man standing next to a red, Nissan Maxima.

Slowly he waves his hand at Kelly, who heads in his direction with Mrs. Harper.

"My husband Fred," Mrs. Harper says as they reach the passenger side door of the Maxima.

Kelly hands Fred the discharge paperwork and goes over some formalities with him, before assisting Mrs. Harper by getting her out of the wheelchair and into the front seat of this car.

When finished, Kelly reaches across Mrs. Harper's front chest area and attaches her seat belt into its holder, when suddenly Mrs. Harper reaches up and gives her a huge hug, to the point, she pulls Kelly into her.

Before Kelly can say or do anything, Mrs. Harper says "God Bless You," and before releasing her hold on Kelly, gives her a soft kiss, on the right side of her face.

Kelly slowly backs herself out of the Maxima, slightly in shock and waves, as the Harper family drives out of the Lutheran Family Center Hospital's Emergency Room parking lot.

A huge smile comes over Kelly's face, as she realizes one of her first instructors at Rasmussen College, where she obtained her nursing degree from, said it best, "Few things in life are as satisfying as when you've played a role in discharging a satisfied customer."

Kelly could stand here all day and take in the sun, which is only surpassed by the cloudless beautiful blue sky, but she knows she's going to be needed back inside the hospital, as her day has only begun.

CHAPTER 15

K urt Thompson was exhausted.
Lying in bed, completely naked, and alone, he thought his heart was going to jump straight out of his chest.

With his left forearm laying across his forehead, he closed his eyes for a few seconds, trying to catch his breath.

He was motionless, hoping it would help his breathing, but in reality, he was just too tired to even think about moving.

Opening his eyes, he looked up at the dark brown colored, five bladed ceiling fan, slowly oscillating in his bedroom.

Slowly, she moved across the bed, until she found her spot.

Laying on the pillow next to his face, she waited for his next move.

"Not now Whiskers," he said softly, and removing his left forearm from his forehead, gave his domestic shorthair, a gentle push away from him.

Sleep was all Kurt Thompson was longing for, a deep, long, uninterrupted one.

Suddenly, the thin white bed sheet was ripped off him, as she crawled into the left side of his bed.

Laying her naked body on top of his, she whispered into Thompson's left ear, "Ready to go animal?" while nibbling gently and slowly on his left ear lobe, with her teeth.

"Animal"? Kurt thought to himself.

"Geeez, if anyone should be called one, it should be her instead of him," he thought.

Kurt had never gone on a blind date before and only did this as a favor for one of his best Southern Illinois University buddies.

Cooper's Hawk restaurant in Arlington Heights was picked as the designated spot for his dinner, with a woman he only knew as Francesca.

Kurt was happy he had dressed appropriately, as Francesca showed up in a beautiful flowered dress and black high heel shoes. His buddy was correct and she truly was as attractive, as his buddy had promised.

The drinks flowed but information was hard to get out of Francesca, who was timid to say the least.

He was able to find out after her second glass of Merlot, she shared a home in Elk Grove Village, with a flight attendant named "Jenny".

Francesca also worked for some bank in Hoffman Estates, as a teller, but had bigger ambitions at this bank in the future.

Kurt was in his glory.

He could date Francesca and see what came of it, while still pursuing the woman of his dreams, Megan O'Brien.

From their first night of love making, at his Mount Prospect townhouse, up to this morning, things had gone totally opposite, of how he thought they would.

His sweet, young Francesca, had become, hot, constantly horny Francesca, who seemed to have developed a huge sexual appetite.

To say he was confused was an understatement.

What man he wondered, would have a problem with a girlfriend who constantly wanted sex?

Plus, she was becoming great in bed and looked as sexy as she did.

"Then what the hell is your freaking problem with all this" he thought to himself, still too exhausted to move.

Kurt Thompson wasn't a prude, but it seemed as though the lovemaking had progressed in a couple of weeks, so had the strangeness of Francesca.

At first, he found himself turned on by the escapades of Francesca, not knowing what to expect.

Blindfolds, bondage through the use of dress ties, ropes, and even handcuffs, were now the toys she was most turned on by.

Strange as well was the fact, Francesca was usually the one bringing these toys to their passionate love making sessions.

Being completely honest with himself, Kurt was a bit taken back by her behavior in the bedroom.

Fifty Shades of Grey phenomenon, Kurt wondered?

Unless you were living in a cave, in some foreign country, the trilogy of books had finished sweeping the   U.S.A. and by June of 2015, a movie had already been out and another book in the series.

Author E.L. James had a hit on her hands, with over one hundred and twenty-five million being sold.

There wasn't a women Kurt knew who hadn't read the books, from police officer, dispatcher, even Animal Control Officer Karen Dunlop, who was in her late fifties, was seen reading the freaking thing, in the lunch room of the Police Station.

One day last week, while at Francesca's place, Kurt waited to hear the shower water starting to run, before he conducted his search.

It only took him two minutes before he found what he was looking for, in a plastic bag, stashed under the very bed they had just made love in.

The Fifty Shades of Grey series, with certain parts of each book highlighted and, in some parts, circled in red.

Since he couldn't exactly ask Francesca if he could borrow them, he did the next best thing.

On his next trip to Costco, for a gallon of milk, whole chicken, box of Hershey almond candy bars, gallon of orange juice, and a twelve pack of Stella's, Kurt bought all three E. L. James books.

Later that night, three empty bottles of Stella sat on his kitchen table, next to the carcass of what had been half a chicken.

Kurt read the first book in its entirety, ignoring any phone calls or texts messages.

Putting the book down, one single thought kept racing through his head.

Was he suddenly playing the role of Anastasia Steele, while Francesca played the role of Christian Grey?

To say Kurt's life was suddenly more confusing after reading the book, was an understatement.

"How the hell could this have happened and was it really a problem" he said to Whiskers, who was rubbing herself against his left leg, as he sat at his kitchen table.

By no means was Francesca ordering him around, like Christian Grey had been to Anastasia in the books, and he certainly wasn't her slave, so again what was the issue which kept him up at night?

Kurt anxiously looked forward to finishing the other two books in the series, when time allowed.

He hoped maybe, just maybe, they would shed some light on this dilemma he was facing.

For now, he would just have to suffer the benefits of being in a committed relationship, with a nymphomaniac.

"Can you give me just a few more minutes honey?" Kurt whispered, as his breathing finally started to return to normal, even with her body on top of his.

"Fine," Francesca responded and, in the process, stopped nibbling on his left ear, rolled off him onto her back, taking the bed sheet with her in the process.

She pulled the sheet up so it covered most of her body, stopping just below her neck.

"How was the bachelor party?" Francesca asked, with total sarcasm in her voice and her arms folded across her chest.

"Shit," Kurt said to himself, tell her the truth about banging the stripper, or lie to her for the first time since their relationship started.

"Typical bachelor party except for the fact we played one of the best golf courses in the world, Black Wolf Run, in Kohler, Wisconsin," he said.

"You guys stayed there the entire time?" she asked, as the sarcasm from earlier, started to diminish ever so slightly.

"Nope, one of the guys you don't know, wanted to go to Door County and check something out, so Bobby Larsen and I went with him. I tried calling you a couple of times from there, but kept getting a busy signal from your phone babe,"' Kurt finished with.

"Aww really honey you tried calling?" Francesca responded, and in the process turned her body slightly to the right.

"Sure did," Kurt said, confident he was winning her back.

Slowly Francesca used her right hand and forearm, to support the right side of her face, which had come off the bed.

Kurt's breathing had finally returned to normal and he was anxious to get started again on round two of love making, when for no apparent reason, Megan's face appeared in front of him.

"Shitttt," Kurt suddenly realized he was supposed to meet Megan in five minutes, at Old Mill Mall, for her new washer and dryer from Sears.

CHAPTER 16

Kurt arrived at the Gilles Food court anticipating the worst. He knew no one wanted to be kept waiting for over 70 minutes, without a valid excuse.

He was sure Megan wasn't going to be the exception either and especially with the mood she had been exhibiting in her messages, this past month.

Extremely agitated, short and terse in both her comments and responses, had become the new Megan.

He was confident more of this would happen to him today, but Kurt had no issue with it, because this was the only woman, he truly wanted to have a long-term relationship with.

She was still the most beautiful woman in the entire food court by far, and easy to find among the crowd, with the ads from some weekend newspaper, spread out on the table in front of her.

How appropriate Kurt thought, she be seated directly in front of the Dunkin Donuts section, in the entire place.

With his large frame, it was difficult to do, but somehow Kurt was able to fit into one of the brown chairs, directly across the table from Megan.

Before he could offer an apology, Kurt was shocked at what he was seeing and smelling, coming from Megan.

A slight, but still noticeable odor of alcohol, to go with her bloodshot eyes.

It had easily been over three weeks since Kurt had seen Megan, simply in passing by each other, when each had a Felony Court case, at the Skokie court house.

As fate would have it, she was leaving the court room, as Kurt was running late and just entering the court room.

Time hadn't been particularly kind to her Kurt noticed, now that he was sitting less than a foot away from her.

Bags appeared under each eye, which had never been on her face in the past and were joined by a general puffiness, not only confined to her face, but overall body in general.

"Sorry Megan," Kurt finally blurted out and then immediately put his head down, like a puppy who had accidentally soiled the new carpet in the living room of their owner's home.

"So, what's this one's name?" Megan responded, with her voice dripping in sarcasm and throwing one last shot in before Kurt could answer, "Meet her on one of your Door County excursions?"

"Finally, some jealousy," Kurt thought to himself.

Kurt picked his head up quickly and pictured a frustrated Francesca, just now leaving his Mt. Prospect place, after getting in touch with an Uber driver, once again.

When he raised his head, Kurt's left hand knocked his set of car keys off the table separating both Megan and himself and on to the food court floor.

Instinctively he bent over to get his keys when he saw them for the first time, scratch marks, as well as bruising on the inside bicep area of her right arm.

"Shit Megan what the hell happened to you," Kurt blurted out, while sitting back up and pointing at her arm.

Megan suddenly turned a bright shade of red and seemed embarrassed by what Kurt had just found, with a confused look appearing on his face.

"Oh that," she said rather sheepishly before continuing, "well some drunken bitch grabbed me in the lockup the other night while I was processing her on T.C. Chambers's Drunk Driving arrest,"

Seeing Kurt Thompson still staring at her, Megan continued, "It was a pretty good free for all for about a minute and we actually went to the ground, which is how my phone got broken."

"You charged her with Criminal Damage to Property for your

phone and Battery for touching you, didn't you?" Kurt asked, as he leaned in closer to Megan.

"Of course, we did," Megan answered and for the first time today, actually smiled at Kurt, before quickly changing the conversation.

"You should talk, how did you get all of those scratch marks on both of your forearms?" Megan asked, with an inquisitive look on her face.

"Thorn bushes got me, while I was looking a couple of times for my Pro V1's up in Kohler, Wisconsin," Kurt quickly came back with.

When Megan didn't respond and still had the strange look on her face, Kurt realized he needed to expand on his explanation.

"Megan, those golf balls are expensive as hell and granted I was a bit drunk, so it was stupid on my part."

In need of some caffeine, Kurt wiggled out of his seat and while standing in front of Megan, asked her, "Do you need anything from Dunkin?"

"No thank you," Megan answered and put her head down, looking at the ads again, in search of her new washer and dryer.

While waiting in line, Kurt heard his cell phone buzz, indicating he had received a new text message.

Since he was next in line, Kurt didn't move, as Megan suddenly reached over and picked up his cell phone.

Kurt watched both in shock and silence, as Megan's hands began shaking, while reading the message.

"Shit," Kurt thought to himself, somebody must have sent a picture of the stripper from the bachelor party.

When Megan began to sob uncontrollably, Kurt realized it was now or never to get his story out, and stepping out of line, walked back to the table, sitting down once again.

"Megan, please talk to me and tell me what's wrong?" Kurt finally asked, with an exasperated tone in his voice.

In between sobs and desperately trying to catch her breath, Megan was finally able to answer his question.

"It's from Mike Antonio of your police department saying they just got the word; Ron Thomas is dead and I think you're the one who killed him, you fucking asshole."

CHAPTER 17

M att O'Neil was exhausted. Lying in bed completely naked, his mind was racing at a speed, he had never experienced before.

With his left forearm laying across his forehead, he closed his
eyes for a few seconds, in hopes his thoughts would slow down and
he could finally fall asleep. Opening his eyes slowly didn't help and
if anything, it made the thoughts multiply in numbers.

In his 27 years, he had faced physical exhaustion numerous
times, as an athlete, in the military and now as a police officer.

This was different, and to say Matt was confused, was an
understatement.

Matt sensed Kelly was starting to have problems with picking
up his share of the responsibilities around their home, even though
she hadn't said anything.

Kelly didn't have to say anything.

Ask any man if he knows he's in his wife's, or girlfriend's
doghouse and the answer will always be "Yesssssssssss."

It's a certain look, a coldness, which all men know, when they're
on the receiving end of it.

Many of the chores Matt used to do—grocery shopping, picking
up the dry cleaning, doing the whites, and cleaning the house—had
now fallen in the lap of Kelly, because he wasn't home.

Which is why tonight was going to be so special.

Probation ended today for Matt, Megan, T.C. and Marc.

No longer would they be called probationary, Greenfield Police
Officers.

In the next two days, each would be called in separately, during their shift, to meet with Lt. Wayne, who would give them the good news.

No big ceremony, just a weak handshake from Lt. Wayne, upon entering his modest office. Next, a ten-minute pep talk and an even weaker pat on the back, as each, individually, left the meeting.

Javier Ortego was a completely different story.

"Javy," seemed to be having problems as far back as the second week of classroom study, at ILETC. Despite the help of his fellow Greenfield Police Officers and each FTO Javy had ever ridden with, he was struggling over different issues.

Report writing, traffic stops, and discretion over issuing tickets, were some of the issues.

Individually, Sgt. Barton and Lt. Wayne each had spoken to him about the problems. Apparently, the chats hadn't worked and even worse, Officer Javier Ortego had started stressing, over fear of losing his job.

You could see it, when you backed him on any call.

You could hear it, in his voice, when he was talking on the radio.

Police work was no different, in some cases, than any other job.

When the job is going well, you're confident, your thought process is smooth and your body reacts properly. The end result, is a finished, properly done job.

Stress on the other hand, destroys the entire job process, both mentally as well as physically.

Pressing to try and improve your production, only screws up the entire finished product.

Probationary Officer Javier Ortego was called in by Lt. Wayne earlier today and was given the bad news.

Three months of extended probation, as well as occasionally having Sgt. Barton riding with him, to monitor his progress.

The Greenfield Police Department was currently down two police officers, due to their untimely deaths.

They had countless dollars, as well as a year of training, invested in Probationary Officer, Javier Ortego.

The Greenfield Police Department needed Javier, as much as he needed them. Officer Javier Ortego didn't take the news well and asked permission to take a few vacation days, attached to his next regularly scheduled days off.

Lt. Wayne, shockingly approved it on the spot.

Upon hearing the approval, Officer Ortego told Lt. Wayne, "I'm going to use this time off to turn things around. I promise you, when I return, I'll be the kind of officer you've been hoping for."

Lt. Wayne was speechless and just sat in his office chair, as Officer Ortego left his office.

Walking down the hallway, as he was leaving the police station to go back to patrolling his beat, Officer Ortego began planning his next seven days off.

After work today, he would meet his girlfriend Juanita for a drink.

She loved the bar Libertad, on Lincoln Avenue, in Skokie, and he would meet her there.

After a couple of great margaritas, he would break the news to her.

They were done as a couple, but could always be friends, if she wanted.

He doubted she would go for this, since they'd argued more in the past month, than any other time in their ten-month relationship.

Because of these arguments, his drinking had increased heavily, as his interest in her sexually, had decreased steadily.

Next, he would fly to Puebla, Mexico and see his mother Maria, and his three sisters, for a couple of days.

Mama Ortego knew how to take care of her Javier.

A few home-cooked meals, as well as a little comfort from his Madre, should make everything better.

Javy wondered how much he should tell his mother, about his situation.

Work, personal life, as well as a new girlfriend in the past two weeks, which he somehow had managed to keep secret from his fellow officers, made for an interesting, upcoming month for him.

The new girlfriend was no Juanita by any stretch of the imagination, but she was partially to blame for some of his recent problems at work.

As he got into Squad 6, in the police station parking lot, Officer Javier Ortego knew he had a ton of shit on his plate, but felt he was up to the task at hand.

Officer Matt O'Neil was concerned about his racquetball partner and fellow Greenfield Police Officer.

But for right now, Matt had his own issues to handle.

With having tonight off, as well as the next two days off, Matt put Operation Treat Kelly, into effect.

Eleven red roses were waiting for her on the kitchen table, when she arrived home from work, at the hospital.

The twelfth rose Matt had carefully trimmed and put delicately in his mouth, for Kelly to see, after she made her way upstairs, to their bedroom.

Matt had already showered, dressed in his only black suit and waited patiently, as Kelly did so.

Like a kid anxious for her birthday surprise, Kelly asked twice while getting dressed, where they were going, but quit after the second time, when Matt refused to say a word.

Roughly thirty minutes later, they were seated at a small table for two, in Kelly's favorite steak house, E.J.'s Place, on Skokie Boulevard, in Skokie.

They sat in the back of the room, with the lights dimmed low and a violinist playing, started the night off right.

A 2003 bottle of Louis Martini Sonoma Cabernet, never tasted so good, as the ninety-minute dinner was filled with hand holding and beautiful smiles by both, as they looked into each other's eyes.

When Kelly turned down the carrot cake, her favorite, for dessert, and gave Matt "the look," the waiter couldn't bring the check quick enough, to please Matt.

A quick exit out of the restaurant and barely obeying the speed limit, on both Harms Road and Dempster Street, found the O'Neil's home, in record time.

Matt dropped Kelly off at the side entrance to their home and started to put his car in the garage.

Matt was so anxious to get inside the house, he almost put his Chevy Camaro, through the back wall of the garage, while backing in.

After closing the overhead door, Matt ran inside the house, using the same door his wife had just used a minute ago. Matt was shocked to find the lights off and pieces of Kelly's clothing, scattered on the floor, every 10 to 12 feet.

Like a hunter, slowly stalking his prey, Matt followed the clothing up the steps, adjacent to the living room.

As he neared the second-floor balcony, the sound of Seal singing, "When a man loves a woman," softly filled the air.

The last piece of clothing Matt found, was Kelly's white lace bra, laying just outside their bedroom door.

He entered their bedroom, to find the only light in the entire room coming from the bathroom, with the door, partially closed.

This light barely silhouetted Kelly, whose face, was the only part of her body visible, because she was lying under a thin, beige-colored, bed sheet.

Not a word was said between the two of them, as Matt watched Kelly reach out with her left hand from under the sheet and turn the volume down on the Sony CD player, located on her nightstand, next to the bed.

Operation Treat Kelly had been a huge success and Matt was ready to complete the mission, as he quickly undressed.

Upon pulling the thin bed sheet back and seeing Kelly naked, just staring up at him, with those gorgeous blue eyes, Matt got into bed and began hugging and slowly kissing, both sides of her neck.

Slowly Kelly tilted her head straight back as her body began to shake.

Blame it on the lack of sleep. Blame it on not getting enough cardio exercise recently and being in terrible shape. Blame it on his stress level, these past months being at an all-time high. Blame it on the fact Matt and his wife, hadn't made love in twelve days.

Whatever the reason, Matt's excitement level came way too early and the mission needed to be scrubbed.

As did the bed sheets, Kelly's pillowcase, and for that matter, Kelly herself.

CHAPTER 18

Kelly O'Neil entered the bathroom and turned the shower on full force, occasionally adjusting the valve.

When the water had reached the correct temperature, she entered the shower.

Kelly closed the curtain behind her and pulled out her white loofah, from her shower caddy, filling it completely with Dial body soap.

She began scrubbing her stomach and groin area, in an effort to get what Matt had just done to her, completely off.

As an emergency room nurse, she had been exposed unfortunately, to every known bodily fluid a person could pass.

She was sure vomit was the absolute worst, due to its smell.

As Kelly moved the loofah, up towards her chest, she was surprised to see the shower water was involved in a race with her tears. Since both were flowing down her face and washing off the makeup she had applied earlier, for their big night out.

Kelly's tears weren't so much for tonight's incident, but instead, over the man she was in love with and losing.

The man she had fallen in love with, wasn't the same man, lying only twelve feet away, in their bed.

The man she had fallen in love with, was a star quarterback, at Gordon Tech High School.

This same man, had entered the Navy and risen up the ranks, going into a Navy Seal unit, she knew little about.

She still loved him with all her heart and soul, and she knew, he loved her.

But Matt had some serious issues right now and appeared to be falling apart, both physically, as well as mentally.

What troubled Kelly the most, was she didn't know what to do about it.

Upon finishing showering and drying herself off, she wrapped her blonde hair into a white bath towel.

Kelly, then put on her pink, terrycloth robe, which had been hanging on a hook, behind the bathroom door.

Silently, she walked past Matt, who was still lying-in bed, with his left forearm over his face, while now looking up at the ceiling fan.

Kelly slowly walked downstairs and went directly to the kitchen.

In the kitchen, she walked over to the stove, turning on the front burner and placing a white and blue porcelain kettle, over the flames.

She slowly turned, looking out a kitchen window, located just above her sink. Looking into her backyard, she was alone with her thoughts.

With the kettle finally whistling, she made herself a cup of Teavana blackberry mojito green tea, in an effort to help her relax.

With her tea cup in hand, she picked up the Catherine Lowell novel she had been reading, from the kitchen table and settled into her favorite old chair in the living room, after carefully placing her bare feet, underneath her robe, in the process.

Kelly was hoping to take her mind off Matt, which didn't work at all.

Looking at their wooden, antique clock, seated on the fireplace mantel, Kelly realized after 45 minutes, she had read exactly three pages and retained none of it.

She left the book in the chair and walked back to the kitchen, placing her cup in the dishwasher.

Slowly, she made her way upstairs, silently praying Matt had fallen asleep, because she didn't know what to say to him, if he was still awake.

Matt was still laying, in the same position she had left him, with his eyes wide open.

As Kelly got closer to the bed, some things had changed, since she had left.

Matt had apparently gotten up and stripped the entire bed.

He put a clean bed liner, sheets and pillowcases, on their bed and the dirty linens lay in a corner, by the clothes hamper.

Also, he had taken a shower, because he and the room smelled fresh, with the scent of febreze still in the air, even with all of their bedroom windows open.

While still in her robe, Kelly got into the bed and laid flat on her back, next to him.

Unlike Matt, she laid with her arms folded across her chest, alone with her thoughts.

Neither Kelly or Matt said a word, lying side by side.

Kelly realized the discomfort level of the silence, was becoming unbearable for her and figured it had to be worse for Matt, who finally broke the silence.

"Kelly, I don't know what," was all Matt could manage, before Kelly rolled over from her back, onto his hairy chest, with her head resting in the middle of it.

Kelly used her left hand, to slowly start stroking, the left side of Matt's face.

"Matt please don't," she said.

"As a nurse, I hear about this stuff all the time," Kelly finished.

"It's never happened to me before damn it, and I'm just fuckin' embarrassed," Matt said, almost in a whisper.

Kelly was now put squarely on the spot.

Quickly, she needed to heal her husband's pride, without doing any further damage, to his ego.

Good luck with all this, she thought to herself.

All of Kelly's girlfriends, married or single, with men in their lives, knew one of the secrets to a successful relationship, was to keep your man's confidence, with the arrow always pointed in the up direction.

"Matt, you've had a hell of a past couple of months," Kelly said, pausing for a second, before continuing. "Yes, your fellow cops at Greenfield have suffered as well, but no one honey, I repeat, no one more than you dear," Kelly stopped to let the words sink in.

Kelly moved her head slightly, so she could see Matt's face and see if her words were making an impact.

Matt remained both motionless and expressionless.

"First, you lose one of your best friends in Chris and yes, I know you had little use for Ron, yet he still was one of yours..." Kelly's voice started to trail off and quiver, at the same time.

"I lost friends in the service," Matt countered.

"Not the same honey, especially after you told me, when you were recovering from your leg injury, how Chris saved your life," Kelly said firmly, adding emphasis to the word "life".

Kelly also moved a few inches, so now her head laid in her favorite position, squarely between the left side of Matt's face and shoulder. She had laid in this spot so often, it was almost like she had a permanent crease in this place, on her husband's body.

Even in this new spot, Kelly continued caressing Matt's face.

"Matt you're my best friend, a wonderful husband and someday you'll be a great father," Kelly said quietly.

"Father, whaaaaaaaaaaat?"

Matt sat straight up in bed so suddenly, Kelly slipped off him.

"Matt, I told you I went off the pill five weeks ago yesterday, plus we've made love six or seven times since then and you know each time it's been wonderful, so who knows, sweetie?" Kelly finished.

Matt laid back down and rolled over, so his face and Kelly's were only inches apart.

"Thank you," Matt said softly and slowly he began giving Kelly gentle kisses.

With her arms around Matt and his lips on hers, Kelly felt a sense of ease fill her.

With her eyes closed, a warm wetness started coming down her face.

Kelly slowly opened both of her eyes and watched as tears streamed from Matt's eyes, to the point the front of Kelly's robe was becoming wet.

Kelly hugged Matt harder and together they drifted off to sleep, in love forever.

CHAPTER 19

Deputy Chief Frank Gyondski leaned back in his black office swivel chair and placed both of his hands behind his head.

Slowly he turned, so he faced the south-side, rear entrance to the Greenfield Police Department parking lot. Being on the first floor of the police station, with two large, ground-to-ceiling windows in his office, allowed him a beautiful view of the area.

Weather wise it was a sunny, 85-degree day.

A huge smile slowly appeared on his face, for the first time in over two weeks.

Officer Mills' Death Investigation, while still ongoing, had become a daily formality, with Deputy Chief Gyondski playing a smaller role, everyday it dragged on.

Officer Thomas's death, on the other hand, barely impacted him.

With the death occurring in Door County, Wisconsin, most of the Chicago news media were advised to contact the Door County, Public Information Officer, which they obligingly did.

Only the reporter, for the *Greenfield Announcement,* wanted additional information on Thomas, for a piece they were running. Deputy Chief Gyondski referred this reporter to Chief Fitzsimons' secretary, Sandy Elloy, who handled it in a professional, timely manner.

A light-skinned, middle-aged, African American woman, Sandy Elloy was easily the most important asset to the Greenfield Police Department.

With her pleasant personality, solid work ethic, and ability to multi-task to the supreme, no job ever assigned to her, failed to get done.

Sandy Elloy was only part of the reason, Deputy Chief Gyondski, was grinning from ear to ear.

Looking at the Ulysse Nardin, gold ban watch, on his right wrist, it showed 1400 hours exactly.

Being Friday, he had earned himself a three-day weekend. He and his wife Beth, could hardly wait.

Both were avid golfers and he would leave work in an hour, head to their Arlington Heights home, where she would be waiting.

Knowing how organized Beth was, his Ping golf clubs, golf shoes, overnight bag, and an Igloo cooler full of Diet Coke for him and Sprite for her, would be packed in her red Audi A4. Thus, allowing them to get on the Indiana Skyway in record time.

The fact they were childless, as well as having no pets, also made trips like these easier and less of a hassle.

They would then take a short trip to the Tracy Chapman Golf School, located in Carmel, Indiana, to work on their golf games.

His weakness being putting, and Beth being fairway woods.

They'd also, would finally catch up on each other's lives.

The number one topic he would tell her about and the main reason for his huge smile, was the Greenfield Village Board Meeting last night.

While the Greenfield Village Board Meeting was 17 hours ago, Deputy Chief Gyondski had started preparation for it months earlier, as if he was General Dwight D. Eisenhower, planning the Normandy Invasion, in World War II.

Other than studying for his one and only sergeant's test, years ago, he never worked as hard on anything in his life.

For this would be the final presentation, on the new Greenfield Police Station, to the Greenfield Village Board of Trustees.

The Lakotta Architect Company had been awarded the bid, to build the new police station, 5 months ago.

Before they finally obtained approval of their blueprints and diagrams, from the Village of Greenfield's Appearance Commission, they had to appear in front of them three times. The first two meetings, were to make revisions and corrections to the blueprints, due to foliage, signage, and lighting.

Only after all of these revisions to the plans had been made, did the Appearance Comission members, finally sign off on the plan.

Twice, the Lakotta Architect Company, had to appear in front of the Planning Commission.

These commission members were more concerned with traffic flow and finances for the new police station. The Planning Comission members finally signed off on the plans, when they were confident their concerns had been fixed.

All five of these meetings, had been recorded by the Village of Greenfield's own cable crew, for the purpose of allowing Village of Greenfield residents, the opportunity to see where their tax dollars were being spent.

Deputy Chief Gyondski requested and received copies of these recorded meetings.

For a solid week, when time allowed, he watched these meetings over and over, until he could practically say the words, which had come out of each commissioner's mouth, verbatim. He even took all of the planning commission meeting tapes home and watched them after dinner, in the basement, while Beth watched her favorite comedy, Modern Family, in their upstairs family room.

Deputy Chief Gyondski analyzed everything he could, while watching the tapes from each meeting.

Which of the commissioners were solidly on board with the plan, which commissioners had voiced concerns about the plans and what their concerns were based on. Of the concerns raised, what had the Lakotta Architect Company and more specifically, their CEO, John Lamond, done to correct them?

Deputy Chief Gyondski was extremely comfortable working with Lamond, who had built five other police stations, (three in Illinois and two in Indiana) in the past seven years. Lamond had solid credentials, to go along with a great personality, which allowed both his employees and clients, to gravitate to him.

Confident the concerns had been addressed properly and thoroughly, Deputy Chief Gyondski wondered whether these concerns would be brought up again, by any of the Greenfield Village Trustees.

The Friday before the board meeting, each trustee on the Greenfield Village Board, was given the revised plans for the police station, as well as the most recent financial analysis, regarding the costs for this facility. All of this information was put inside a large brown envelope, which had been hand delivered to their homes, by a Greenfield Community Service Officer.

Exactly two days before the Greenfield Village Board Meeting, CEO John Lamond and Deputy Chief Gyondski lunched alone, in Deputy Chief Gyondski's office.

Sitting directly across from each other, at a small conference table, very little was said during their meal.

Once their lunch was over, it was all business for the next two hours, with facts and figures checked and then double-checked. More than anything, Deputy Chief Gyondski wanted no surprises to be presented to the trustees at the board meeting.

Deputy Chief Gyondski had seen firsthand how this could almost derail a project, at a Greenfield Village Board Meeting, roughly a year earlier, when he happened to be in the audience, for his own budget request of five, Ford Police Interceptors.

At the time, the Greenfield Fire Department, had received permission from the Greenfield Village Board of Trustees, for bids on a new fire station, on the west side of Greenfield.

Dalti Builders, of Northfield, Illinois won the bid on this project, due to their solid reputation and low bid.

Appearing at what should have been their final, Greenfield Village Board Meeting, was the head of the firm, Bruno Dalti. The company was named after his departed father, Sal Dalti.

Because Bruno Dalti inherited the company, as opposed to busting his ass to earn it, he took it for granted.

Sal Dalti had worked 14-hour days, building an architecture firm known throughout the entire northern part of Illinois. Sal Dalti was known as a micro manager, leaving no detail untouched. He died at the age of 74, due to lung cancer.

Unfortunately, Sal had only one child to leave the business to, Bruno Dalti.

While Sal Dalti was a micro manager, Bruno Dalti, didn't have a managerial bone, in his entire body.

Bruno delegated every task he could, while he spent his summer golfing and sailing all over the United States. Winters were spent skiing, all over the world, without a care.

Bruno Dalti, as the saying goes, "Was out over his skis," on his knowledge and preparation for the Greenfield Fire Station project and he was about to take the worst fall of his professional life.

As each trustee sitting on the dais, looked at the small video screen in front of them, Bruno Dalti put his first Power Point slide up, for Village President Kerry Conte and all of the Village Trustees to see. It took no more than one minute, before a Village Trustee, Paul Dementris, raised his hand after viewing the slide and was given permission by Conte to speak.

Calmly, Trustee Dementris stated, "These figures don't match the figures each of us received in our packets over the weekend, Sir."

Deputy Chief Gyondski immediately looked directly at both the Greenfield Fire Chief, Wayne Glober and his Deputy Fire Chief, Ralph Lynch, who were seated next to each other, one row below, where he was seated.

Both of these men had fought terrible house fires, which resulted in them dealing with dead people in their stellar careers, yet each had turned a shade of white, which matched their highly starched, uniform dress shirts.

Calmly, as if he was ordering a cheeseburger from McDonald's, Bruno Dalti replied, "Trustee Dementris, my staff and I had a meeting this morning and you are correct, in fact you don't have the figures from the Power Point, I'm currently showing you."

Barely pausing for everyone in the audience to catch their breath, he continued, "As you can see sir, we are currently thirty-nine thousand dollars over budget, due to additional building material costs, which weren't properly budgeted for."

Everything else Bruno Dalti said for the remainder of the board meeting, fell on deaf ears.

At the conclusion of the meeting, a small crowd had gathered around Bruno Dalti, in the hallway outside the village board room. This crowd consisted of the Fire Chief, Deputy Fire Chief, Greenfield

Economic Development Commissioner, Mary Sak, and Bruno Dalti's staff.

There was so much yelling and finger pointing, Deputy Chief Gyondski was afraid someone was going to lose an eye.

Deputy Chief Gyondski couldn't wait for the next Greenfield Village Board Meeting, in two weeks, to see how this mess would be straightened out.

The Village of Greenfield was in between a rock and a hard place.

They were too heavily invested in this project, to suddenly scrap it and start over.

Deputy Chief Gyondski fortunately, found an excuse to attend the next Greenfield Village Board Meeting, and even got there a few minutes early, to secure a prime seat in the section reserved for village employees.

First item on the agenda, the new Greenfield Fire Station, located at 1615 Revere Avenue.

All of the same players from the last meeting, fire personnel, Mary Sak, and the Dalti Firm, were present. Or were they really?

As two members of the Dalti Firm stepped forward to the microphones, he noted one significant absence, Bruno Dalti.

Instead, the budget director of the Dalti Firm, Brad Steigel, handled the presentation, assisted by Village President Conte. Both sides wanted this project to succeed and they pulled it off with accurate figures and clarification about where they were financially.

The Village of Greenfield Board, unanimously approved the new Greenfield Fire Station that night, with little opposition.

Bruno Dalti was never seen again, in the Village of Greenfield.

Deputy Chief Gyondski made a promise right there, in the Greenfield Village Board Room that night, he would not be another Bruno Dalti.

With Chief Fitzsimons' permission, Deputy Chief Gyondski had changed his daily work hours, for the day of his presentation on the new police station, to the Greenfield Village Board and was excused from the daily Chris Mills briefing.

It was a good thing he did.

The night before the presentation, Frank Gyondski tossed and turned, while Beth was sleeping peacefully next to him, even occasionally snoring. Frank realized one thing, his future career rested solely on him being perfect, in roughly 18 hours, in front of the Greenfield Village Board.

Finally, he turned to look at the clock radio, located on the nightstand next to his bed. In bright, red numbers, 2:45 Am shined on its broad face.

Frank Gyondski said one word, softly to himself, into his pillow, so as to not awake Beth, "Shit."

Slowly, he got out of bed, tired and frustrated, over his inability to sleep.

Opening the medicine cabinet in their bathroom, he instantly found what he had been looking for, because he had used it three nights ago, Advil PM.

After opening the bottle, he turned it with his left hand, quickly pouring two tablets into his right hand.

Throwing them into his mouth, he washed them down with three gulps of water, from a small, multi-colored Dixie cup.

Upon finishing, he silently put the Dixie cup into the wastebasket under the bathroom sink, as opposed to dropping it, so as not to awake Beth.

Silently, he returned to bed, slowly getting in. Once in bed, he glanced over at Beth, who continued to snore softly on her side of the bed, while being curled up in a fetal position. Her snoring, combined with the way she was lying in bed, brought a small smile to his face.

Within 20 minutes, the Advil PMs had kicked in, allowing him to join Beth, in a relaxed state of sleep throughout the remainder of the night and, for that matter, half of the morning.

When he finally woke up and looked at the same clock on his nightstand, this time it read 10:00 Am.

With Beth off, at her job as Vice President of Finances, at the Chase Bank in Bloomingdale, he pondered his breakfast options.

Making his way downstairs, he stopped at the island, in the middle of the kitchen.

Located on top of it was a single piece of loose-leaf paper, with red cursive on it.

Slowing, to pick up the note, a huge smile came across his face, as he realized Beth had written it, before leaving for work. The note read:

Frank,

I wish I could be there tonight to see you shine in your moment of glory, but you know I can't due to work. I know how hard you've worked on this, and there is no doubt in my mind you'll knock it out of the park. Please, please call me when it's over. I'll be thinking of you my love.

Carpe Diem,
Beth

Frank put the note back on the island and shook his head slowly from side to side.

Twelve years of marriage and his wife was still the amazing woman he met in a statistics class, at University of Illinois, Chicago. Was she the sexiest student at the school? Not a chance in hell, Frank Gyondski thought, the minute he sat down next to her and asked her a question concerning, mean, median, and mode.

But he didn't care, due to his lack of success in the women department. Shit, it had been a long time since Frank Gyondski had spoken to any woman, tall, short, White, Hispanic, African American, Asian Pacific—all had turned a cold shoulder to him, and probably with good reason.

Simply put, he brought nothing to the dance, in the looks department.

In the traditional Polish mode, he was tall, with blonde hair and brown eyes. In the untraditional Polish mode, he was skinny, big nosed, with a receding hairline, and brown-rimmed glasses.

So, when Beth Wankovsky answered his question, in an easy-to-understand way and finished with a smile on her face, his day was made. For what he wanted besides beauty, was a woman of intellect, who could match his and challenge him on a daily basis, regarding his beliefs and values.

Frank Gyondski found this in Beth.

A brief, seven-month courtship, filled with tours of Downtown Chicago's favorite sights, Art Museum, Field Museum, Operas and Symphonies, only confirmed in his mind, and heart, she was the one for him.

The only problem which stood in the way of a future of love and happiness, was both of their religious believes.

Frank was Roman Catholic, with an aunt who was a nun, in Cincinnati, Ohio. Beth's father was a Rabbi, at a synagogue in Buffalo Grove. For marriage to happen, someone was going to have to give up their religion and convert, or was this necessary?

One night, over cups of coffee, at the Starbucks, in Rand Hurst Mall, they discussed their future and realized both were devoted to their jobs and children were not a necessity for either of them.

Problem solved, just like that. Beth's father, Rabbi Wankovsky, and pastor Edward Shea, at St. Timothy's Church, in Arlington Heights, conducted the service. As the years passed, both became even more devoted to their jobs and each other.

Dropping the note from Beth, back on the kitchen island, he found the remote control for the 26-inch Panasonic television, located high up on a wall, in their kitchen and hit the on switch.

Instantly, a CNN's weather analyst filled the screen, wearing a deep purple-colored dress and talking about rain, somewhere in the lower plains.

He paid little attention to anything the analyst was saying, as he turned his Cuisinart coffeemaker on and headed towards the front door. Upon reaching it, he stopped and checked to make sure his Nike gym shorts, weren't hanging too low.

While no neighbors should still be home, at this hour of the day, there could still be a landscaping crew working, or someone walking a dog, which didn't need to see his ass sticking out of his shorts. Certain they weren't, he opened his front door, to a sea of sunshine, which momentarily blinded him.

After his eyes had adjusted to the light, he walked gingerly in his bare feet, due to a few loose pebbles lying on the driveway. At the driveway, he found what he was looking for immediately, as both of them were only lying a foot apart, wrapped in identical, clear plastic.

Unwrapping the first one, he quickly gazed at the front page for anything which could affect both Beth's and his financial future. Typical, he thought to himself, the *Wall Street Journal* was reporting the price of gas and milk were rising, while their stock investments, were falling in value.

Before walking back inside the house, he wiped his bare feet three times, on a brown-colored doormat, his wife had placed outside the front door. Beth was a cleanliness freak and had trained her husband well.

Everything had a designated place in their home and Frank Gyondski was amazed how much time it saved in their daily lives, never having to search for things. Confident, he had removed any debris attached to the bottom of his feet; he went back inside the house, through the open front door.

He walked directly to the kitchen table, where he dropped both of the newspapers, along with the plastic wrapper from the Wall Street Journal. Instantly, he reached down and grabbed the plastic wrapper with his left hand and went to a tiny, white holder Beth had put in a cabinet, under the kitchen sink, designated just for these items.

Next, he walked over to a kitchen cabinet and pulled out a brown coffee cup. Walking over to the Cuisinart with the coffee cup in his right hand, he pulled the coffee pot from its holder with his left hand and filled the cup to its rim. Sipping the coffee slowly, so as not to burn the inside of his mouth, the caffeine seemed to jolt him awake. With this new energy, Frank Gyondski made himself breakfast of a bowl of Kellogg's raisin bran with an onion bagel, which he covered with Philadelphia cream cheese.

He slowly ate his breakfast, while going through both of the newspapers, killing the remainder of his morning. Upon finishing his breakfast, he rinsed out his cereal bowl, coffee pot, coffee cup and plate holding the bagel, before putting them and his utensils in his silver-colored, Sears Kenmore dishwasher.

Carefully, he stacked the newspapers and then left them on the kitchen island, for Beth to read, when she returned home from work.

Frank Gyondski walked upstairs to his bathroom, directly off their master bedroom. In the bathroom, his daily work ritual for the past 17 years began. Teeth flossing, brushing, showering, finally followed with slowly shaving, with a new triple blade Schick handheld razor. In record time, Frank Gyondski was finished and dressed in a clean uniform.

Grabbing his lunch from the refrigerator, he stopped by the interior door leading to their garage and opened the panel for his ADT alarm. Slowly, he punched in the code to activate the alarm, that began beeping, indicating he had sixty seconds to open the door, exit and then close this door, for the alarm to be set.

For the first time, since he had ever activated the alarm, he turned around and looked at all of the rooms he was able to see, from where he was standing, realizing his life would never be the same, when he returned home tonight.

Satisfied everything was fine, he closed this door.

Once inside the garage, he hit the Genie overhead garage door button and slowly, the overhead garage door raised. As if synchronized, the overhead garage door stopped at exactly the same time, the ADT alarm quit buzzing, which brought a quizzical look to his face.

Getting into his silver-colored, Chevy Malibu, he turned the car on and immediately turned off both the Norcom Radio and Greenfield Fire Department radio channels with his right hand. If Armageddon hit Greenfield, Illinois today, he was confident he would be contacted on his Verizon phone.

One of the few things Chief Fitzsimons hadn't changed, when

he took over the Greenfield Police Department, was allowing both of his Deputy Chiefs, to take their department-issued cars, home with them.

The fact both Deputy Chiefs lived pretty close to Greenfield, Deputy Chief Bart in Wilmette and Deputy Chief Gyondski in Arlington Heights, also made the decision somewhat easier.

Switching the radio dial to his favorite classical station, 98.7 FM, he was alone in his private world, as the car filled with Vivaldi's Four Seasons. Between listening to Vivaldi, occasionally daydreaming and traveling down Euclid Ave, he was parked in his designated spot, in the Greenfield Police Department parking lot, in no time.

With his blue lunch bag and a green Polo travel bag, which contained his suit for the board meeting, Deputy Chief Gyondski walked through the front door of the police station.

Without delay, he went directly to the one person who would determine his schedule for the remainder of this workday, Sandy Elloy.

Seated behind her desk, which was situated just outside the chief's office, Deputy Chief Gyondski found her speaking on the telephone, which was firmly pressed next to her left ear.

Upon seeing him, she raised the index finger on her right hand, while still speaking on the phone.

"Aww shit now what?" he said softly to himself and turned his body away from Elloy, so she wouldn't hear him.

Seeing Chief Fitzsimons' office door open, he stuck his head in, only to find no one inside.

"Someday prick, this will be all mine," Deputy Chief Gyondski thought.

"The Chief and Deputy Chief Bart, are at the monthly, North Shore chief's luncheon, at the Skokie Hilton," Sandy Elloy said, in a direct, matter of fact style, while still seated behind her small desk.

Stepping back from the Chief's office, he turned so he was now standing directly in front of Sandy Elloy, who suddenly stood up from behind her desk.

Both Deputy Chief Gyondski and Sandy Elloy just smiled at each other, as each knew what would be happening in seven and a half hours.

Sandy Elloy finally broke the silence. "Frank, I know you're ready and I just wanted to wish you good luck," was all she could get out, before he interrupted her.

"There's always a chance of a screw up with the Power Point..." was all he said, before she quickly stopped him with a stern look on her face, again pointing the same index finger, on her right hand, straight at his face.

"Bullshit," she blurted out, which startled him, since he had never heard her swear before.

Sandy Elloy then reached down to the right side of her desk and picked up a card, which Deputy Chief Gyondski recognized immediately, as one from Hallmark, due to the gold-colored, distinctive seal located on the back of it.

"Thank you," he said taking the card and slowly lowering it inside the green travel bag.

"You're welcome Frank," Sandy Elloy responded, "and you have no appointments or phone calls to follow up on."

Sheepishly he responded with a quiet, "Thank You," before turning and heading down the hallway, past the dispatch center, to his office.

Since Deputy Chief Gyondski's office was located just down the hall from Chief Fitzsimons, he reached it in less than a minute.

Standing outside his locked office door, Gyondski stared at it, as if by doing so, the door would somehow magically open.

"If only we were in the new station," he thought to himself.

For now, he would need his key to get inside his office. But if things went well tonight at the board meeting, this wouldn't be an issue in roughly 18 months. In the new Greenfield Police Department building, every employee would be given a key card, enabling the holder of the card access to particular doors.

Every key card would be programmed, depending upon the individual's assignment, or rank in the department.

For example, the Chief and both Deputy Chiefs, would have access to the entire building.

All detectives and their bosses, would be the only ones to have access to their office. For maintenance, or repairs, a master key would be kept in the dispatch center and anyone using it would have to sign out for it.

But for now, Deputy Chief Gyondski reached inside his left pants pocket and fished around, until he found his silver key ring and struggled to finally open his office door. Once inside his office, he split the lunch bag and green travel bag between the two old cloth chairs, positioned directly in front of his desk.

Walking behind his desk, he dropped his keys on the corner of it and then checked his office phone, making sure Sandy Elloy was correct, there weren't any phone messages waiting for him.

As usual she was right, and he was pleased no one needed him to call them for the first time in a very long, long, time.

Since he'd never turned his computer off when he left yesterday, he simply hit the space bar to view the screen. This would allow him an opportunity to check his Greenfield Department emails, as he tried to figure out what he could do worthwhile, for the next few hours, before the Greenfield Village Board Meeting. After reading only three emails, he found exactly what he was looking for, quarterly range qualifications were being conducted this week.

"Perfect," he said softly and slowly to himself.

After carefully checking the remainder of his department emails and finding nothing of significance, he went to his own personal email account, on Microsoft, Outlook.

Mixed in with the traditional jokes, he found three emails from friends, all in law enforcement, wishing him good luck with his presentation tonight.

Satisfied, nothing else needed his immediate attention, he stood up and walked around to the front of his desk.

Reaching down to both chairs, he picked up the items he had placed on them, only a few minutes earlier.

Leaving his office, his first stop would be the Greenfield Police Department's lunchroom.

After locking his office door, he went back down the hallway, toward Sandy Elloy's desk.

Stopping just short of her desk, he turned right and went through an exit door, which could be used to reach either the front lobby of the Greenfield Police Department, or a flight of stairs, leading to the basement.

He used the stairs and after reaching the basement, made a series of turns, which took him to the lunch room.

It was your typical lunchroom, for a small-sized police department, anywhere in the United States.

A couple of small tables, requiring only four chairs each, were located in the rear of the room while a large, round table, was situated in the center of the room.

The room contained all of the normal essentials, refrigerator, stove, dishwasher, two different vending machines and, most important of all, a microwave, as well as coffee maker.

Due to the time of day, the room was empty and Deputy Chief Gyondski actually stood in the doorway, thinking about the social dynamics of it.

The small tables were usually occupied by the non-sworn members of the Greenfield Police Department, such as the PSOs, or Social Worker Debra Santiago, or probationary officers with their FTOs.

This was due to the unwritten department rule, the large round table, was to be used only by the cops on the force.

Granted, there was no assigned seating, but just like roll call seating, everyone usually sat in the same chair, during both of these instances.

Except, whenever Chief Fitzsimons stopped by the lunchroom, at exactly 1200 hours, whenever his schedule allowed it. Then everything was up for grabs in a number of different ways.

The whole dynamics of the table seating was something a sociologist, or psychologist, would love. This was especially true now, with a sergeant's test coming up in three months, when the current list expired.

Every prospective Greenfield Police Officer who was going to take the test, and usually ate at a different time other than 1200 hours, were now changing their lunch times, to the same time Chief Fitzsimons ate.

Cops were sitting so close to the Chief; he could barely raise his hand to eat.

Deputy Chief Gyondski just shook his head in the doorway, as he walked over to the refrigerator and put his lunch bag on the empty top shelf. Then he left the lunchroom and headed to the men's locker room, which was located directly next door.

Arriving at his locker, he gently placed his green travel bag on the brown bench, which separated the lockers in the aisle.

He fumbled with the combination on his Master lock, which didn't seem to want to open.

Three separate times he tried the numbers 17 left, 43 right, and then 17 left with no success.

Frustrated, he tried once more, before the hinge of the lock, finally separated itself from the cylinder.

Removing the lock, from the front of his locker, he put it on top of his green travel bag.

Quickly he opened his skinny locker, anxious to get started at the range.

Apparently, Beth's training at home had carried over to her husband's professional life as well.

The inside of Deputy Chief Gyondski's locker, could be summed up in one word, immaculate. Every single item from shampoo, to used ticket books on the top shelf, were straight, with nothing loose anywhere inside the locker.

Carefully, he took off his Kimber Model 2145 holster, which was designed specifically to hold his 40 Caliber Kimber. He stopped momentarily, with the holster containing his weapon, still in his left hand and looked at the full-length mirror at the end of his aisle.

The mirror had a 45-caliber size hole, near the bottom of it, due to someone at shift change dropping their off-duty gun, while removing it carelessly from its holster.

Upon hitting the ground, the weapon discharged one round, resulting in the hole in the mirror.

The Greenfield Police Department had gone through two additional and similar incidents in Deputy Chief Gyondki's career, where duty weapons had gone off, either inside the police station, or in one case, a shotgun round, through the floor of a squad car.

Fortunately, the bullets hurt no one, in all of these incidents.

Although, a few people involved, had to change their underwear immediately afterwards.

When he took over the Police Department, Chief Fitzsimons decided not to replace the damaged mirror in the men's locker room.

His message was clear, he wanted it to serve as a daily reminder to all his personnel, to practice weapon safety, everywhere they might be.

Deputy Chief Gyondski's eyes went from the damaged mirror, to the top of his locker, as he gently placed the holster and weapon in a designated spot for this item. He then removed his Sam Browne duty belt from the silver hook it had been hanging on, from the locker door.

Remembering the damaged mirror, he carefully checked the holster carrying his department-issued, Berretta 92SB, confirming it was locked properly and the weapon was secure.

It had been months since he had actually worn his duty belt and it was a bit harder getting it on, around his bulging waist. With the duty belt on, he moved items, such as his OC spray, radio holder, and his ASP Baton, to the correct spots on the belt.

Finally, he took four, black-colored basketweave keepers, from the top shelf of his locker.

Strategically, he put them on his Sam Browne belt, which resulted in the belt being secure, against his uniform pants belt.

Upon finishing, he picked up the lock from on top of his green-colored travel bag and held it in his right hand.

He then picked up the travel bag by its strap and hung it inside the locker.

When finished, he slammed the locker shut, attached the lock to it and paused for a moment, to make sure he had everything he needed for qualifications.

Confident he did, he exited the locker room, walked past the lunchroom, and down the hallway. At the end of the hallway, he turned left and walked past the evidence room, until he was standing outside the door leading to the range.

Opening this door, he passed through another door which he wasn't sure why was in the open position, and then found himself standing at the rear door of the Range Master's booth.

Silently he stood there, watching Range Master Dietz writing notes inside some type of log, apparently for an officer who had just left the range.

Deputy Chief Gyondski came to this conclusion based on the fact he could smell burnt gunpowder in the air and saw spent shell casings from his vantage point, on the floor of range booth two.

It didn't take long for Dietz to sense someone was standing behind him, as he quickly turned around and seeing Deputy Chief Gyondski said "Pleasure to see you boss, may I help you?"

Without hesitation Deputy Chief Gyondski responded, "Well Range Master Dietz, could you somehow fit me into your schedule today and allow me the opportunity to qualify?"

A huge grin appeared on Range Master Dietz's face as he answered enthusiastically, "Sure," followed up with, "I'll even call the radio room sir and let them know you're with me in case someone needs to contact you."

"Thanks," Deputy Chief Gyondski answered, as he knew exactly what he needed to do next.

Leaving the booth, he went through a singular glass door, which allowed him access to the shooting range. He was surprised by the burnt gunpowder smell, considering there were two huge installed wall fans going at full blast, located at opposite ends, of the shooting area of the range.

Deputy Chief Gyondski walked over to the shooting booth with a large black number 3 decal located on the front of it. With his left hand, he lowered a panel that completely covered the entire front of the booth and prevented him from going any farther in this booth.

With his Beretta still holstered, he found the magazine release for the weapon and pressed it, allowing the magazine to slowly slide out of the weapon and fall into his left hand. He took this magazine and put it on the same panel, he had just lowered.

Next, he carefully removed the Beretta from his holster and pulled the slide back on the weapon, with his right hand, while holding the weapon tightly with his left hand.

When the slide on the weapon was fully back and in the locked position, the last 9mm round inside the weapon ejected, landing by his right foot.

With the weapon still pointed down range, he carefully tilted it so he could inspect the interior, as required by department procedure and formality more than practicality. He knew it was almost physically impossible for another 9mm round to still be in the weapon, without a magazine still inside of it.

Satisfied the weapon was safe, he placed it alongside the magazine, on the panel inside the booth.

He turned around in the booth, intending to go to a table and empty the other two magazines for the weapon, which were still inside their pouches, on his Sam Browne belt.

But then he found Range Master Dietz standing at the rear of the range, holding different items, in each of his hands.

In his right hand, was a black plastic case, with the word Glock on the side of it.

In his left hand, were two plastic bags, which Deputy Chief Gyondski could clearly see contained a black-colored, leather holster, as well as new magazine pouches.

Deputy Chief Gyondski was getting his birthday present early.

With all of the craziness in the past months, he was aware the Department had ordered new Glock 22's, Gen 4 for all duty personnel, along with new magazine pouches, for the weapons.

He wasn't sure when these weapons would be delivered, or if a qualification course had been designed by Range Master

Dietz, and approved by the Director of Training, Sgt. Jack Paskiewiecz.

Unknown to Gyondski, some squads such as Lt. Wayne's, had already been issued their Glocks, passed the qualifications course and were carrying them on the street for a while.

While Gyondski was excited to fire the new Glock 22 Gen 4, he was actually more excited to try the new attachment this weapon would have, the Koldttette, 300 flashlight.

In the old qualification course for some reason, he always had problems in the stage where he had to fire 12 rounds, while holding his Terra Lux, Model Lightstar, 220 in his right hand.

Not being the strongest physical specimen in the first place, played a major role in this problem, but he never felt confident, no matter how much Range Master Dietz worked with him, on different techniques and grips to use the flashlight and shoot at the same time.

With the purchase of this flashlight, those problems should be a thing in the past. The Glock 22 Gen 4 was capable of having the flashlight attached to the bottom of it and activated by a simple switch, located on the grip of the weapon.

Gyondski hated to admit it, but Chief Fitzsimons had spared no expense in this situation.

The last item purchased for the Glocks, was probably the most important of all.

Each officer would now be using a level three holster, made specifically for the Glock 22 Gen 4, with the Koldttette, 300 flashlight attachment.

Obviously, no police officer wanted to be killed in the line of duty. More specifically, no police officer wanted to be killed by an individual, who was able to get the officer's duty weapon, out of that officer's holster and kill them with it.

The previous administration felt strongly about getting their officers properly equipped, when they purchased the Berretta for them, with a level one style holster.

Some officers loved it, due to the simplicity of it and the ability for the officer to get their weapon out easily.

Unfortunately, this wasn't lost on convicts as well.

While still a rookie, Deputy Chief Gyondski was introduced, by his FTO John Shay, to a series of Caliber Press Books, called *Street Survival* and *The Tactical Edge*. The pictures in these books showed convicts at penitentiaries across the United States, on prison exercise yards, practicing how to disarm and kill police officers.

Many of these pictures showed the major problem was that the officer put the prisoner in a poor search position. When the opportunity allowed, the prisoner would turn around and far too often, be able to get the officer's duty weapon, in only a few seconds. The outcome would often be a headshot by the suspect, resulting in instant death to the police officer.

These new level three holsters were designed to prevent such an incident from occurring, due to a multi-step process the officer would have to use, before the weapon could be released from the holster.

"Ready to go through our department qualification round with your new toys?" Range Master Dietz asked, confident he already knew what Deputy Chief Gyondski's answer would be.

Gyondski surprised him by instead of answering, looked at his wristwatch.

Then, with an inquisitive tone in his voice he asked, "How long does it take my friend?"

"With the way you shoot, should have you done in 75 minutes," Dietz answered.

Deputy Chief Gyondski knew Dietz was blowing smoke up his ass, since he wasn't even close to being an accurate shooter.

Deputy Chief Gyondski's watch showed, 1500 Hours exactly.

If Dietz was correct, he would have plenty of time to get the new gear on his duty belt, have a brief training session on all three new toys, as Dietz called them, shoot, clean the weapon, shower, eat and still be ready for the Greenfield Village Board Meeting.

"Let's do it," Deputy Chief Gyondski said enthusiastically, realizing this was the perfect opportunity to get this over with today and kill some time.

"Excellent Boss," Dietz answered and followed up with, "Take the two remaining magazines for your Beretta and put them on the panel, next to the weapon please."

Deputy Chief Gyondski did exactly as instructed and quickly removed both of them. When finished, he turned back around again to find Dietz's left arm extended directly in front of Deputy Chief Gyondski's body, while still holding the clear plastic bag.

"Boss, take this into the men's locker room and swap it out with your old stuff." Pausing only a second, Dietz continued, "When you finish doing it, come back in here and I'll run you through the entire process."

"Got it," Deputy Chief Gyondski responded and then grabbed the plastic bag and headed for the men's locker room.

While walking quickly down the hallway and nearing the lunchroom, Deputy Chief Gyondski could see Lt. Wayne conducting roll call for his shift, through a small glass window, in the training room door.

"Fuck," Deputy Chief Gyondski suddenly realized, this might not be the best idea after all.

The last thing he needed right now, was to have contact with any Greenfield Personnel about a particular issue, or problem they were experencing. He made a quick 180-degree turn and headed directly back to the range; thankful he hadn't encountered anyone in the hallway.

Range Master Dietz's face showed a look of confusion, as he watched Deputy Chief Gyondski enter the back of the range, while still holding the clear plastic bag, he gave him only a few minutes earlier.

"Tell you what," Deputy Chief Gyondski said. "Let's do everything right here for now."

With an inquisitive tone in his voice, Dietz answered, "You're the boss."

Before the word "boss" had even come out of Dietz's mouth, Gyondski was taking his basketweave keepers off his duty belt and dropping them on a table. For roughly the next 20 to 25 minutes he took off his old duty gear and then put on his brand-new holster, as well as magazine holders. It took a tad longer than he wanted, due to the new leather. Both items were rigid and hard to adjust properly.

Upon finishing and getting them both in the exact spot he wanted, he again attached his basketweave keepers, to his Sam Browne belt.

Quickly, he glanced at his watch, which read 1547 hours.

He felt comfortable with the time and believed he was in good shape, if everything went the way Dietz had promised.

Apparently, no one had ever explained Murphy's Law to him.

Things started out innocently enough, with Dietz showing him the proper procedure for using the new level three holster.

Next, using his own Glock 22 Gen 4, Dietz showed him how easy it was to use the new Koldttette, 300 flashlight. Deputy Chief Gyondski was amazed at what little pressure he needed to apply to the switch, located on the Glock's grip to activate the light.

"Any questions?" Dietz asked, after completing this particular part of the training process.

With a direct tone in his voice, Deputy Chief Gyondski answered, "No."

"Good, good," Dietz answered, "Let's go shoot and get you done."

Dietz immediately headed to the shooting area of the range, followed closely by Gyondski.

While passing again through the glass door, to get to the shooting area of the range, Deputy Chief Gyondski glanced at his watch and was comfortable things were on time. His watch read 1622 hours, and his stress level decreased noticeably.

When he and Dietz reached booth number 3, Gyondski noticed his old items had been replaced by his new Glock 22 Gen 4, with the Koldettette, 300 flashlight.

The Glock 22 Gen 4 was in the locked back position.

"The weapon's safe, Boss, so go ahead and pick it up," Dietz said.

Deputy Chief Gyondski did just that and felt like he was holding something out of a Star Wars movie.

The weapon looked like nothing he had ever seen before in his law enforcement career. Being made entirely of plastic had something to do with it, plus the fact it was empty.

But what really made it look like some type of laser weapon, was the flashlight attached to the bottom of it.

"You ready to qualify?" Dietz asked, which suddenly brought Deputy Chief Gyondski out of his world of fascination and back into the world of reality.

A meek "Yes," was all Deputy Chief Gyondski could mumble, mainly due to his embarrassment of playing with the Glock 22 Gen 4, which he handed back to Dietz.

"Good, good but before we do, you're going to notice the new holster rides a bit higher than the old one you used for years. Don't fret, after maybe a week to ten days at the most, it should be broken in and you'll be fine," Dietz said.

"10-4," Deputy Chief Gyondski responded.

Apparently, Dietz was going to go the extra mile, due to Deputy Chief Gyondski's rank, because he continued talking about the new holster. "Now, when you're really going to notice the new level three holster, is when you're sitting down, or obviously driving. But again, it's like anything else new, it will simply take some time to get use to."

Deputy Chief Gyondski had no response other than to give Dietz a death stare. As in the past, when he used this look on other Greenfield personnel, it had an immediate impact.

"Hey, hey, enough talk," Dietz responded. "Why don't we get you qualified?"

"Thank you," Deputy Chief Gyondski answered dryly.

Apparently, Range Master Dietz was busy, while Gyondski had been switching out his old equipment for new. The entire floor of the range was clear of every single shell casing, which he hadn't seen before and both fans had been turned off, allowing for better communication between the two of them.

Secondly, silhouetted nicely down range, was the traditional paper target, of a male upper torso, which the Greenfield Police Department had used for years, in qualifying their personnel.

Only this time, Deputy Chief Gyondski noticed a small change in the appearance of the target. A green-colored piece of paper, had been placed squarely in the middle of the head of the target.

"Okay, follow me," Range Master Dietz said with newfound enthusiasm and energy.

Deputy Chief Gyondski proceeded to follow him down range, stopping when they both reached a black line painted on the ground, which ran the width of the range.

While standing side by side, with their toes on the line, both turned, so they were now facing each other.

"You noticed the green paper in the middle of the target's head?" Dietz asked

"Yup," was all Deputy Chief Gyondski mumbled for a response.

"From this distance Boss, and with your new Glock, you should have no problem easily hitting green with all of your head shots, which you're going to need to do, to qualify and pass this course," Dietz said.

"Then God dammit, let's get started," Deputy Chief Gyondski responded tersely, wanting to make sure Dietz was getting the message, he needed to get this show on the road.

Instantly, Dietz began reading from a typed piece of paper, which was laminated, and turned out to be the total course of fire, Deputy Chief Gyondski would be doing with his new Glock 22 Gen 4. This instruction took close to three minutes due to explaining how many rounds would be fired, righthanded, lefthanded, but also walking off the distance they would be fired from.

To emphasize the proper distance, Dietz walked Deputy Chief Gyondski, starting from the five-yard line, backwards and stopped at each distance the shooting would take place from, until they had reached the rear of the range, before the shooting booths, which was a total distance of 25 yards.

Upon finishing reading off the laminated sheet, Dietz asked very nonchalantly, "Any questions about anything I just covered?"

"Not... a ...one," Deputy Chief Gyondski answered.

The tone in Deputy Chief Gyondski's voice was a sudden wake up call for Dietz.

Upon hearing it, Dietz practically ran back to where they had started, at the five-yard line.

Deputy Chief Gyondski didn't run, instead, he walked slowly and collected his thoughts. Probably out of habit, he again glanced at his watch. It showed 1700 hours and he began to worry a bit. When he reached the five-yard line, he found Dietz standing there again, with both of his hands full of items. In Dietz's left hand were three brand new, fully loaded magazines, for Deputy Chief Gyondski's Glock 22 Gen 4. In his right hand, was a set of earmuffs, black in color, along with a clear pair of shooting glasses.

Deputy Chief Gyondski took two of the magazines out of Dietz's left hand, putting them instinctively in their pouches, located on the right side, of his Sam Browne duty belt. Next, he took the ear muffs from Dietz and placed them over his ears. He finished by putting on the shooting glasses, which would protect his eyes in the event of a cartridge somehow ejecting, in an awkward fashion and hitting him in the face. When he was satisfied the glasses were fitting properly, he took the remaining magazine from Dietz.

Turning his body so he was now standing facing the paper target, Deputy Chief Gyondski removed his Glock 22 Gen 4 from the top of his holster. Aiming the weapon forward, he slid the magazine into the weapon and dropped the slide in the process. He then fully secured the Glock 22 Gen 4 in his new holster.

Slowly, he began taking full, deep breaths, in and forcefully blowing them out of his mouth, in an attempt to totally relax his body, improve his shooting and qualify on the first attempt.

"Okay, your first course of fire will be a total of eight rounds, six of them center mass, with the remaining two going to the head," Dietz said, reading it off the laminated sheet.

"Is the line ready?" Dietz said, from his new position, which was behind Deputy Chief Gyondski and off to the right.

Quickly, Deputy Chief Gyondski raised his left hand indicating he had heard the request and was prepared to shoot.

With only a slight pause, Dietz continued. "The line is ready.... fire," Dietz yelled.

On the word, fire, Gyondski put his left hand on the black colored grip of the Glock, pushed down hard with the weapon, then pulled it back, while releasing the safety on the holster in the process, as he had been trained.

The Glock never moved more than two inches, remaining in his holster.

"Fire," Dietz yelled again.

Once more Deputy Chief Gyondski pushed down on the weapon, only this time pulling it directly back towards Dietz, in an effort to get it out of its holster. No such luck and after two separate attempts to shoot, he had been unable to get his freaking gun, out of his holster.

A combination of anger and embarrassment flowed through him, as he quickly raised his left, weapon-free hand into the air, indicating there was a problem.

Deputy Chief Gyondski slowly turned around, took off his earmuffs and placed them on top of his head.

Sheepishly, Dietz walked over, so he was now standing face to face, with Deputy Chief Gyondski.

Raising his earmuffs so they were now on top of his head as well, Dietz said, "You need to push down hard then pull the weapon directly back towards you, while releasing the safety on the holster sir."

"I did it just the way you trained me," Deputy Chief Gyondski responded, with clear signs of his frustration evident on his face.

"Okay, okay, watch me," Dietz said and then turned his entire body so he was now standing, facing the east wall of the range.

While Deputy Chief Gyondski looked on intently, in one quick, fluid motion, Dietz used his right hand to push down hard on his Glock and in less than 2 seconds, the weapon had cleared his holster and was pointing directly at the east wall in front of him.

"Again," Dietz said and for the second time, he went through the proper procedure and had his weapon out and pointed at the east wall again.

"You want to try again Deputy Chief, or call it a day?" Dietz asked.

Quickly, Gyondski brought his left arm up in front of his face and through his clear, plastic glasses, looked at his watch, which read 1717 hours.

"Hmm," he said, trying to decide in his mind what to do.

In a little over two hours, he would be presenting the future building of the Greenfield Police Department, to the Greenfield Village Board.

But he was already here, dressed, ready to get this done, even if the window for getting it done, showering, and eating, was getting smaller by the minute.

The getting it done now argument won out.

"Let's do it right now," he said rather enthusiastically, to the pleasure of Dietz, who once again resumed his previous position.

Again, Deputy Chief Gyondski turned, so he was facing the silhouetted target, five yards directly in front of him and then lowered his earmuffs, adjusting them, so they fit perfectly.

For the second time in less than a half hour, Dietz said, "Is the line ready?"

Again, Deputy Chief Gyondski raised his left hand, indicating he was ready.

As he was lowering his left hand, Dietz yelled as loud as he could, "Fire."

Smoothly, this time Deputy Chief Gyondski pushed down hard on his Glock, pulled it back and released the safety properly.

His new Glock 22 Gen 4 moved even less than the first two previous attempts.

He could feel the sweat starting to form on his upper lip. This time, Dietz walked over so he was standing next to him and also facing the target, directly in front of them.

"Boss, fold your arms across your chest for a minute, I want to try something," Dietz said.

He did as he was asked, but was rather curious, as to what Dietz was going to do next.

He didn't have long to wait as Dietz used his right hand and pushed down hard and back on Deputy Chief Gyondski's Glock 22 Gen 4. After releasing the safety, the weapon should have come out of its holster, but Gyondski's gun never moved never moved.

"Okay, okay, Sergeant Paskiewiecz and I were aware this might be an issue with this flashlight and holster arrangement."

Deputy Chief Gyondski immediately turned, so once again he was facing Dietz, this time their faces were only inches part.

"Explain," Deputy Chief Gyondski stated.

"This combination of flashlight, with this type of level three holster, has a minor, minor, history of sometimes not releasing the Glock 22 Gen 4 properly," Dietz said.

"What?" Deputy Chief Gyondski yelled, right into Dietz's face.

"Boss, boss, I can fix this. Trust me, it's not the gun which is fine" Dietz answered.

"How?" Deputy Chief Gyondski asked.

"Just take your duty belt off and let me use some sandpaper to smooth out your holster, after I carefully remove your Glock, of course," Dietz said.

Deputy Chief Gyondski wasn't convinced at all and stared at Dietz.

"Deputy Chief, really, I have the sandpaper in the rear of the range, back by the cleaning supplies," said Dietz. "Trust me, this will work and hardly damage the holster in the process."

Deputy Chief Gyondski didn't need to hear another word and immediately began taking his basketweave keepers off his Sam Browne duty belt. When finished, he handed the belt to Dietz, who took it and walked toward the rear of the range.

Deputy Chief Gyondski was standing alone, on a partially lit shooting range, holding four black-colored basketweave keepers, in his left hand.

He decided to follow Dietz, whom he found seated at the

cleaning table, behind the range booth, working feverishly on the holster, with a piece of sandpaper.

He saw his new Glock, laying back in the original case, with the lid up, next to Dietz's left foot.

Dietz must have felt Deputy Chief Gyondski watching him and while still working on the holster, Dietz said, "About ten more minutes Boss."

Gyondski saw an old metal chair, orange in color, off in the corner and headed directly for it.

When he reached it, he turned and slowly lowered himself into it.

He dropped his head, opened his legs, and stared directly at the brown-colored, concrete floor.

Slowly he closed his eyes, trying to collect his thoughts.

Deputy Chief Gyondski was totally enervated over the craziness of the past two and a half hours.

He began controlling his breathing and trying to rest.

"Okay sir good as new," an exuberant Dietz yelled, as he stood over Deputy Chief Gyondski, holding the Sam Browne duty belt in his right hand.

The brief rest apparently helped, as Gyondski jumped out of the chair and looked straight at Dietz, who had a huge, shit-eating grin on his face.

"Watch Boss," Dietz said.

Gyondski looked on, as Dietz took the Glock 22 Gen 4, placed it in the holster and then, with little effort, pulled it out.

He did these three consecutive times, without an issue.

Deputy Chief Gyondski grabbed his own duty belt, complete with the Glock 22 Gen 4 back in the holster and, after moving his OC spray and radio holder around for a minute, applied the basketweave keepers.

When finished he looked at Dietz and said, "Let's do this."

"Yes Sir," Dietz yelled and headed for the door, which would lead them back out to the five-yard line.

"Deputy Chief Gyondski, 4312, 4312," Melissa Prezlicke's voice came over the police station page.

Deputy Chief Gyondski headed for the nearest phone, which was located inside the range booth, while Dietz waited for him.

Dialing in the code 4312, he waited patiently, refreshed from his short nap.

Melissa Prezlicke picked up, after the second ring and in a soft voice asked, "Deputy Chief, is that you?"

"Yes Melissa," he answered patiently.

"Deputy Chief, there is a John Lamond waiting for you in the lobby," she said softly into the telephone.

"Excuse me," he said into his phone.

"Sorry, but he said he tried calling you on your cell a number of times and you never answered."

Transferring the phone to his right hand, he looked at his watch, which read 1855 hours.

Covering the telephone mouthpiece with his left hand, he looked directly at Dietz and yelled, "What the hell?"

Dietz responded by cocking his head to the left and raising both his hands, as if he was surrendering.

Taking his hand off the mouthpiece, Deputy Chief Gyondski said as calmly as he could, "Tell Mr. Lamond to grab a seat in the lobby and I'll be up as soon as I can."

"Yes Sir," she replied.

Deputy Chief Gyondski breezed past Dietz and headed straight to the men's locker room, taking his Verizon phone out of his left pants pocket in the process.

He then realized; the phone was on vibrate only.

The screen showed three missed phone calls, one from Beth, two hours ago and two from John Lamond, within the past 20 minutes.

Reaching his locker, he calmly put his combination in and pulled the lock hard, hoping it would actually open for once on the first pull. It did and he let out a sigh of relief.

Taking his Sam Browne duty belt, he checked to make sure the Glock 22 Gen 4 was safely secured inside its holster, before hanging it on the hook inside his locker. Next, he took off his white uniform dress shirt in record time.

He never thought his night would blow up like this.

While taking off his white Hanes t-shirt, he realized he didn't have time to shower and put on the beautiful, Joseph A. Bank suit, which was hanging in the travel bag directly in front of him.

Even though his stomach was growling, the possibility of eating dinner had passed him over an hour ago.

With the t-shirt off, he held it in his left hand, while picking up his uniform dress shirt, from the locker room floor with his right hand. He rolled them together into a ball and threw them into the floor of his locker, which was a completely uncharacteristic move for him.

"You can still save this Frank, c'mon," he said softly to himself.

He quickly grabbed a clean white, Hanes t-shirt, from a hanger in his locker and followed the same procedure with a dress uniform shirt.

Next, he grabbed his Sam Browne duty belt, off its locker hook, before suddenly stopping.

"Fuck," he said softly, afraid someone in the bathroom might have heard him.

He didn't have a duty weapon, since he hadn't qualified with his new Glock 22 Gen 4 and his Beretta was still on the range, with Dietz.

Instinctively, he reached for his off duty 40 Caliber Kimber, which was still laying on the top shelf of his locker. Carefully, he slid it onto his uniform pants belt, moving it to the left-hand side of his body.

He glanced once more at the top shelf of his locker, verifying that it contained nothing else he would need for tonight's meeting, which would start in 24 minutes. Convinced he had everything he needed, he started to close the locker door, but stopped when he saw something taped to the inside of the door.

He couldn't remember when he had put it on the door and he hadn't glanced at it for quite some time now, but if ever there was time for needing it, the time was right now.

It was an old prayer card, with a picture of Jesus Christ on the front of it, with the saying, "Jesus, I trust in you," on the bottom of the card.

Ripping the card off the locker door, he turned it over and saw a prayer for Divine Mercy on the back.

Slowly, he read the prayer to himself, while holding the card in his left hand.

When finished he said, "Amen," and quickly crossed himself.

He then reattached the card to the locker door.

Violently, he slammed the locker doors shut, put the combination lock back on the locker and pulled on it once to guarantee, the lock didn't open.

The lock was as secure, as his faith and love in Jesus Christ.

He walked out of the locker room, down the corridor and up the stairs, until he was standing outside his office door.

Unlike earlier today, his hands were free, so he was able to get his keys out and his door opened quickly.

He walked directly to his desk, and picked up an accordion style folder, which contained all the plans for the new Greenfield Police Station.

He then walked back, with the folder in his right hand, to his office door.

Since he had left the key in the lock, he was able to save time and lock the door quickly, putting the keys into his right pants pocket.

Walking down the corridor, he stopped quickly in the dispatch center and yelled to Susie Patz, "I'll be at the Village Hall for a Board Meeting."

"Kick ass Boss," she yelled back.

He took five steps, turned right, and walked out the exit door, which led to the main lobby of the police station.

Sitting in a black suit with polished black shoes and a white dress shirt with a grey and charcoal-colored tie was John Lamond.

If looking good was the only issue Gyondski thought, then the new police station was a sure thing. Deputy Chief Gyondski walked up to Lamond, who stood up instantly when he saw him approaching.

He stopped when he was within two to three feet of Lamond, and they stood face to face for possibly the last time ever.

Strangely, not a word was said between the two of them.

For some reason, each had a goofy smile on their faces.

After about five seconds, Deputy Chief Gyondski simply said, "You ready?"

"Ready," was all Lamond responded with and then followed Deputy Chief Gyondski out the front door of the police station toward the Greenfield Village Hall.

Because it was located directly next door to the Greenfield Police Station, their walk took less than three minutes.

Upon reaching the door leading to the boardroom, Gyondski stopped and pulled out his Verizon phone, which showed 1926 hours.

He turned off the phone, put it back in his left pants pocket, and confidently strolled into the boardroom with Lamond right behind him.

As they headed for the front row for seating for Village employees, he was momentarily caught off guard to see Chief Fitzsimons and Deputy Chief Bart already seated side by side in the second row.

Deputy Chief Gyondski reached his seat and put the accordion folder between himself and Lamond, who took the third seat in the front row.

As if someone had put a firecracker up his ass, Gyondski immediately jumped up, walked over to the lectern where the village employees' laptop was located and reaching into his left pants pocket, removed a small silver and black thumb drive.

Quickly, he installed the thumb drive into the laptop and within a minute the screen located behind where the Village President, Village Attorney and six Village Trustees would sit, lit up with the wording, Greenfield Police Station Proposal.

He closed the proposal and replaced it with the generic slide showing the Village of Greenfield Village Board Meeting, with today's date on the bottom of it. He had perfect timing because just as this slide was up, all the Village Trustees were taking their seats on the dais.

The Greenfield Police Station proposal was first on the agenda so after the pledge of allegiance and some other formalities he was called.

Deputy Chief Gyondski did all of the talking and his Power Point presentation, backed by his few additional comments, was flawless.

Only Village Trustee Phillip Black had one comment and Deputy Chief Gyondski was ready for anything this trustee would throw at him.

Trustee Black had taken on the responsibility of being the guardian of all Greenfield spending up for approval by the Greenfield Village Board. He had acquired a reputation of watching every bid brought in front of them as if the money was coming out of his very own pocket. Shockingly, his question was so innocuous, Deputy Chief Gyondski was able to answer it easily.

After having his question answered, Trustee Black motioned to approve the Greenfield Police Station proposal, which was seconded by Trustee Dementris.

The approval passed unanimously and the new Greenfield Police Station was a go.

Now, leaning back in his swivel office chair, Gyondski couldn't wipe the shit-eating grin off his face as he relished his accomplishment from last night and looked forward to a great weekend ahead with Beth.

"Nice job last night Frankie," a voice said and he recognized it immediately from their telephone conversation the day of Chris Mills' death.

Quickly, Deputy Chief Gyondski turned his swivel chair towards the open door of his office and watched as the figure approached his desk.

"Trustee Coconato?" Deputy Chief Gyondski asked, which was strange due to each of them being acquaintances for the past three years.

"Relax Frankie, I was over at the Village Hall picking up some mail I forgot last night and I thought I would stop in and tell you again what a great job you did with the new police station proposal," Coconato said as he stopped walking and stood on the left side of Deputy Chief Gyondski's desk.

"I've been singing your praises to anyone who will listen like I did last night to all my fellow Village Trustees," continued Coconato.

Deputy Chief Gyondski had an uncomfortable feeling about this whole situation and stood up, trying to figure out whether to close his office door or not.

Trustee Coconato could see the fear on Gyondski's face for he commented," Frankieeee c'mon relax and enjoy your achievement.

Apparently, his comments were having very little impact on Gyondski, who was still looking like a cat in a room with nine rocking chairs.

Again, Trustee Coconato attempted to ease Gyondski's nerves by stepping a bit closer and saying, "Hey, I spoke to the pricks secretary before I walked down here and she told me he's at some luncheon for a while".

"Who you calling a prick?" Chief Fitzsimons asked, while standing in the open office door.

CHAPTER 20

"Hi, this is Megan. I can't get to the phone right now so please leave a message at the beep unless you're that asshole Kurt Thompson, who can go fuck himself."

"Bitch," Kurt yelled out loud in his Gilles squad car.

Fortunately, he wasn't driving. Instead, he was parked behind Zechmeister's Deli, on Milwaukee Avenue.

Holding his cell phone in his right hand, Kurt actually stared at it, confused by the whole situation.

Exactly two weeks ago, to the minute, Megan had held a similar cell phone belonging to Kurt in her small, delicate, quivering hands, when she learned her fellow Greenfield Police Officer Ron Thomas was dead.

Shortly thereafter, Megan totally lost her mind, accusing Kurt of Ron Thomas death.

"Based on what Megan?" Kurt asked. "The fact we both were in Door County at the same time?"

As he looked on in amazement, Megan stood up, took his phone, and threw it as hard as she could on to the floor, causing it to shatter in the process.

"You hated all of us Greenfield cops the first time you met us at ILETC, didn't you asshole?"

Megan then turned and walked quickly towards the east exit doors of the food court. Kurt walked two steps behind Megan, confused as hell as what other patrons were thinking, as well as worried about what he would do when he finally caught up to her.

Kurt stopped at the last set of doors leading to the parking lot of Old Mill Mall.

As he watched, Megan got into her car, threw the gear shifter into drive and gunned it. Within seconds she was flying out of the lot without any regard for parked cars in the parking lot, customers walking, or other motorists. In a flash, Megan was gone from Kurt and possibly his life.

That was the last time Kurt Thompson had any contact with her for the past two weeks. During those two weeks, Kurt had called, texted and emailed Megan nonstop after he had gotten his new iPhone from Verizon. No response is what he got despite trying every method.

In a move he feared could backfire, he drove out to her Antioch townhouse, checking for her Volkswagen Passat, twice in the past six days, with negative results.

Finally, he decided to give it a rest and see if she would regain her sanity. Kurt had to admit she was correct about his hatred for the entire Greenfield cadet class, except for Megan of course. All it took was him meeting all of them one time. Secondly, the fact he wasn't really bent out of shape over either Chris Mills' or Ron Thomas's deaths didn't exactly help their relationship. But to actually think he would go as far as to play a role in the killing of one of them was a bit much, to say the least.

He had bigger, more serious problems to deal with right now, besides Megan. His job with the Gilles Police Department was in jeopardy. Ever since he and Francesca had become serious, Kurt's work performance had steadily declined.

With his FTO, Kurt was second on his entire shift in tickets written and arrests made for three straight months. But after being free from his FTO, he was near the bottom in these same categories. Worse, Kurt was having trouble concentrating at work mainly due to exhaustion from sex and constant text messages from Francesca.

As a result, his supervisors were rejecting his police reports due to a lack of essential information on a daily basis. Everything seemed to be falling apart at once for him.

In the past month, he even had a complaint made against him from a Wilmette citizen. This complaint should never have taken place because he had received eight hours of training in Verbal Judo at the Illinois law Enforcement Training Center. The consensus among most of the cadets, when they talked over a beer or meal in the cafeteria, was Verbal Judo was the best course they had received at ILETC.

Taught by a retired Elmwood Park cop, Joe Trunkale, the course centered on dealing with an irate public in a wide variety of situations, such as traffic stops, field interviews, and even arrest situations. A heavy-set Italian, in his early sixties, Trunkale might not have been the most gifted speaker, but he had the attention of every cadet in the classroom the day he introduced them to Verbal Judo. Every cadet realized it was a rarity to learn something they could use in their professional lives on a daily basis and maybe even occasionally in their personal lives as well.

Through a series of different instruction techniques, role playing, squad car videos of traffic stops and lecture, Trunkale was able to get his message across to the entire class. A key point in Trunkale's message was, "It's the one extra comment—even under your breath—which is said after the incident has been settled. It is totally unnecessary, and it will jam you up and may cost you your job." Kurt nodded his head in agreement when he heard this said in class.

Earlier today, Kurt shook his head in disgust, as he read the result of the department's investigation into his complaint. Written Reprimand, based on the findings of his Commander Al Billings, with the last sentence stating, "Any future complaints, if found to be sustained, will result in harsher disciplinary actions taken by this Police Department."

Kurt realized it was time to get his head on straight and forget Megan. He needed to save his career. Old Mill Mall was having a problem with non-handicapped parkers, taking the parking spots of handicapped parkers. So, the property manager for the shopping center, William Coyne, did what anyone else would do in a similar situation. Coyne called the only government official he knew, a Village Trustee, who got the ball rolling.

This trustee then called the Village President, who called the Village Manager, who called the Police Chief, who then called in his Deputy Chief of Operations. The Deputy Chief of Operations put out a memo to all uniformed personnel, asking for special attention to this issue and citations written, when appropriate. Two days after the memo was put out, Kurt finally had Old Mill Shopping Mall in his beat.

William Coyne had been 100% correct. People with no disabilities, some as young as their thirties, were parking in clearly marked handicapped spots, so they could be closer to the front door of stores.

"Lazy assholes," Kurt said to himself, as he watched this happening frequently.

In the span of three hours, in between hot calls, he wrote six tickets, using the same method for each one. Kurt would drive by the offender's car, looking to make sure the handicapped placard wasn't hanging from their rearview mirror and they didn't have a handicapped license plate.

When confirmed, he got the 10-28 off the vehicle, and then he drove away to a quiet spot in the next aisle to write out the citation. Upon finishing, he drove back to where the violator was parked, quickly got out of his Dodge Challenger, put the ticket under the windshield wiper, got back in his squad car and drove away. It was a fool proof system.

After finishing his lunch at his favorite hamburger place, Goodies, he headed back across the street to the Shopping Center and started looking for his next violator. Parked near the entrance to JC Penny, on the Milwaukee Avenue side, he found an ugly diarrhea-colored Lincoln Mercury with a non-handicapped Illinois License plate number of SOP 27.

Using the same method from earlier, he ran the 10-28, which showed the vehicle belonged to a Stanley Pietrowski of 1727 Lincoln Avenue, Elmhurst, Illinois. Pietrowski's date of birth showed him to be 89 years old. In three minutes, Kurt had the ticket written, with Pietrowski's copy inside the attached envelope of the ticket.

Getting out of his squad car, Kurt walked quickly to the driver's side of the Mercury and foolishly looked in and saw the blue-colored handicapped placard laying on the console of the car, next to the gear shift lever.

"Fuck me," he said out loud.

Without hesitation, he put the ticket under the driver's windshield wiper and turned to get back inside his squad car. This time his plan had failed.

"Officer, officer please wait," a man yelled at him, as he came out of the front door of JC Penny.

Kurt stood next to his squad car in a slight state of shock. Slowly moving at a snail's pace toward him, was an elderly individual with a huge, unlit cigar in the corner of his mouth. This individual was dressed in a black baseball cap and old blue jeans, which were held up by the widest, brown belt Kurt had ever seen. Even though it was 1430 hours and the temperature was in the high 70s, the man wore a tan, zipped jacket.

A normal person would have made the trip from the front doors of JC Penny to Kurt in about a minute or two minutes at the most. It took this individual a good five to six minutes, as he shuffled more than walked toward Kurt.

"Here comes trouble, I can feel it," Kurt said out loud to no one in particular.

This individual stopped directly in front of him. Before either party could say a word, the elderly man raised his right hand and put the palm of it directly in Kurt Thompson's face.

The individual said, "Let me catch my breath for a minute kid."

Kurt stood there motionless but confident he could easily handle this problem with his Verbal Judo Training.

Roughly a minute later, the elderly individual was finally able to speak. "Stanley Pietrowski, so what's your name Officer?"

Before Kurt could answer, Pietrowski extended a shaking right hand which Kurt grabbed also with his right hand.

"Parkinson's," Kurt thought to himself because his Uncle Tommy Thompson had it years ago and he eventually died from it.

With a somewhat soft tone in his voice, Kurt introduced himself to Pietrowski. Upon having Pietrowski's right hand firmly joined with his, he realized just how weak and fragile Pietrowski truly was. Kurt had gotten firmer handshakes from his six-year-old niece Annie. It felt cold and slippery, like he was holding on to an old washcloth, Kurt thought to himself.

"Soooooooooo, Officer Thompson, why are you standing by my car?" Pietrowski asked.

Too late, before Kurt could say a word, Pietrowski had seen the ticket.

"What the hell is that shit under my wiper blade?" he yelled.

In a calm, monotone voice, Kurt said, "Sir you need a handicapped placard issued by the Secretary of State's office if you're going to park in a handicapped parking spot."

"But I have one, really, just look at the mirror," Pietrowski said as his voice became both louder and higher.

Kurt Thompson and Stanley Pietrowski both turned simultaneously and stared at the inside front mirror area for the handicapped placard, which Kurt already knew wouldn't be hanging there.

"What the hell? Some asshole must have stolen it because I know I had one when I went inside Old Mill Mall, Officer Thompson, I swear," Pietrowski blurted out.

He slowly shuffled three steps past Kurt so he was now directly next to the driver's side window of his own car. Slowly bending at the waist, Stanley Pietrowski peered inside.

"Why wouldn't he simply use his car key, which he had in the right pocket of his blue jeans?" thought Kurt.

"There it is! There it is!" Pietrowski screeched so loudly, Kurt thought his ears were going to bleed.

As Kurt looked on, somewhat amused, Stanley Pietrowski had managed to transfer most of his weight onto the left side of his body, which was supported by his brown walking cane. With his right hand free, Stanley Pietrowski continued pointing at the placard, lying inside his car.

"There it is! There it is!" Pietrowski yelled with his voice rising in pitch.

Kurt then broke the cardinal rule of Verbal Judo Trunkale had preached over and over at the Illinois Law Enforcement Training Center: "Never ever lie to the person you're dealing with."

Kurt took two steps from the open door of his squad car so he was now standing directly next to Stanley Pietrowski.

In a calm and professional voice, free of attitude, Kurt said, "My job isn't to look inside your car; instead, it's to enforce the law."

Satisfied with what he had just said, Kurt took two steps back to his squad car and got in. He attempted to close the door, only to find Pietrowski holding it open with both of his arms and his cane laying on the ground.

"Sir, let go off my door," Kurt yelled at Pietrowski while still seated inside his squad car.

"Noooooooooooo," Pietrowski yelled back. "Not until you take that God damn ticket off my car!"

Quickly, Kurt got out of his squad car, pissed off about how things were going. Unbeknownst to him, a small crowd had gathered due to Pietrowski's yelling. Kurt Thompson put his arms on the squad car door to try and pull it away from Pietrowski. No luck and Kurt couldn't figure out where the hell Pietrowski had found this new strength from.

"Time to go to Plan B," Kurt thought.

Using the index finger on his right hand he pointed it directly at Pietrowski's face and said sternly, "Mr. Pietrowski, if you don't let go of my squad car door, I'm going to arrest you for Obstruction of Justice."

The words didn't faze Pietrowski one bit. Then, Kurt made a foolish decision, which he would regret later. Taking two steps forward, Kurt Thompson lightly grabbed hold of Stanley Pietrowski's tan jacket.

"Police Brutality, Police Brutality," Pietrowski began to yell, as his unlit cigar finally fell out of his mouth.

Pietrowski's yelling was so loud, every person in the JC Penny parking lot stopped and stared at the commotion.

"Mr. Pietrowski, please stop yelling," Kurt found himself pleading.

"Attica, Attica," Pietrowski yelled even louder than before.

"Attica?" Kurt Thompson said out loud, confused as to why Pietrowski was yelling it now.

As the parking lot crowd began to swell and move in closer, Kurt sensed their presence for the first time and because of them said, as loud as he could.

"Mr. Pietrowski, this is your final chance to let go of my car door before I arrest you."

"Noooooooooo," Pietrowski shrieked before suddenly going strangely quiet. Pietrowski's hands slid down Kurt's car door.

Before Kurt could say a word, he watched as Stanley Pietrowski's eyes rolled into the back of his head and he fell backward. Fortunately, Kurt still had both of his hands on Pietrowski's jacket and was able to grab hold of him as he fell. With no place to put Stanley Pietrowski's now limp body, Kurt had no choice but to lower him onto the open parking spot.

"Gilles 712," Kurt Thompson yelled into his Motorola shoulder mic.

"Go ahead, 712," Dispatcher Joanne Fontany responded quickly.

"I need an ambulance as well as a supervisor sent to the Milwaukee Avenue side of JC Penny," Kurt yelled.

"10-4," Fontany answered quickly and then realized she had forgotten important information.

"Identify the medical need for the ambulance, 712," Fontany asked.

"Heart Attack," Kurt responded.

"Heart Attack, 10-4, Gilles Fire is on the way," Fontany said.

Instinctively, Kurt left Stanley Pietrowski's left side and ran to the trunk of his squad car. Opening the trunk, with a spare squad car key, he began throwing things around in the trunk until he found what he was looking for. A red, hard case, with the wording, Polous Automated Defibrillator, on the front of it.

He ran back quickly, carrying the defibrillator in his right hand to where Stanley Pietrowki was laying. Pushing his way through the crowd, Kurt kneeled down again on the left side of Pietrowski, placing the defibrillator between Pietrowski and himself.

Looking up quickly at the crowd, which seemed to have doubled in size, Kurt said, "Folks, you need to please back up, immediately."

Kurt then unzipped the case holding the defibrillator. Taking the defibrillator out, he put it on the ground halfway between Pietrowski's belt and face. Next, he took two white pads out of their tin foil packets along with the grey cord they were connected to and plugged the cord into the bottom of the defibrillator.

Kurt Thompson could hear the sound of sirens coming northbound down Milwaukee Avenue. He knew he couldn't wait for them as Pietrowski appeared to have stopped breathing. He opened Pietrowski's tan jacket, to find a green and blue, short sleeve dress shirt.

Without hesitation, Kurt ripped Pietrowski's shirt open, only to find another layer of clothing—the traditional white, sleeveless t-shirt. Kurt grabbed his folding knife, which was clipped on his left pants pocket. While still holding the white t-shirt, he cut it open, straight down the middle, with the folding knife. This entire process took no more than ten seconds, as the edge-bladed knife went through the shirt like a hot kitchen knife going through butter.

With Pietrowski's chest fully exposed, Kurt was able to apply the two, white defibrillator pads to the upper right chest of Pietrowski and down low on the left-hand side of Pietroski's chest.

As loud as he could, while waving his hands like an umpire signaling safe, Kurt yelled, "Stay clear, stay clear!"

It was time to save Pietrowski's life. Kurt firmly pushed the clear, plastic yellow button located in the middle of the defibrillator.

NOTHING.

He pushed the button twice more, only harder each time, in case of a loose wire or battery. Both times he got the same result.

NOTHING.

"Why isn't it working?" an elderly Hispanic woman yelled while standing directly over Kurt and watching.

"He's dying," yelled another person standing in the crowd, on the right side of Pietrowski's body.

For many, they were witnessing something they had never seen before and hopefully would never see ever again—a man dying directly in front of them, with a cop present, doing nothing to save his life.

Kurt was so involved with trying to fix the broken defibrillator, he never saw Lt. Morris, or his Fire Department personnel walking towards him, until he heard, "Let us through please."

As if the Red Sea had parted, the crowd stepped aside and allowed, Lt. Morris, his paramedics, and the engine company personnel through.

Kurt stood up and watched as Lt. Morris' crew quickly took up a position around Pietrowski's body. With one swift move, two of the engine company personnel picked up Pietrowski by the legs and shoulders and placed him on a stretcher, by the two paramedics.

Upon finishing, Lt. Morris and his four engine company personnel walked in a direct path toward the rear doors of the ambulance, while the two paramedics pushed the stretcher behind them.

Kurt looked on in amazement as not a word was said by anyone in the crowd and they easily stepped aside of the oncoming Fire Department personnel.

As soon as the stretcher was put inside the ambulance, a paramedic Kurt had never seen before, started doing chest compressions on Pietrowski, while the other paramedic got the defibrillator inside their ambulance ready.

A member of the engine company left their rig and ran to the cab of the ambulance. Because the ambulance and fire truck had been left running after arriving at the scene, all this fireman had to do was shift the gear lever and the ambulance sped off. Now since the engine company was short a man, they followed the ambulance to Lutheran Family Center Hospital to pick up their missing man, instead of returning back to their firehouse. As both Fire Department vehicles sped off, lights and sirens wailing in the air, the crowd of on lookers began to disperse.

After roughly two to three minutes, Kurt found himself standing alone with the broken defibrillator in his right hand and Pietrowski's tan jacket in his left hand. That's when he saw him standing alone, with his arms folded across his chest, staring at him—the Gilles Watch Commander, Al Billings.

Standing no more than 5'9" and weighing easily 220 pounds, Billings had earned the nickname, "Fireplug," at the Illinois Law Enforcement Training Center years ago and it had stuck with him ever since. Al Billings wasn't someone a criminal, or for that matter a Gilles Cop, wanted to mess with. Al Billings ran his squad with a unique style.

He allowed his two sergeants to handle most of the menial work, such as giving roll call, reviewing reports, and even going on minor calls. But if there was a major crime in progress which could require some hands-on treatment, or the traditional "cluster fuck," you could count on him being at the scene, often in the background and observing until needed. Such as what was occurring right now in the Old Mill Mall Shopping Center parking lot.

Billings never moved the entire time the paramedics had been working on Pietrowski. Even now he just stood there as Kurt approached him. Slowly, he walked toward Billings as if he was going to the electric chair. Kurt was looking for any kind of sympathy Billings was willing to throw his way.

With Billings' first statement to him, Kurt knew sympathy wouldn't be coming in any manner. "Give me the facts quickly, Thompson, before you head over to LFCH," Billings barked at him.

"Really not much to say Boss," Kurt started.

Because Billings didn't move or say anything, Kurt continued. "Victim's name is Stanley Pietrowski, and he didn't like the fact I gave him a P ticket for parking in a handicapped spot."

Once again Billings didn't move or say anything, so Kurt figured he better say more. "Pietrowski became extremely agitated over this whole P ticket thing to the point of yelling and screaming at me, which witnesses can verify."

Finally, Billings spoke two simple words, "Heart Attack?"

"Looks that way," Kurt said as more of a question than a definitive answer.

Then everything went south in a hurry.

"Strange," Billings said, "I saw the AED pads on Pietrowski's chest when ambulance crew 9 wheeled him by me on the stretcher."

Now, it was Kurt's turn to shut up and think about his next statement. But Billings beat him to it.

"So, how many times did you shock him to bring him back?" Billings asked.

Kurt stood there for a few seconds and actually thought about lying, before he returned to his senses.

"Couldn't boss, since the defibrillator wasn't working properly due to the battery being dead," he said.

As soon as the word "dead," came out of Kurt's mouth, Al Billings jumped on it like a big mouth bass going after its bait.

With Billings left eyebrow raised in a curious manner he asked. "Hmm, was it working properly when you field tested it as you're required to do at the start of your shift, Officer Thompson?"

Kurt quickly realized he was digging his grave deeper and deeper with every statement and lying would only make the matter worse.

"I never checked it Sir, when I checked out my squad car," he answered.

"Really," Billings said with notable sarcasm in his voice, his arms still folded across his chest and a strange look of disbelief on his aged face.

"Which car is Pietrowski's?" Billings asked.

"The ugly brown Lincoln Mercury parked over there," Kurt said and turned to point at it with his right hand, which had become free after transferring Pietrowski's tan jacket, which contained car keys, into the same hand holding the defibrillator case.

Without hesitation, Billings suddenly took Pietrowski's tan jacket away from Kurt. Once Billings had Pietrowski's jacket in his hands, he started to go through its pockets until he found what he was looking for. Pulling out Pietrowski's car keys, he hit the remote-control button until the lights and horn sounded on the Lincoln.

As Kurt Thompson looked on in horror, Billings walked over to Pietrowski's vehicle until he was standing next to the passenger door. Unknown to Kurt, Billings was simply going to Pietrowski's vehicle as an act of kindness to put Pietrowski's jacket inside the vehicle for safekeeping. Kurt found himself closing his eyes for a few seconds, too scared to look at what was going to happen next.

Opening his eyes, Kurt's problems, as impossible as they may have seemed, were actually getting worse. Billings was rapidly walking toward him with the sternest look on his face imaginable. The look on Billings face wasn't the issue—what Billings was holding in his right hand was—Stanley Pietrowski's Illinois handicapped placard.

Stopping directly in front of Kurt Thompson, Billings held the placard up in such a fashion it almost hit the tip of Kurt's nose. Both Al Billings and Kurt Thompson stared at the placard, each with different thoughts racing through their heads.

"Officer Thompson, did you or didn't you see this placard when you were writing Pietrowski his parking ticket?" Billings asked.

"No Sir," Kurt Thompson answered emphatically. "If I had, Sir, I wouldn't have written the ticket."

"Good, good," Billings answered with a sense of relief in his voice as he cleared his lungs of air.

"You want me to go to LFCH Boss, and check on Pietrowski?" Kurt asked.

"Yeah, go ahead and then call me on my cell as opposed to putting it on Norcom when you find out what his condition is," Billings said.

"You got it, Boss," Kurt Thompson said before quickly turning and walking to his squad car.

As Kurt walked, he felt a state of numbness come over him. Never ever, did he think a situation would come up where he would find himself lying to a supervisor. Yet the words, "No Sir," continued bouncing around in his head.

Finally reaching his squad car, Kurt got in and slammed the door in frustration. Quickly, he looked to where he had just been standing to see if Commander Al Billings had seen him slam the car door. Commander Al Billings had apparently left the shopping center, probably with Pietrowski's handicapped placard lying on the seat next to him in his Gilles Chevy Tahoe.

As Kurt shifted the car from park to drive, he was totally unaware of the firestorm which would be coming down hard on him over one parking ticket and one huge lie.

CHAPTER 21

E xiting Old Mill Mall Shopping Centers parking lot, Kurt turned left on to Greenwood Road.

Kurt was so deep in thought; he never saw the American Republic Cab coming straight at him.

Fortunately, the taxi cab driver honked his horn and slammed on his brakes at the last moment to avoid hitting Kurt's squad car, squarely in the driver's side door.

Otherwise, the crash would have killed Kurt instantly.

He turned his head, looking sheepishly at the driver of the cab, who was a bald, middle-aged Russian man wearing a black t-shirt. For only another second, Kurt looked at this driver, who started to raise his middle fingers on both hands but then quickly put his hands down, when he realized who he was about to flip off.

Kurt sped up, trying to get away from the cab and his near-death experience, as quickly as possible.

Driving in complete silence, his mind raced with ideas and thoughts.

With his car radio off and surprisingly no Norcom traffic since he pulled out of the shopping center, he was actually able to think. There was little doubt in his mind, he was going to get banged by Billings for the defibrillator issue.

But otherwise, he felt pretty good about their conversation roughly twenty minutes ago.

Then he remembered the lie he told Billings.

Suddenly, he realized only one other person knew if he had looked inside Pietrowski's car and the person was currently at Lutheran Family Center Hospital.

Kurt allowed himself a small smile, confident things were improving.

Since Old Mill Mall Shopping Center and Lutheran Family Center Hospital were only ten minutes apart, Kurt got to the hospital in no time at all.

He couldn't help but notice, as he pulled around the rear of the hospital, Gilles Ambulance 9 and Engine Company 27 were in the parking lot spaces designated for emergency vehicles only.

Carefully, he pulled into a parking spot marked, "Police Vehicle Parking Only," which was on a small, red and white sign posted on the wall directly in front of him.

"Gilles 712 is out at LFCH," Kurt said into his Motorola shoulder mic because he had turned off the engine to his Dodge Challenger, killing the power to his Norcom Radio.

Dispatcher Fontany answered with the same low, monotone voice as earlier, "10-4."

Getting out of his squad car, he took a deep breath and then blew it out of his lungs forcefully in an effort to calm his nerves.

Briskly walking up the wheelchair ramp, he headed for a double set of glass doors, which he had entered way too often in his short career.

As he neared these double doors, he looked up at a large sign with white lettering which stated, Emergency Personnel Only.

As he was about to enter these doors, he was nearly bowled over by Lt. Morris, who was coming out of them with a full head of steam.

The look on Lt. Morris' face said it all.

"Who pronounced him and at what time?" Kurt asked.

"Not sure Thompson, because there were two doctors working on him once we got him inside," Morris answered.

Kurt was momentarily caught off guard because he didn't think he had ever met Lt. Morris and wasn't sure how Lt. Morris knew his name.

"Curious, did you guys ever get a pulse when you put him inside your ambulance?" Kurt asked.

"Nothing," Lt. Morris answered dryly. "Flat lined the entire time."

"Thanks Boss," Kurt said before extending his right hand.

"No problem kid," Lt. Morris answered and shook Kurt's right hand firmly, before walking away.

If Kurt could have jumped for joy right now without causing a scene, he would have.

In his young mind, the only witness to his major fuck up was dead and would take his version of the incident to his grave.

Kurt stopped for a minute to make sure the smile from his face was completely gone and a look of concern had replaced it.

Going through the emergency room doors, he went directly to the large, nurses' station, located just to the left of the entrance.

Like every other time he had been here, all three nurses stationed at the desk were writing down information on pink-colored note pads, or entering information into computers, while talking on the phone.

Kurt saw two or three doctors walking by in their light blue scrubs and white-colored lab coats.

Each of these doctors were carrying an iPad and seemed to be involved with something. He knew better than to bother either the nurses or doctors while they were busy, so he stood quietly in front of their desk until one of the nurses was done.

"Well, well, what have we here," the female voice said loud enough to be heard easily by Kurt and all of the nurses at their station.

Kurt didn't turn around; confident he knew who was calling to him.

Then, fearful he was being viewed as being rude, he turned 180 degrees until he was standing face to face with, Wanda Miller.

In her early fifties, Wanda Miller was the nursing supervisor currently working in the emergency room.

Other supervisors filled in for her when she was ill or on vacation, but none of them had the talents Wanda Miller did.

Wanda Miller had the most beautiful smile, with a personality to match, as long as you knew your place in her emergency room.

She was a legend in police stations and firehouses on the North Shore for her ability to bust any cop or firefighter whom were either hitting on one of her nurses, giving them a hard time, or just wasting their time asking stupid questions.

Yet, she was also known for placing a hot cup of coffee down next to a cop who was finishing up his paperwork on a Death Investigation or Sexual Assault case in the early morning hours.

"So, what brings you in today, Sunshine?" Wanda Miller asked, with her arms folded across her multicolored scrubs and her head cocked to the right.

"Ambulance 9's heart attack, which turned into a DOA from Old Mill Mall" Kurt answered.

Seeing a puzzled look on her face, he said one additional word, "Pietrowski."

"Oh, ok, now I know who you're talking about," she said before continuing. "Don't move baby, while I go get the file and tell you who pronounced and at what time."

"10-4," Kurt said dryly as he watched Wanda Miller walk away.

He knew better than to move an inch and have her come looking for him.

Bored, he stood there for a moment before pulling his cell phone out of one of the vest pockets of his dark blue-colored, bulletproof vest.

Suddenly, Kurt realized he was in an area of the hospital where cell phones couldn't be used.

But honestly, he didn't really care.

After dodging a major bullet earlier today, he wanted to see how far his current good luck would take him.

Putting in Megan's cell phone number, he texted, "How are you?"

Quickly, he put the cell phone back in his bulletproof vest pocket and looked around, making sure no one was watching.

Within a minute, his cell phone beeped loudly.

Kurt was so excited he dropped his cell phone, while pulling it out of his bulletproof vest.

"Shit," he screamed out loud, not caring who heard him in the process.

Reaching down, he quickly picked up the phone and checked it to make sure it wasn't damaged.

A smile came across his face as he saw the message was from Megan.

The smile turned into a frown as he read the message, which was in capital letters: "NOTHING HAS CHANGED SO GO FUCK YOURSELF ASSHOLE, YOU COP KILLING PRICK."

So much for good luck he thought, as he put the cell phone back after deleting the message.

Turning to his right, he saw Wanda headed his way with a full head of steam, carrying a tan manila file in her right hand.

"I'm so fucked," he said softly, under his breath.

Instinctively, Kurt used his right hand to open the upper right breast pocket of his bulletproof vest, pulling out a small, blue-colored, spiral note pad and pen.

"Stanley Pietrowski, 1727 Lincoln Avenue, Elmhurst, Illinois, with a DOB putting him at 89 years old was pronounced dead at exactly 1601Hrs today by Dr. Murphy, who will obviously have signed the death certificate. Also, sunshine, one of my nurses will call the Cook County Medical Examiner's Office, notifying them of Pietrowski's death."

Wanda was able to say all of this in one complete breath.

"Thank you, Wanda, and if you need me for anything, I'll be around for a few more minutes," Kurt said while still looking down at the note pad, he was feverishly scribbling notes into.

"Going to call the station?" Wanda asked.

"Yeah, I have to call Lt. Billings and give him an update," Kurt mumbled while still writing in his notebook.

"Fireplug?" Wanda let out a short snicker before saying, "When's that old timer going to hang it up?"

"No idea, since he never responds when we bust him about it at roll call," Kurt said.

Before Wanda could say anything, a middle-aged Polish nurse, who seemed flustered, walked up to both of them and said, "Wanda, we need your help in Exam Room #12."

"Take care Officer Thompson," Wanda Miller said and with that both of the nurses were gone.

Kurt walked in the opposite direction of both nurses, down a long hallway, turning left at the end of it and entering a room marked, "Families Only."

Once inside this room, he quickly locked the door and walked over to a couch, taking a seat next to an old-fashioned, white telephone.

Before calling Lt. Billings, Kurt pulled out his note pad and prepared himself for the series of questions he knew would be asked.

After dialing Lt. Billings' cell phone number, it rang twice before he answered.

"Go ahead Thompson," Lt. Billings answered with a terse tone in his voice.

Kurt was surprisingly taken back by both the tone in Lt. Billings' voice and the way he had answered his cell phone.

Before he could say a word, Lt. Billings jumped back on the line. "I'm assuming Pietrowski is dead," Lt. Billings said.

"Yes Sir," Thompson responded.

"Shit," Lt. Billings yelled into the phone and before Kurt could respond he continued, "Okay, okay, call into the station and tell Dispatcher Fontany to start a CAD ticket if she hasn't done so already and make sure she labels it Death Investigation, not Fire Department Assist, since you were in the process of giving out a P Ticket."

"10-4 Boss," was all Kurt Thompson could respond with as the words, Death Investigation, kept bouncing around inside his brain.

"Thompson, I'm not sure you've been monitoring our radio traffic while you were at LFCH, but we're swamped out here," Billings said, but this time in a much softer tone, "so I need you to go back to Pietrowski's car and handle the tow, before you come in and do your report, understood?"

"Got it Boss," was all Thompson could mumble into the phone before asking "do you want an Evidence Technician to come out and take pictures of Pietrowski?"

"Great question, but due to Pietrowski's age, plus the fact you were with him for a considerable length of time and saw no injuries or wounds we can go without one on this case." Pausing for a second to catch his breath, Billings continued, "just articulate it properly in your report and yes you can put in your narrative I told you no pictures were needed." Billings answered.

"Yes Sir," Kurt answered.

"Also, regarding the tow, tell you what, I'll save you the trouble and have Dispatcher Fontany Call Red's Towing for you. Forget that, I'm two blocks away from Red's and have the car keys. I'll stop in and arrange the tow myself," Billings said.

"Thanks Boss," Kurt Thompson said before hanging up the phone.

Standing up, Kurt flipped the pages of his small, spiral note pad making sure he could decipher what he had just written down for the report he had been assigned.

Taking only a couple of steps he needed to open the room's door, Kurt flung it open in a hurry to get to his squad car.

In the process, he startled a young woman in her early thirties, who had her hands over her face.

Apparently, she never expected someone to be in the same room she was trying to get into.

The minute she removed her hands from her face, Kurt knew instantly who she was but still needed to prove it to himself.

"May I help you Miss?" Kurt asked.

"I don't think so since I'm looking for my mother and she obviously isn't in this room from what I can see," the young woman answered, while glancing inside the room, while still standing at the entrance to it.

"No, I was the only one in the room this entire time," Kurt answered and took one step out of the room before stopping, so he was now standing face to face with this woman.

"By chance is your last name Miller?" he asked.

The woman had calmed down considerably.

"Not even close, my name is Anna Pietrowski. I'm trying to find my mother, Helen Pietrowski, who is around here somewhere," she said.

Anna Pietrowski turned her head to the right and then left in an attempt to find her mother, who was walking down the hallway.

Then, she looked straight ahead at the empty room, where Kurt had once stood.

But Kurt was walking at a record pace down the hallway of the hospital to get away from Anna Pietrowski.

If Kurt could have run, he would have.

Finally reaching his squad car and getting inside, he slammed the door with such force he thought he had broken the passenger side window.

"What the fuck!" he screamed at the top of his lungs as he threw the gearshift into reverse and flew out of the Lutheran Family Center Hospital parking lot.

"Okay, okay, calm down, they may be alive but the only fuck who can jam me up is dead," he found himself saying in an effort to reassure himself.

When Kurt had finally convinced himself, he was going to be okay, he was pulling back into the Old Mill Mall parking lot, next to Pietrowski's Lincoln Mercury.

It wasn't hard to find Pietrowski's car because a red-colored tow truck from Red's Towing was parked next to it. Without hesitation, the tow truck driver got out the minute he saw Kurt's squad car pull up.

The driver then walked over to the driver's side door of Kurt's vehicle.

Kurt knew all of the drivers for Red's Towing, but not this one apparently, with multi-colored tattoos covering both of his forearms, which stood out distinctively.

The Red's driver wore the distinctive grey-colored overalls, rolled up to his bicep area on each arm, with the towing company's seal over his left breast. The name "Rico," stood out prominently on a nametag which was sewn over his right breast.

When Rico was near shouting distance, Kurt yelled at him, "Tow it back to your lot and a family member will be by for it sometime soon."

Rico gave Kurt the traditional thumbs up signal acknowledging he had heard him before turning and walking back to Pietrowski's vehicle.

The Gilles Police Department, like other police departments on the North Shore, had been using Red's Towing long before Kurt Thompson had joined the force.

While some of Red's drivers were on the creepy side, due to their appearance, their service was quick and reliable, which made every cop happy on a rainy or snowy night.

Kurt knew this for a fact.

On one of his first midnight shifts alone without a field training officer, he responded to a multiple car 10-50 personal injury accident, at Milwaukee Avenue and Oakton Street.

Quickly, Red's Towing was dispatched and got to the scene.

The number of tow trucks they were able to supply to his accident is what impressed Kurt Thompson the most.

But today, all he cared about, was filling out the tow report for Pietrowski's crappy Mercury and getting it towed out of the parking lot.

Kurt carefully checked every box on the tow report, to make sure he had filled in the lines properly but stopped filing out the report when he got to the second to last line which read, "Release the car to,"

Kurt had no idea who to put down, so he left this box empty and, on a line, wrote, "Contact Gilles Police Department before releasing this vehicle."

Satisfied the tow report was completed properly, he looked up just in time to see Rico hoisting the Lincoln Mercury onto the back of his flatbed tow truck.

When finished, Rico wiped both of his dirty hands on the pants of his overalls.

He approached Kurt's squad car, pulling an old, thin pen from his right pants pocket in the process.

Kurt Thompson stayed seated behind the wheel of his squad car and simply handed the tow report, which was still attached to his metal clipboard, to Rico through the open driver's side window.

In record time, Rico signed the form and removed it from the clipboard, ripping off the pink back page of the form for the record keeper in the Red's Towing office.

Rico didn't say a word as he handed Kurt his metal clipboard and walked slowly back to his tow truck.

Kurt just sat there in silence, before finally saying out loud, "All of this over a fucking P ticket."

In less than a minute, the tow truck carrying Pietrowski's car was out of the Old Mill Mall parking lot and headed for the Red's Towing impound lot, via Milwaukee Avenue.

Kurt foolishly thought the vehicle was out of his sight and his life for good.

He had no idea how wrong he could be.

CHAPTER 22

Kurt Thompson couldn't figure things out for the life of him. His Police Station was only 11 months old, and while it wasn't the mecca the new Greenfield Police Station was rumored to be, it still held its own as a fine piece of architecture.

"Then why the hell," he thought to himself, "was he working at a desk, which had been around since the Korean War?"

Grey in color and completely metal, it easily weighed between 25 to 30 pounds.

Stopping for a minute after finishing his General Case report, he looked around the report writing room and saw three more of the same desks. The things some police departments do in an effort to save money seemed confusing as all hell.

But this wasn't his biggest worry at the moment.

All that mattered was making sure all the facts, the way he had presented them to Commander Billings, were in this report.

Reading the report off the computer screen took him roughly five additional minutes, but it was well worth it.

Upon finishing, he leaned as far back as his chair would allow him.

Crossing his arms over his bulletproof vest, he let out a sigh and a small smile came across his face.

Everything was done and he was satisfied it would meet the approval of Billings, who had already left for the evening after their shift ended at 1800 Hrs.

Since Kurt hadn't worn a watch since his high school days, he pulled out his phone and saw the time was 7:45 Pm.

Using his right hand, he pulled as hard as he could on the stuck second drawer of the desk, to get an overtime slip. Due to the age of the desk, condition of the drawer, or force he used, the drawer came flying off its track and landed on the floor, next to his right foot.

"Figures," Kurt mumbled to himself.

While still seated, he reached down into the drawer and grabbed an overtime slip.

He thought about putting the drawer back inside the desk somehow and then changed his mind, leaving it on the floor.

He filled out the overtime slip at record speed, pausing only for a second to decide whether he wanted his overtime to be in pay or compensation time.

"Compensation time," he said out loud, not caring at this particular moment who heard his snide comment.

Grabbing two small paper clips, from a black plastic dispenser on top of his work desk, he attached the overtime slip to the case envelope, which he threw into a tray outside the supervisor's office. Walking to the men's locker room, he quickly changed out of his uniform and into an old pair of blue jeans, faded top-siders and a light blue t-shirt, with a superman logo on the front of it.

Picking up his dirty uniform from the locker room floor, he quickly stuffed the uniform into a black-colored Nike workout bag, while saying out loud, "Nice fucking way to start my three day weekend."

No one heard him due to everyone being out of the police station working or, at the very least, having dinner somewhere in town.

Within minutes he was out the side door of the police station, into his double-waxed, black, Ford Cobra and flying out of the parking lot heading home.

For a June night, it had turned remarkably cool in the lower seventies, with no humidity.

Kurt looked out his driver's side window while at a stoplight and couldn't find a single star in the sky.

Only a full moon, which bothered him for a minute "Premonition of bad things to come or just an old wife's tale," he thought to himself.

With his cell phone turned off and Nickelback's, "All the Right Reasons," CD blasting through his six Boise speakers, located throughout the interior of the Cobra, his thoughts turned to what had easily been the worst day of his career.

With roughly only 14 months on the job, today was a day of firsts in many ways for him.

He had committed two separate, but related acts, which he never thought he'd have to do.

For the first and hopefully only time, he'd lied to the face of Commander Al Billings during a Death Investigation of all things.

Secondly, and more significantly, he played a role in the death of Stanley Pietrowski over a freaking handicapped placard.

"Jesus Kurt, what the fuck were you thinking today?" He mumbled softly to himself.

Kurt was forced to admit, he had reached a new low in both his law enforcement career and now with the apparent loss of Megan, his personal life as well.

With the roads surprisingly empty for a Friday night, he made it home in record time.

Carefully, he pulled his Cobra into the single-car, attached garage just as the last Nickelback song on the CD was ending.

Before getting out of his car, he reached over to the sun visor on the passenger side of the Cobra and hit the garage door opener.

He watched his garage door close slowly through his rearview mirror.

Finally getting out of the Cobra, he went directly to the backseat behind the driver's seat and retrieved his Nike workout bag. With the Nike bag thrown over his left shoulder, he entered his townhouse through the door leading from the garage into the laundry room.

No sooner than two to three seconds after doing so, he heard the ADT alarm activate. The screeching sound of the alarm seemed to vibrate off the walls and appeared to grow louder by the second.

Quickly, he walked over to the control panel, opened it and punched in the code 1234, which immediately deactivated the alarm.

Kicking off his top-siders, he left them directly underneath the control panel for the alarm.

Shoeless, he walked back inside the laundry room and removed the Nike bag from his left shoulder and placed it on top of the dryer.

Carefully, he pulled his uniform from the Nike bag and dropped both the shirt and pants inside the washing machine, which already contained dark colored clothing.

Next, he removed both his sweat-stained t-shirt as well as sweat socks from the bag and threw them in a separate laundry basket, which he used for only white clothing. This laundry basket was on the floor of the laundry room, tucked in a corner of the room.

With the Nike bag completely empty of clothing, he left it on top of the dryer, turned off the light to the laundry room and walked towards the stairs leading to the upstairs bedroom.

Upon reaching the stairs, he slowly climbed them, slightly surprised at how tired he was.

At the top of the stairs, he turned to his right and entered his blackened bedroom.

Kurt's plan was simple as could be.

He would grab a 45-minute nap, then eat a slice of Rosatti's deep dish sausage pizza he had wrapped in tinfoil in the refrigerator, while downing two, ice-cold Tsingtao beers and seeing who Kimmel or Fallon had on tonight.

He walked straight towards his king-sized bed and fell face first into it, falling asleep almost on impact.

His plans for the evening as well as his life were changed forever, seven minutes later.

At exactly 9:04 Pm, both his iPhone and his home telephone, located down in his kitchen, seemed to explode simultaneously, causing him to roll over on to his back.

Grabbing his cell phone from his rear pants pocket, he held it up next to his face due to still being partially asleep.

The light from the phone seemed to light up his entire bedroom.

Kurt saw the message was from one of his Southern Illinois University buddies, John Pozniak.

In capital letters the message read, "DUDE JUST SAW YOU ON THE CHANNEL NINE NEWS, YOU'RE A FREAKIN CELEBRITY."

Before Kurt could figure out what this message meant, his telephone downstairs began ringing again.

Unlike the first phone call, which he didn't pay much attention to, he actually rolled over onto his side after the third ring so he could hear the caller's message on the answering machine.

"Kurt, honey are you home?"

"Megan?" Kurt said, but he seemed to be asking himself his very own question.

Kurt found himself yelling her name out loud and, in the process, rolled off his bed, scaring the hell out of Whiskers as he made a beeline for the stairs.

In record time he made it downstairs and grabbed the receiver just as Megan was saying good-bye.

"Megan don't hang up," Kurt yelled into the phone.

"Well, well, Mr. Celebrity," Megan said with both a sexy childish tone and bit of sarcasm in her voice.

There was so much Kurt wanted to say, he just didn't know where to start.

So, Megan started for him.

"You all right baby?" she said in her sexiest voice ever.

"Baby?" he thought to himself as he actually pinched the upper part of his right thigh to make sure he wasn't dreaming.

He wasn't dreaming because his thigh started to throb.

For some unknown reason, he answered with a strong, convincing tone in his voice to show Megan he was still king of the jungle.

"Yeah, I'm fine and curious why you would think I wouldn't be."

"I just watched the first part of Fox 32 News and you were all over it, honey," Megan said slowly and with the sweetest tone in her voice Kurt had ever heard coming from her lips.

Kurt had a hard time swallowing due to the lump in his throat and was afraid to ask Megan the next question.

He paused for a second to work up his courage.

"They had some interesting cell phone footage of you at Old Mill Mall earlier today' she said and the sweet, sexy, Megan O'Brien, was completely gone. The new bitchy Megan O'Brien of the past couple of weeks had taken her place.

Again, Kurt couldn't speak due to what he was hearing and how it was being delivered to him.

"Really Kurt?" Megan yelled into the phone. "GRABBING SOME OLD FART BY HIS JACKET AND THROWING HIM TO THE GROUND, HOW LOW CAN YOU GO YOU PIECE OF SHIT?" Megan yelled into the phone.

"Fuck you Bitch," was all Kurt could blurt out, before slamming the phone back into its holder.

Kurt found himself standing in his kitchen shaking.

There was a combination of hatred and anger roaring throughout his body.

Raising both of his clenched fists into the air over his head, he yelled, "Fuccccccccccccck," so loud he was sure one of his neighbors had heard him, even though all of the windows in his townhouse were closed.

He opened his mouth slowly, inhaling as much air as his lungs would allow him.

Convinced his lungs couldn't't hold any more air, he slowly blew it out of his lungs as the instructor of the Stress Management Class at ILETC had shown them.

Since he never had a need to use this technique before, he was surprised at how effective it was.

Within a matter of five minutes, he found himself almost back to a state of normalcy.

During this time of anger, he had received five more text messages, three from fellow Gilles cops and two from college buddies.

All five weren't identical but of the same general message, "Hey, you okay? Just saw you on the news."

Slowly, he walked back upstairs to his bedroom and took his Glock 17, still inside the safariland basket weave holster off his right hip.

Due to the day, he was having, he walked gingerly to the nightstand next to his bed and gently put the weapon down on top of it.

Changing out of his clothes, he left them where he dropped them, to join a pile of other clothes and two magazines laying on the floor of his bedroom.

Laying his iPhone 6 on his bed, he saw he had received four more text messages, which he ignored for now.

"What the fuck people? Get a life," he yelled out, frustrated as hell.

Apparently, this new round of yelling had frightened Whiskers.

The Siamese jumped off his bed and ran out of the bedroom, down the stairs, heading for a quieter spot.

Walking over to his bedroom closet, he grabbed a yellow-colored Under Amour shirt off one of the top shelves.

Kurt looked at the front of the shirt, which read, Illinois Law Enforcement Special Olympics Torch Run. It was his favorite running shirt, and he threw it on quickly.

Walking over to his bedroom dresser, he grabbed a jock, Champion black-colored gym shorts and pair of New Balance white sweat socks. In less than a minute, he was dressed but still needed two more essential items.

Carefully, he opened the nightstand drawer removed his iPod Shuffle, which was still in its case and located exactly below his off-duty weapon.

He strapped this iPod on his left bicep, causing him to raise his Under Amour shirt in the process.

Walking downstairs, he walked around his townhouse and turned on all his outside lights.

Once they were on, he only needed his Asics running shoes, which he found exactly where he had left them. Lying on the floor of the family room, in front of his Sony Bravia 60-inch television.

With his shoes on, he walked over to his alarm panel for the second time tonight and activated it.

As the alarm beeped in the background, he opened the door leading to his garage.

Hitting the switch on his Lift Master garage door opener, he watched as the overhead garage door rose slowly, with the same clanking noise as if it were the drawbridge to a castle.

Then, he walked over to the passenger side of the Cobra and through the open passenger-side window, took the remote for the overhead garage door off the visor.

Standing back up, with the remote in his left hand, Kurt walked out of his garage and turned left, pressing the remote for the overhead garage door to close it.

With two huge flower planters on the front step of his townhouse to choose from, he picked the one holding beautiful pansies and put the remote control behind it for safekeeping.

For the first time in his life, he didn't stretch before starting a run.

For today was like nothing he had ever experienced before.

Kurt started running from his townhouse toward James Jennings Park, located two miles east of him.

He ran due to his bitter hatred for Megan O'Brien.

He ran for the sympathy he felt for the Pietrowski family.

With the original soundtrack from the first Rocky movie blasting through his ear pods, he ran past Jennings Park in sixteen minutes and ten seconds, his best time ever.

He ran past dogs barking from their fenced-in yards and lovers in back seats of cars, silhouetted by the full moon.

Finally, he ran to put his story together for Chief Dennis McKinley.

He was sure by now Chief McKinley knew what had taken place in the parking lot of the Old Mill Mall Shopping Center earlier today.

A number of thoughts went through Kurt's mind as he ran, ranging from who would represent him during this process, his Fraternal Order of Police attorney or would he have to hire his own, the actual process, would there be a lawsuit brought by the Pietrowski family and what his ultimate punishment would be.

He knew he was in a shit load of trouble; he just didn't know how much.

Roughly 45 minutes later, he arrived back at his townhouse, totally covered in sweat, despite the temperature now being in the low sixties.

For the second time in less than three hours, he entered his townhouse after retrieving his remote control from behind the flower planter.

Removing his Asics running shoes once he got inside, he waited a few seconds as the ADT alarm continued to sound.

He wasn't sure why he let the alarm continue ringing, but his mind continued to race with a wide variety of thoughts on a number of different topics. With only ten seconds left before the alarm would go off, he punched in his deactivation code.

With the alarm finally off, he walked over to the answering machine and looked to see how many calls he had missed while running.

The number eleven flashed repeatedly on the small screen.

Walking over to his refrigerator, he opened it and found what he was looking for immediately on the bottom ledge of the refrigerator door—lemon lime Gatorade.

He was so thirsty; he downed the 12-ounce bottle in only three gulps.

Leaving the empty bottle on the kitchen counter, he returned to the refrigerator and pulled out a second bottle of Gatorade.

He drank half of this bottle and upon stopping, went to check his text messages on his cell phone, which showed he also had eleven of them.

These eleven messages would have to wait, he thought.

During his run, he decided to handle the phone calls on his answering machine first.

Finally, properly hydrated after nearly finishing his second bottle of Gatorade, he continued to hold the bottle in his left hand.

With his free right hand, he hit the play button on the Panasonic answering machine.

"Kurt, it's your father. Please call me when you can so we can talk about what you went through today. I'm willing to help you with whatever you need son, just call."

"For years I don't hear from you and you decide to call me now, you fuckin' prick," Kurt said in a disgusted tone.

Kurt Thompson was exasperated. Looking up at the ceiling of his kitchen, he screamed, "WHAT THE FUCK, FIRST MEGAN AND NOW MY FATHER, WHAT THE HELL COULD GO WRONG NEXT?"

Physically shaking, he hit he button on the answering machine for message number two.

"Kurt, this is Chief McKinley and I will be quick."

Kurt's heart seemed to stop beating and he held his breath.

"Needless to say, the mayor, village manager and I have watched the incident a few times now and to say we're a bit confused is an understatement. Your report, which I have a copy of here on my desk, tends to contradict what we've seen on the video," Chief McKinley said.

"Jesus," is all Kurt could mumble to himself since there was a brief pause by Chief McKinley on the tape.

With a sudden rougher tone in his voice Chief McKinley continued. "We need to talk about this incident. From looking at your schedule here on the computer, I see you're off until Monday. Don't come in for your shift that day, instead, report to me at 0900 hours and we'll try and sort this out then,"

Kurt just stared at the answering machine; glad the message was over.

Or was it, Kurt thought?

"Officer Thompson, I'm placing you on Administrative Leave effective immediately until we can get to the bottom of this mess and trust me Thompson, this truly is a mess for all of us right now. See you Monday and if you want your FOP representative fine, pick one. Don't be late," Chief McKinley finished as the message ended.

Blood on the Badge

Kurt could barely stand. With his left hand, he dropped the empty bottle of Gatorade into the kitchen sink.

Walking over to his kitchen table, he pulled out one of his wooden chairs and flopped down into it.

The words "Administrative Leave," seemed to echo in his mind over and over as he sat motionless in this chair, for a good two minutes.

She moved silently on the linoleum floor, taking every step so carefully, Kurt never heard her coming as she approached him.

When she finally made it next to him, she gently began rubbing up against him in one continuous motion.

Somehow, she knew the pain he was in and hoped to relieve it.

Maybe in another time or place this would have worked, but not today.

For only a few men in their lifetime would ever have the kind of day Kurt had just experienced.

With a rage he never felt before, he stood up.

His right hand flew from his side, finding its spot at the base of her neck.

He watched excitedly as her head flew back and her beautiful green eyes seemed to grow wide with fright.

She gasped for any kind of air to fill her lungs, but her effort was futile.

She soon realized she would be no match for him due to this newfound strength he had acquired from the horrific rage and hatred flowing throughout his body.

As quickly as it started, it ended.

With one last squeeze, he could feel her neck breaking in his hand and her body suddenly go limp.

In one last fit of rage, he yelled the word "Asshole," as he hurled her into the air and watched as her body hit the interior door, leading to the garage.

He looked at her for only a few seconds as her body lay motionless on the floor and a stream of blood dripped out of the right side of her mouth.

In a move that scared even him, he began laughing hysterically.

He laughed so loud and with such intensity, his whole body shook.

For he hadn't killed for some time now and the sheer joy of doing it, especially to someone he loved so much, made the act so much sweeter.

One final time, Kurt looked at her lifeless body lying on the floor and his laughter suddenly stopped.

Kurt was too exhausted, both physically and mentally, to move her body and figured he would dispose of it in the morning.

"Good-bye Whiskers," he said softly and finally turned his head away.

Kurt Thompson didn't even realize it until the first one ran down his left cheek and the taste of salt violently hit his lips.

Sitting back down, he bent over in the chair and put his head into his hands.

He began to sob uncontrollably, rocking back and forth in his chair.

Unknown to him, in a small two-flat, located off Route 83 in Elmhurst, Illinois, Anna Pietrowski was doing the exact same thing.

CHAPTER 23

Trustee Coconato and D.C. Gyondski immediately diverted their focus on Chief Fitzsimons, who hadn't moved from the open office door.

The silence in the room was deafening, with all three of them not knowing what to say or do next.

Deputy Chief Gyondski finally decided he needed to say—if not do—something, as he saw his career quickly fading over a comment he didn't even make.

With his voice cracking he mumbled, "Trustee Coconato stopped by boss, to congratulate us for all of the hard work with the new police station presentation last night."

"Really?" Chief Fitzsimons answered quickly.

His head was tilted slightly back with a mock look of disbelief on his face and his arms were folded tightly across his uniformed chest.

"That's right, that's right" Trustee Coconato answered as he must have realized this could be his only opening, he and Deputy Chief Gyondski probably had to escape the mess he had caused.

"Apparently none of your phones are working?" Chief Fitzsimons asked with a matter-of-fact tone in his voice and a look on his face to back it up, as he stared at Trustee Coconato.

"You know Chief, I was over at the Village Hall picking up some items I forgot from the Village Board meeting last night so I thought I would come over and see you, but Sandy told me you were out," Trustee Coconato said, with his strong Italian accent.

Apparently, the comments made little impact on Chief Fitzsimons, whose look from only a few minutes earlier hadn't changed one bit.

Deputy Chief Gyondski realized Chief Fitzsimons smelled

something wasn't quite right with the entire situation and once again, the entire room fell silent.

"Chief, you have an urgent phone call from Chief McKinley of the Gilles Police parked on line two," Sandy Elloy said.

She had walked down the corridor from her desk and was now standing directly behind Chief Fitzsimons.

"Thank you, Sandy," Chief Fitzsimons said as the tone in his voice finally started to lighten up.

Chief Fitzsimons finally left his position in the doorway and headed right toward Deputy Chief Gyondski's desk.

Seeing Chief Fitzsimons headed his way, D.C.Gyondski moved from his position of standing behind his desk to now standing next to Trustee Coconato.

Once he reached Gyondski's desk, Chief Fitzsimons walked around it so he was now facing the open office door.

Using his left hand, he picked up the black-colored phone located on the left side of the desk. Finally, ready to talk, he punched in *02 on the phone's keypad, which connected him immediately to Chief McKinley.

"Dennis," Chief Fitzsimons said into the phone with a nonchalant tone in his voice.

Deputy Chief Gyondski stood there in total awe.

For as long as he had worked for the Chief, this was easily the longest he had seen the man silent.

Glancing at his watch, he guessed it had been close to six or seven minutes without Chief Fitzsimons saying a word.

Finally, Chief Fitzsimons said, "Thank you, Dennis, for all of the information. By all means, let me know if you hear or learn of anything else, I need to know about."

Hanging up the telephone, Chief Fitzsimons lowered his head and it remained in this position as he gathered his thoughts.

Finally, he raised his head and turned it to the left, looking directly into the eyes of Deputy Chief Gyondski.

"Officer Ortego was found dead in Gilles today," Chief Fitzsimons said.

"Holy shit" Trustee Coconato said out loud before shutting up and realizing he probably shouldn't even be in this office.

"Shit," Gyondski said, while slowly shaking his head, from side to side.

"Chief McKinley just told me what he knows about the incident. Due to the fact it was one of our own, he personally went to the crime scene to find out as much as he could before calling me."

Both Deputy Chief Gyondski and Trustee Coconato continued to stare at Chief Fitzsimons, wanting to see if he would share any more information about Officer Ortego's death with them.

Surprisingly, he did, apparently in shock over the loss of his third officer in such a short period of time.

"Gilles Police are working with NORTAF on the case, because they have reason to believe it's a suicide due to a note and Ortego's service weapon was found at the scene," Chief Fitzsimons said.

"Jesus," Deputy Chief Gyondski said softly.

"Unbelievably it's even worse than just Officer Ortego's death," Chief Fitzsimons said, this time for some unknown reason, looking directly at Trustee Coconato. "Details are still a bit sketchy, but our very own Officer O'Neil found the body and has already told a Gilles Commander, they can expect to find his fingerprints on the grip of Ortego's gun."

CHAPTER 24

Waiting in the interrogation room, of the Northland Police Department, Matt O'Neil sat with his arms folded and a warm can of Diet Coke on the table in front of him.

"How you holding up?" Kevin Kray asks him in a slight whisper due to the fact there is probably a microphone somewhere in the room and anything he or Matt say is likely being recorded.

"Fine, really fine," Matt answers with notable sarcasm in his voice as he turns his face and looks directly at Kevin Kray, who is sitting next to him.

Matt is by no means fine, and both he and Kevin know it.

Matt had to admit his stress level has been slightly eased by the help and comfort he's getting from Kevin, who is his appointed Fraternal Order of Police attorney.

From the moment they met in a corner booth, at the Northland Starbucks, two hours ago, Matt was put at ease by the professionalism Kevin Kray had displayed.

With his black leather binder containing a legal pad with over 50 questions, to his three-piece Brooks Brothers suit, there wasn't any doubt as to what occupation Kevin held.

Matt puts Kevin's age somewhere in the late fifties, due to all of the grey hair and wrinkles.

Age is critical to Matt because he definitely wants someone with experience to handle this shitball, which doesn't seem to make sense to him.

He is actually numb over the events that had transpired in the past 12 hours.

"Hell, the past months and the loss of three of his fellow officers are the real issues," he thinks.

While Kevin ignores the Styrofoam cup of coffee directly in front of him and writes something on his legal pad, Matt looks around the room.

By no means is this his first experience being in an interrogation room due to his occupation as a police officer.

But this is his first experience being in one as an individual who needs to talk to the police about a particular incident.

Matt is sitting on the wrong side of the table in his mind.

As interrogation rooms went, it is your standard room.

Battleship grey painted walls with whatever leftover paint being used for the huge metal table located in the middle of the room and chairs located on either side of the table.

A typical clock hangs over the only door in the room, with the traditional light hanging directly over the middle of the table.

A pretty good-sized two-way mirror is located on the wall that Matt is facing.

He wonders how many NORTAF personnel are currently standing behind it right now.

Most police departments on the North Shore have neither the manpower nor experience to handle a homicide investigation in their village.

Thus, they created the North Regional Major Crimes Task Force (NORTAF).

Made up of police departments all surrounding Greenfield and similar to MCAT, the personnel who made up NORTAF bring different specialties—crime scene collection, interview and interrogation to name a few—to this unit for cases of serious magnitude.

Matt knew two members from the Greenfield Police Department who were members of NORTAF, Crime Scene Technician Steve Edelman and Detective Eric Schulte and had been called out twice already due to homicides in Evanston.

As most cops in Greenfield, Matt had never used, or for that matter needed NORTAF and hoped he never would.

Matt glances at his watch and realizes he and Kray have been sitting in this room for close to 75 minutes, and he knows why.

Whichever NORTAF detective is going to interview Matt wants to show who has all the power in this situation.

Second, the detective is trying to increase the anxiety level.

Matt had already used the same technique himself on a couple of follow ups for hit-and-run traffic accidents in hopes of getting a confession from the driver.

"Shit," Matt says out loud, bored and cold due to the temperature in the room.

He figures the temperature is easily in the low 60's and wonders if lowering the room temperature is some new interview or interrogation technique, he isn't aware of.

With nothing else to do, he glances at the clock again and realizes it had been now 80 minutes since he put his ass in this crappy chair.

Because he has nothing but time on his hands, Matt tries to figure out when and where he'd been sitting longer than today.

He quickly surmises it was in the military and either in a truck convoy, or a C 130.

His figuring comes to a quick end.

After exactly 81 minutes, they walk in, single file.

Two NORTAF detectives who don't have smiles on either of their faces.

As these detective's head for the metal table, Matt pushes his chair in so he can easily rest his hands on the table in a partial prayer position. His hands come together with all of the fingers interlocking, hopefully giving an image to both Detectives that he is relaxed in this setting.

Nothing can be further from the truth in Matt's mind.

He then quickly unlocks his fingers and using his right hand, Matt gently moves the Diet Coke can aside so it is next to the untouched Styrofoam cup by Kevin.

Both detectives drop their black binders on the table in front of their chairs.

While each of the detectives pull a chair out from under the table, Matt's mind races at what technique they are going to use on him.

"Good cop, bad cop, or sympathetic, nurturing cop," all fly through his head.

After each of the detectives is seated, Matt thinks it's strange they copied him by pulling their chairs close, so their bodies are up against the table and easily within arm's reach of both Kevin and himself.

"I'm Detective Jeff Lyons from the Wheeling Police Department," he extends his right hand to Matt.

"I'm Detective Bill Golden of the Wilmette Police Department," he also extends his right hand to Matt.

Talk about two totally opposite looking individuals.

Jeff Lyons is rather young, in his mid-thirties, tall, thin, with bright red hair and dressed impeccably.

Bill Golden looks like he just got out of bed, is easily in his mid-fifties, short, with a bit of a gut and a two-day-old beard.

Golden looks nothing like a detective and could pass as a member of a motorcycle gang.

The one similarity each of them have are the clammiest hands and weakest handshakes Matt had ever encountered.

Neither detective makes any effort to shake Kevin's hand.

Foolishly, a small grin appears on Matt's face over this lack of a handshake for his attorney.

"You find something funny going on here Matt?" Detective Golden says with a tone that makes Matt feel even colder than he did a few minutes ago.

"No Sir," Matt responds as if he's back in the service.

Matt then glances over at Kevin, who also gives him a look as if someone had just pissed in his cereal.

It doesn't take Detective Lyons very long to get the ball rolling.

While all of the handshaking was taking place, Detective Lyons had opened his black binder, pulling out completed police reports, along with a police supplemental report.

Both of these documents are lying on the table in front of Kevin.

"As you can see Matt, I have a copy of the Gilles Police Department General Case Report of this incident as well as a Supplemental Report on the very, very brief statement you gave Commander Billings at the crime scene of your involvement in this incident."

Immediately, Detective Lyons pushes both of these documents across the table into the hands of Kevin, who is ready for them.

Matt turns and watches as Kevin reads both of them.

When finished he nods his head once at Matt, approving the documents as legitimate.

Then, Detective Golden continues as if he is reading something off a card. "Matt, since you came in on your own free will and obviously can leave at any time you wish, there isn't any need for Miranda warnings in this instance."

"I understand," Matt replies.

"Good, good," Detective Lyons responds and after pausing for only a few seconds gets started. "So, take your time and tell us everything you can remember about this horrible, horrible tragedy," he finishes with an almost pleading tone in his voice.

Again, Matt looks at Kevin who simply says two words, "Go ahead."

Matt turns and looks directly at Detective Lyons.

Unexpectedly, Detective Golden spouts off like a parent who had just caught their child's hand in the cookie jar. "You can leave out the part about meeting Attorney Kray across the street at the Starbucks, if you wish."

If this comment is intended to upset Matt, it has just the opposite effect.

Inside of Matt, a small fire starts to burn.

"Javier Ortego and I had a scheduled racquetball game set for 0800 hours today at Leaning Tower YMCA in Gilles, where he's a member," Matt starts out.

The tone in his voice has changed dramatically, becoming more forceful.

"So, according to this report, he texted you and said there was something wrong with his car?" Detective Lyons responds and also matches Matt's newfound confident tone.

"Correct," Matt responds.

"So, what time was that?" Detective Golden asks.

Matt pulls out his new phone from his right front pants pocket, a gift he had rewarded himself with for all of the overtime he'd been pulling in these last couple of months.

Quickly, he scrolls down and finds the message, which shows the text was sent to him at 0700 hours and reads, "Dude, I need a jump for my car. It's dead in my driveway. Can you do it after racquetball?"

"The original plan was to just meet Ortego at Leaning Tower?" Detective Lyons asks.

"That is correct Sir," Matt responds and quickly realizes this is how the two detectives are going to play him, each taking turns asking him questions.

"I responded by texting I would be there in roughly 20 minutes and to be ready to go because I'll just beep the horn."

"First time going to his house?" Detective Lyons asks, toning it down considerably from before and this time with a more inquisitive voice.

"Been there before for a Bears versus Vikings shift party," Matt answers.

"So, you're familiar with the total layout of his place?" Detective Lyons asks.

"Not really Detective, since I came in through the front door and spent the majority of time in his family room watching the game," Matt says.

"C'mon, never went to the bathroom, kitchen for a beer and snacks, or joined any of your guys on the rear patio," Detective Golden jumps in and then follows up with a death stare.

"I was tired and only stayed the first half and doubt any of our guys went out on the patio Sir," Matt says.

"Why would that be?" Detective Golden quickly asks.

"Game was played in late December, and the temperature was about ten degrees at kickoff," Matt says.

"Okay, okay, let's get back to today," Detective Golden mumbles loud enough for everyone at the table to hear him.

"What time did you get there today?" Detective Lyons asks.

"I got there at exactly 0730 hours because Mike Mulligan on the SCORE was just going to a scoreboard update," Matt says.

For the first time since the interview started, neither detective says anything.

Both of them just stare at Matt.

Seeing a possible opening in controlling the interview, Matt starts talking.

"I beeped my horn a couple of times, expecting Javier to come out either through the front door of his townhouse or his overhead garage door," Matt says before being interrupted by Detective Lyons.

"But he didn't come out, so how long do you figure you waited before you got out of your car?"

"No longer than four or five minutes because I was worried about being late and losing our court," Matt answers and then realizes his honesty just opened the door for either one of these detectives, if not both, to pounce.

Detective Lyons realizes it before Detective Golden.

Any advantage Matt had obtained in regards to controlling the interview is suddenly lost.

"Not a real sympathetic guy O'Neil?" Detective Lyons is back on Matt in a second.

Before Matt can say a word, Detective Golden jumps in, "Hardened by all of the Navy Seal stuff you did in the military, O'Neil?"

"Excuse me?" Matt says mainly in an effort to buy time.

At this moment he realizes what these two detectives prior 80 minutes had been used for, going through his background step by step.

"What part of that last statement didn't you understand?" Detective Golden asks, still glaring at Matt.

"All of it, because if I didn't care about him, I would have just called him on my phone instead of getting out of my car," Matt replies angrily.

"So, you see his car in the driveway, he's not answering his phone or coming outside, what are you thinking is happening?" Detective Lyons asks.

"I didn't think he fell back asleep or could be on the toilet. I'm a bit unsure," Matt answers and finds himself, for the first time since the interview started, raising his hands off the table and holding them about shoulder-width apart in an open position, as if he is saying the Our Father during mass.

"Tell us what you did next, please," Detective Golden says.

The word please, catches Matt's immediate attention and temporarily throws him of track, before he continues.

"I started walking around the outside of his townhouse, starting at the front door and traveling to my right looking in every window in hopes of seeing something significant," Matt answers calmly.

He then pauses and waits for their next question.

Again, both detectives play the waiting game and neither of them presents a question to Matt for nearly a minute. The silence in the room is hard on Matt as he feels three pairs of eyes all focused directly on him.

Finally, Detective Lyons says simply, "Continue."

"I got to the rear patio sliding glass doors and looked in but again, I don't see Javy or anything unusual. So, I walked over to where his Weber grill is located. Taped behind the left wheel is a key to the front door of his place," Matt says.

"How did you know the key was there?" Detective Lyons asks.

"When he moved from his crappy apartment in Bolingbrook, he told T.C. Chambers and I he was going to place a spare one there in case of emergency. It really wasn't too big of a secret on our shift," Matt answers.

Again, with no comment or question coming from either detective, Matt continues. "I returned to the front door of his place, finding no signs of forced entry and let myself in using this key. Once inside, I called out his name and got no response."

"Obviously, his home alarm wasn't in the on position or it

would have activated," Detective Lyons says as if he is just making a statement as opposed to asking Matt a question.

"Correct," Matt replies.

"Kind of curious about that," Detective Golden asks rather nonchalantly.

For the first time, the other three individuals direct their attention to Detective Golden as if he has some new, huge information regarding this case.

"Besides knowing the whereabouts of the key, did you or T.C. Chambers also have his code to deactivate the alarm?" Detective Golden asks and leans across the table so he's now even closer to Matt.

"No Sir," Matt answers calmly.

"So, what was your plan if the alarm was in the on position and you activated it when you walked in?" Detective Golden follows up and a slight grin appears on his face.

"Wait for the Gilles Police Department to respond because I was legitimately concerned about Jav," Matt says.

"So, you're in the hallway of his townhouse, concerned about his safety. I assume you took out your off-duty weapon?" Detective Lyons asks.

"No," Matt answers in a matter-of-fact style.

"Why not?" Detective Golden asks.

"I never carry when I'm going to work out because I'm not going to leave it in a gym locker or inside my car Sir," Matt answers.

"Then what did you do next?" Detective Lyons asks.

"I walked up the stairs to the second floor and headed directly to his bedroom," Matt says very calmly and slowly because he knows what's coming next and, in his mind, he's trying to prepare himself for it.

"That's when you saw him?" Detective Golden asks.

"Yes," Matt says very softly.

"Continue," Detective Lyons says.

"Before I reached his master bedroom, I glanced to my right as I was passing the guest room, which also served as his office. There he was, sitting in a chair." Matt says.

All eyes are now squarely focused on Matt and he feels as if the two detectives' looks are burning a hole right through him.

"Take your time if you need to compose yourself Matt," Detective Golden says in a gentle tone.

Matt doesn't need any additional time.

He had spent the first hour while waiting with Kevin, in this very room, going over in his mind the probable questions he would be asked by whoever the NORTAF detectives would be.

"Javier was leaning to his right in the chair with a sizeable, bleeding wound on the right side of his head and still holding his department-issued Glock in his right hand," Matt is able to get this out in one complete sentence.

Suddenly, Detective Lyons picks up the police report of this incident with his left hand and is now holding it close to his face when he says, "Confirm for us what you did next."

"When I saw Javier in this condition, both my military and police training kicked in. I took the weapon out of his right hand in case there was an intruder or offender still on the premises," Matt answers and sits up a bit straighter in his chair.

"You hadn't seen the note on the desk, had you?" Detective Golden asks.

"No," Matt responds.

"Continue Matt," Detective Golden says.

"I cleared the second floor, finding nothing unusual at all and then returned to Javier's office where I laid the Glock on his desk. At this time, I saw a hand-written note slightly covered in blood," Matt says.

"Did you read the note Matt?" Detective Lyons asks.

"No, due to not really having a reason and obviously realizing this was now a crime scene and didn't want to touch any evidence, like the one shell casing from the Glock which was still in its present position on the floor just to the right of the chair Javier was seated in."

"What did you do next?" Detective Lyons asks.

"I called the Gilles Police Department on my cell phone, advising them of the situation and telling them my description and where I would be upon their officers' arrival at the residence."

Matt answers in such a manner it's almost as if he is reading it off the police report Detective Lyons is still holding.

"How well did you know Javier?" Detective Golden asks.

"Pretty well considering there is a slight age difference," Matt responds.

"Apparently, he didn't take the extended probation handed down to him all that well, Lt. Wayne told us roughly two hours ago," Detective Golden says and the smirk from earlier is back on his face.

"Don't really know detectives, since he took some time off after being told of the department's decision and now this," Matt answers and then quickly realizes it's his first semi-truthful statement he's given them so far.

"C'mon, Matt who the hell would be freakin' happy being told you're still stuck on probation?" Detective Lyons yells and Matt realizes his one less-than-truthful answer might have opened the door to some doubt about his credibility.

"What about his social life, such as his girlfriend?" Detective Golden asks.

"All of his family are still somewhere in Mexico and believed he was dating a girl named Juanita, a beautiful Hispanic girl from Skokie. But I'm not sure of her last name," Matt says calmly.

"Anybody else on the force tight with him?" Detective Golden asks.

"I think him and Thomas were close, but—" Matt feels confident he's back on track with this answer.

He couldn't have been more wrong if he tried.

"I guess we'll never know, will we?" Detective Golden says and his voice trails off after the word we.

"Guess not Detective," Matt answers.

"You and Thomas were never close, were you?" Detective Golden asks.

For the first time since the interview started, Kevin jumps in saying, "Not sure where you're going with that comment, Detective."

"Just asking your client a question counsel," Detective Golden follows up with.

Matt immediately looks over at Kevin, waiting for his permission, before he answers the question.

Problem is Kevin is still staring at Detective Golden, trying to figure out his angle with the Thomas question.

A minute passes and the stare down continues.

Kevin finally realizes Matt is looking for some sign from him as to whether to answer the question or not.

While still playing stare down with Detective Golden, Kevin says softly, "Go ahead Matt, and tell him your true feelings about Ron."

"Yes, Thomas and I really didn't have much in common other than working for the Greenfield Police Department," Matt says.

"Where were you the day Thomas died?" Detective Golden asks.

"YOU HAVE GOT TO BE FUCKING KIDDING ME," Kevin yells at Detective Golden, who has suddenly stood up and walked around the table so, he's now standing on Matt's left side.

"ANY REASON YOU MIGHT HAVE BEEN IN DOOR COUNTY, PENINSULA STATE PARK TO BE EXACT THE DAY YOUR SOMEWHAT FRIEND THOMAS WAS FOUND FLOATING IN THE LAKE?" Detective Lyons yells at Matt while standing up suddenly.

For the second time in less than a minute Matt turns to look at Kevin, who has a look on his face like he just sat in a pile of dog shit.

Again, Kevin nods his head once, indicating to Matt he has permission to answer the question.

"Jav and I played racquetball that day and then worked out in the weight room at Leaning Tower YMCA, before I went home and did a number of chores for the remainder of the day," Matt says with a matter of fact tone in his voice.

"Hmm and the witness to verify some of this is dead with your fingerprints all over the weapon used in his death," Detective Lyons says.

"Confirming your fingerprints wouldn't be found on the note since you never touched it or read it when you put the Glock back on the desk?" Detective Golden asks.

"Correct to both of those comments, Sir," Matt says.

"The suicide note Javier Ortego wrote isn't very complimentary to you at all Matt," Detective Golden says and once again, a huge grin appears on his face.

"Sir?" Matt responds and he is stunned momentarily by both the last comment and current look on Detective Golden's face.

"The suicide note says even though you're married, you betrayed Javier by cheating with his girlfriend Juanita, which played a part in his suicide," Detective Golden responds.

Before Matt can respond, Detective Lyons fires the next salvo, "Yeah, the note also says he suspected you played some part in Thomas's death, and he was letting us know in hopes we could figure this whole mess out."

"THOSE ARE A BUNCH OF LIES," Matt screams and stands up.

"This interview is over gentlemen," Kevin says as he also stands up.

Detective Golden is standing so close to Matt their faces are almost touching.

Now its Matt's turn to play stare down with Detective Golden.

No one obviously wants to lose.

The game goes on as both Kevin and Detective Lyons watch in silence.

Kevin apparently has seen enough and walks over to Matt, grabbing him by his left elbow and whispering in his ear, "This is accomplishing nothing, so put your fucking dick back in your pants and let's get the hell out of here."

Handshakes are out of the question at this point as Matt falls behind Kevin and they head out of the room.

As Kevin reaches the interrogation room door, Detective Golden yells out, "We'll be in touch Matt."

Neither Kevin or Matt acknowledges the comment as they continue out of the room and down a narrow hallway.

After only one right turn, they come to the lobby of the Northland Police Department.

She is standing all alone.

The frown on her face turns upwards into a scared smile, the minute she sees Matt.

Kevin briskly walks past her and then suddenly stops to wait as Matt walks up to her and gives her a hug.

"I'll wait for you two out in the parking lot because I need to go over a couple of things with you Matt," Kevin says and then walks out the lobby doors and turns right, headed for the visitor's parking lot.

Matt puts his arms around Kelly and says nothing as they try and outdo each other in giving the most forceful hug to each other.

Kelly soon realizes she is easily losing at this silly game so she goes to Plan B.

While her left arm is still around Matt's waist, she takes her right hand and begins to massage his upper back and neck area.

"Feels wonderful babe," Matt says softly into her left ear.

No other conversation is exchanged between the two of them as the hugging and massaging continues.

Soon, Matt has this creepy feeling they are not alone and stops, breaking their embrace while standing straight up.

Oblivious to it when he entered the police station with Kevin earlier today, Matt now realizes the left side of the lobby, which is covered in bulletproof glass, is the records center for the Northland Police Department.

Matt and Kelly both turn and look at this area when Matt sees both Detective Lyons and Golden standing behind the glass.

As Matt looks on in awe, both Detectives give him a thumbs up simultaneously and have huge grins on their faces.

Grabbing Kelly's right hand, Matt heads out of the front door of the police station and heads toward the visitor's parking lot, where his car is parked.

"You hungry?" Kelly asks as they keep walking.

"Nope, just tired and pissed off honey it's been quite a day, to say the least," Matt mumbles.

Pissed off really doesn't describe the mood Matt's in right now after the comments made by both detectives in the interview.

"There couldn't be any way Jav wrote those things in his suicide note, could there?" Matt is playing these thoughts over and over in his tired head.

Matt doesn't say a word to Kelly and only grips her hand tighter, thinking about the "Juanita comment" and wonders if he should even bring it up with her when they get home.

Finally, they reach the visitor's parking lot and find a clearly frustrated Kevin standing at the entrance.

Kevin, seeing Kelly holding onto Matt's hand, realizes the sensitivity of the situation and carefully chooses his words. "We'll meet in a couple of days whenever is best for you Matt, to see if there's anything more you need me to do."

Matt is totally focused on every word coming out of Kevin's mouth.

Kelly grips his hand even tighter, sensing things may not be right with this entire situation.

Matt suddenly senses something is going on as Kevin's focus goes from Matt to a person approaching from behind him.

With the conversation stopped between Kevin and himself, Matt hears footsteps approaching on the grey colored, gravel stones of the parking lot.

Matt lets go of Kelly's hand and quickly turns around.

"Hello Officer O'Neil," Deputy Chief Bart says disgustedly.

CHAPTER 25

"**B**oss?" Matt O'Neil responds with a tone of shock in his voice.

He is totally blown away by the head of the Operations Division of the Greenfield Police Department standing in front of him at this hour of the night.

"Mrs. O'Neil, Attorney Kray," Deputy Chief Bart acknowledges both of them and they stare back at him, also apparently confused by his appearance.

"How you holding up, Officer O'Neil?" Bart asks without a thread of compassion or concern in his voice.

"As best to be expected Sir," Matt responds, which is one of the biggest lies he has ever said to anyone.

Matt lies because he is scared shitless right now and has no other avenue to express it.

"Really sorry to hear about Officer Ortego," Deputy Chief Bart says and then to emphasize the point, slowly lowers his head for a moment.

"What's being done at his residence?" Attorney Kray jumps in, having the distinct advantage over the other three people of never having the opportunity to meet Officer Ortego. Consequently, he can be professional as opposed to emotional.

"Scene has been turned over to the NORTAF team to handle and we're confident they will do a very thorough job," Deputy Chief Bart answers.

"We Boss?" Matt asks.

"Matt, both Chief Fitzsimons and I were present at the crime scene and, Deputy Chief Gyondski has been in continuous contact with us," Deputy Chief Bart says.

"Any Greenfield personnel on the team handling this case?" Attorney Kray asks.

"None counsel, and we wouldn't want any of them at the crime scene to guarantee there wouldn't be a conflict of interest," Deputy Chief Bart says calmly while for some strange reason, continuing to stare at Matt.

Attorney Kray seems satisfied with the answer, which is good enough for both Matt and Kelly.

"Jav's family been notified, Sir?" Matt asks with a rather timid tone in his voice.

"Yes, this matter was taken care of roughly ninety minutes ago."

"Thank you, Sir. I really appreciate it," Matt says.

"Not a problem Matt. So, tell me how your interview with the NORTAF detectives went," Deputy Chief Bart responds ever so nonchalantly.

"I thought it went extremely well, Boss, until the end quite frankly, when they came up with some goofy scenarios about Officer Thomas death and my possible involvement in it," Matt answers.

"WHATTTTTTTTTT?" Kelly yells.

"AWWWWWW FUCK," Matt yells, not caring who he is standing with.

Matt turns to find a visibly upset Kelly, who has even started crying slightly.

"Honey, none of it is true and you more than anyone else should know where I was the entire 36-hour period before he died," Matt answers.

Matt reaches out to hold Kelly by her upper arms as he looks into her moist eyes.

"Funny they should bring Thomas up since I also spoke with Detective Kenbridge earlier today," Deputy Chief Bart says with a hint of doubt in his voice. "His death is still classified as an open Death Investigation."

Suddenly, Matt has a strange feeling overcome him as he lets go of Kelly and turns back so he is once again facing Deputy Chief Bart.

Apparently, Attorney Kray must have had the same feeling as

he quickly moves from standing behind Kelly to his new position of standing on Deputy Chief Bart's left side.

"Officer O'Neil did extremely well in the interview Sir," Attorney Kray says, sounding like he is giving a closing argument in a trial. "I'm positive the detectives can furnish your Chief with a copy of it, if you request one."

"Excellent Counsel, I'll pass that on to Chief Fitzsimons, who expects nothing but the best from all of our Greenfield personnel," Deputy Chief Bart answers. "Speaking of Chief Fitzsimons, he's part of the reason I'm here right now, Officer O'Neil."

"Sir?" Matt is totally confused by this latest comment and is worried what could be coming next.

"The Chief and I had a lengthy discussion earlier this evening," Deputy Chief Bart says. "We agree it's in everyone's best interest— NORTAF, our department, et cetera if we remove you from your squad and have you work records for the next couple of weeks"

"The words, 'Remove you from your squad,'" stun Matt to the point he can't respond.

So, Attorney Kray talks for both of them.

"Are you saying Officer O'Neil is under investigation in some way for the death of Officer Ortego or Thomas, Sir?"

"I did not Counsel, unless you know something I don't," Deputy Chief Bart raises his right hand in the direction of Attorney Kray and points his index finger in Kray's face.

Matt sees this whole thing spinning out of control and knows he needs to do something before it is too late.

Instantly, he moves himself in front of Attorney Kray so he stands directly in front of Deputy Chief Bart.

"Boss, it would help all of us if you could give me some explanation for this move please," Matt asks.

His comment works immediately as Deputy Chief Bart lowers his right hand and seems to quickly regain his composure.

"Matt, Chief Fitzsimons and I aren't oblivious to what the hell's been happening. With Officer Ortego's death now making it three of our police officers deceased, we're also aware of the stress and your indirect involvement in each of these deaths so we simply want you to catch your breath a bit and stay off the street for a short period of time until things get back to normal, if they ever will. Understood?" Deputy Chief Bart says with a rather sympathetic tone for the first time since he has shown up.

"You don't think this will paint a picture of Officer O'Neil being a possible suspect in all of this?" Attorney Kray asks with a rather exasperated tone in his voice.

"Counsel, the Chief and I have looked at every possible scenario regarding this situation. We even weighed the option of giving Officer O'Neil some time off, but we believe it would paint him as a possible suspect in one of these deaths and force him to go into hiding from his fellow personnel," Deputy Chief Bart answers calmly and seems to put Attorney Kray at ease for the moment.

"Bullshit," Matt thinks. "Somehow Chief Fitzsimons and Deputy Chief Bart know about Javier's suicide note allegations and it's the reason for the move to records."

For thirty seconds, Matt stands there, trying to keep his composure. His stress level is nearing the breaking point.

"Matt can we get going?" Kelly says softly as she is bending over slightly at the waist while holding her stomach. "I'm really not feeling well right now."

"Sure babe," Matt says and again turns his body as well as his attention away from both Deputy Chief Bart and Attorney Kray and back on the most important person in his life.

With Matt being only inches away from Kelly when she asks him to leave, it only took him a few seconds to spin around and again be face to face with her.

With his size advantage in both height and weight, he dwarfs her and prevents both Deputy Chief Bart and Attorney Kray from being able to see her.

"Kelly, what is it?" Matt asks. "What's wrong?"

"Really not sure since I've never been pregnant before Matt," Kelly says with a huge grin and stands straight up. "So, take me home, Daddy to be."

CHAPTER 26

"Thank you, thank you, thank you, Officer Ortego," Deputy Chief Gyondski says softly to himself, even though his office door is closed and he's alone.

Seated behind his desk, he realizes he has a few minutes before he needs to make his next phone call.

"Idiot, you can make the next phone call whenever you fucking want," he says to himself as he hangs up his telephone.

He more than anyone on the Greenfield Police Department, has benefited from Officer Ortego's death, as he crosses himself and says a quick Our Father and follows it up with a Hail Mary as well.

Deputy Chief Gyondski figures Officer Ortego is going to need every prayer he can get.

By committing suicide, he has partially broken the Fifth Commandment of the Catholic Church and is headed straight to a life in Hell.

Sister Theodore and Father Blaski at St. Roberts, where young Frank Gyondski had gone to grade school, are easily rolling their eyes in heaven right now. Sister Theodore, in particular, had drilled the Ten Commandments into young Frank and his classmates repeatedly his entire year in third grade.

To this day, he can recite each of them verbatim.

"Poor Bastard," Deputy Chief Gyondski mutters to himself and then he laughs out loud, starting to sound more like Francis Underwood from *House of Cards* than himself. *House of Cards* was the only show he and Beth watched together on Netflix.

They both couldn't wait for season four to see what sinister actions President Francis Underwood had planned next.

The real reason he prayed for Officer Ortego was because his death had for the moment, taken Deputy Chief Gyondski's career out of a life in hell and given it a second chance after the fucking debacle Village Trustee Coconato had just pulled.

Immediately after getting the news of Officer Ortego s death, Deputy Chief Gyondski jumped on it, hoping to save his career as well as to show the Chief what type of Deputy Chief of Support Services he had in Frank Gyondski.

As Chief Fitzsimons escorted Trustee Coconato out of the Deputy Chief's office, Frank Gyondski grabbed his office phone from its cradle on his desk and hit programmed button #5. Listening as it quickly punched in the numbers for Beth's cell phone.

Beth's phone rang twice before she answered it. "Just finished loading up my car babe. Are you on your way home?" she asks with a sweet tone in her voice, making Frank's comments even more painful.

He knows what he has to say, but doesn't know how to say it.

Any spouse can sense trouble with their mate, whether through body language, tone of voice, or lack of words. Beth, being an exceptionally smart woman, senses it the minute her husband doesn't respond to her comments.

"Frank, what's the matter?" Beth asks, alarmed at the silence on the other end of the phone.

"We've lost another one honey," he mumbles into the phone.

"OH MY GOD WHO?" Beth yells into the phone.

"Officer Javier Ortego," he answers meekly.

"Did I ever meet him?" Beth asks, still with a tone of shock in her voice.

"No, his shift was working the day we had our department Christmas Party and only Officers O'Brien and O'Neil stopped in for a meal on their dinner break," he answers.

"Okay, I'll call the golf school when we're finished," Beth answers.

"Thanks babe," Frank answers, always impressed by his wife's thoroughness.

"Frank, please be careful," Beth says. "This is getting really, really, crazy."

"I promise I will," he answers. Then, he quickly goes into work mode, saying, "Beth, don't wait up for me since I have a ton to do now and I will just crash here and be home late tomorrow."

"Okay," says Beth. "And Frank, remember, I love you."

"I love you as well Beth and believe me, I will be careful," Frank answers.

After hanging up the phone, he turns in his chair until he is directly in front of his computer.

In record time he finds the file in Microsoft Works 2010 labeled, "Greenfield Police Documents" and opens it.

Scrolling down, he finds the department roster which lists every employee's name within the Greenfield Police Department as well as their address, home and cell phone numbers and date of hire.

Halfway down the roster, he found Javier Ortego of 8223 Ozark Avenue, Gilles, which is all he needed for now.

He pulls out his department cell phone and puts this information into the notes app. Standing up, he grabs the keys for his Chevy Malibu off the desk and puts them into his left pants pocket. With his right hand, he grabs his department portable radio from its battery charger located behind him on a separate table.

Confident he has everything; he leaves his office to meet up with the Chief when his phone rings.

Checking the neon green panel on the phone shows the caller to be Chief Fitzsimons from his cell phone.

"Boss...?" is all he could say before the Chief starts up.

"Deputy Chief Bart and I are headed to Officer Ortego's residence, and I've already contacted the Village Manager and given him a brief idea of what's going on. He will contact all the remaining Village Trustees," Chief Fitzsimons barely pauses long enough to catch his breath before continuing talking at record speed. "I need you to call Village Attorney Katt and give him a quick overview. Obviously, you'll also prepare a press release, any chance you know the PIO for the Gilles Police Department?"

"Yes Sir. Her name is Sergeant Nichole Price. I've worked with her before. She's very competent and extremely professional, like all of the Gilles Command Staff," Deputy Chief Gyondski gets in and waits for anything additional from Chief Fitzsimons.

"Okay, sounds like a plan. I will send Deputy Chief Bart back to brief you when I don't need him anymore with me in Gilles, understood?" Chief Fitzsimons finishes.

"Understood Chief," Deputy Chief Gyondski is able to get these last words out before all he is left listening to is a dial tone.

Hanging up his phone, he sits back in his chair for a minute.

He hates to admit it, but his current Chief has his shit together.

Chief Edward Angeli would never have been able to handle the death of three of his police officers without losing his mind.

Chief Angeli portrayed the friendly grandfather figure to most people when everything was going according to plan or nothing out of the ordinary was taking place.

But when the proverbial "shit hit the fan" a few times, such as an officer involved traffic accident, or a bullet discharging accidentally in the locker room, Chief Angeli would lose his freaking mind for days.

Frank Gyondski had recently been on the receiving end of Chief Fitzsimons' outburst, and he still thought this Chief was a pompous asshole. With all that being said, Chief Fitzsimons still got the best out of his people and demonstrated leadership throughout the entire department.

The day of Chris Mills' death, Chief Fitzsimons made a promise to "Get his police department healed from today's tragedy." Deputy Chief Gyondski was sure the Chief never envisioned the additional loss of two other police officers that he would have to endure in the coming months.

But to the Chief's credit, he had lived up to his word and busted his ass every day while dealing with this ongoing tragedy. He was dealing with personnel, who were stressed, frustrated, angry, in shock and actually scared about who might be next to die. Roll call visits, extended time talking to his officers in the lunch room and parking lot conversations with Greenfield patrol personnel, were just some of the techniques he used in an attempt to heal his police department.

Frank Gyondski couldn't recall a medium-sized department losing this many police officers in such a short time frame, but then the killing of four police officers came to mind.

All D. C. Gyondki could recall it was only a few years ago and it was somewhere out west.

The killer was found the next day and was killed in a shootout with local police. In the killer's possession was a gun belonging to one of the officers he slayed the day before. Frank Gyondski shuddered, thinking how a police department and their command staff, could suffer that kind of carnage and still function.

Leaning forward in his chair, he hit the programmed button #4 and waited as his phone dialed Katt's phone number automatically.

"Good afternoon and thank you for calling the law firm of Katt, Cooper, and Montgomery, Mary Ellis speaking."

"Mary, this is Deputy Chief Gyondski from the Police Department, is Attorney Katt in?"

"He's meeting with the head of Public Works right now Deputy Chief. If you want, I can interrupt him."

"No, just have him give me a call when he's available, either on my cell phone, or here at the police station. He has both of those numbers and please let him know, I definitely need to speak with him today," Deputy Chief Gyondski says.

"Will do and have a great weekend Deputy Chief," Ms. Ellis finishes.

Hanging up the phone, Deputy Chief Gyondski laughs mildly at her last comment.

"Have a great weekend, another dead cop with a fellow cop's fingerprints on the gun used in the act. What the hell is going to be so great about this weekend?" Frank says halfheartedly to himself.

Getting up, he goes over to a file cabinet located in a corner of the room. Bending over slightly, he pulls out the second drawer of the file cabinet, which consists entirely of thin manila folders. Each individual folder has a white piece of tape across the top of it, with a current Greenfield police officer's name typed on it. Every officer updated these files every year, for a very sorrowful purpose.

On a form in the file, the Greenfield Police Officers had to list who they wanted contacted first, in case they died on the job.

Using his left hand, he goes through these files until he finds the one, he's looking for—Officer Javier Ortego. As he is pulling this file out, the one in front of it somehow comes with as well and falls on his office floor. Quickly, Deputy Chief Gyondski bends over and picks it up, glancing at the name on it.

The file read, Officer Matt O'Neil.

Deputy Chief Gyondski holds both files in his hand, staring at them and slightly freaked out.

Two men who are totally different in race, age, and personalities, but yet, they are tied together in death.

Deputy Chief Gyondski knows little about Javier Ortego as well as the recently departed, Officers Mills and Thomas.

"Jesus Frank, you don't know anything about Dombrowski or Chambers either so who are you trying to kid," he thinks.

He knew about Megan O'Brien only vaguely because she was the hottest female officer, he had ever seen his entire time in law enforcement.

Deputy Chief Bart filled him in more about Officer O'Brien after Officer Mills' burial when her apparent boyfriend, Kurt Thompson, showed up at the gravesite and caused a bit of a scene.

Granted, what any police officer does in their free time is entirely up to them, as long as it isn't illegal, against department policy, or interfering with their on-duty work performance.

Deputy Chief Gyondski handled the paperwork for vacation hours as well as sick leave taken by Greenfield police personnel. Yes, O'Brien had taken a significant number of sick days, compared to her fellow officers, so he would have to monitor her situation more carefully.

Finally, there was Officer Matt O'Neil, who was a total enigma after hearing about his involvement in Javier Ortego's death.

Before today, Deputy Chief Gyondski had little problem with Officer O'Neil.

While a college education was a must for many police departments nationwide, a potential candidate who had a military background usually had a slight advantage above the other candidates. Maturity, excellent physical shape, self-defense, along with weapons training, but more importantly, these candidates had decision making skills some college grads often didn't have. In the little over a year Deputy Chief Gyondski had observed Officer O'Neil's action, he quickly realized O'Neil possessed all of the before mentioned qualities.

Apparently, he wasn't alone with his feelings because Lt. Miler had picked O'Neil for the coveted Greenfield Police Department Honor Guard, over more senior officers in the department who also had military experience as well.

Following both Officers Mills' and Thomas's deaths, O'Neil had gone through the proper chain of command and received permission from the Chief to clean out each of their lockers.

It was an unusual request, but word had already spread earlier throughout the entire department about O'Neil's so called "Golden Boy" image, which was enhanced when the Chief sent him personally to Door County, instead of one of the detectives, to identify Thomas's body.

Officer O'Neil may have gone from Golden Boy to being in the doghouse, but only time would tell.

It wasn't of particular concern currently to Deputy Chief Gyondski who had a desk full of work to dive into.

He opened the manila file for Officer Ortego which would help him prepare both his press release as well as notify next of kin regarding whom to release his body to. He decided to do the press release first because it should be the easier of the two and he'd have the information in case PIO Price needed it to help with her press release.

He almost finishes the press release when his office phone rings. Recognizing the telephone number as being the same one he called roughly seventy minutes ago, he answers.

"Attorney Katt," he answers.

"Deputy Chief how you hitting them these days?" Katt asks with a strong, confident, voice.

"Suppose to be on my way to the Tracy Chapman golf school right now Counsel," Deputy Chief Gyondski responded dejectedly.

"Was there roughly three or four years ago and helped my game a ton. Hey, ask for Teaching Pro Russ Francis, great instructor, as well as great sense of humor," Katt came back with.

Deputy Chief Gyondski could believe it since he had been in the same foursome as Katt in a couple of village golf outings over the years. Katt couldn't have been taller than 5'6" and weighed roughly 140 pounds but could bomb a golf ball off the tee and putted like Tiger Woods.

"Wait you said you're supposed to be on your way...and you're still in your office at 6:15 on a Friday. I'm not getting good vibes Deputy Chief so please fill me in," Katt asked with a slight sound of fear in his voice.

"Counsel, Chief Fitzsimons wanted me to give you a brief overview of an incident that has occurred, involving two of our newer officers," Deputy Chief Gyondski answers.

Overview apparently is the wrong terminology when dealing with any kind of attorney, Deputy Chief Gyondski would find out.

Forty-five minutes later, he was finally hanging up his telephone and tired from filling Attorney Katt in.

Besides being tired from the marathon phone call, Gyondski had a new issue to deal with—hunger.

He realizes he still has food in the refrigerator from yesterday which he never ate due to the range issue and stood up to go downstairs and grab some dinner.

But then he heard a loud knock on his office door, and he sat back down.

"C'mon in, it's open," Deputy Chief Gyondski yells.

Opening the door, Deputy Chief Bart came in with a look of frustration he hadn't shown for quite some time.

Sitting down in one of the two chairs in front of Deputy Chief Gyondski's desk, he pauses for a minute.

Finally, he opens a black binder he had brought with him to the crime scene.

"Really bad?" Deputy Chief Gyondski asks.

"Worse than we thought, according to Chief McKinley, who briefed the Chief and I when we got to Ortego's place."

"How so...." is all Gyondski is able to say before Social Worker Debra Santiago knocks on the open office door.

"Deputy Chief Bart, I have a text message asking for me to come in and meet you in Deputy Chief Gyondski's office?" Santiago asks inquisitively.

The look on her face says she knows something terribly wrong has taken place or she wouldn't have been called in this late on a beautiful Friday night.

Quickly, Deputy Chief Bart jumps out of his chair and takes a couple of steps to reach Santiago.

"Debra, Debra, please come sit down. I'll fill you in on the reason I contacted you," he says as calmly as possible.

Deputy Chief Bart extends his left arm to Santiago and guides her toward the same chair he just got out of only seconds ago. Santiago, who is in her early twenties, shuffles more than walks toward this chair, possibly afraid of what she will find out once she sits down.

There isn't any doubt in Deputy Chief Gyondski's mind Santiago never dreamed when she started working for the Greenfield Police Department a year and a half ago, she be handling police officers' death notifications so quickly in her career.

When Santiago's predecessor, Brenda Williamsburg quit after a period of roughly four years, the Village of Greenfield opened up the job search for her replacement. Eighty-seven candidates applied for the job, some from as far away as Colorado. Fresh out of DePaul University with her Masters in Social Work, Debra Santiago was chosen and every Greenfield Police Officer really didn't care.

Debra Santiago would make the fourth Social Worker hired by the Greenfield Police Department since Deputy Chief Gyondski began working there. The other three being, two men and a woman, who all started out like a ball of fire. Then marriage, private practice, burnout, frustration with management, all resulted in them finding the door on their way to a different career path.

Clearly, there is a tremendous need for a social worker on a police force of any size. Plus, their purpose and functions had only expanded, as the years went by, to the point some North Shore Police Departments had two full time social workers. Every cop worth his salt could think of numerous times they came to his or her aid, on a wide variety of circumstances or calls.

When Debra Santiago finally is seated, Deputy Chief Bart sits down in the chair next to hers and then moves his chair so he is now directly facing her.

Pausing for a second to collect his thoughts, Deputy Chief Gyondski looks on from behind his desk.

"Debra, there's no easy way of saying this, but earlier today Officer Ortego was found dead in his townhouse."

"'OHHHH MY GOD NOOOOOOOOOOOOO," Debra Santiago yells out before covering her mouth and nose with her hands and slowly begins to weep.

As her crying seemed to intensify, she says, "He was just so young and ...and so full of life."

Both Deputy Chiefs Bart and Gyondski know better than to say anything.

They both look on as Santiago's cries slowly start to diminish after a short period of time.

By the time Santiago's crying is about to stop, Deputy Chief Gyondski has put a box of Kleenex tissues on the front of his desk for her to use.

Quickly, she pulls three of these tissues out with her right hand and uses them to blow her nose and gently dab her eyes.

When he is confident Santiago has stopped crying, Deputy Chief Bart asks her, "How well did you know him?"

"Only a little bit on a professional basis, but the few times I saw him in the lunch room, he seemed happy and told me about his girlfriend, I think her name is Juanita."

Deputy Chief Bart quickly glances at Deputy Chief Gyondski and mouths the word, "no," as he shakes his head slowly from side to side. Gyondski picks up on this right away, realizing Santiago apparently doesn't know Officer Ortego hardly at all, because it isn't any secret how upset he was when Lt. Wayne extended his probation.

Furthermore, they both knew just how stressed-out Officer Javier Ortego had become based on his radio traffic and the few encounters each had with him.

The question in each of their minds was, "Could Ortego have been stressed out to the point of actually killing himself?"

"Can you please tell me how he died?" Santiago asks rather sheepishly.

"I wish I could but I can't due to it still being an ongoing Death Investigation," Deputy Chief Bart answers quickly, knowing this question was coming sometime from Santiago.

Deputy Chief Gyondski sees an opening because the conversation between Deputy Chief Bart and Santiago had stopped.

Grabbing Officer Ortego's Death File from the middle of his desk he says, "I need your help tonight Debra."

"Regarding notifying his family," Santiago responds.

"Yes," is all Deputy Chief Gyondski needs to say.

"Then let's do it for Javy," Santiago replies and waits to be handed the telephone.

Deputy Chief Gyondski dials the telephone number on Officer Ortego's form and then, he hands Santiago the phone, along with a note pad and Bic pen in case she needs to take notes.

For the next fifteen minutes, both he and Deputy Chief Bart look on as Santiago speaks in fluent Spanish, pausing only occasionally to jot down a few notes.

"Gracias, Buenas noches," Santiago says before handing the telephone back to Deputy Chief Gyondski.

As both Deputy Chiefs look on, Santiago reviews her notes and writes down a couple of additional comments.

Deputy Chief Bart's stress level has gone up because after only a minute he blurts out, "So fill us in," with a notable agitated tone in his voice.

"Maria Ortego was pretty shaken up by the news of the death of her son to the point she could barely speak at all," Santiago says.

"Shit," Deputy Chief Bart says before following with, "Now what do we do?"

"She gave me a telephone number and address of her sister, Consuelo, who speaks English and lives in North Ridge, California. Maria believes she could both help us as well as come and take possession of Javier's body," Santiago says.

Instantly, Deputy Chief Gyondski turns his chair so he is once again in front of his computer and opens up Goggle Chrome. He goes to whitepages.com and types in, "Non-Emergency Number Northridge California, Police Department."

Gyondski says the number out loud twice, as Santiago writes the number down on her notepad.

Next, he turns his chair so once again he is facing both Santiago as well as Deputy Chief Bart.

With his left-hand Deputy Chief Gyondski dials the telephone number and waits.

"North Ridge Police Department, Dispatcher Prims."

"Deputy Chief Frank Gyondski of the Greenfield, Illinois Police Department, may I please speak to your on-duty Patrol Supervisor?"

"One moment Deputy Chief, while I transfer you," Prims responds.

"Thank you," Deputy Chief Gyondski says and then waits patiently.

He doesn't have long to wait.

"Sergeant Schafer, may I help you," the voice on the other end of the phone says.

"Sergeant, this is Deputy Chief Gyondski of the Greenfield, Illinois Police Department. We need your help doing a Death Notification for us."

"Sorry, I got the Deputy Chief part but could you spell your last name for me?"

"Sure thing, it's G.Y.O.N.D.S.K.I."

"Okay, I got it. I assume you're going to send me a Type 3 LEADS message with all of the information, Deputy Chief?" Schafer says.

"Sergeant Schafer, we're in a time restraint over here and this is also a rare occurrence for us," Deputy Chief Gyondski responds.

"How so Deputy Chief? Our department policy states we don't move on these until we can verify it with the Law Enforcement Agency requesting it?" Schafer comes back with a doubtful tone.

"The notification is for the aunt of one of our police officers, who was found dead earlier today," Deputy Chief Gyondski says.

There is a long pause on the other end of the phone as Sgt. Schafer has a decision to make. After roughly a minute of thinking it over, he comes back on the line.

"Deputy Chief, I'm sorry for your department's loss and out of respect for this officer, I will honor your request. So, go ahead and give me all of the information we're going to need to carry this notification out."

"Sarge, I'm going to have you speak to our Social Worker Debra Santiago, who has all that you're requesting," Deputy Chief Gyondski says and then hands Santiago the telephone.

"Sergeant Schafer, I am Debra Santiago."

Gyondski zones out when he sees Deputy Chief Bart stand up while Santiago is talking.

Deputy Chief Bart walks toward the open office door and then stops upon reaching it.

With his right hand he motions for Gyondski to join him. Santiago is now referring to her notepad for the address of Consuelo. Gyondski leaves his seated position and catches up to Bart, who has moved out into the hallway.

While standing next to Deputy Chief Bart, Deputy Chief Gyondski asks, "What's up?"

"The Chief just texted me and wants me to head over to the Northland Police Department, where NORTAF Investigators are going to be questioning our very own Officer O'Neil, who walked into that station, about an hour ago, with his FOP Attorney."

"Really?" Deputy Chief Gyondski responds, more than a little bit surprised.

"Yeah, but before I go, I just want to confirm you don't need my help with any of this," Deputy Chief Bart says.

"Go, go, between Santiago and myself we're pretty much done, as long as Sergeant Schafer lives up to his word," Deputy Chief Gyondski answers, confident the situation is under control.

Gyondski watches as Bart walks down the long corridor between his office and Chief Fitzsimons' office.

Quickly, Deputy Chief Gyondski returns his focus to Santiago when he hears her say loudly, "Sergeant, thank you again for your help with this matter. You said you'll be contacting Deputy Chief Gyondski in roughly forty-five minutes or so with an update?"

Only then does she see Deputy Chief Gyondski, watching her from his position at the open office doorway. Both of them return to their previous seated positions.

Gyondski makes sure his office door is still in the wide-open position, which is his practice anytime he is alone with any female employee or female visitor.

"Debra, can I get you anything to eat or drink? Maybe a bottle of water?" He asks gently, appreciative of what she's doing for the Greenfield Police Department.

While still seated, she reaches down on the right side of the chair and pulls out a 12-ounce bottle of Ice Mountain water from her purse and holds it loosely in her right hand.

"Boss, thank you, but I'm pretty good right now, since I was in the middle of dinner when I received the text message from Deputy Chief Bart to come in," she says.

Before he can say anything, she asks rather sheepishly, "May I ask where Deputy Chief Bart went, since technically, he is my boss."

"Chief Fitzsimons gave him another assignment, so you probably won't be seeing him anymore this evening," Deputy Chief Gyondski responds.

"Okay, understood and if you don't mind, I just want to sit here for a bit, close my eyes and try and relax, as opposed to going to my office since it would be way too tempting to lay down on the couch I use for clients," Santiago says.

"Sounds fine to me," Deputy Chief Gyondski says in a matter-of-fact tone. "Trust me, when Sergeant Schafer calls, I'll wake you up if you're sleeping."

Anyone walking by his office right now might have been slightly freaked out by what they would witness if they looked in. Social Worker Debra Santiago is sitting in a chair with her head in her left hand and her body leaning to the left. Seated across from her and sitting behind his desk, Deputy Chief Gyondski's head is in his right hand. Gyondski's left hand is gently tapping a pencil on his desk so as not to distract Santiago, who appears to have fallen asleep.

Few things still amazed Deputy Chief Gyondski at this stage of his law enforcement career, such as when he got together with golfing buddies or college professors from UIC, who Beth and him still remained close with after graduation.

Often during the conversation, they would ask, "Got any really great stories for us?" He would just smile and shake his head in amazement.

Every cop had his or her favorite bizarre Death Notification story, which they couldn't wait to share.

Officers at retirement parties would go until the early morning hours, retelling these stories over beers and slaps on the back. Frank Gyondski racked his brain for a few minutes and then a smile crossed his face as he remembered the Debbie Dunhham case.

Four years ago, he had just made Lieutenant when he was dispatched to meet Social Worker Williamsburg at 98334 Winnetka Road, Unit A, who was on a Death Notification call.

This address of 98334 Winnetka Road was located on the far northern side of Greenfield and directly across the street were homes belonging to the Village of Northfield.

He remembered it was a busy Friday night, which had tied up both street sergeants.

It was particularly crisp for an early fall night.

When he arrived at the scene, he needed to park almost five townhouses down, due to all of the emergency vehicles in the parking lot. A Greenfield ambulance, fire truck, one squad car and the Evidence Technician vehicle all blocked his access to the residence.

He started to get out of his squad car, when he saw Williamsburg practically running toward his vehicle.

"Lieutenant, I'm glad they sent you because I have a bit of a mess inside with the victim," Williamsburg blurted out.

He stayed inside his squad car and let Williamsburg continue because she looked like she was ready to explode.

"Victim's name is Frank Dunhham, only 55 years old, and died apparently of a heart attack during some passionate love making," Williamsburg said.

"Okay," Lt. Gyondski mumbled, still not seeing an issue.

Williamsburg must have sensed this confusion because she brought out the good stuff the next time she spoke.

"Problem is Frank lives over at 27754 East Ridge Lane, according to his Driver's License. The woman he was here with on Winnetka Road is his mistress, when she was finally able to stop crying long enough to talk and apparently know Frank's wife from church."

"Ahh, now I see your problem," Lt. Frank Gyondski said.

"Your boys inside are going to be busy on this for quite a while, so would you mind going over with me to East Ridge Lane to make the notification?"

Williamsburg asked so sweetly, he could feel the cavities forming inside of his mouth.

"Not a problem," he replied. "Just give me the numbers on East Ridge Lane again, please?

"27754," Williamsburg said dryly and upon finishing, was off to her green Volvo.

Lt. Frank Gyondski waited until Williamsburg entered her vehicle and was leaving the townhouse complex, before he got on Norcom.

"Greenfield 308," he said.

"Go 308," Dispatcher Pat Brenan answered.

"Social Worker Williamsburg and I are enroute to 27754 East Ridge Lane on a follow up to this call. Check PIMS to see what calls we've had at that address," he requested.

"10-4 308, I'll check so standby," Brenan came back.

Since 27754 East Ridge Lane was only three miles away, he quickly reviewed in his head the proper procedure for handling this type of call.

He had it down as he pulled up in front of the house, directly behind Williamsburg's car.

"Greenfield 308, we're out on East Ridge Lane, at the address I gave you earlier," he said.

"10-4, 308 and be advised I'm checking PIMS and we've had a couple of domestics reported there as well as an Involuntary Committal for a Debbie Dunhham," Brenan said. The way he was speaking into his headset sounded like he was reading the PIMS information off his computer screen and transmitting at the same time.

Slowly Lt. Frank Gyondski and Brenda Williamsburg walked, practically side by side, up the short driveway until they reached the front porch of the residence. They needed to move old newspapers, still in their purple or blue colored plastic wrappers off the porch with their feet, to find a level place to stand.

A black, metal plant holder was located in the corner of the porch with three layers of shelves for individually potted plants. Each plant on the shelves were dead and looked like they had been so for quite some time.

Just as he was getting ready to ring the doorbell, he heard it.

He turned to look at Williamsburg, who apparently heard it as well due to the puzzled look on her face.

Whoever was home was vacuuming and the sound made it seem like it was taking place on the other side of the front door. Lt. Frank Gyondski rang the doorbell twice and waited.

When no one answered the door after roughly two minutes, he rang it again, three times.

Still no answer as the vacuuming seemed to have moved from the front door to the back of the house.

Removing his Motorola portable radio from its holder on his duty belt, he brought the radio up to his mouth, pressed the transmit button and firmly said, "Greenfield 308."

"308?" Dispatcher Brenan answered sounding totally surprised he would be getting another transmission so soon.

"Greenfield, we're not getting any answer at the residence so can you please call the house plus if anyone picks up have them come to the front door?"

"10-4 308, just give me a minute to pull up one of these reports and get the telephone number off it," Brenan responded.

Lt. Frank Gyondski put his head down and waited for the sound of the telephone ringing, if it was even possible through all the vacuuming noise.

"308 Greenfield, I have the telephone number and I'm calling it right now," Brenan said.

Lt. Frank Gyondski didn't need to acknowledge this on the radio, instead, he moved as close as possible to the front door and listened.

Remarkably, the vacuuming stopped, while the sound of footsteps could be heard approaching and then stopping on the other side of the door.

"Who is it?" a female voice yelled out from inside the house.

"Lieutenant Frank Gyondski of the Greenfield Police Department, Ma'am, could you please open the door and let us in?"

"WHOOOOOOOOOOO DO YOU WANT AND WHY THE HELL ARE YOU BOTHRING ME AT THIS HOUR," the voice yelled only louder and in a higher pitch.

"Once again lady, I'm Lieutenant Frank Gyondski of the Greenfield Police Department and I really need to talk to you, it's pretty important," he said.

Suddenly, the deadbolt on the door was unlocked and the door was moved from a closed position to a partially open one. Seeing the door slightly open, Lt. Gyondski walked inside the house, followed by Williamsburg.

No sooner had they entered, when they saw a short female, roughly in her early fifties, walking away from them.

Williamsburg closed the door behind her to keep the chill out while Lt. Gyondski followed the female in an attempt to get her attention.

No luck, while he was almost behind her, she stopped and turned on her vacuum again, moving it across the dining room carpet.

Dressed in an old fashioned, two-piece, grey sweat suit, the woman was unique by two distinct factors.

First, the longest baby blue fingernails anyone had ever seen.

Second, enough make-up on her, she looked like the late comedian Phyllis Diller in her prime.

Back and forth she moved, oblivious to the fact she had two total strangers standing inside her house, watching her every move.

Lt. Gyondski moved so close to her that they were almost face to face, but still needed to yell.

The vacuum was so old it seemed to scream.

"Ma'am, you need to sit down because we need to talk to you," he said as diplomatically as possible.

Nothing changed as she continued vacuuming.

Again, he said to her with a bit more anger showing in his voice, "Ma'am, I have some important news we need to talk about, but you need to come over and sit on a couch."

Frustrated, he looked over at Williamsburg, who was cleaning a stack of newspapers and books off one of the couches in an attempt to make some room for everyone to sit.

Finally, he had no choice and took immediate action to end the problem.

He walked over to the wall socket and unplugged the vacuum, in hopes she would join him. Next, he walked over to the couch and sat down next to Williamsburg.

In the calmest voice he could muster, Lt. Gyondski simply asked, "Is your name Debbie Dunhham?"

The woman stared at both of them.

"Ma'am, we need you to confirm you're Debbie Dunhham," Williamsburg asked this time.

"Yes," was all she said.

"Then you're married to Frank Dunhham," Williamsburg continued since she seemed to be building a slight rapport with Debbie.

"Yes," she answered and then quickly added, "He's not home right now, if you're looking for him."

"Well, that's the reason why we're here," Williamsburg responded.

"If you need to talk to him, he's probably at 98834 Winnetka Road, Unit A, FUCKING HIS GIRLFRIEND THE MOTHERFUCKER," Debbie screamed.

Both Williamsburg and Lt. Gyondski were stunned and said nothing for a brief moment.

Debbie Dunhham wasn't stunned and she quickly walked over to a table where her purse was sitting, wide open.

As Lt. Gyondski and Social Worker Williamsburg watched, Dunhham reached inside of it and pulled out a 38-Caliber Colt Detective Model.

With this weapon in her right hand, she put it in her mouth and pulled the trigger.

"Deputy Chief Gyondski, you have a call parked on line 2," Dispatcher Brent Renolds says over the intercom.

Deputy Chief Gyondski awakes and nearly falls out of his chair in the process.

"Renolds, why is he working?" Deputy Chief Gyondski says so loud it wakes up Santiago, who had also fallen asleep.

Quickly, he looks at his watch and it shows 2315 Hours, meaning a new shift had come on.

Then, he picks up the telephone with his left hand and hits *2 saying calmly, "Deputy Chief Gyondski, may I help you?"

"Deputy Chief, this is Sergeant Schafer with the North Ridge Police Department. I'm really sorry for the delay, but our on-duty Social Worker Becky Pollock had another issue come up and I needed to wait for her. We're at the house talking to Consuelo and things are fine. If you want to put your social worker on with Pollock, we can take care of this."

Deputy Chief Gyondski hands the phone to Santiago and whispers, "North Ridge Police Department."

Santiago speaks to Pollock for roughly 25 minutes, during which time Deputy Chief Gyondski hands her Ortego's Death Notification file, after placing a yellow sticky note on it, with the telephone number for the Cook County Medical Examiner's office.

He listens to Santiago's conversation only halfheartedly; confident she knows what she's doing.

Instead, he stares at Matt O'Neil's Death Notification file for the longest time.

He feels it holds some deep secret to everything which has been strangely happening with the Greenfield Police Department lately.

"You're a smart man Frank, what are you missing here?" he says softly so Santiago can't hear anything.

Apparently, he is staring at it a bit too long.

"I'm finished, Deputy Chief Gyondski and leaving," Santiago says.

From the tone in Santiago's voice, he can tell she is indeed finished and had enough.

"I'll walk you to your car," he says as they both get up and head for his open office door.

Not a word is said between the two of them due to exhaustion, as they leave the Greenfield Police Station and walk quickly to the parking lot, where her black colored, Nissan Murano is parked.

Right before they make it to Santiago's car, Gyondski stops to make sure his intentions aren't being misinterpreted.

Apparently, Santiago is so tired she doesn't even realize he had stopped until she has taken another ten steps.

She quickly turns around, looking at him as he says, "Debra, are you sure you're not too tired to drive?"

"Deputy Chief I'll be fine, trust me," replies Santiago.

"Okay, then thank you for all that you did for so many of us tonight," he says. "Try and enjoy the rest of the weekend," he finishes up with.

"I will give it my best," and she gets into her vehicle and slowly drives out of the parking lot.

Deputy Chief Frank Gyondski has a final decision to make as

he turns to his right and sees his silver Chevy Malibu alone in the parking lot.

Go home and inevitably, Beth will wake up and they will play twenty questions.

Or sleep at the station tonight and get up to finish the press release for Price as well as start one new project.

It doesn't take him long to make his decision as he walks back into the police station.

CHAPTER 27

"What a difference a few months could make in some-one's life," Matt thinks to himself as he drives home on Willow Road, deciding to take a short cut and go through the Village of Northfield.

It seemed like only yesterday he was a rising star for the Greenfield Police Department with a bright future and unlimited possibilities.

Roughly an hour ago he was being questioned by two NORTAF investigators about a friend's death with some comments being made about infidelity, which he will never forget.

Matt's emotions were like a sawed-off shotgun round, all over the freaking place.

"Juanita, c'mon man" he says to himself.

"Had to be a joke to try and see if I would overreact." he says while rubbing his chin with his left hand.

Overall, Matt thought he held his own throughout the interview and was impressed as well with the actions of his FOP attorney, Kevin Kray, who never backed down.

Finally, he didn't have a clue as to how much information Deputy Chief Bart knew about the entire incident or which side of the fence he was standing on.

Still supporting Matt by offering him some time in the records division?

Or needing to keep an eye on Matt and be prepared for possible further questioning by NORTAF?

The only thing Matt believes he's guilty of, is being in the wrong place at the wrong time.

He looks over at Kelly who is either sleeping or pretending to sleep.

After putting on her seatbelt once inside Matt's Camaro, she laid her head straight back on the black, leather headrest and closed her eyes.

Matt can't wait to find out more about his beautiful wife's pregnancy.

How far along is she?

When did she find out?

Hell, who is her obstetrician?

Racing home tonight isn't even close to being a possibility.

Matt had flown home from E.J.'s Place breaking speed limits and even cruising through one stop sign on the corner just west of his house, when he cleared his probation period.

Not today, for father-to-be Matt O' Neil.

Not with newly announced, mother-to-be Kelly O'Neil, sitting next to him.

Matt drives like an 80-year-old woman done with Sunday mass and heading home for breakfast, slowwwwwwwww.

He never believed Sunday drivers existed until joining the force and seeing them with his very own eyes.

Matt could tell story after story of their children—bankers, lawyers, doctors—coming to the Greenfield Police Station and looking for advice on how to take away their elderly parents' driver's licenses.

They would suggest: "Could you sit down the street from their house and stop them for a traffic violation?" Or Matt's personal favorite: "Could you maybe teach me how to disable their car, like taking off the distributor cap?"

Matts answer would always be, "No," but in his mind, he was worried about being put in a legal bind.

Every cop's responsibility is the safety of the people using the village, town, or city where they patrol. Now, Matt had first-hand knowledge of a possible threat to their safety.

He wasn't sure he could live with himself if they left their homes and got involved in a traffic accident, which resulted in them, or another motorist's death.

Three times in the past six weeks, he found himself going to the elderly motorist's home and letting them know the concerns their children had about their driving ability.

In two of the cases, he was able to convince the elderly driver to surrender their license to the Illinois Secretary of State's Office.

In the final case, the daughter came to the house and put her foot down.

She convinced her 88-year-old father, how much he was loved and how dangerous his driving had become. After she and her dad had cried for ten minutes and then hugged, he gave his daughter his driver's license.

The light turns yellow at the intersection of Willow Road and Sunset Ridge Road as Matt approaches it.

Even being a late Friday night, with only a few cars on the road, Matt slows his Camaro and brings it to a gentle stop.

He looks to his right to check on Kelly and sees the most beautiful, lighted soccer field he has ever seen in the suburbs.

Slowly, he turns into the parking lot and reads the sign, "Willow Park." He realizes he is at the Northfield Park District Community Center.

As if some powerful magnet is pulling the Camaro, Matt slowly drives through the parking lot of the facility.

Due to large ground floor windows, he can see the glistening blue water of a gigantic indoor swimming pool. Being an avid swimmer like Kelly, summers in the future will be spent going on family picnics, near a beautiful lake so they could all go in for a dip.

Located just west of this facility is a huge church, which has a marking on its exterior wall, reading "Northfield Community Church."

Matt smiles when he sees monkey bars and swing sets on the church property.

He can't wait for the day when he can push his son or daughter on the swings, or maybe chase them around the monkey bars and hear squeals of laughter coming from him or her.

Matt makes a wide left turn and drives at the same speed he used to enter the parking lot as he is exiting it.

He is anxious to get Kelly home and to bed for some rest.

On the other hand, Matt knows a bottle of Jameson, on a shelf in his kitchen pantry, which is calling out his name.

He needs to sort this day out if possible, with all the craziness attached to it.

Unbeknownst to Matt, the crazy train is just leaving the station and he's in for the ride of a lifetime.

CHAPTER 28

hief Fitzsimons stands over the body just staring at it. Finally, he sees enough and says softly, "This is getting to be a bad habit."

He slightly nudges the couch his Deputy Chief of Support Services, Frank Gyondski is sleeping on.

Startled and awoken from a deep sleep, Frank Gyondski yells, "What the hell?" as he rolls over from his left to his right side.

While still lying on the couch, Frank Gyondski looks up to find Chief Fitzsimons standing over him with both arms fully extended and a Styrofoam cup of coffee in each hand.

"I did it for Sergeant Garza, and now I'm doing it for you sunshine," Chief Fitzsimons says calmly as he extends his left hand.

"Bad habit Sir?" Deputy Chief Gyondski asks calmly, while still half asleep.

"Never mind Frank, apparently just a private joke," Chief Fitzsimons says as he waits for Frank to accept his offer of a fresh cup of coffee.

Slowly, Deputy Chief Gyondski takes the coffee out of his Chief's left hand with his own left hand. Both of them drink their coffees in complete silence.

It doesn't take the Chief long to figure out his Deputy Chief isn't enthralled about being awoken from a surprisingly deep sleep on Debra Santiago's office couch.

Wearing a Chicago Cubs blue t-shirt, with grey gym shorts, hair totally messed up and a one-day-old beard setting in, Deputy Chief Gyondski is a complete mess.

"So, you really spent the night sleeping here on Santiago's couch?" Chief Fitzsimons asks nonchalantly, in between sips of his coffee.

"Yes Sir," his Deputy Chief answers.

"Why?" Chief Fitzsimons asks.

"Boss, by the time Santiago and I finished up the Death Notification and working with the Northridge Police Department, it was past 2300 Hours, soooo?"

"You didn't want to go home to Beth and get grilled by her, not to mention you still needed to finish the press release for us and work with Price from the Gilles Police Department," Chief Fitzsimons said with a matter-of-fact tone in his voice.

"How did you know?" Deputy Chief Gyondski asks.

"Saw your car in the parking lot when I pulled in at 0630 hours this morning and knew the only office with a full-size couch besides mine was Santiago's. I let you sleep a bit and I went downstairs to the lunch room to make some fresh coffee. By the way, there isn't a need for a press release," Chief Fitzsimons answers.

Deputy Chief Gyondski looks up at his Chief like he had just been told the moon was made out of cheese.

"Apparently, everyone involved either has been able to keep it from the press but more likely the press has other issues to cover, such as Hillary going against Donald Trump for president and no interest in this case," Chief Fitzsimons says with a matter-of-fact tone reflected in his voice.

The coffee hasn't kicked in yet because all Deputy Chief Gyondski is able to mumble is, "How?"

"Not really sure, to be honest with you, since the Cook County Medical Examiner's office came out and took custody of the body," Chief Fitzsimons says.

"I guess this wouldn't be the first time our Police Department had employees die of suspicious causes. The press called and had no interest in their deaths," Deputy Chief Gyondski answers as he finally starts to wake up.

"What else do you have to do today Frank, since the press release won't be one of your jobs?" Chief Fitzsimons asks.

"Hire three more police officers to replace the loss of Mills, Thomas, and now Ortego," Deputy Chief Gyondski says as if giving a subordinate an order.

Slowly he gets off the couch and begins to stand.

With his position as Deputy Chief of Support Services, he's responsible for the hiring, training, and equipping of any new Greenfield Police Officer.

He's also fortunate he has an active eligibility list with eight names on it, based on their overall scores, from the Greenfield Police and Fire Commissioners.

"Fantastic Frank, and I'm well aware you've busted your ass these past two days with the new Police Station presentation and now this," Chief Fitzsimons says.

"Thank you," Deputy Chief Gyondski replies.

"No Frank, thank you for your dedication and service. By the way, I dropped off a dozen bagels from the Corner Bakery in the lunch room if you're hungry," Chief Fitzsimons says.

"Thanks again Boss," Deputy Chief Gyondski says and stands there as the Chief leaves Santiago's office through the open office door.

Suddenly, the Chief returns. "Want to make sure your aware Officer O'Neil is going to be placed under your command and will be spending the vast majority, if not all of his time, in the Records Division," Chief Fitzsimons says in a surprisingly calm voice for a decision of this magnitude.

"Why Boss?" Deputy Chief Gyondski asks.

"Officer Ortego's passing is still classified as a Death Investigation with Officer O'Neil playing a major role in this incident. I figured it would be much easier for NORTAF, if they needed to speak with him again, to know exactly where he is," Chief Fitzsimons replies.

From the look on his Deputy Chief's face, Chief Fitzsimons knows instantly how this decision is being taken.

Gyondski replies meekly, "Okay."

Chief Fitzsimons then leaves Santiago's office and doesn't return.

Deputy Chief Gyondski walks over to Santiago's desk.

From a corner of the desk, he grabs his phone and keys, which he uses to lock Santiago's office door.

The small cup of coffee hasn't helped, and he slowly walks down to the men's locker room.

Standing in front of his now open locker, Frank had his first decision of the morning to make—wear his uniform or street clothes.

Being a Saturday, technically, he isn't even supposed to be here.

Also, all he really needs to do is make a series of phone calls to candidates for the three open police officer positions, which shouldn't take more than 90 minutes.

But the way things were going and with the possibility of NORTAF stopping by for some unknown reason, makes his decision much easier for him.

Changing out of his sleeping clothes, he quickly puts back on the same uniform he'd worn all day yesterday, or looking at his watch, roughly 7 hours ago.

Taking his red health kit from the floor of his locker, he walks over to the bathroom of the locker room.

Standing in front of the first sink he comes to, he looks into the mirror and scares the shit out of himself.

Puffiness and slight blackness are forming under both eyes.

His hair is a mess and his one-day beard appears as though he is testosterone laden with blotches of hair forming all over his face.

In succession, he brushes his teeth, combs his hair after throwing some water on it and returns his health kit to his locker. Finally, he locks the locker.

He is ready to take on the day until his stomach says to him, "Feed me."

He heads for the lunchroom for another cup of coffee and to get a couple of those bagels the chief had brought in. Upon getting to the lunchroom, he finds an empty coffee pot and one bagel left inside the Corner Bakery box.

"Shit," he yells, not caring who hears him.

Changing the coffee filter with a fresh pack of grounds, he fills the coffee maker with water and hits the on switch. While the coffee pot slowly fills, he practically inhales the sesame seed bagel long before the coffee is ready.

Walking over to the refrigerator and opening it, he finds his lunch bag, which has been pushed to the rear of the top shelf. Removing his lunch from the refrigerator, he places it on a counter.

From his lunch bag, he pulls out a Yoplait Greek yogurt and spoon he has brought from home.

He hears the coffee pot start beeping to indicate it is done. Filling a Styrofoam cup with fresh coffee and grabbing it with his right hand, he picks up the yogurt and spoon with his left hand and heads toward his office.

Carefully, he walks up the flight of stairs leading from the basement to the first floor.

Upon reaching his office, he puts the yogurt with spoon on the floor outside his door.

He searches and finds his keys in his left pants pocket, allowing him to quickly open the door and head inside. Once inside his office, he decides to leave the door open, but isn't sure of the reason why.

In record time he finishes both the coffee and yogurt, which leaves him feeling filled for the moment.

Turning in his chair he throws the empty food items and plastic spoon in a garbage can underneath his desk. He turns again while still seated and finds the file he is looking for instantly on a table behind his desk.

Inside the file, he has the candidates placed in the order they are on the eligibility list with the first pick being on top, followed by candidate number two and so on. Picking up the first candidate packet, he checks out the name, Michael Hood, and then finds a phone number for him.

The Michael Hood phone call redeems Deputy Chief Gyondski's faith, the system is working the way it is supposed to.

The yelling by his family members in the background when young

Michael says, Yes Sir, I would be honored to be a Greenfield Police Officer," brings huge smile to Deputy Chief Gyondski's face as he sees, hopefully good things down the road for Officer Michael Hood, Badge #377.

The phone call for candidate number two, Steven Holl's, unfortunately, doesn't go as well.

Getting Holl's' phone number off the cover sheet for his packet, Deputy Chief Gyondski dials it and waits patiently for the phone to be answered.

After the fourth ring, a female answer with a soft, "Hello."

"Steven Holl's please?" Deputy Chief Gyondski asks.

"Who the hell is calling?" the female yells into the phone.

"This is Deputy Chief Frank Gyondski of the Greenfield Police Department Ma'am. Who am I speaking with?" is all he can get out before the voice explodes to the point, he needs to move the telephone away from his left ear.

"IS THIS SOME KIND OF SICK JOKE?" the female yells into the phone.

"Excuse me," Deputy Chief Gyondski responds with a curious tone in his voice.

"HE'S DEAD YOU ASSHOLE AND IT'S ALL BECAUSE OF YOU AND THE FUCKING GREENFIELD POLICE DEPARTMENT," the female screams louder, this time before quickly hanging up the telephone.

Upon hearing the dial tone ringing in his ear, Deputy Chief Gyondski looks at the phone in disbelief of what he has just heard.

The fact that someone could yell at him and get away with it, pisses him off to no end.

Secondly, how could the Greenfield Police Department play a role in the death of Steven Holls, who lived in Davenport, Iowa?

Should he call her right back?

Should he wait an hour before calling back? All these questions are racing through his mind.

He spends the next thirty minutes going through all his emails— both his professional and personal and finds nothing of substance.

Next, he calls Beth on her cell phone but gets her voicemail.

He decides against leaving a message. Then, he realizes with all the shit going on, he better say something.

The minute he gets the beep for voicemail, he jumps in with, "Hi babe, just wanted to see how you were doing. All is okay here, which is the best I can say for now. If things go the way they're supposed to, I should be home no later than noon. Can't wait to see you sweetie. Love you."

Hanging up the phone, he looks at his watch and realizes it has been exactly thirty minutes since the last phone call to the Holl's family and it is time for another one.

He punches 563, the area code for Davenport, Iowa, into the phone, followed by the 7-digit number. Deputy Chief Gyondski has his game face on this time and knows the phone call will be on a recorded line.

Again, the phone rings exactly four times and he is confident he is about to get the Holl's' answering machine when a male pick up the phone and says, "Hello?"

"Sir, this is Deputy Chief Gyondski of the Greenfield, Illinois Police Department. I'm trying desperately to get in touch with a Steven Holls."

"He's my son Deputy Chief," the male voice says calmly. "Correction, he was my only son."

"Sir, I'm very confused as to what's going on out there, I'm just calling to tell him the great news about us wanting to offer him a position as a police officer with our department," Deputy Chief Gyondski finishes.

"Amazing," is all the voice on the other end of the phone answers with.

Deputy Chief Gyondski doesn't know what to say next.

He does the obvious and just shuts up and waits.

The silence must have been too much for the male because roughly thirty seconds later he begins talking.

"I apologize for my wife Angela screaming at you earlier today. It's just the fact we've been through so much this past month and truly your profession is a big part of the reason why," says the man.

Between still being tired and truly sympathetic to this stranger, Deputy Chief Gyondski simply says, "Could you please fill me in on what exactly happened?"

Clearing his throat, the male begins, "I'm Eric Holls and Steven was my son and a truly great one at that, Sir."

Deputy Chief Gyondski remains quiet, allowing Eric Holl's to tell his story completely.

"All Steven wanted was to be a police officer in the worst possible way," says Eric. "Even though we have great Law Enforcement Schools here in Iowa, he learned the best school around for being a Police Officer was Western Illinois University in Macomb, Illinois. So, he enrolled there, got his degree and started taking police applicant tests like yours, I believe, roughly ten months ago."

"This is correct sir," Deputy Chief Gyondski says.

"After graduation, he worked at our local Ace Hardware and stayed in shape for police tests by using the Christmas gift Angela and I got for him, a membership at a World Fit Center," continues Eric.

Deputy Chief Gyondski sits quietly on his end of the phone, staring at a picture of Steven, which is paper clipped to his application.

"No sooner than two weeks after joining World Fit, he met a personal trainer named Sally Summers, who was also from Davenport. Steven fell literally head over heels for her in every possible way. Both Angela and I even liked this girl, shoot."

Deputy Chief Gyondski starts to get an idea of where this might be headed but decides to still keep his mouth shut.

Mr. Holl's continues, "Things seemed to move real fast between the two of them. After roughly two months, Steven confided in his mother he was going to start looking at rings and propose to her when Valentine's Day came around."

Deputy Chief Gyondski gets so caught up in the story he blurts out, "Did he?"

"He did and told her she was the one and confirmed for her, the first time apparently, his desire to be a cop. He said she would be a great cop's wife," Mr. Holl's says in a direct style, before quickly continuing. "She told him she wouldn't have anything to do with being a cop's wife with the goofy schedule and crazy hours, and if he didn't think about changing careers, they were through."

"Deputy Chief, I came home from work the day after they had this meeting and found his Dodge pickup in the driveway even though he was supposed to be working. So, I came inside the house and repeatedly called his name but didn't get a response," Eric Holl's suddenly stops talking.

Deputy Chief Gyondski doesn't like where this story is going.

Like being on a roller coaster ride, he can't get off and they are headed for another twist and turn.

In a tear-filled voice, Eric Holl's continues. "So, I continued walking throughout the house and decided to check our garage, which is attached off the laundry room. I opened the interior garage door and felt something hit me on the top of my head. I turned on the garage lights."

Eric Holl's stops due to the need to compose himself once more. Deputy Chief Gyondski can hardly hear his words due to his sobbing.

Eric Holl's suddenly gets back on the phone. "Steven hung himself using some old rope I had in the garage and ran it through one of the garage rafters."

Moving the receiver away from his mouth and to make sure he isn't heard, Deputy Chief Gyondski puts his right hand completely over the mouthpiece before mumbling, "Unfucking believable."

"Later on, I checked Steven's bedroom. On his desk was a suicide note Steven had written to Sally saying he wanted to teach her a lesson. Can you believe it?" Eric Holl's is able to get this last sentence out before completely losing it on the phone.

Deputy Chief Gyondski doesn't know what to say or do because he'd never had a situation such as this before. He decides his best course of action is to keep his mouth shut and let Mr. Holl's cry. After a good five minutes, Gyondski can hear Mr. Holl's crying start to slow down a bit, so he decides to say something.

"Mr. Holl's, I am deeply sorry for your loss. I promise to keep Steven and your entire family in my prayers."

"Thank you Deputy Chief. You seem like a very kind man. I truly believe Steven would have loved working for you, Goodbye." Eric Holl's hangs up the phone.

Deputy Chief Gyondski does so as well and shakes his head in amazement at what he has just heard.

"Frank you have a minute?" Chief Fitzsimons says as he knocks on the open office door.

"Always for you Boss," Frank replies.

"So how many of the three openings have you filled?" Chief Fitzsimons asks.

"Only one Boss, due to the second candidate killing himself over a girlfriend issue," Frank replies.

"Holy shit, can't wait to hear that story sometime, but for now, I have more important news you need to be aware of," Chief Fitzsimons says excitedly.

"Sir?" Deputy Chief Gyondski answers with an inquisitive tone in his voice, due to the excitement his Chief is showing.

"I just got off the phone with the head of NORTAF, Chief John Calvey, of the Farlingten Police Department and they have the gunshot residue report from the Cook County Morgue regarding Officer Ortego's hands."

"Please don't tell me negative results Sir?" Deputy Chief Gyondski asks.

"Absolutely none found on either of Ortego's hands," Chief Fitzsimons says.

"Shit," Deputy Chief Gyondski says disgustedly.

"Yes, they just changed the classification on Ortego's Death Investigation from a suicide to a homicide."

"Let me guess who their primary suspect is?" Deputy Chief Gyondski asks.

"Officer Matt O'Neil," Chief Fitzsimons says.

CHAPTER 29

"**G**reenfield Police Department, Officer O'Neil speaking," While holding the telephone up to his left ear, Matt waits patiently for the caller to finish her question before answering.

"No Ma'am, we're not under attack," Matt responds apathetically. "Those are the tornado sirens you hear behind your home, which we test the first Tuesday of the month, at exactly 9:30Am, all across the Village."

Again, he waits for the woman to finish her comment before he responds.

"Well, you may have a point. If we do it the same time of the day every month, the KGB could launch an attack on the Greenfield Residents. Well, I shudder to think of the consequences," Matt says and can't help but grin after finishing.

"Big fan of the show, the Americans, with Kerri Russell, are we?" Matt asks, which results in him speaking to a dial tone.

"Might have pushed the envelope on that one a little bit," he says to Records Supervisor Linda McMillon, who just smiles at him before returning to sorting the huge stack of Y Tickets on her desk.

Matt desperately needs a laugh, considering he's at the center of his own personal tornado and knows no way out of it.

On a good note, the Records assignment has gone much smoother than he thought it would.

On their first day of working together, Linda McMillion had shown him everything he needed to know in roughly 45 minutes.

When finished she asked Matt, "Do you have any questions for me about anything I just showed you?"

Matt answered, "I think you explained everything properly. Just give me a couple of days to get acclimated to working in here."

"We're happy to have you Matt and feel free to pick any desk not being used," Linda answered.

"Thank you, Linda," Matt answered.

Linda McMillion was a pleasant, Irishman, in here early fifties, and after only two days of working in the Records Division, it wasn't hard for Matt to see Linda ran a tight ship and the majority of her workers responded well to her management style.

Matt's favorite job in the Records Division was answering non-emergency phone calls, usually on a wide variety of topics. The phone calls were often so bizarre, every night during dinner he and Kelly would swap stories to see who had the strangest day at work.

Matt had already won this contest, 18 out of 19 times.

There wasn't any doubt Kelly's pregnancy had brought them closer together.

Last week on Tuesday, Kelly told him she was nineteen weeks into her pregnancy and wanted to be surprised about the sex of the baby.

Nights were spent with the two of them lying in bed, yelling out possible names for the baby.

Matt also started reading a bedtime story slowly and softly into Kelly's belly. As he put it, "So the baby would get use to his voice."

Another benefit of the records job was it enabled Matt to have lunch on a regular basis with either T.C. or Marc and find out what was going on in their lives.

Matt wasn't the least bit surprised Megan O'Brien had not stopped by the Records Division to check on him.

On one occasion, she came by to get her misdemeanor cases for court.

Since Matt was seated at the time and Linda McMillion was already standing at the front counter, she simply handed the cases over to Megan.

Not a wave, text, or voicemail came from Megan, the entire

time Matt was removed from the patrol division and he didn't know what to make of it.

Ever since Matt had seen her with Kurt Thompson at Chris's funeral, the slight friendship they shared seemed to have vanished between the two of them.

"Hell," Matt thought, "I'm not sure if she hangs with anyone on the force since she usually takes her meals by herself."

Of course, with any new situation, there will always be the bad side to it as well.

In this instance, he was desperately trying to dispel the rumors circling amongst his fellow Greenfield Police Officers.

Matt was appalled at how far members of CAVE would go to totally destroy his career.

The word was out regarding the results of the GSR test as well as other information regarding Jav's death. Both T.C. and Marc would pass the latest gossip to Matt so he would be aware of it and start working to dismiss it.

Matt didn't know what he would do if the rumors about him and Juanita started to surface.

He knew he was on extremely thin ice with Chief Fitzsimons and he needed to, as the saying goes, "Keep his nose clean." But if anything upset Kelly to the point of having problems with her pregnancy, or God forbid, losing the baby, then the gloves would indeed come off.

Finally, his two patrol shift supervisors and their behavior towards him weren't any different than they had been from the first day he started working for them.

Lieutenant Wayne, in the few chance encounters he had with Matt, simply ignored him.

In one instance, when he saw Matt walking down the hallway towards the lunch room, he actually turned and walked in the opposite direction.

Sergeant Barton was just the opposite.

Every day, he would find some type of excuse to stop into the Records Division and check on Matt.

In the latest incident, with two members of CAVE standing at the Records Division front counter, Sergeant Barton walked next to them and motioned for Matt to come see him with his right hand. As Matt approached the three of them, Sergeant Barton raised his left hand from below his waist and handed Matt a can of Coke.

The look on the faces of the other two Greenfield cops was priceless.

Sergeant Barton topped it off by saying, "You need anything else O'Neil, just contact dispatch. No, better yet, you have my cell phone number, just give me a call."

As Sergeant Barton walked away, Matt could hear him softly say in a sing-song voice which only Matt could understand, "Complain about virtually everything!"

In his relatively young life, Matt had encountered numerous leaders in both his personal and professional careers.

Matt put Sergeant Reginald Barton at the top of the list with no one coming close to him.

Linda McMillion had finished sorting the Y tickets and stood by Matt's desk with them in her hand, when a phone rang on a nearby vacant desk.

While still seated, Matt rolls over to the vacant desk and picks up the phone.

"Greenfield Police Department, Officer O'Neil speaking."

For the second time today, he waits patiently for the person to finish their story as he watches a woman in her late 50s, wearing a light blue dress, which is out of style and black high heels, approach the front counter.

"Sir, let me check with our dispatcher. I'll put you on hold for only a minute to see what is occurring in your neighborhood," Matt answers.

Matt does exactly what he told the caller he was going to do.

After placing the caller on hold, he calls dispatch and is a bit surprised when he hears, "Communications, Karen Jenkins, may I help you?"

"Karen, it's Matt O'Neil and curious but when did you get moved to days?"

"Hi, Matt" Karen says. "To answer your question, about two weeks ago when I came back from my extended leave from work."

Matt knew what the extended leave was for and didn't want to go down that road with her today, not with all of his own issues pending.

"Karen, I have a caller on the line who claims we have five squad cars on his street right now and believes Armageddon has started."

While still chuckling, Karen Jenkins says, "Let me guess, he lives on the 800 Block of Joy Road?"

"Yes, so we do have something going on over there?" Matt asks with a tone of surprise in his voice.

"Yup, domestic battery with some pretty significant injuries to the victim, which is why Fire is also on the scene."

"Okay Thanks," Matt replies and suddenly looks up.

While still holding the phone, he looks in the direction of the front counter to see Linda McMillion suddenly start to back up as the woman in the blue dress is reaching inside her purse for something.

Fortunately, the telephone is in Matt's left hand and, while still holding it, he puts his right hand on top of his Glock 22 Gen 4.

Matt's a few seconds too late, for the woman is prepared for today and removes the item from her purse without taking her eyes off McMillion.

In no time at all, she has it out and drops it on the counter in front of McMillion.

It is a piece of loose-leaf paper with red cursive written on it.

Matt removes his hand from the top of his Glock.

Linda McMillion moves back toward the counter where this woman is still standing.

"Yes Sir. We have a call regarding one of your neighbors, which unfortunately is all I can tell you at this time," Matt tells the caller.

Needless to say, this doesn't satisfy the caller one bit.

He keeps Matt on the phone, asking him another set of questions.

Matt puts his head down this time, trying to figure out exactly what the caller really wants when Linda McMillion taps him on his left shoulder. Looking up, Matt now finds Linda standing in front of him.

Placing his hand over the mouthpiece, Matt asks, "What's up?"

"The woman at the front counter is asking for you," she says.

Uncovering the mouthpiece Matt says, "Sir, you can walk down to the address and try and talk to the supervisor on scene, or wait until the next Greenfield Journal comes out and read about it in the crime blotter, but I have to go. Good bye, Sir."

With that accomplished, Matt hangs up the phone and says, "Thank you Linda."

He walks directly to the front counter and watches as the woman standing their stares at him.

When he reaches the counter he says, "I'm Officer O'Neil."

The woman now holds the note in her right hand.

Quickly, she stashes the note back inside her purse. Then, she extends her right hand to Matt, who grasps it firmly.

While still holding Matt's right hand with her own, she says, "I really need your help Officer O'Neil."

"Regarding what, if I may ask?" Matt replies.

"Solving the death of my nephew," the woman says.

"Well, so we're all working off the same page, what's your nephew's name?"

"Officer Ron Thomas," the woman answers.

CHAPTER 30

M att knows he can't continue this conversation while standing at the front counter.

"Ma'am, please don't move. I'm going to find us a room where we can keep talking in private," he says.

"I understand," Marge Thomas answers with a slight Irish accent.

Matt turns and walks straight back to Linda McMillion's desk.

Linda is entering some information off an arrest report into PIMS, when he reaches the front of the desk, she stops typing and only turns her head away from the computer screen, keeping her fingers on her keyboard.

"Linda, I'm really not sure what I have with this woman, so I'm going to move her to the front interview room for some privacy," Matt says.

"Sounds like a plan, just let me know if you need anything." Linda says.

Matt quickly walks past her desk.

Once he is out of the records section, Matt starts making a series of three right turns, while rubbing his forehead. Call it an educated guess or intuition, but something tells him this is going to be the traditional cluster fuck.

He finally reaches the lobby and once again extends his right hand to the woman, "Hi, I'm Matt."

"Marge Thomas," she replies as she also extends her hand.

"Great Marge so please follow me since we really can't talk here."

All Matt needs to do is take a few steps back toward where he just came from as the interview room is just off the lobby.

Once inside, he proceeds to close the curtains, which were put in the room just for this purpose.

When he finishes, he turns around and sits down in an old, metal chair on one side of a small, brown desk.

"Please be seated, Marge," he asks and even goes as far as to point at the chair across the table from him, which he wants her to use.

As she starts to sit, Matt suddenly jumps up, walking around the desk and opens the room's door roughly three quarters of the way.

Then, he returns to his seat and while Marge looks on, he pulls a small notebook from the right breast pocket of his bulletproof vest to go along with the pen which is already lying on the desk.

Confident Marge is comfortable; Matt decides it is time to get started.

"So, you made a pretty incredible statement a few minutes ago regarding your nephew," Matt states.

"He was murdered Officer O'Neil, I just know it," she blurts out, not allowing Matt to finish his sentence.

He stares at her, trying to figure out what Marge Thomas is all about.

"Perhaps I need to fill you in on a couple of things, which may help my credibility with you," she said calmly.

"It can't hurt," Matt replies.

"My nephew Ron is an exact duplicate of his father, Nick Thomas, who had the nickname of Fast Nickie. Granted, he was a bar owner in Willowbrook, but it wasn't the total reason for the nickname."

"Liked women I take it?" Matt asks.

"On the day Nick married Sharon, I caught him and a bridesmaid getting a little too cozy in a closet at the reception," Marge says.

Matt decides to keep his mouth shut and see where Marge is going with this.

"Needless to say, Ron decided to follow in his father's footsteps when it came to women as well as hard drinking," Marge continues.

"How often did you see him?" Matt asks, trying to establish a foundation for their relationship.

"Until recently, rarely due to my husband's fight with lung cancer. I really couldn't travel and nothing was really appealing for Ron in Rensselaer, Indiana."

Again, Matt remained silent, waiting for Marge to get to something he could use.

"Things seemed to change though," Marge says. "Both Sharon and Nick passed within two months of each other."

"How so?" Matt asks, believing he might have something finally to work with.

"Ron vowed to keep in touch more, and he actually lived up to his word this time," she answers before quickly continuing.

"He would post on Facebook every couple of days—what he was up to. He also started to send me pictures of his newest I'll call them girlfriends. Other people may call them one-night stands."

Matt is impressed with the openness Marge is demonstrating about her recently departed nephew's sex life.

"But things really started to change just recently when he met, who he called, 'the love of his life,'" Marge says.

"Really?" Matt asks because he wasn't aware there was a new love in his deceased, fellow patrolman's life.

"Yes, she is adventurous, athletic, and had impacted him to the point he had cut down significantly on his heavy drinking. So, when he brought up the possibility of taking her to Door County in the future and showing her his property on Washington Island, I finally believed him," Marge says.

The minute Matt hears the words, "Door County," his credibility level for Marge went straight up.

"So, he talked about this mystery woman and Door County and you're well aware, this is where he died, so you believe she's the one who killed him or at least played a role in his death?" Matt says with a noticeable new interest in Marge's information.

"No, Officer O'Neil," says Marge. "I said earlier he really started to open up to me recently. A week before he died, he actually came to Rensselaer, and we had the best time together."

Matt looked on as Marge starts to tear up a bit. "He was so

relaxed the day he came to visit. We had a great time laughing at old pictures of him when he was a child and it continued all the way through lunch. Heck, we even went grocery shopping together and got the oil changed in my car," Marge says before pausing for a while as she starts to lightly dab both of her eyes with a Kleenex.

"Then, everything suddenly changed," Marge says. "An hour before we were set to go out for dinner, his whole demeanor was different."

"What happened to affect him so strongly?" Matt asks as he finds himself leaning forward and sitting up straighter in his chair.

"He received a text message from the new girlfriend and it said an old boyfriend had found out about them and was so angry he threatened to kill both Ron and her if she didn't end things," Marge says and this time the eyes opened up as the tears start to flow.

Matt knows better than to try and talk to her when she is in this condition, so he just sits there quietly and marks down a few things on his notepad, until Marge is able to compose herself.

"Ron was just a totally different person that night when we went to his favorite Italian Restaurant called Arni's over on South College Avenue," continues Marge. "I mean he always loved going there because of their deep-dish sausage pizza."

Matt desperately wants to get Marge back on track talking about Ron's possible killer, but he doesn't know how.

"He hardly ate a thing and barely spoke at all," says Marge. "He played with his glass of beer and then right before we ordered a couple of cannoli's, he opened up."

"Marge, this is really important so tell me exactly what he said," Matt pleads.

Marge must have realized it as well as she pulls her chair closer to the table and leans forward so her face is only inches away from Matt's face.

"He told me, 'Aunt Marge, this guy is the real deal when it comes to being vicious and if I let my guard down and continue seeing this girl, I believe he would go as far as doing it.'"

"So, Marge, you're telling me you believe this guy killed your nephew at Peninsula State Park a few months back over some girl?" Matt clarifies.

"YES," Marge yells in frustration this time instead of whispering it.

"I'm curious, how did he do it?" Matt asks.

"Officer O'Neil, I'm a libarian, in a relatively small, Indiana town, you're the cop."

Marge finishes, obviously upset and pissed off.

"All right, all right, I'm sorry if I've upset you, but you seemed to have so much of this figured out," Matt says and opens both of his hands and arms up as if to give up.

Marge continues staring at Matt, waiting for him to ask the right question.

"Okay, so why am I involved in all of this?" Matt asks, as he moves his arms so they are now resting on the table with his hands clenched together.

"The day he died, I received a telephone call from a Deputy Chief Bart, after the Rensselaer Police Department had come to my home to fill me in on Ron's death," Marge answers.

"How did things go with Deputy Chief Bart?" Matt inquires, more than a little bit interested due to his own recent encounter with him.

"I didn't care for his cocky attitude and the tone of his voice one bit," Marge answers. "I had just been told of my nephew's death. Then to be peppered with all of these questions and not, excuse my language, giving a shit about Ron, was galling to me, to say the least."

Again, Matt sat quietly, afraid to push Marge for the answers he was so desperately seeking but too afraid to even ask the right questions.

A good five minutes passes as he allows Marge to both catch her breath as well as regain her composure. When he is confident, she has done both, he starts up again.

"Why did you come here and ask for me, when as you know, your nephew was killed in Wisconsin?" Matt asks calmly.

"Over dinner at Arni's, he said to me, 'Aunt Marge, if anything happens to me, then promise me you'll contact an Officer in Greenfield named Matt O'Neil. He will know what to do in regards to finding my killer,'" Marge states.

Matt makes a noticeable sigh in front of Marge, only this time to try to calm his nerves as he attempts to figure out his next move.

Confident he has a game plan established, in his mind at least, he starts once again.

"I'm truly flattered," Matt starts, "I really am Ron thought so highly of me. I will need your information first, such as your Driver's License as well as any information you may have on his new girlfriend and, of course, her possible old boyfriend."

Instantly, Marge reaches across the desk and touches the top of Matt's right hand while softly saying, "Thank you."

Matt waits patiently as she opens her purse and quickly finds her wallet, laying it on the desk.

Instead of opening it, she starts looking back inside her purse for another item.

He glances at his watch, suddenly realizing this has been going on much longer than he originally thought and he still needed to grab lunch before heading off to Skokie for his 1330-hour Felony Court appearance.

When Matt looks back across the table at Marge, she is holding a cell phone in her left hand.

"Ron sent a picture of the new girlfriend while she was sleeping at his house in Waukegan one morning," Marge says. "I'm sure she wasn't even aware he did it."

She then hits a button on the phone to make sure the picture is still on the cell phone.

Satisfied, she quickly hands the phone to Matt, who grabs the phone and looks at the picture.

Marge then opens her blue wallet and quickly pulls her Indiana Driver's license from the clear plastic tab holding it in place.

After retrieving the Driver's License, she holds it in her right hand and is ready to give it to Matt, but she can't because he's still holding her cell phone in both of his hands and staring at the picture on the screen.

Marge becomes a bit startled due to Matt's hands shaking mildly, while still holding the phone.

After a minute has passed and Matt is still staring at the picture on the phone, Marge blurts out, "I believe Ron told me her name is…"

"Megan," Matt blurts out. "Her full name is Megan O'Brien."

Marge is happy now with Matt finally speaking again and interested in the information she is able to provide for him.

Matt puts the cell phone on the table and quickly picks up Marge's Indiana Driver's License.

He starts to write her Driver's License Number on to his notepad, when Marge interrupts him.

"I also have the name of Ron's killer or, should I say in police jargon, possible suspect?"

"I'm pretty sure Marge, I know who it is. But to make sure we're on the same page, tell me the name you have," Matt responds.

"Kurt Thompson," she says emphatically, putting the final piece of the puzzle in place.

CHAPTER 31

"That's your last case envelope I see on your Felony court sheet Officer Thompson and please make sure you check your disposition cards also and confirm you have all of them," Records Clerk Jackie Stone says.

Not wanting to take any chances, he proceeds to do as Stone has instructed and meticulously goes through all three case envelopes, making sure each of them are complete.

"Looks good and thanks for having them ready for me Jackie," says Kurt.

"Not a problem Officer Thompson and by the way, it's great to have you back," Jackie says.

The minute she finishes, she begins blushing as she brushes part of her short brown hair behind her left ear.

"Why thank you, Jackie, it's really good to be back," he answers.

With the entire records division personnel looking on, Kurt can feel his face turning red due to his embarrassment.

Quickly, he grabs the three case envelopes off the front counter, which are wrapped in a brown rubber band.

He tucks them under his left arm and heads for the front door of the Gilles Police Station.

Walking away, he makes a mental note to give Ms. Stone a bit more attention in the future.

Granted, she is the perfect age for him, being in her early 20s.

She's also hot looking, with a great body and totally into cops, being a Law Enforcement Major at Oakton Community College, in Des Plaines.

"Hell, it's been so long since I had any contact with a woman, of any age, in a complimentary fashion," thought Thompson.

He has to admit it's good to be back at work after the past thirty days, which were some of the hardest days of his life.

Quickly, he comes out of the front glass doors and heads toward his squad car, with a full head of steam.

Apparently, a bit too much steam, fueled by two cups of Starbucks coffee.

As he walks down the winding cement staircase, Kurt Thompson stumbles on one of the last steps, and yells out, "Shit!"

The case envelopes drop to the ground, and he is momentarily airborne, twisting to the right before he is able to reach out with his right hand and catch himself on a railing adjacent to the steps.

He stands momentarily with his back to the railing, which he holds onto with both hands in between two steps.

Frantically, he attempts to catch his breath while thanking God he isn't actually hurt in what would have been one of the freakiest, on-duty injuries, in the history of the Gilles Police Department.

Then, he does something totally uncharacteristic for him.

It starts out as a slight giggle, but before he knows it, he breaks out into a full bellyaching laugh.

He stares up at the cameras stationed over the front doors of the police station, not really knowing why.

Is it the fact he has returned after being off work and almost breaks his neck five hours into his shift?

Or is it simply symbolic he would be airborne, if only for a few seconds, as his career had been only a month earlier?

He took his eyes away from the cameras and instead puts his focus on the same front doors he had left only a minute earlier.

He walks to his squad car, and begins to reminisce about what those doors meant to him.

For those are the same doors he entered roughly 80 hours after getting off the phone with an obviously pissed off Chief Dennis McKinley, regarding Stanley Pietrowski's death.

It all starts coming back to him as he drives over to Popeye's Chicken for a quick snack.

Within 20 minutes of getting off the phone, Kurt Thompson dragged his exhausted body, both mentally and physically, back upstairs and stripped his sweat-soaked clothes off, throwing them into a corner.

He crawled into bed and pulled on the only sheet he had on the bed, until it rested just below his neck.

He never set the alarm clock, instead hoping to fall asleep and not wake up until Monday morning, for his meeting with the Chief.

No such luck and almost on instinct, he awoke on Friday morning, at 10:00Am.

He only did five things of significance the entire weekend.

First, he walked over to where Whiskers' body laid and quickly bagged her broken body in a black, Glad garbage bag. Then, he put this bag inside another Glad garbage bag of the same kind.

He opened the door leading out to his garage and put Whiskers' body in a garbage can, making sure to cover it with a couple other garbage bags, which were already inside. He wanted to make sure Whiskers' body wouldn't be the first one, the trash collector would see when he came early Wednesday morning.

Second, he went to YouTube with a yellow notepad on his lap and pulled up all the videos he could find on his Old Mill Mall encounter.

He watched the Channel 32 version first. He did this while munching on a monstrous peanut butter and jelly toasted sandwich, which he washed down with a glass of orange juice.

Like an NFL Head Coach watching game film, on a Monday morning after a game, Kurt watched the videos over and over with two main purposes in mind.

First, he wanted to see what everyone else had seen of this terrible incident, to make sure he was on the same page as them. Second, he wanted to start putting together his defense for his upcoming meeting.

"Of course," he said to himself, as Fox 32 led off their newscast, talking about the Old Mill Mall incident as the video footage played on the screen.

As he watched in amazement, Fox 32 showed the incident from him looking inside Stanley Pietrowski's car, all the way through to the Gilles Fire Department taking Pietrowski away.

Whoever had taken the video was no more than 20 to 30 feet from them.

Kurt was amazed at the quality of the picture and audio of the video.

Over and over, he watched the video, playing it at times in slow motion.

He would even pause it, looking for a loophole or an out.

When he was satisfied, he had watched it thoroughly and seen everything he needed to, he glanced down at his yellow notepad to review what he had written down for a defense.

He wasn't surprised by what he found.

The yellow notepad was completely blank, with not one notation on it.

Lunch had long passed and surprisingly he wasn't the least bit hungry. Next he watched the Channel 9 version. Since he had nothing but plenty of time these next three days, he also watched the Channel 2 version of it also.

Whoever had taken the video was smart and made copies of it because each television station was playing the same version of what he had watched first, on Fox 32.

"I'm so fucked," Kurt said as he stopped watching the tape.

He realized what he had feared the most before sitting down. He had no valid defense or explanation for his actions with Stanley Pietrowski and would take the punishment Chief McKinley would give him.

Third, he called his Dad in an effort to get him off his ass.

It had been so long since they had spoken, Kurt couldn't remember the phone number and didn't even have it in his phone.

Going through a small black and white phone book, he kept in a drawer in his kitchen, Kurt turned to the letter A.

He found his dad's name immediately under the word asshole.

The same way he had been while Kurt was growing up, John Thompson wasn't there as the phone call went directly to his voice mail.

"John, just returning your phone call from last night and, yeah, I'm in a bit of a mess at this time. Tell you what, don't call back since I have a meeting with the Chief on Monday. I promise to call you after the meeting so we can discuss getting together based on the number of days off I will surely get from this incident. So, take care, and I promise to call you soon."

Kurt knew he would never call John Thompson, "Dad" after the way he had abandoned his wife, Susan, and daughter, Ella, when Kurt was only five years old. Granted his mother Susan was no picnic being both bipolar as well as schizophrenic. But there had to be another way other than the way John Thompson handled it.

Fourth, Kurt Thompson spent all of Saturday, cleaning everything he owned.

All his property, both inside and out, was vacuumed and dusted.

He stripped his bed of linens and did three loads of laundry.

He checked all of his household goods to see what he needed.

Finally, he worked on the Cobra.

Kurt was surprised how long everything took.

Finally, he went to Heartland Animal Shelter, located on Milwaukee Avenue in Northbrook, early Sunday afternoon.

It took him hours as he played with a wide variety of puppies of mixed breeds.

Each of these puppies hoping to impress him so much, he would buy one of them and they could wind up sleeping on anything other than the floor of a cage that evening.

He finally chose a puppy and named him Max.

Twenty-five minutes later, a black and brown German Shepard puppy headed to the Thompson residence.

If only the meeting with Chief McKinley had lasted this long or gone as smoothly the next day.

Granted, Kurt realized he was doomed from the start on Monday, when he started to get dressed in the only suit, he owned, which he had purchased earlier in the year from J&G Clothiers.

The address for J&G Clothiers was 2710 Old Mill Mall Court, Gilles, Illinois.

Not having any viable defense for his actions, Kurt decided against bringing his FOP Representative to this meeting.

Unknown to Kurt, was the verbal beating Chief Dennis McKinley had been receiving since the Old Mill Mall video hit the news waves.

His fellow chiefs on the North Shore, every Village Trustee, and even Mrs. Chin, the owner of the dry cleaners where he brought his clothes, had mentioned it to him.

As he returned to his unmarked, white Ford Explorer, with his six neatly pressed uniform shirts and pants, Chief McKinley decided he would be transferring the shame he felt for his police department from his shoulders, to those of Officer Kurt Thompson come Monday.

Kurt barely had time to sit down across from the Chief before the accusations came out in the form of Department Regulations.

"87-10 Actions Unbecoming an Officer, 87-23 Violation of Code of Ethics, and 89-10 Failure to Maintain Equipment," flew from Chief McKinley's mouth.

Kurt Thompson tried to figure some of this out and interject some of his own thoughts into the conversation while his Chief was talking.

Instead, he figured his best option was to keep his mouth shut, and look at the documents his chief handed him.

"You're just lucky as hell the autopsy showed Mr. Pietrowski suffered from severe stages of Parkinson's, but actually died of myocardial infarction which is code for Heart Attack. He was dead the minute you had to grab him or you would be in even more trouble Officer Thompson are you clear on this "? Chief McKinley asked.

"Yes, sir I am," Kurt answered him.

It was only when Chief McKinley said the words, "Commander Billings" that Kurt regained his focus on what his boss was saying.

"Yes, Officer Thompson, I've spoken to all of your bosses," Chief McKinley said. "Believe it or not, they're all-in agreement on one thing."

"Which is Chief?" Kurt was finally able to say.

"For some God damn reason, they believe you have the capabilities of becoming an excellent Police Officer," Chief McKinley said.

"Thank you Chief," Kurt said boldly as a bit of his self-confidence began to return.

"I believe so as well, even after this major screw up on my part." Kurt said.

"Then what exactly is it Kurt, which has taken your career and thrown it in the toilet?" Chief McKinley asked while taking his hands and placing them palms up.

Kurt knew exactly what, as well as whom, but was too afraid to come out and say her name.

"I've seen solid futures in law enforcement destroyed by the four evils so let's see if we can narrow this down," Chief McKinley stated.

"Four evils Boss?" Kurt asked inquisitively.

"Hell, yeah Kurt!" Chief McKinley said and suddenly stood up as he began walking around to the front of his desk. "Gambling, drugs, alcohol and of course the most dangerous one of all, women."

Again, Kurt chose to remain silent and see where this whole thing was headed.

"None of your bosses believe it has anything to do with the first three since they've never seen you hung over at work, granted you were still on probation most of the time and it could have ended your career," Chief McKinley said as he took a seat on the front of his desk.

Sitting in this new position gave him a huge psychological edge of looking straight down at Kurt.

Not a word was said between the two of them as they stared into each other's eyes as each in their own peculiar way was attempting to figure out what the other one was thinking.

Kurt still refused to speak, wanting to see if Chief McKinley knew anything more.

"It's the red-haired Greenfield Officer you stood next to at Officer Mills' funeral, isn't it?" Chief McKinley finally asked with a gentle, grandfatherly tone in his voice.

Kurt's mouth was open so wide in shock, you could have dropped a 12-inch submarine sandwich into it and not even hit the sides.

"I was there, Kurt and yes I got there later than I wanted, but I had to go out of common courtesy to Chief Fitzsimons and his Command Staff," Chief McKinley said while keeping the quiet, grandfather tone in his voice.

Sensing Kurt was too confused, embarrassed, or afraid to discuss this issue, Chief McKinley continued.

"Kurt, people break up or fall out of love," said Chief McKinley. "Heidi and Seal, Kid Rock and Pam and, of course, the on again off again relationship my kids can't stop talking about, Justin and Selma Gomez."

"Selena sir, her name Chief, is Selena Gomez, not Selma, Sir," Kurt quickly interjected and then put his head down after realizing he had just corrected his boss.

"Excellent Kurt, you were paying attention," said Chief McKinley.

For the first time since this meeting started, the tension in the room started to be lifted.

"Kurt, I'm not going to start telling you how to live your life until it affects my life or the lives of any of my Police Personnel or the citizens of Gilles," continued Chief McKinley. "But this obviously has made a HUGE negative impact on a number of us and we're better than this," Chief McKinley said.

Barely pausing to catch a breath and preventing Kurt from speaking, Chief McKinley stood up and continued speaking, but lost the grandfatherly tone. "Officer Thompson, I'm giving you a 30-day suspension, effective immediately and obviously if you had still been on probation when all of this took place you would have been immediately terminated," Chief McKinley paused for a second before continuing

"Your other supervisors and I are hoping when you return, we will see the Kurt Thompson who first impressed us with his stats and arrests, as opposed to the latest version who seems to be confused."

"Do you have anything you wish to say or do you wish to appeal this suspension?" Chief McKinley finished.

"No Sir," Kurt answered affirmatively, standing straight up and shot his right hand out.

Chief McKinley grabbed Kurt's hand with his own right hand before bringing his left hand over so his hands completely covered Kurt's right hand.

Looking directly at Kurt, with the most passionate voice he could muster, Chief McKinley slowly said, "I don't know you very well Kurt and truth be told, this position prevents me from knowing a ton of my new personnel. A number of Chiefs would have fired you for your actions at Old Mill Mall last Thursday, but I'm giving you a golden opportunity to quite frankly, get your shit together. So, don't disappoint us, understood?"

"Yes Sir. I promise I won't let you down," Kurt Thompson replied while vigorously shaking Chief McKinley's hands.

Then, Kurt quickly exited the Chief's office.

Kurt started out with a bang by reconnecting that night with his father, John.

It happened so fast, just three days after telephoning his Dad, he was sitting in a canoe with him for a week of fishing at Polar Bear Provincial Park.

Kurt had never seen water so blue with so many speckled trout willing to practically jump into their canoe.

Located along the Hudson Bay Providence in Ontario, it allowed Kurt to get everything he wanted out of a vacation—relaxation, meditation, and great exercise.

There was also plenty of time to allow John to fully explain his side of the divorce in detail.

Kurt came back a new man with a renewed relationship with his father, which he had so desperately wanted growing up.

He promised his father he would try and attend a Fourth of July barbecue if he wasn't working

When he picked up Max from Carriage Hills Kennels after his trip, he was almost knocked over and layered in kisses.

"Sir, may I have your order please," a voice asked him over the intercom at the drive thru of Popeye's Chicken, located on Golf Road just west of the Skokie Courthouse.

"Sorry about that," Kurt says with an embarrassed tone in his voice.

Yes, it was good to be back with a second chance to make a difference and to prove to Chief McKinley he'd made the right decision after all.

CHAPTER 32

Marge Thomas had just caused a major dilemma for Officer Matt O'Neil.

On the one hand, he believed everything she told him, especially the part concerning Kurt Thompson's possible involvement in her nephew's death.

Since there were no secrets in police departments, Marc Dombrowski had over lunch, recently told Matt about the Old Mill Mall fiasco, resulting in Kurt Thompson's suspension.

Matt was so happy he gave Marc a high five so hard, he was afraid he had broken his hand in the process.

As Matt continued scribbling into his notepad, with his head down, his thoughts were filled with "Who the hell do I go to with Marge's suspicions?"

Someone, besides him who was actually handling this case needed to be aware of this information.

The questions on Matt's mind were: "Who would this person be?

Should he call either Detective Golden or Lyons from NORTAF?"

If he had time, could he get in touch with and, more importantly, get a quick answer from his attorney, Kevin Kray?

Marge obviously had no use for Deputy Chief Bart so he was out of the equation.

Matt was sure NORTAF was in the process of or had already obtained a subpoena for all his phone records.

Thus, calling his Attorney would certainly raise questions.

Sgt. Barton was still in Matt's corner, but he wasn't directly involved in any part of this investigation.

Why drag him into this?

Finally, it came to Matt when he realized who indeed was involved, especially with the death of Officer Ron Thomas. "Lieutenant Alderman," he blurted out as he raised his head.

"Who?" Marge Thomas asked and you could tell she obviously had never heard this name mentioned before by her nephew.

For the next five minutes, Matt felt obligated to give Marge Thomas a quick overview of who was handling her nephew's Death Investigation from the Door County side of it as well as the Greenfield Police Department's side of it.

Matt emphasized exactly the role Detective Kenbridge was playing and specifically Lt. Alderman's involvement as well. "So, Marge, I'm going to get Lieutenant Alderman for you, not Deputy Chief Bart, and you can explain to him everything you've just told me. Please take your time making sure you don't leave anything out."

"But Ron said you would be the one to solve his death," Marge Thomas said as tears started forming in the corner of her eyes.

Matt reached over with his right hand and grabbed her left hand before saying, "Marge, I'm going to be playing a role in solving his death. But we have different states and jurisdictions involved so I need to get a bit of help from a few people."

Marge Thomas let go of Matt's hand as she reached inside her black Coach purse for a couple of tissues to dab her eyes.

"Okay," she replied, "Can you please get me a glass of water?"

"Not a problem Marge," Matt responded as he stood up and looked directly down at Marge blowing her nose. "I'll be attempting to locate Lieutenant Alderman as well."

Matt O'Neil was damn proud of the way Marge Thomas was holding up so far.

He was sure this was much more difficult than she thought it would be when she walked into the Greenfield Police Department, roughly 30 minutes ago.

Matt had his head down and was scribbling the sequence of events into his notepad for the Police Report he needed to do when he returned from court.

Consequently, he was slightly off balance as he walked out of the interview room and quickly turned left, heading toward the front counter of the police station.

He never saw the person who was also headed toward the same front counter, until the very last moment before they collided.

"Sorry about that Officer," this person said in very broken English and with a strong Russian accent.

Matt was more than a bit pissed as he regained his balance and started to give this individual the death stare, before saying out loud, "Ivan Drago?"

This person chuckled a bit before extending his right hand to Matt, saying, "No, Ivan Petrov, but I tend to get the Ivan Drago a ton from, how you say, Rocky fans."

"Hmm, what exact Rocky movie was it again?" Matt asked and actually stared at him, wide eyed like he was looking at a real movie star.

"Rocky IV," Petrov answered and smiled broadly, showing off the most crooked teeth Matt had ever seen in another human being's mouth.

"Say, I'm here to see a Lieutenant Alderman of your Investigations Unit. Could you help me find him?" Petrov asked and stared at Matt, waiting for his response.

"Sure," Matt answered and walked over to a phone located on the front counter of the Records Division.

Picking up the handle of the phone, he turned and looked at Petrov, "Who should I tell him you're with?"

Slowly Petrov pulled back the right side of his blue sport coat revealing a gold shield hooked on to the front of his brown belt.

Matt had never seen a shield this big before in his entire life.

Petrov must have been pissed at Matt for staring at his shield because he replied in a loud and strong voice, "Secretary of State Police, Investigative Unit."

Matt realized he might have made an error and turned back quickly to the panel on the phone, hitting the button for the intercom. Knowing everyone in the building would hear him, he spoke in his most professional sounding voice, clearly saying, "Lieutenant

Alderman, call the front desk, please." Then, he repeated himself once again, saying, "Lieutenant Alderman, front desk."

Almost as if he was sitting at his desk, waiting for the page, Lieutenant Alderman responded.

Grabbing the phone after only the first ring and barely getting it to his right ear, Matt couldn't get a word out before Lt. Alderman calmly said into the phone, "What's up O'Neil?"

"Lieutenant, I have an Investigator Petrov here from the Secretary of State Police attempting to find you," Matt said slowly and calmly into the phone.

"Shit, he wasn't supposed to be here until tomorrow and every one of my detectives are either out of town on follow-ups or at 26 and California on a Grand Jury Indictment," Lt. Alderman said roughly into the receiver.

"Is he going to use me for doing something besides sharpening pencils and paging people?" Matt wondered to himself.

"Let me talk to Petrov," Lt. Alderman said.

Matt turned and handed the phone to Petrov saying, "He wants to talk to you,"

Grabbing the phone out of Matt's hand, Petrov was only able to get the words, "Yes, Lieutenant Alderman," out of his mouth, before he spent the next minute listening.

Lt. Alderman spoke so loudly, it was easy for Matt to overhear most of the conversation.

"Look, Investigator Petrov, I must have gotten the days screwed up for when you were coming over. Not a problem, I have the address we talked about the other day. I'll send the beat car and roving car with you to check things out. So just head out, be careful and they will probably beat you to the address," Lt. Alderman finished.

"Understood Lieutenant. I see the officer who just paged you has his hand in the air. I believe he wants to speak with you," Investigator Petrov said.

Handing Matt back the telephone, Investigator Petrov slapped him on his right shoulder as he walked past him and headed out of the police station.

"Do you have a minute for me Lieutenant Alderman?" Matt asked.

"Of course, O'Neil, whatever you need," Lt. Alderman answered with the most sarcastic tone imaginable.

Matt tried the best he could to keep it short concerning Marge Thomas and her reason for coming to the Greenfield Police Station.

Unfortunately, it still took him two minutes to try and explain everything.

When finished, he waited patiently for Lt. Alderman to come to some type of decision.

"Shit O'Neil, just tell her to stay seated and I'll be up as soon as I can to interview her," Lt. Alderman said disgustedly into the phone.

"Roger that," Matt answered. "I'm headed to Skokie for Felony Court in case you need to get in touch with me."

Apparently, Lt. Alderman had heard enough from Matt today as he said, "O'Neil, O'Neil, just go to court and I'll take it from here."

"Roger that, Lieutenant," Matt replied.

As he hung up the phone, he wondered what he did exactly to piss off the head of the Greenfield Investigations Unit.

Matt couldn't worry about it for right now because he had more than enough on his plate for the rest of his shift.

Matt started walking back around the counter to the desk he had picked out his first day assigned to the records section.

Being short on time, he quickly picked up his four court cases off the middle of his desk and headed back to where he had just come from.

As he passed Linda McMillion's desk, he paused for a second, telling her, "Headed out to Felony Court. I'm going to grab some lunch when I'm done."

"Enjoy the freedom Matt," Linda replied and then looked up at him and smiled broadly.

Since Matt was headed to court, he was fully suited up with a bulletproof vest as well as his Sam Browne belt. The minute he stepped out the front door of the police station, he turned on his portable radio and immediately looked down to make sure he was on the correct frequency of Channel 3.

"Greenfield 321," T.C. Chambers said.

"Go for Greenfield," Dispatcher Susie Patz answered.

"Start me a CAD Ticket and make it for Assist Outside Agency at 524 Short Street," he said before quickly jumping back on the radio to say, "also put 323 on it."

"524 Short Street, got it," Patz answered.

Walking quickly toward the rear parking lot of the police station, Matt grabbed his phone from the front pocket of his bulletproof vest and quickly scrolled through it, finding the number he wanted.

After dialing the number, he waited patiently until the other party finally picked up.

"Shit, look who escaped Records and is on the loose," T.C. Chambers joked.

"Yeah, headed to Felony Court right after I find a squad car out here," Matt said as he had reached the parking lot and was looking around for which one to take.

Since T.C Chambers had no response and Matt was curious about something, he decided to keep talking.

"What's the deal with this Investigator from the Secretary of State Police Investigative Unit named Petrov?" he asked.

"All I know is Lieutenant Alderman called me a few minutes ago on my cell and said to meet Petrov over at 524 Short Street but not really sure why," T.C. answered.

"Greenfield 323 is out on Short and waiting for 321," Megan O'Brien said.

"10-4," Susie Patz replied.

"Shit, Megan's already there so I have to go," T.C. said. "Hey, let's try and grab lunch tomorrow."

"Got it," Matt responded.

Hanging up on T.C., a smile came on Matt's face as he saw it sitting there.

Squad four, his assigned squad car, unoccupied and recently washed.

Slowly he walked around the Ford Interceptor, checking it out for any new damage. If he didn't report the damage, it would be the last thing he needed at this stage of his career. Confident his car was fine; Matt got in the car and threw his court cases on the passenger seat.

Finally, he put on his seatbelt adjusting it over his shoulder microphone.

As Matt carefully began to back up, he heard T.C. Chambers come on the air. "Greenfield 321 is out on Short also."

As she would for easily 70 times today, Patz calmly said, "10-4."

Matt pulled out of the parking lot and turned left on to Waukegan Road, before deciding to get on the radio.

"Greenfield 327," he said into the squad's microphone as if it was his first time using it.

"Go ahead, 327," Patz responded.

"327 is headed to Skokie Court," Matt said. "I am driving Squad 4."

"10-4, 327 and enjoy it," Patz said, knowing Matt's situation and how good it must feel to actually be back out on the road, if only for a little bit.

"Jenkins must be on her lunch break which is why Patz is on the radio" Matt found himself saying slowly out loud.

Matt could take two different ways to court but decided on a path which would take him somewhat close to Short Street, if needed.

It actually felt good to be driving a Greenfield Police car again, he thought to himself.

As opposed to his Camaro, he rode so much higher off the ground in the Ford Interceptor, which allowed him to see everything.

Matt crossed over the railroad tracks on Greenfield Road, just east of Harlem Avenue and barely moved at all in his driver's seat, due to the beefed-up suspension. He knew if he had been in his or Kelly's personal cars, they would have been bumping all over their seats.

"10-13, 10-13, shots fired and officers down," Megan O'Brien yelled into her Motorola microphone.

"10-13, 10-13," she yelled again before a shot went off, close to her microphone.

CHAPTER 33

M att O'Neil can feel his heart beating so rapidly he thinks it is going to jump right through his Second Chance, Monarch, Level Two bulletproof vest.

He is amazed at how quickly the palms on both of his hands have gone from bone dry too sweaty.

Matt's head is pounding from the radio traffic coming over his Norcom radio.

Every Greenfield Police Unit on the street was yelling into their respective radios at the same time. Each of them desperately trying to tell Susie Patz they were headed to 524 Short Street.

Instead, they were talking over each other and nobody's radio traffic could be recognized.

Matt knew better than to try and get on the radio.

He focuses like he never has before on driving quickly and safely.

Over and over the words of his defensive driving instructor at the Illinois Law Enforcement Training Center, Mike Mazur, with his slow Texas drawl, rang in Matt's head.

"You aren't any good to any of us, Ladies and Gentlemen, if you get killed trying to come save another officer's ass, so you have to get there safely people."

Matt is fortunate in the fact every intersection he comes to had a green light so he can move quickly through the lights without having to turn on his lights or siren.

This also wouldn't be his first time on Short Street, which would work to his advantage.

FTO Carll had pointed out 524 Short Street to Matt on their second day together.

As they had done earlier that day at every Greenfield Bank, FTO Carll created some type of crime scenario.

He was assessing Matt's decision making and tactical skills.

524 Short Street was unique in a number of different ways.

First, it's the only street in Greenfield with only two homes on it. One of the homes sits only two tenths of a mile from Waukegan Road as you go westbound on Short Street.

The other home was located at the end of the street.

Second, the entire street was completely blacktopped and exactly one mile in length. This could possibly be the reason why it obtained its name from the early village officials of Greenfield, Carll had told Matt.

Third, the street was a dead end and the backyard of 524 Short Street was so big, the Chicago Bears could have used it as a practice field.

Behind the backyard was a small hill with Metra Railroad tracks on top of it.

Last, the two houses on Short Street were Lustron style houses.

They were the only ones of their kind left in the entire village. Built at the end of World War II, these enameled steel homes were a public eyesore. But they were easy to construct and could withstand any type of weather.

To the north of Short Street was a condominium complex called Orchard Park.

The vast majority of residents of Orchard Park were wealthy, but elderly.

Matt couldn't recall ever seeing anyone under the age of sixty, exiting their parking lot.

The management of Orchard Park wanted to guarantee its residents wouldn't see the ugliness of Short Street. Consequently, a beautiful tree embankment had been installed many years ago in an attempt to block out those two homes.

To the south of Short Street was a hair salon simply called Stage.

The Stage management were also concerned about their patrons parking in the rear of their establishment, getting out of their cars and looking at the worst street in Greenfield.

Consequently, they had a ten-foot wooden fence installed in the rear of their building and it ran the length of their property.

Knowing he wouldn't be able to scale the wooden fence or come in from the rear of Short Street left Matt with only one viable option, to approach from the parking lot of Orchard Park.

Turning right off Waukegan Road into the parking lot of Orchard Park, he slowly drove his Ford Interceptor at a snail's pace.

Frequently, he kept glancing to his left in an attempt to see where T.C. Chambers and Megan O'Brien had parked their Greenfield Patrol Units.

It only took him a few seconds of inching forward before he saw both of them parked, one behind the other, in the street, in front of 524 Short Street.

Parked in the driveway of the residence was an all-white Ford Escape, with so many radio antennas, the driver could easily have contacted Russia without an issue.

Matt assumed this vehicle belonged to Investigator Petrov, from the Secretary of State.

With the radio finally free of Greenfield Units' Radio Traffic, Susie Patz's voice broke the silence.

"Greenfield Unit 321?" she asked in a patient voice.

T.C. Chambers didn't respond to his call sign.

"Greenfield Unit 323, come in please," Susie Patz asked, this time making her request a plea.

Megan O'Brien also didn't answer her call sign.

"Greenfield 327, out on Short Street," Matt said into his car microphone and didn't even wait for a response from Patz before placing the microphone quickly back into its holder.

"10-4 and be careful," Patz answered, with a surprised tone in her voice.

Then it dawned on Matt why Patz had answered him the way she had. He would be alone at 524 Short Street for some time.

After being assigned to Records Duty, one of the first things Matt would do every morning was to sign onto New World at his desk computer and see which beat each Greenfield Police Officer had.

This morning had been no exception. Megan O'Brien had been assigned the beat where 524 Short Street was located, and T.C. Chambers was the roving car for the east side of town.

With it being lunchtime, both the Traffic Unit and Detective Unit were nowhere to be found

With Sgt. Barton in the station on an issue, the nearest Greenfield Unit responding to 524 Short Street was coming from the west side of town.

Matt certainly didn't like his odds or his present tactical position, but he had no choice.

To wait for a back-up unit was out of the question.

He needed to get onto 524 Short Street and do it as quickly as possible.

Matt has two weapons available for him to use. His Glock 22 Gen 4 or his Bushmaster Modular AR 15.

Due to the unknown circumstances, there possibly being more than one assailant, and maybe needing to go inside a house, it is an easy decision to make.

Hitting the release button on the dashboard of the Ford Interceptor, he waits less than two seconds for the metal band holding his AR 15 in its port to release.

The loud click indicates it released.

Grabbing the weapon with his right hand, he gets out of the Ford Interceptor.

Immediately, he kneels behind his driver's side door and starts the process of preparing this weapon for use.

Quickly, he releases the black rubber clip, which holds the shoulder harness for the weapon together. With the shoulder harness now free, Matt pulls the Velcro apart, allowing him to slip it over his head and his left shoulder. Then, he clips the tip attached on it to the bottom of the AR 15.

Now, the weapon rests comfortably in the middle of his bulletproof vest with the barrel facing the paved parking lot.

Next, he flips open the AR 15's rear sight, hitting the right button to activate the EO Tech's 510, red holographic. With the index finger on his left hand, he repeatedly pushes the small button located on the left side of the sight until the red hologram shines brightly.

Finally, he clears the lower receiver on the weapon, guaranteeing a 223 round is in place.

Carefully, he moves the grey weapon's stock two clicks, comfortable it will fit properly against his right shoulder when he is ready to use it.

Satisfied, he stands up half way until he can easily peer at 524 Short Street from his open squad cars driver's side window. No movement, noise, or suspects could be seen from his vantage point.

Next, he looks for where he can safely advance to and finds it with his first glance.

Kneeling back down, he makes the weapon ready for use by switching the safety on the AR 15 from the off position to ready for fire position.

Carefully balancing the weapon, he gets back inside his Ford Interceptor.

While crouching down behind the vehicle's steering wheel, he shifts from park to drive and the vehicle slowly begins inching forward.

He almost crashes into the rear trunk of an unoccupied, brand new Mercedes Benz, GLE SUV, but he cranks the steering wheel to a hard left at the last second.

The passenger side of his squad now faces 524 Short Street at a 45-degree angle, giving him maximum cover.

Throwing the gearshift into park, he opens his driver's side door with his left hand and practically rolls out of his seat.

The minute his Reebok Krios Tactical Boots hit the ground, he sprints around to the rear of his vehicle and gets directly to the front passenger side of the Benz, kneeling behind its engine mount.

This new position puts him less than 30 feet from the front door of 524 Short Street.

Raising his head barely above the engine area of the Benz is when he saw them for the first time—two bodies lying next to their vehicles.

One of them wears a Greenfield Police Department uniform.

The second body is dressed in a blue sport coat with part of his right hand blown off.

Both lay motionless, with blood slowly running from their bodies.

Being so close to them, it's easy for Matt to recognize who they are immediately—Investigator Petrov and Officer T.C. Chambers.

Momentarily, Matt finds it hard to breathe, and swallowing is out of the question due to the lump which has formed in his throat.

The wail of police sirens in the distance snaps Matt back into reality.

Instantly, he rises to his feet bringing the AR 15 straight up as well.

As Navy Seal trained, he cocks his head slightly to the right so he is able to use the EO Tech 510 sight properly.

He knows it is a waste of time, but he carefully makes his way around the Mercedes Benz until he is kneeling next to T.C. Chambers' body.

A shotgun blast had struck him in the jaw.

Part of T.C.'s face is missing and his trachea and esophagus are totally exposed.

The AR 15 rests nicely on Matt's right shoulder and points it toward the house. Matt uses his left hand and makes the sign of the cross on what remained of T.C. Chamber's face.

Quickly, Matt glances at Investigator Petrov's body.

He soon realizes it is in even worse shape than Chamber's.

If this were the movies, Matt would go charging through the front door of 524 Short Street, killing the bad guys in the process.

Instead, he sees his best tactical advantage is to go around to the north side of the home, which he currently is closest to.

The fact that there are no doors or windows on that side of the house also plays a significant role in his decision.

Quickly, he gets up and runs to that location, waiting for the sound of gunfire coming at him from inside the house.

Not a shot is fired at Matt, which surprises him.

Slowly, he walks on the balls of his feet with his AR 15 raised and pointed directly ahead.

He is amazed how well his traction is as he walks through tall grass and occasional mud.

Matt never looks down, focusing entirely on the rear sight of his AR 15, waiting for a possible offender to emerge from the house, yard, or anywhere in a split second. His right index finger rests lightly on the trigger of the weapon.

The sound of multiple police sirens, now seem to be coming from every direction.

Matt figures they are only a few blocks away, but he can't stop and wait for them.

He needs to find Megan and the killer or killers of his best friend.

As he finishes walking around the north side of the house, Matt temporarily freezes at what sits in a corner of the backyard.

A light green vinyl carport, which holds one vehicle.

It is the vehicle inside the carport which has taken Matt's breath away.

Someone had pulled a dark green tarp off the rear portion of this vehicle, apparently trying to identify it.

"Holy shit," Matt says out loud.

Matt is staring at the trunk of a White, Ford Bronco, complete with the faded White Sox sticker still attached to the rear window.

Matt wants to run toward the Bronco, but all of his tactical training kicks in.

That's when Matt momentarily sees a figure on the top of the Metra tracks.

The dark, navy blue police uniform gives him away immediately.

"Matt, look out," Megan yells from the driver's side of the Ford Bronco.

These momentary distractions are all it takes.

Matt never sees his assailant until the very last second, when he finally transfers his attention from Megan, and the figure on the Metra tracks, to a white male, standing behind the open passenger door of the Ford Bronco, pointing a handgun at him.

Almost on cue, this individual behind the passenger door and Matt fire simultaneously at each other.

In the span of no more than 3 seconds its over, as Matt falls to the ground in the backyard of 524 Short Street.

CHAPTER 34

He had no idea how people traveled before GPS devices were created.

This morning he walked out to his vehicle, took his Garmin Nuvi 54 out of the glove box, and put in the address of 1011 Alpine Road, Rockford, Illinois.

With a sweet female voice telling him where to go, he was off.

Being a Saturday afternoon, in the early days of August, helped speed up his journey.

Since traffic was light, he wasn't surprised how quickly he was able to get to his destination of American Legion Post 1207.

The building was huge and so was the parking lot for it.

Granted it was a Bar and Grill, but how many customers did the management really expect?

Also, what's with the roof that looked like it belonged on a building in Tijuana, Mexico?

Needing more time to think about all of this, he looked to his left and found just what he'd hoped for. A huge, three-story parking lot with plenty of empty spots.

Quickly, he drove over to it and after a series of right hand turns inside of it, found himself on the third floor, without another car in sight.

Slowly, he pulled into a spot that was on the opposite side of Alpine Road.

Due to it being 90 degrees he lowered every window in his car, before turning off the engine.

Complete silence engulfed him and allowed him to ponder his next move.

He was actually apprehensive as he sat in his dirty Chevy Camaro.

These past 16 months had been like nothing he had ever imagined he would experience, when he last saw this group.

He had to admit he was apprehensive about the reaction he would receive from them.

Marc Dombrowski had passed on the invitation, which didn't surprise Matt.

For some reason Marc never connected with anyone in the class and spent most of his time only with the entire Greenfield group from day one.

Matt's iPhone beeped.

He reached for the iPhone, which was lying on his front passenger seat.

He took off his Ray Ban Aviators, in an effort to see who was trying to get in touch with him.

A huge smile crossed his face when he realized it was Kelly.

Reading her text made him smile even more since she had written, "Have a great time and enjoy every minute of it, my love. See you in a couple of days when you come home to us. Xoxoxo, Kelly."

"Us," Matt said out loud and slowly started to shake his head from side to side.

Everything this past week in conversations with Kelly had been put as "us" because the baby was less than five months away.

Granted she was the love of his life and his feelings were biased, but Kelly was actually glowing while carrying their baby.

With Matt in attendance at their last visit to their obstetrician, Dr. Neva Lewis, the results were everything they had been hoping for.

Kelly had gained only 18 pounds so far, and the baby had been the most active on the fetal monitor since they had been going in for their appointments.

Matt respected Kelly's decision and hadn't pushed on wanting to know the sex of their baby.

Dr. Lewis knew this as well and had helped in trying to keep the baby's sex a secret.

This obviously created a problem when it came to decorating the spare bedroom they had set up as a nursery.

Matt figured they would wallpaper instead of paint for right now and he could fix up the room on the maternity leave he would be taking.

"Man," he thought to himself, "how lucky could one man be?"

There was little doubt many a man's wives would have said screw it and moved on, when the crap came out about Javier Ortego's girlfriend and Matt, even though it was lies.

Not Kelly who told Matt the thought never crossed her mind he was the killer or he could be cheating on her.

Instead, she comforted him in every way possible whether it be emotionally, physically, sexually and finally, spiritually.

Their strong Catholic upbringing and faith in Jesus Christ, had never wavered while all of this craziness was happening.

If Matt's regularly scheduled days off included Sunday, mass at St. John Brebuf in Gilles was always on the agenda for the day.

Both Kelly and Matt loved the way the pastor, Father Ray Barlog, ran the parish, as well as said mass. Never had they been in church longer than forty-five minutes and left spiritually refreshed after a powerful sermon.

Matt placed his phone back on the Camaro's front passenger seat and put his Ray Ban Aviators back on. Slowly, he placed his head against the headrest of his driver's seat, for the first time in a very long time.

With his left hand he found the seat adjustor and slowly moved his seat so it was tilted slightly back.

In this new position, Matt was looking directly at the sun visor positioned directly over the steering wheel. Closing his eyes, he attempted to catch a quick nap.

Instead, Matt caught much more—Megan's voice crying for help at 524 Short Street.

The soggy combination of both grass and mud had caused Matt to slip, and in all probability, saved his life.

Rising instinctively after the shot had passed him, he brought his AR 15 to shoulder level and advanced on his target—the assailant behind the passenger door of the Ford Bronco.

Only this time, two things had changed since he had fallen earlier.

His AR 15 was now covered in mud and the assailant wasn't standing behind the open passengers' door of the Ford Bronco.

Matt's training kicked in and, without hesitation, he let go of the AR 15.

Due to its harness, the AR15 now rested, muzzle facing down, on the front of Matt's bulletproof vest.

In seconds, Matt had his Glock 22 Gen 4, out of his holster, raised and pointed directly at the passengers' door.

Slowly, Matt walked towards this door, holding his breath. His right index finger was next to the trigger of the weapon until he had reached the door and saw the body lying behind it.

"Tyler," Matt said loud enough for only him to hear.

With the Glock still pointed directly at Tyler's head, Matt reached down and removed a Glock 22 Gen 4, from the right hand of his assailant, Tyler Hale.

As trained, Matt cleared the Glock and then wedged it between his duty belt and bullet proof vest on the right side of his body.

Within seconds, Kurt Thompson arrived, weapon in hand. He went directly to the driver's side door of the Bronco.

"Clear, O'Neil," Thompson yelled.

"Got it," Matt replied.

"HOLY SHIT MEGAN," Kurt Thompson yelled.

"Greenfield 327," Matt yelled into his Motorola shoulder mic.

"Go 327," Susie Patz responded, yelling into her headset for the first time ever in her career.

"Greenfield, we have officers both down as well as injured," Matt said. "Tell Greenfield Fire Personnel they are needed immediately at the rear of the residence for the injured Greenfield officer."

"10-4," Patz answered, much calmer. Then she asked, "What is the status of the assailants?"

"The assailant is also down and tell Lieutenant Alderman he and a NORTAF team will be needed at this address ASAP," Sgt. Barton answered.

Being the true professional or possibly seeing the portable Motorola's identification number on the screen in front of her, Susie Patz answered, "Roger that, Sergeant Barton."

"You okay, O'Neil?" Sgt. Barton asked as he slowly holstered his Glock 22 Gen 4, from his position on the right side of Tyler Hale's body.

"Yes," Matt answered as he returned to the area, also holstering his own weapon.

"Greenfield 327," Susie Patz called.

"Go ahead Greenfield," Sgt. Barton answered for him, as calm as if he was placing an order at McDonald's.

"Greenfield Fire Battalion Six is insisting the Crime Scene be secure before their personnel enter," Patz responded.

"Tell him God damn it, to get in here now. The crime scene is secure and he has my word on it," D.C. Bart replied.

"Roger that, 302," Susie Patz answered. "His personnel, along with ambulances from both Morton Grove and Gilles Fire Departments, are coming in."

"Fucking fire guys," Deputy Chief Bart said out loud, to no one in particular, as he put his Motorola radio back inside its case, on the right side of his Sam Browne duty belt.

He then started walking closer to where Sgt. Barton and Matt were standing.

Deputy Chief Bart easily stood out in the crowd which were now entering the backyard because he was the only one carrying a blue-plated, Remington 870 Tactical Express Model Shotgun.

If the word pandemonium, could be used in police work, the next 5 to 10 minutes, in the backyard of 524 Short Street resembled it.

A team of Greenfield paramedics, led by their Battalion Chief Jim Gancher, ascended on the area and headed directly toward the area of the Bronco where Kurt Thompson was standing over the body of Megan O'Brien. Kurt was waving at them frantically with his left arm in an effort to get them to hurry up.

Every law enforcement officer who was working anywhere in the area of 524 Short Street, when the call came out, were now standing in the backyard of the residence.

As Matt looked on in amazement, he saw three Cook County Sheriff's Officers walking around with their service weapons drawn, but held against their legs.

Two K9 German Shepard's, one being from the Skokie Police Department, stood at opposite ends of the yard with their handlers having a devilish time trying to control them.

Deputy Chief Bart saw this occurring at his crime scene and quickly ordered Matt and Sgt. Barton to regain control over the craziness.

"Stay with the dead guy O'Neil," Sgt. Barton said. He turned to go over to the other side of the Ford Bronco and check on Megan.

"The dead guy is Tyler Hale," Matt said to Sgt. Barton who apparently, didn't hear him, because he continued to walk away. Sgt. Barton obviously cared for Megan O'Brien and wanted her to get the best medical attention possible for her injuries.

But he also knew he needed to try and maintain some type of order for his NORTAF Evidence Technicians. The biggest threat to maintaining order was the Greenfield Fire Department, which was roughly 20 feet away and closing quickly. The Greenfield Fire Personnel had one mission, which was to stabilize the patient and them get to the nearest medical facility quickly and safely.

Cops could talk for hours about guns, or knives, which were moved by fire personnel at crime scenes, shell casings which became stuck under a paramedic gurney, or a hypodermic needle filled with heroin, that was picked up with other syringes by a paramedic in a rush to get out of the area.

Sgt. Barton would have his hands filled with getting names and badge numbers of the fire personnel who would be on scene, for the crime log he needed to fill out.

Meanwhile, Matt continued staring directly down at Tyler Hale's dead body.

His attention was drawn away from Tyler as he heard Kurt Thompson repeatedly saying, "Megan, you're going to be okay, just hang in there."

As Matt watched, two of the biggest paramedics from the

Greenfield Fire Department had decided against rolling Megan through the mud and grass and, instead, picked up the stretcher she was on and carried her towards the front of the house.

Kurt Thompson was on the right side of the stretcher, holding onto her right hand.

The remaining Greenfield Fire Personnel were walking on the left side, or rear of the stretcher.

Each were carrying either a drug box, defibrillator, or backboard.

What Matt could see of Megan O'Brien's left shoulder didn't look good.

Someone had removed her gun belt, bulletproof vest along with uniform shirt, and her white Under Amour shirt was drenched in blood.

A small, green oxygen bottle was placed inside the stretcher.

Two small prongs on a plastic nasal cannula were placed inside Megan's nostrils, to assist her breathing.

A bloody tourniquet had been applied as well to her left upper arm.

Matt smiled slightly as the Greenfield Fire Personnel passed Lt. Wayne, who was carrying boxes of both yellow and red crime scene tape and was frantically looking around for some fixed objects to attach his tape to.

"You okay O'Neil?" Lt. Alderman asked.

Matt quickly turned his attention away from Lt. Wayne to Lt. Alderman, who seemed to have brought the cavalry with him.

Behind Lt. Alderman stood two of his detectives, Paul Sutherland and Steve Liske.

Behind these two detectives, stood an entire squad, from the Morton Grove Fire Department.

Matt was surprised to see the Greenfield Detectives, including their boss, in bulletproof vests, with "Police," stenciled on the back.

None of the bulletproof vests seemed to fit properly and looked peculiar on them, due to their dress shirts and silk ties.

Matt was also totally shocked to see the entire Morton Grove

Fire Personnel on scene, had been outfitted also in bulletproof vests.

"I'm asking you again, are you doing okay, O'Neil?" Lt. Alderman asked.

Matt was taken back because he believed Lt. Alderman was being sincere by the tone he used when he asked Matt the question and the body language he displayed.

"Yeah, not hurt," Matt replied, which probably surprised most of them because the right side of his uniform had splatters of dried grass and mud on it from his fall.

Satisfied Matt was fine, Lt. Alderman pulled out his cell phone from a pocket of his bulletproof vest and pointed it directly at Tyler Hale's face.

"You don't have to take a picture of him Boss, I know who this guy is," Matt said with a confident tone in his voice.

All three investigators, along with Sgt. Barton, who had walked back over to where Matt was standing, just stared at him.

Sgt. Barton recovered faster than the others and broke the silence. "Who is he Matt?"

"Tyler Hale, Boss, from..." Matt started. He would have finished his sentence if it weren't for Deputy Chief Bart, who had suddenly pushed his way through the crowd of Morton Grove Fire Personnel and Greenfield Police Personnel to ask one simple question.

"You guys cleared the house, correct?"

Every cop, including Matt, immediately put their heads down, afraid to look Deputy Chief Bart in the face when he got the bad news.

"Holy shit, its Tyler Hale," a new voice blurted out from somewhere amidst the crowd which had gathered around the body, by the passengers' side door of the Ford Bronco.

Marc Dombrowski didn't care about crime scene procedures.

He knew the last remaining member, of his Greenfield ILETC class, who was still alive, was standing in front of him.

Matt was totally caught off guard as Marc walked over and put his arms around him.

Not knowing what to do, Matt returned the hug and the two stood in each other's arms, realizing the significance of the situation.

"Love you man," Marc said, his voice breaking up in the process.

"Same brother," Matt responded and increased the pressure of his hug while saying it.

"Excuse me people, but we still have work to do," Deputy Chief Bart barked. "O'Neil, you're with me. Sergeant Barton, you as well with Sergeant Garza."

Sgt. Garza was standing behind the Morton Grove Fire Personnel. Both Sgts. Garza and Barton barked out, "Got it," at the same time.

"Lt. Alderman, this crime scene as well the front of the house is in your capable hands. You have my authority to utilize any personnel as well as NORTAF teams at your disposal."

"Got it, Boss," Lt. Alderman replied, suddenly energized.

In single file, with Matt in the front and Sgt. Garza in the rear, the four of them walked straight toward the back door of 524 Short Street.

The crowd of law enforcement personnel in the backyard had doubled, yet the four of them had no problem getting through.

The cops stepped aside the minute they saw the look on Matt's face. While passing through the crowd, Matt was amused how the crowd had broken down into groups of four or five. The conversations in each group went something along the lines of "Hey, does Steve, Bill, or John, still work for you guys?"

With the response generally being, "He took the early buy out, retired, or yup still with us."

Finalized by the first group saying, "When you see him tell them hi from…"

Matt was surprised how quickly cops went into a relaxed mode at crime scenes.

In the military, you always seemed to be on edge, until you heard the order to stand down.

Since the distance from the Bronco to the rear door of the residence was roughly 45 feet, the four of them covered it in less than a minute.

Matt's approach had put them on the left side of the door, which is where they stood in single file.

Matt thought the old wooden door, which had gone through countless Illinois winters, without a screen door to protect it, wouldn't be a problem. With his free right hand, Matt removed his Glock 22 Gen 4 , which seemed to have a domino effect on the three others behind him.

Matt moved one step closer to the door and started to use his left hand to see if the gold doorknob was locked when he froze, due to the most terrifying sound he had ever heard coming from directly behind his head.

Deputy Chief Bart had chambered a round in his shotgun.

The sound was so distinctive and the weapon being so close to Matt's head, made the situation even worse.

Quickly, Matt turned his head until his eyes and those of Deputy Chief Bart's were locked.

Deputy Chief Bart didn›t budge an inch, and Matt wasn›t prepared to get into it with the second highest ranking officer on the Greenfield Police Department.

Deputy Chief Bart wasn't apparently amused by Matt's look and simply said, "Let's go O'Neil."

Begrudgingly, Matt started to turn his head back around when he saw them.

Roughly half the crowd in the backyard, who only a minute ago had been laughing or telling stories, were now down on one knee with their weapons pointed at the rear door of the house.

Matt again focused on the doorknob, which he slowly turned to the left.

It was unlocked and he slowly opened the door about 1/3 of the way.

Matt raised his left hand in the air and with the thumb on that hand raised he moved this hand towards the sky so Sgt. Garza, who was in the rear, could realize what had just taken place.

Seeing this, Sgt. Garza tapped Sgt. Barton's left shoulder. Sgt. Barton, in turn, tapped Deputy Chief Bart on his left shoulder. Upon receiving his tap, Deputy Chief Bart moved his head until he was practically over Matt O'Neil's left shoulder.

"Go," Deputy Chief Bart whispered into Matt's left ear.

In four seconds, they were all in the house, veering left and clearing the kitchen.

Sgt. Barton and Sgt. Garza were right behind them when they entered the home, but they immediately went to the right toward the bathroom and bedroom area of the home.

Deputy Chief Bart yelled, "Clear," as he and Matt found no one in the kitchen.

Sgt. Barton yelled "Clear," as he and Sgt. Garza found no one in the bedroom or bathroom of the residence.

All four Greenfield officers continued walking toward the living room area, coming from different directions.

As they entered the living room, still with their weapons raised, they stopped and lowered their guns due to what they were witnessing.

CHAPTER 35

"So, tell us about your connection to Tyler Hale," Detective Bill Golden asked calmly.

"Limited at best," Matt replied.

Neither Detective Golden nor his partner, Detective Jeff Lyons said a word.

Both Detectives sat there, hands resting in their laps, waiting for Matt to say something.

"An occasional cup of coffee, Pike Place Venti, at the Starbucks over at the Student Union before class at the Illinois Law Enforcement Training Center, was the extent of it," Matt responded in a relaxed tone.

"Man, what a difference a few days can make in a person's life," he thought.

It was exactly 12 days—almost to the minute, he killed Tyler Hale in the backyard of 524 Short Street.

As was customary, wherever Chief Fitzsimons was in charge, if one of his officers was involved in a shooting, the Illinois State Police Public Integrity Task Force was brought in to handle the investigation.

This was the case with the Tyler Hale shooting.

Matt had been cleared by this Task Force yesterday of any wrongdoing and the shooting was classified as a "Clean Shoot." But the NORTAF Investigation involving Matt hadn't been closed yet due to a few loose ends still needing to be tied up.

Located between Chief Fitzsimons and Deputy Chief Gyondski's offices was a conference room used mainly for Command Staff meetings or a meeting of great significance. Today's meeting definitely met this criterion.

Matt sat directly across the table from Detective Golden, who shocked Matt by wearing a suit, tie, and even shaved.

On Matt's left sat Deputy Chief Bart, who consequently was seated directly across from Detective Lyons.

On Matt's right sat Chief Fitzsimons, who was sitting across the table from a man Matt was seeing for the first time.

Dressed in a navy-blue suit with the traditional red and blue striped tie, this individual looked more like a bank president as opposed to a cop, due to his frail appearance.

Also, gathered around the table, in different chairs were Lt. Alderman and Deputy Chief Gyondski.

It was the guy across the table from Chief Fitzsimons who gave Matt the creeps for right now.

Matt was the last one to make it to this meeting. Because he already knew everyone in the room except for "Mr. Blue Suit," there hadn't been any introductions.

But Mr. Blue Suit kept staring at Matt, giving him weird vibes.

Each person at the table had a bottle of water, cup of coffee, or can of soda, as well as a stack of files, in front of them.

"So, give us your thoughts on these pictures," Detective Golden said, pointing at two stacks of 8 by 12 black and white pictures.

Sitting on the table, directly in front of Matt, is what Deputy Chief Bart, Sgts. Garza and Barton and he encountered when they entered the living room, from different directions, at 524 Short Street.

From wall to ceiling, there were pictures of every member of Matt's class at ILETC, who had graduated as members of the Greenfield Police Department.

Some of the pictures were group shots, such as the night they spent at P.J.'s Sports Bar, only 36 hours before graduation. Other pictures were of the entire class when they would gather before their daily run.

A few of the pictures were headshots of individual members of the Greenfield Cadets.

The headshots of Chris Mills, Ron Thomas and Javier Ortego were different than the others due to one significant feature.

A huge red "X" had been put through their faces, which put a chill through every person seated at the table.

"Fucking Tyler Hale," Matt said softly, believing no one else had heard him.

Apparently, he was wrong as Deputy Chief Bart leaned over in his chair and said directly into Matt's left ear, "Keep it together, O'Neil."

"So just who the hell was Tyler Hale?" Chief Fitzsimons asked, totally exasperated as he raised both of his arms into the air

"Just a total drifter in every sense of the word," Detective Lyons answered quickly.

"Explain?" Chief Fitzsimons responded and then leaned forward in his seat, closing his hands together and placing them on the table in front of him.

"The Internal Revenue System, through tracking Hale's pay stubs with his Social Security Number, has been able to put him at odd jobs in states such as Wisconsin, Indiana, Ohio and even Michigan within the past three and a half years," Detective Lyons said.

"As you pointed out Matt, he was a barista at the Starbucks and a desk clerk at the Days Inn located over on West Street in downtown Champaign during the day," Detective Golden answered with his matter-of-fact voice.

"What about at night?" Chief Fitzsimons asked.

Pausing for a minute before answering, Detective Golden replied, "Bartender at P.J.'s Sports Bar."

"What the fuck," Deputy Chief Gyondski blurted out, which brought him stares from everyone gathered around the table.

"What do you have on him besides that and give me his motive for all of this?" Chief Fitzsimons asked with a harsh tone in his voice.

Matt was a bit surprised as both Detective Golden and Lyons suddenly turned and looked at each other.

It was apparent to everyone seated at the table, neither detective appeared very anxious to answer Chief Fitzsimons' question.

Finally, Detective Golden took the initiative.

Turning his body in his chair and looking across the table at

Chief Fitzsimons, he said calmly, "We have hardly anything on him at all Chief."

The news must have made an impact on Chief Fitzsimons, who suddenly sat back in his chair, leaning to his right side and raising both the index and middle fingers on his right hand to his face. Opening a manila file seated in front of him, Detective Lyons looked down at a typed report inside of it and began skimming the report before speaking.

"We went back as far as we could, to him graduating from Stoughton High School."

"Where?" Deputy Chief Bart blurted out.

"Stoughton, Wisconsin, located roughly 19 to 20 miles east of Madison," Detective Lyons answered calmly and professionally.

"No priors?" Chief Fitzsimons asked suddenly seated back where he was only a few minutes before, straight up in his chair with his hands locked together and resting on the table.

Without having to even look at the report in front of him, Detective Lyons answered, "not even a parking ticket."

Chief Fitzsimons wasn't satisfied as he turned to his right and looked directly at Lt. Alderman, who nodded his head up and down in apparent agreement with Detective Lyons.

While Matt was paying attention to the conversation around him, he couldn't take his focus off "Mr. Blue Suit" who also continued staring directly back at Matt.

"Speaking of parking tickets, explain the whole Bronco situation to me," Chief Fitzsimons ordered, totally exasperated with the way things were developing.

"The owner of the Ford Bronco is LTJG Ben Zimmerman," Detective Lyons answered quickly.

"U.S. Navy?" Matt asked. Since the Bronco was being discussed as well as the military, his interest was stoked.

"A Lieutenant Harmon of N.C.I.S worked with us to verify Officer Mills was a Navy Seal, which seemed to open a ton of doors," Detective Lyons said.

"Continue," Chief Fitzsimons said as his interest also seemed peaked since he was hearing things for the first time, he could wrap his brain around.

"Lieutenant Harmon was able to produce the flight manifesto signed by LTJG Zimmerman when he took a C5 Galaxy out to Hawaii to catch up with his fleet, which has been stationed in the South China Sea for the past 6 months," Detective Lyons said and everyone seated at the table could see his confidence growing.

Surprisingly, no one seated at the table said a word as they apparently were trying to figure out what to ask next to get to the bottom of this Bronco mystery. Chief Fitzsimons was suddenly a step-in front of the group.

"The Bronco was parked somewhere at the Great Lakes Naval Academy when Hale stole it months ago," Chief Fitzsimons blurted out.

"CORRECT," Detective Golden yelled out for some reason.

"Proof?" Chief Fitzsimons asked.

"We have a picture of the Ford Bronco going through the Willow Road Toll booth apparently on its way to Greenfield this past spring," Detective Lyons answered.

Then to emphasize his point, he held the picture up with his right hand up high enough for everyone in the room to see.

"Let me guess, Ben Zimmerman crashes at 524 Short Street for some extra rest or......?" Deputy Chief Bart said.

"Apparently, since his parents, Ira and Ethel Zimmerman are the owners of the residence and they're snowbirds," Lt. Alderman said calmly.

Sensing a couple of people at the table were puzzled by his statement, Lt. Alderman tried to clarify. "For the past five months the Zimmerman's have been in Miami, Florida, where they own a condo," Lt. Alderman said in an effort to clear up the confusion over the term, 'snowbird.'

No one said anything as they waited for him to give them more information.

"I checked with our building department and they informed me the Zimmerman's have a house in Glencoe as well when they're not in Florida," Lt. Alderman finished.

"They've been trying to sell the house at 524 Short Street on their own by placing ads on owners.com, which is how our building department got wind of it," Lt. Alderman continued.

"Explain sir," Matt said this time as he had shifted his focus from "Mr. Blue Suit" to Lt. Alderman.

"Apparently, the building department uses an intern or the newest person they hire and one of their jobs is to monitor these types of transactions, for whatever reason Don Schblansky didn't seem too interested in telling me why."

"How did he..." Deputy Chief Gyondski started to ask before he was cut off by Lt. Alderman.

"Hale removed the For Sale sign and apparently Ben Zimmerman left a small Eddie Bauer Leather Shooters Bag with the keys to the residence inside of it, since both of these items were found in the trunk of the Ford Bronco," Lt. Alderman countered.

"Is the Glock 22 Gen 4 in Hale's possession at the time of his death, the same weapon our personnel are currently using?" Deputy Chief Gyondski asked.

"Merely a coincidence," Detective Lyons answered this time before finishing with, "purchased over six months ago at Gat Guns, 970 Dundee Avenue, East Dundee, Illinois."

Not to be out done, Detective Golden jumped in, "Yeah, ATF Agent Terry Shields offered his and his office's assistance but we didn't need it since the owner of Gat Guns, Greg Tropino, bent over backwards to help us in every way possible. They showed us the sales receipt and copy of Hale's FOID Card when he made the purchase, so obviously they did nothing wrong"

"Speaking of the Bronco, are we sure it was involved in Officer Mills' death?" Matt asked with doubt in his voice.

Slowly and carefully, Detective Golden pushed a manila file folder across the table using his right hand.

Matt could feel the pressure of everyone at the table staring at him.

It suddenly dawned on him he was probably the only person in the room who hadn't read this report.

As Matt started reading the report from the Northern Illinois Crime Laboratory, Detective Golden tried to speed things up by interjecting, "Hale never took the Bronco to get the right fender repaired and Officer Mills' DNA was recovered from this area of the vehicle."

Chief Fitzsimons realized this was probably the best time if ever to get other sensitive information out and looking at Matt, said "We also have conclusive evidence linking Hale to the death of Officer Ortego."

"Sir?" Matt said as he stopped reading the report to look at Chief Fitzsimons.

"Hale's fingerprints were found on the suicide note, as well as two other vital locations inside his townhouse," Chief Fitzsimons said.

As Matt pondered his next question, Deputy Chief Bart attempted to close the door on the Ortego case by saying, "We also found a duplicate key to Javier's townhouse in the glove box of the Ford Bronco."

"So, the case is no longer being classified as an open Death Investigation," Matt asked as his head started to throb.

"Correct," Lt. Alderman said and figuring he had the most information of anyone else in the room, he decided to keep the information coming on recent Greenfield Police Officers who had died in the past five months. "I spoke with Detective Kenbridge earlier today, and the Thomas investigation is still on going."

Lt. Alderman saw everyone staring at him and quickly said, "I know what you're all thinking and he confirmed for me, Hale's fingerprints weren't found on any piece of evidence they are currently holding."

Suddenly Marge Thomas's face appeared in front of Matt, saying repeatedly, "Find Ron's killer, Officer O'Neil. Find Ron's killer, Officer O'Neil."

Matt sat straight up in his Camaro so quickly he almost struck his head on the roof of the car.

Granted it was August and all his car windows were down, but he was totally covered in sweat with his shirt being soaked all of the way through.

Slowly, he got out of his car and did a simple set of stretching exercises to loosen his muscles.

Matt finished by doing the best exercise of all, roughly 7 or 8 deep squats, with his hands firmly behind his head. When finished, he took off his wet t-shirt and threw it on the floor, directly behind the driver's seat.

He put on a light green Polo shirt with the traditional orange Polo player emblem on the left side of the shirt.

Getting behind the wheel of his Camaro, he turned the key in the ignition and listened to the 8-cylinder beast roar as he hit the gas, with the vehicle still parked.

Shifting the vehicle into drive, Matt drove slowly through the parking garage, which was now filled with cars.

As Matt left the parking garage and pulled into the parking lot of the VFW, he made a mental note to personally thank Officer Tim Ferguson, of the Rockford Police Department, for setting up this party.

Sometime tonight he would find out what Ferguson was drinking and grab him one or two of those beverages, in recognition for setting up PTA CLASS 15-213's first class reunion.

What a job it must have been for him to try and contact the remaining 22 members of Matt's class, in organizing this event.

Matt was fortunate to find a parking spot near the front entrance to the VFW.

Getting out of his car, he watched his shadow from the bright sunlight, as he made his way toward the entrance. Upon opening the front door, he walked through another set of doors and went down a long, dimly lit hallway.

He didn't need any signs to tell him where to go, because the sounds of yelling and laughter came from a large room, which was immediately to his left.

Before getting to this room, he paused for a minute to collect his thoughts.

Matt wanted so desperately to be attending this with Chris, Ron, Javier and, of course, T.C. Chambers. Matt wasn't sure how he would be able to handle the comments and questions about their deaths.

Matt actually prayed Kurt Thompson wasn't here today. Even though he helped save Megan's life, he had little use for him and believed he was somehow involved in Ron's death.

Time was up and he decided it was time to go in before someone came out of the room and found him standing in the hallway, looking stupid.

Matt took two steps and turned left, entering the biggest ballroom of any VFW he had ever been in. The laughter and yelling, which had come from this room only seconds ago, suddenly came to an abrupt stop.

Instead, a steady stream of applause filled the room, led by Mark Dugan, who walked over to Matt giving him the hardest bear hug.

For some reason, Matt had never appreciated a bear hug like this one and he savored every second of it as the applause started to die down.

When the applause stopped, Matt and Mark Dugan separated themselves from each other and the words, "speech, speech" filled the entire hall.

Matt looked on and his fellow classmates had formed a gauntlet, which required him to walk through. Slowly he did, first turning to his right and then to his left, shaking the hand of every person.

Matt was stunned when he turned to his left and the hand, he shook was Detective Robert Kenbridge of the Door County Sheriff's Police.

"Nice job kid," Kenbridge said with a matter-of-fact tone in his voice.

Matt didn't know what to say since these past five minutes had been so overpowering.

As he let go of Detective Kenbridge's hand, he turned so he had a clear view of a number of booths directly in front of him.

Kurt Thompson was seated and holding the hand of a heavily bandaged, but giggling Megan O'Brien, who was seated across from him. What had been one of the greatest moments of Matt's life had suddenly turned into a pile of shit.

CHAPTER 36

K urt Thompson couldn't stop smiling as he held Megan's hand. His love for her had only intensified somehow, while serving his suspension from the Gilles Police Department.

To think he would have a chance of reconnecting with her, in such a way, was unfathomable only weeks ago.

Before the suspension, Kurt would have his Norcom portable radio turned to the Greenfield police frequency on Channel 3 and keep the radio in his Dodge Challenger tuned to the Gilles frequency.

He did this with the hopes that somehow or some way their paths would cross on a call in Greenfield's Beat 3-0, which was located near the far northern part of Gilles.

To be able to see that sexy ass, in her Blauer navy blue pants would be enough for him, for right now.

He got to see more than just her sexy ass, due to Tyler Hale at 524 Short St.

When Megan started yelling for assistance, Kurt Thompson had just left the drive through window of the Popeye's, in Morton Grove.

Fortunately, he had the green turn arrow and within seconds was on Goggle maps, typing in the address of 524 Short St. Greenfield, Illinois.

"Shiiiit" he said to himself, as a black and white picture of the house he was headed to came on his MDT.

It suddenly dawned on him, two nights ago he'd played in a coed softball game at Lakeview Park, in Greenfield.

Lakeview Park was located only three blocks west of 524 Short Street, so he knew exactly where he was headed.

Kurt had never heard Megan scream the way she had on the radio a minute ago, which meant she was in deep shit.

With his mars light flashing and siren screaming, he headed down Waukegan Road, trying to look closer at the picture of 524 Short Street, while cutting in and out of traffic.

It was either the second or third time he glanced at the picture, when he saw it.

Some type of vehicle, tucked away at the far west side of the property.

"Holy fuck the Bronco?" He found himself saying out loud.

He looked up from his MDT, just in time to avoid rear ending a Dodge Caravan, full of kids.

The driver did what most people tend to do when a police car is behind them, with all of its emergency equipment activated, stop in the middle of the road.

As Kurt swerved around the Dodge Caravan, he looked up from the seat of his squad car, to see the driver, and elderly woman, who looked like she had no clue as to what she was doing.

He didn't care and flipped her off, using the middle finger on his left hand, as he continued going balls to the wall down Waukegan Rd.

Kurt knew coming down the street of 524 Short St. would give a huge advantage to the assailants, so he picked the safest option available to him, coming in the rear of the property, which would mean crossing the railroad tracks.

He looked at his watch as he pulled up and remarkably from the second Megan had yelled for help, to the time he arrived, was exactly four minutes.

"Gilles 712 is out at 524 Short St. Greenfield," he yelled into the Norcom radio of his squad car.

An understandably confused Debbie Steille, who was handling the dispatching for the Gilles Police Department, answered "10-9 Gilles 712?"

Kurt never answered her, as he grabbed his blue trauma bag by its belt, from its position of hanging over the headrest, of the passenger seat of his squad car.

Running through a backyard, he faced his first obstacle, a five-foot high metal cyclone fence.

All of the cardio work he did on his suspension paid off and he was over it cleanly.

He carefully climbed the embankment of the Metra Railroad tracks, trying to avoid slipping on the assortment of rocks.

While doing so he decided to pull his Glock, Model G43 from its holster to be prepared for the unexpected.

Bad move on his part and by doing so it caused him a new problem.

Just as he reached the top of the embankment, he looked to see where exactly he was in relation to the backyard of 524 Short St and took a step forward to improve his view.

This caused him to trip over the first Metra train rail he encountered and he fell forward into an almost downward dog yoga position.

In an effort to catch himself, he opened the palm of both of his hands and was pretty successful in preventing injury.

He wasn't as successful in regards to his Glock, as it went flying out of his hand, hit a large rock and unexpectedly fell back down the embankment he had just climbed, bouncing off the rocks in the process.

"FUCCCCK ME," Kurt yelled out loud, as he and every cop who had ever lost their weapon in a situation such as this realizes.

"I'm headed to a shootout without my freaking gun,"

Kurt was up and after his gun, fearful of what could happen to him, if he didn't get it in the next minute or two.

In record time he was back down the embankment looking for his Glock.

Thankfully he found it, lying next to a fresh pile of dog shit.

Apparently, a few Greenfield residents had been using this area as their own dog kennel and with good reason.

Secluded by the train tracks and with only a few homes to worry about, it was the perfect location for letting your dog run free and not have to pick up after.

"Whewwww," Kurt realized how lucky he was as he bent down and grabbed his Glock.

As if someone had put a lit M80 in his ass Kurt flew back up the train embankment with this Glock secured in his right hand.

When Kurt again reached the top of the embankment, he was shocked at what he was witnessing.

Like something out of an old John Wayne movie, Matt O'Neil and the person behind the passenger door of the Bronco were shooting at each other.

As trained at ILETC, Kurt immediately looked for cover and found it just east of his location, in the form of an old elm tree. For a full minute he stood behind this tree while still holding his Glock Model 43 in his right hand.

Finally, with calmness in the air he peeked around the left corner of the tree and was stunned at what he was seeing.

Asshole Matt O'Neil was advancing on the passenger's side door to the Ford Bronco and someone was lying, motionless behind it.

On the driver's side door of the same vehicle, withering in pain, was Megan O'Brien.

Slowly he came down the other side of the train embankment, with his gun raised to a firing position.

Good thing Matt O'Neil was so preoccupied with the dude lying on the ground behind the Bronco's door, because when Kurt first raised his weapon and released the safety, it was pointed in the direction of Matt's head.

Kurt could see when he got close enough to the body the guy was dead with a sizeable hole in his forehead.

Even with the slightly disfigured face of this dead individual, Kurt Thompson knew who it was the minute he saw him. "Tyler fucking Hale," he yelled out immediately.

As he had been trained and even with Megan on the ground dying, his personal safety, as well as Matt's was the most important thing right now.

Consequently, he checked the backseat of the Bronco for any potential threat and fortunately found none.

"Clear O'Neil," Kurt Thompson yelled.

"Got it," Matt replied.

Only then did Kurt have a chance to focus directly on Megan and what he saw wasn't pretty.

She was seated on the ground, against one of the poles for the canopy of the carport.

Megan was leaning to her left and using her right hand to try and stop the bleeding which was coming somewhere from the upper shoulder area of her left arm.

Her specially made Armor Corr, Ladies Ranger bulletproof vest was half way off, as if a struggle between her and the assailant was the result of it.

"Kurt?" Megan said with the softest voice he had ever heard coming from her lips, as he approached her.

Upon reaching her, Kurt dropped to his knees, so he was positioned directly in front of her.

He realized if he didn't do something quickly, she would die of blood loss from her wound and appeared to be going into shock.

As gently as he could, he completely removed her bullet proof vest, gun belt, as well as her Greenfield uniform shirt.

"Jesus fucking Christ," Megan yelled out, as she began kicking her legs, while writhing in pain.

Kurt didn't need a medical degree to figure out what specifically was causing her so much pain.

A sizeable hole was noticeable and bleeding just above her collarbone in her left shoulder area.

Quickly he opened up his blue colored trauma bag and digging to the bottom of it, found what he needed the most.

He pulled out the Nitro Pak and ripped open the outer package.

Faced with a vacuum sealed second package he mumbled "what the fuck," as to not in any means damage its contents.

Upon being opened he removed the 70-inch elastic bandage.

Carefully he applied the gauze side directly over the bullet hole.

He was pleased the bullet had gone through her shoulder and didn't hit any bone in the process.

He then wrapped the Nitro Bandage as tight as he could through her armpit area and then directly over the wound.

"Fuckkkkkkkkk Kurt," she yelled with her last bit of strength as he used every inch of the bandage to make the tightest tourniquet he could.

Satisfied he'd done all that he could, he stood up and turned to his left, when he saw them headed his way.

"They're here Megan," he yelled excitedly before looking down at her.

Unfortunately, the combination of pain, as well as loss of blood must have been too much for her, as she was no longer seated, but now laying face first in the grass.

Kurt motioned continuously with his left hand at the Greenfield Fire Department personnel trying to get them to speed up their response in getting to them.

Granted, he would have preferred Vinny Cedeno and the crew out of Fire Station 2 on Dempster Street, but would have to make do with these guys.

Kurt stepped aside as the Greenfield crew got about 10 feet from him.

He did so because he wanted them to have immediate access to Megan and save her life, but also due to the fact two them could have played offensive tackle for the Bears; they were so big.

As Kurt looked on, he was impressed at how good these guys were.

In record time they had put a new bandage over his Nitro one, had Megan on a gurney and had put some type of tiny oxygen tubes in her nose.

The two paramedics who could have played for the Bears were on opposite ends of the gurney and remarkably, instead of rolling it, each had picked up their respective ends and were carrying it through the backyard of 524 Short St. Kurt was with them, headed for the front yard of the residence.

Kurt found his role in all of this now reduced to hand holding and offering encouragement to Megan.

Only once they reached the Greenfield Ambulance and were lifting her into the back of it, did Kurt feel a hand on his left shoulder.

Quickly he turned around to find Battalion Chief Jim Gancher, of the Greenfield Fire Department, standing directly in front of him and staring him in the face.

"Confirming you're not family, correct?" Gancher asked, but with a tone in his voice which made it seem like more of a command than a question.

"Yeah, I'm only a former boyfriend at this stage," Kurt said for some reason, with a rather shy tone in his voice, before turning to try and look into the rear windows, on the back doors of the ambulance.

"Thought so but wasn't quite sure," Gancher mumbled and upon finishing used the palm of his left hand to slam twice on one of the rear doors of the ambulance.

In a flash the ambulance carrying Megan headed down Short Street, with its lights and siren in full form.

Kurt just stood there flabbergasted and thought for a second of actually running after the ambulance and jumping on the rear panel of it.

"FUCKERRRRRRRR," Kurt yelled at Gancher and then turned and started running towards the back yard of 524 Short Street.

He had never run this fast in his entire life, while wearing combat boots.

As he entered the backyard, he noticed a number of cops down on one knee with their weapons pointed towards the back of the house.

He didn't have time to stop and help and quite frankly didn't really care.

Kurt only cared about getting to the hospital Megan was being transported to.

"FUCK ME, FUCK ME, FUCK ME!" he yelled at himself and it suddenly occurred to him, he had no clue as to which hospital they were taking Megan to.

Glenbrook, Evanston, LFCH, were all possibilities and each offered advantages as to why they should be the chosen one to save Megan's life.

Kurt got to the top of the Metra tracks and could barely see his squad car and some type of individual by it.

Carefully he came down the other side of the Metra tracks vowing not to fall down this time and with his blue colored health kit swinging in every direction, in his left hand.

Clearing the metal cyclone fence and coming out of that home's backyard enabled him to clearly see the individual by his squad car.

Kurt never stopped running until he'd reached the driver's side door of his squad car, which for some odd reason was running, but with no key in the ignition.

The individual he'd seen from the top of the Metra tracks was standing adjacent to the driver's door of Kurt's squad car, with his arms folded across his chest.

Strangely, Kurt couldn't catch his breath and bent over in an effort to help him with this.

While still being bent over, Kurt suddenly felt an arm draped over his sweaty neck.

This individual then bent down as well so his head was next to Kurt's left ear.

With hardly any emotion in his voice, the individual said "They took her to Glenbrook Hospital,"

Turning his head to the left, Kurt found himself face to face with Commander Al Billings.

Neither one of them spoke as the perspiration was falling off Kurt's face and on to his mud-covered boots.

Finally, Commander Billings broke the awkward silence by saying "What are you waiting for son?"

"Thank you, sir," Kurt said before standing up.

In less than 30 seconds he was behind the wheel of his squad car and headed towards Glenbrook Hospital.

The minute he turned the corner and was going northbound on Harlem Avenue and more importantly out of the sight of Commander Billings, his right hand found its way to his Unittrol Control Panel.

Turning the light switch to the fourth position, turned on all of his overhead Mars lights

Quickly he turned left on to Central Rd. and headed west roughly only 7 to 9 minutes away from Glenbrook Hospital.

"Kurt can you get me another Pinot Grigio," Megan O Brien said louldly in the crowded VFW Hall, which was filled with their classmates from ILETC, but also some local veterans who had stopped in for a drink on a beautiful summer night.

Using her right hand, she gently pushed her wine glass across the table until it was sitting directly in front of Kurt's bottle of Miller Lite.

"Sure, Megan not a problem," he said as he picked up her wine glass with his empty right hand and grabbed his empty beer bottle with his left hand.

Slowly he began to smile broadly, as he was looking at the face of a woman who in the past 20 days had brought happiness and love back into his life.

After being released from Glenbrook Hospital, a week after the shooting, Megan shocked Kurt by agreeing to move into his Mt. Prospect townhouse, to recover from her injuries.

Kurt found nursing qualities he didn't even know he possessed.

It helped Megan was on so many pain pills and in such dire need of help; she was actually a pretty good patient.

For the first five days all she did was sleep, barely eat and take her pills.

Kurt was proud of himself for being on his best behavior and acting like a total gentleman.

From the day he brought her home from the hospital to his place, he tried nothing remotely sexual and been sleeping on his fold out sofa bed in the family room.

Every night, when he was sure Megan had fallen asleep, he would slowly open her bedroom door and just stand there with Max, his German Shepard puppy, watching her for about five minutes.

He loved having her back in his life, even in this physical condition, with the left side of her body wrapped in bandages.

It was almost surreal how on the 9th day, Megan had made remarkable progress it seemed to Kurt in both the movement with her left shoulder area and in her overall disposition.

For on this day Kurt brought Megan the same breakfast she had eaten the previous five days of Rice Chex, a glass of tomato juice and a cup of black coffee. Only this time he found Megan instead of still asleep sitting up in bed, with an actual smile on her face.

Kurt was shocked to see Megan had removed the sling for her left arm and a couple of bandages also appeared to have been taken off.

As he gently placed the tray holding her assortment of food and drink across Megan's lap, Kurt felt a soft, gentle kiss on his left cheek, which momentarily stunned him.

He moved his head so his face and hers were only inches apart and looked her directly in the eyes to see if he was imagining this, or getting the go sign from her instead.

The fact she tried to move the tray with her one good arm was the only sign Kurt needed and the tray was off the bed and resting comfortably on the floor, in a matter of seconds.

Kurt didn't know what to expect from a badly injured Megan, but was amazed at what she could still do sexually.

He'd never made love before to such a physically injured woman, so he was extremely slow and careful and allowed her to take the lead, in showing him exactly what she wanted.

Roughly 25 minutes later, they laid barely touching, but both with smirks on their faces for what they had been able to do in this bed.

Kurt was all set to say something sexy but it would be a waste of time right now, as the gentle snoring of Megan filled the room.

Kurt didn't realize how late it was as he found a number of their fellow ILETC classmates had already gone home, without stopping to say goodbye to Megan and him.

But not Matt, who was still sitting at the bar, drinking nothing at the moment, but deeply involved in a conversation with the bartender.

Kurt didn't know who the bartender was, but the way Matt was hanging on every word he was being told by the bartender, was more than a bit intriguing,

It got even stranger to Kurt, when he got closer to both Matt and the bartender and they both stopped talking, and turned their heads, as if they both were giving him the stink eye.

Something was going on between these two and Kurt was fearful he was the focus of their conversation.

If only he knew how correct he was in his assumption.

CHAPTER 37

Robert Kenbridge saw Kurt Thompson approaching the bar and because he'd served him only a half hour ago, he knew what he would be asking for.

By the time he reached him, a new round was waiting for Kurt, preventing any wasted time, as well as a possible conversation among the three of them.

As Kurt slowly walked back to his booth, Kenbridge leaned closer to Matt and whispered, "Something is definitely off with that guy."

"Agree," is all Matt could whisper back, as his right foot kept shaking on his bar stool.

Matt waited until Kurt was seated across from Megan before he exploded like a teakettle, whose steam had built up to the point, of the lid coming off.

Leaning across the bar, Matt's face was only inches way from Kenbridge's face.

As sternly as he could manage, Matt said, "With all due respect, what the hell do you mean the Thomas case has been designated as inactive?"

Not to be intimidated by some kid from Illinois, Kenbridge's face didn't budge as he answered and Matt listened intently, "For right now son, we don't have dick to go on with regards to any fresh evidence or possible leads. No more canvases to be done. We haven't had any new security video to watch for over two months."

Sensing he had slowed Matt's onslaught and wanting to keep his momentum going, Kenbridge continued, "Granted we're not Chicago—what did they have by the end of July? 345 Homicides? I saw that somewhere, anyway, we actually have crime in Door County and a pretty good case load for me to work on," Kenbridge finished.

"What about all of those latents you were finding on the canoe and Thomas's vehicle?" Matt asked.

"Nothing to compare them to," Kenbridge answered "Most of them my crime techs told me were partials anyway. Even using the FBI's AFIS database didn't get us anywhere."

Knowing Matt would be throwing it at him, Kenbridge beat him to the punch by saying, "We ran Tyler Hale's prints and don't have them on anything at Peninsula State Park or on items belonging to Thomas."

Matt wasn't finished as he countered with, "Have you figured out where the Coors Light was purchased the day of the drowning?"

"No sales receipt for the liquor was found at the crime scene or inside his vehicle," Kenbridge answered.

"Soooo," Matt said realizing the combination of liquor, along with frustration over the answers he was getting from Kenbridge, were starting to ramp up his anxiety level even more.

"What do you mean so?" replied Kenbridge. Now, his voice had an edge and sharper tone to it.

Before Matt could get another word out, Kenbridge came back at him. "Do you have any freaking idea just how many places sell liquor in Door County?"

Matt had no idea and finally realized this was going nowhere fast. He casually asked, "What did the search warrant of Thomas's cabin turn up?"

"Great question. We didn't need one due to your new best friend giving us consent to search," Kenbridge answered.

The edge in his voice was gone and a small smile suddenly appeared on his face.

"Marge Thomas?" Matt asked and was surprised how meek he answered Kenbridge.

"Of course," Kenbridge said. "She's a big fan of yours my friend."

Finally having something to work with, Matt thought and actually sat up a bit taller on his bar stool with some new enthusiasm.

"So, what did you find?" Matt asked eagerly.

"Nothing out of the ordinary," Kenbridge said rather dryly.

"Meaning the killer had all the time they wanted to get to the cabin on Washington Island, get inside and take whatever they wanted?" Matt asked with the stern look back on his face.

"I think you've been watching a little too much Criminal Minds Matt," Kenbridge answered and leaving the bar area, headed toward the men's bathroom, of the VFW Hall.

"Fine," Matt said softly to himself as he downed the last of a partially filled glass of Jameson whiskey, one of his classmates had bought him.

Another full whiskey and a bottle of Stella sat on the bar in front of him.

Matt turned his bar stool to the left.

He figured he would do the right thing and see how Megan was convalescing under the watchful care of her nurse, Kurt Thompson. Looking directly at the booth they had been sitting in only a few minutes ago, he was shocked to see it empty and only a couple of beer bottles, with a single wine glass sitting on the table.

"Figures," he thought, knowing Kurt Thompson had no use for him and Matt hadn't reached out to Megan to see how she was doing since the day she had been shot.

Matt still couldn't figure what a sweet, innocent, Irish girl, could see in a goon like Kurt with all the other guys out there. But it was her life and as long as she was happy, then more power to her he thought.

Turning his bar stool back so it was again facing the bar, Matt could see Kenbridge slowly walking back toward him while drying his hands on a white towel, draped over his left shoulder.

Matt waited patiently until Kenbridge was standing directly in front of him, before asking him the most powerful question of the night, "So what's your next move?"

"When my case load lightens up, I will go back and start looking at this case page by page," Kenbridge said.

"Need a fresh set of eyes?" Matt asked.

"What are your plans for tomorrow?" Kenbridge answered.

"Supposed to head up your way and get some fishing in with Trooper Dugan, but we could put that on hold if need be," Matt responded, hoping Kenbridge would come back with the answer Matt was looking for.

Matt never heard Trooper Dugan slowly creep up behind him.

From over Matt's left shoulder, a singular key dropped in front of him on the bar.

"What's this?" Matt asked, holding up the key.

The key had a tag on it which stated Waterbury Inn, Ephraim, Wisconsin.

"My gift to you for a job well done," Kenbridge replied.

"I don't understand," Matt said and was totally confused as to what was going on.

"Two law enforcement officers' minds are better than one, so let's do this," Kenbridge said, holding a pamphlet for the Waterbury Inn in his left hand. "You're roughly three hours away from Ephraim, Wisconsin."

"So, stop drinking for the night. When you feel up to it, drive to this place. The key laying on the bar in front of you is your room for the night," Kenbridge finished.

"For the purpose of…?" Matt asked but was pretty confident he already knew the answer to his question.

"I will swing by my office in the morning and pick up the Ron Thomas case files and will be knocking on your Waterbury Inn door between 10 and 10:15 tomorrow morning," Kenbridge said.

Matt stood up so quickly he stunned both Kenbridge and Dugan, who had recently moved to the right side of the bar.

"Thank you," Matt said enthusiastically, as he headed for the same set of doors, he'd entered roughly four hours ago.

Just as he was about to go through those doors, Marge Thomas's face appeared in front of him again and the words: "Aunt Marge, if anything happens to me, then promise me you'll contact Officer Matt O'Neil of the Greenfield Police Department. He will know what to do in regards to finding my killer."

"I'm coming Ron, trust me, Brother, I'm on my way."

CHAPTER 38

Matt hadn't slept like this in months.

In a strange way, Kelly started to have some funky dreams, two months into her pregnancy.

Peculiarly, she would talk out loud during the dreams, as if she was actually participating in the event.

At first, they both laughed about it and found it cute.

They noted the dreams in a memory book Kelly had started, to someday share with their son or daughter, when he or she was older and could read.

Last week, Matt had to admit it was starting to become more than a bit annoying when it kept him up at night. There were even a couple of nights Matt became so frustrated he gently poked Kelly a couple of times, in the middle of the night, because he needed a good night's sleep before going to work.

It helped to be in a bed by himself and be able to stretch out as opposed to getting an accidental knee or elbow in the back.

"Hey, easy on dumping on the wife O'Neil," he thought to himself.

"Shit, he had put Kelly through some unbelievable hell these past months, with hardly a peep of frustration coming from her."

Instead, she had rewarded him with a get-away to re-energize, catch up with classmates and possibly even catch a few fish. Well, the fishing part would have to wait for now.

Matt would be meeting with Detective Kenbridge in a few minutes to try to shed some new light on Ron Thomas's death.

Rubbing his eyes, he sat straight up in bed and looked over at the old Panasonic clock radio, shocked to see it was 9:50 am.

Too late for a quick shower, he figured it wouldn't bother Kenbridge a bit, since he had probably seen it all in his Coast Guard career.

Walking over to the blinds, in his ground floor room, he opened them to a rainy, gloomy day.

Slowly, Matt walked over to the small bathroom to pay it a visit.

He was surprised he hadn't awoken in the middle of the night to pee; with all the liquor he had consumed last night at the VFW.

Matt was confident this wouldn't be the case when he hit his late 50s or early 60s.

Finished in the bathroom, he headed for the kitchen of the condo and decided a pot of coffee would do both him and Detective Kenbridge some good, when they reviewed the countless pictures, diagrams and reports from the crime scene.

Matt was surprised at how anxious he felt about all of this.

Suddenly, the burden of solving a fellow copper's death fell on his shoulders, even though he never even cared for the guy from the first day he met him.

Quickly, he found a small pack of coffee filters in the cabinet directly over where the coffee maker sat. Matt was almost hypnotized as he stood there with both hands on the counter, slowly watching the clear glass coffee pot fill with the darkest, coffee he'd ever seen.

For whatever reason his stomach began to growl.

He grabbed his iPhone and Googled breakfast places in Ephraim, Wisconsin.

"Old Post Office" was the first restaurant that popped up on his phone. "Great service with a fantastic breakfast, as well as a spectacular view of the lake," was the review which immediately caught his eye, as he scanned the other reviews for similar comments.

Matt was so engrossed in the reviews; he didn't hear the knocking on his front door until it had grown into a heavy pounding.

"Finally," Matt said out loud in a half joking tone so Detective Kenbridge would hear him.

Matt decided to turn his phone off so he could fully concentrate on what Detective Kenbridge was bringing him.

The kitchen counter was practically next to the front door of the condo, so it took him all of two steps before he was ripping open the front door and sticking his head out, so his face would be only inches from his visitor.

"Mark Dugan?" Matt asked, confused.

The blank look on Dugan's face, combined with dark circles under his eyes said it all.

"He's dead, isn't he?" Matt asked, still needing some confirmation.

"Yes," Dugan answered in a low, monotone voice, with an unchanging expression on his face.

The moment Matt heard the word "Yes," he dropped his coffee cup and it shattered on the multi-colored, linoleum floor of the condo.

Matt didn't care because not only was his coffee cup shattered, but so were his hopes of catching the killer of Officer Ron Thomas.

CHAPTER 39

Slowly, Mark Dugan walked into the condo and stopped after three steps, to unlace and remove his Merrell hiking boots.

Matt remained in the doorway, too stunned to move, after hearing Detective Kenbridge was dead.

Realizing he was dripping water all over the light brown carpeted floor, Mark took off his Eddie Bauer rain slicker and hung it over a kitchen chair.

Finally, Matt closed the door of the condominium and took a few steps so he was now standing only a few feet from the back of Mark.

Matt waited patiently for Mark to collect himself, but wasn't sure how long this would take.

With his coffee cup still lying broken on the floor, Matt walked over to the kitchen cabinet, pulling out two new coffee mugs and filling them to the brim with the last drops of coffee.

Mark walked over to the kitchen counter and picked up one of the coffee cups with both of his slightly trembling hands.

Matt looked at him, who slowly raised the coffee cup, taking a sip.

Even though Mark couldn't answer him with a coffee cup pressed against his lips, Matt asked anyway, "How do you know?"

Barely moving the coffee cup from his lips and not changing the expression on his face, Mark answered slowly, "I've seen the pictures from the accident scene."

"Holy Mother of God," Matt said out loud, before he made the sign of the cross.

Mark still hadn't moved from his original spot at the kitchen counter.

He seemed to be in some kind of daze, as he looked straight ahead, staring at the kitchen wall.

Matt wasn't sure what to do next so he waited patiently, knowing Mark would eventually come around.

Four to five minutes later, Mark finally put his coffee cup on the counter and walked over to the table Matt was now sitting at.

Forcefully, he grabbed a chair and sat down, putting himself directly next to Matt.

Time was up in Matt's mind in regard to getting all of the facts about Detective Kenbridge's death. "If it means harming the psyche of Mark, so be it," Matt thought.

"Where?" Matt asked, without even turning his head to look in Mark's direction.

"On 43, about six miles past Manitowoc," Mark answered rather dryly, with no emotion in his voice.

Matt's brain was working hard to try to process all of this.

The good night's sleep he'd just experienced enabled him to vaguely recall seeing a sign for Manitowoc last night, as he drove through the town, on his way to the Waterbury Inn.

"He hit the biggest fucking buck I've ever seen," Mark said this time, with a slight bit of emotion, before standing up and heading over to where the coffee pot was in the kitchen.

Matt was wide awake due to the combination of both caffeine and adrenalin and couldn't wait for him to return, so he yelled, "Maybe the pictures were wrong."

Matt yelled this loud enough for Mark to hear him, but not so loud as to upset the other residents.

"He was pronounced dead by the coroner for that county, who happens to know him better than anybody else," Mark replied.

"Former Coast Guard buddy?" asked.

"No, his twin brother Eric," Mark said in the same tone he had used when entering Matt's condo.

"Holy shit," Matt said before putting his head down between his legs and saying softly to himself, so Mark Dugan couldn't hear him, "You're an asshole, O'Neil."

For Matt realized he didn't care about Detective Robert Kenbridge personally, or even how he died. He only cared about the fact Kenbridge had taken pertinent information to his grave, which Matt needed to solve Ron Thomas's death.

"What the hell has happened to you?" he thought to himself. "With less than two years on this job, have you really turned into an asshole over a case, which in all probability is an accidental drowning?"

He kept his head lowered, contemplating his next move when a loud knock on the front door of the condo startled him for a few seconds.

Matt stood up and was headed for the door, but was beaten to it by Mark, who was closer to it when the knocking started.

Mark opened it quickly, which seemed to catch the person on the other side of the door off guard, momentarily.

Mark and Matt found themselves towering over a woman in her early seventies who was wearing the traditional green and gold sweatshirt of her beloved Packers with a huge letter "G" in yellow, on its front.

With her white hair in an old-fashioned bun and cheater glasses on her face, she could have passed as Mrs. Claus.

Either the way Mark had opened the door, or the fact two large men were towering over her, made the woman move both of her hands over the letter G on her sweatshirt and act like she was having a heart attack.

Consequently, the three of them found themselves just staring at each other and waiting for the other person to speak.

Finally, the woman asked in a very soft tone, "Which one of you gentlemen happens to be a Mr. Matt O'Neil?"

"I am," Matt answered, curious as to why this woman would be asking.

"Apparently, your wife has been frantically calling your cell phone and can't get through," she said. When finished, she raised both of her arms, opening her hands as if to indicate that she didn't understand why Matt couldn't or wouldn't answer his phone.

Matt didn't say a word but instead turned and ran to his bedroom.

Once inside the bedroom he realized he had left it in the kitchen and raced back to that room, finding it on the counter.

Instantly, he hit the button located on top of the phone to turn it on and waited.

Nothing happened and he hit it again.

The reality finally set in after trying to turn it on for the third time, realizing his phone was worthless to him if the battery was dead.

Matt was shocked when Mark walked over to him and handed him his Motorola phone.

Instinctively, he punched in the area code of 847 and stopped, because he didn't know Kelly's cell phone number.

Ever since they had been married and he purchased a new cell phone, Kelly was automatically #1 in his contacts. Now, when he needed to get in touch with her the most, he only remembered 847 --- ----.

Matt looked away from the phone for a minute and stared at Mark, wondering if he had Kelly's telephone number, before realizing Mark wouldn't have a need for it.

Suddenly, all of the numbers appeared in Matt's brain.

Without hesitation, he typed them in and hit the send button. Kelly must have been carrying her cell phone around with her because it only rang twice before she answered with a puzzled, "Mark?"

Matt was stunned for the second time in the past five minutes and yelled into the phone, "NO IT'S MATT."

Before Kelly could say anything back, he asked, "Honey is the baby okay?" before looking straight up at the ceiling of the room, afraid of what Kelly's answer would be.

Kelly said nothing, which only made him tighten his grip on Mark's phone.

After only 15 to 20 seconds, Kelly came back on the line and said calmly, "The baby and I are fine dear, but I called because I have some terrible news."

"What?" was all Matt could say, as he was still dwelling on the fact the baby was safe.

"You need to come home babe as soon as you can."

"Why?" Matt asked, curious as to what was going on.

"Matt, another Greenfield Officer is dead," Kelly said.

CHAPTER 40

"**O**kay, Cub fans, here we go! It's a typical Cubs-Sox cross-town classic with the bases loaded, top of the 7th inning, Jose Abreu at the plate and Carl Edwards Jr on the hill," Pat Hughes says.

"Here's the 3-2 pitch to Abreu," Hughes' voice rises with excitement. "Strike three called! Abreu angrily drops his bat and is barking at Home Plate Umpire Brian Wysocki."

"Typical Wysocki call," Chief Fitzsimons says, "Had to be outside the strike zone by at least a foot."

Slowly, Fitzsimons gets up off his huge dark brown leather couch, in the family room of his 17th floor, Lake Shore Drive condominium. To wake up a bit and stimulate some blood flow through his large body, he stretches both arms out to each side.

He's watching the game on WGN with the sound turned off and his favorite baseball announcer coming over the stereo system, set up in the same room.

Chief Fitzsimons chuckles a bit as Abreu is now being restrained by his manager, Robin Ventura, while Brian Wysocki walks away from both of them and heads towards the Cubs dugout.

Chief Fitzsimons is amazed by the quality of picture on his Samsung 70-inch Plasma television screen as it hangs directly over his fireplace.

Picking up a note pad and pen, from a large marble coffee table, located directly in front of him, he scribbles, "Call Billy from Abt on Monday and thank him for the sweet deal on this bad boy."

"Time for the seventh inning stretch and guest singer Vince Vaughn," Pat Hughes says.

"Was great in Wedding Crashers and Old School ..." Chief Fitzsimons thinks but can't remember another thing Vaughn was good in.

He ambles toward the Amana refrigerator in the kitchen, for the first of possibly a few cold Smithwicks. He figures with Vaughn singing, *Take Me Out to the Ball Game,* and at least two or three commercials, he's a good three minutes before he needs to get back to his leather couch.

He loves watching Cubs baseball this way, with Pat Hughes calling the game on WSCR radio.

There was something about Pat Hughes which was so special, and the way he and the late Ron Santo would carry on in the booth, was so genuine and sincere.

If truth be told, he's also a big fan of John Rooney, the current voice of the St. Louis Cardinals.

Chief Fitzsimons listened to Rooney when those damn White Sox were winning the World Series, back in 2005, and he was their play-by-play man.

For some reason, he barely got into the whole Harry Caray thing.

Chief Fitzsimons loved the uniqueness of him sitting in the bleachers with a fishing net, while broadcasting Cub games years ago. Plus, Harry Caray with color analyst Jimmy Piersall, was by far the craziest broadcasting duo of all time.

There wasn't a White Sox game they would broadcast where they didn't crack up talking about their former wives and the amount of alimony they were paying.

Chief Fitzpatrick starts laughing thinking about some of those telecasts from the old Comiskey Park.

Man, it feels good to laugh again and he suddenly realizes it's been a long time since he has.

This has been a good week in a number of different ways, but mainly because he hasn't lost a member of his Department. In all of his years as a Police Chief, he never lost four of his people and there was a fifth suffering from a severe gunshot wound to her shoulder.

Was Tyler Hale capable of doing all of this carnage without a viable motive?

Nothing had been turned up yet by Lt. Alderman and his detectives.

As Police Chief, he had requested all the files on this case. He reviewed them independently and had also come up with the same conclusion of the NORTAF Investigators.

Tyler Hale was a Serial Killer, who took his motive with him, to the fiery gates of hell.

It seems strange something could have happened at the ILETC to set Tyler Hale off to the point of him coming to Greenfield and killing three of his police officers before being stopped by Officer Matt O'Neil.

Speaking of which, it will be very interesting to see what the future holds for Officer Matt O'Neil with the Greenfield Police Department.

Talk about a cop's career having some major ups and downs, all in the span of months. Then to become an instant hit with both the local and Chicago media was fascinating to watch. In the past month, he recalled seeing Officer O'Neil being interviewed separately by reporters from Channels 9, 2, 5 and Fox 32 about the heroic shootout with Tyler Hale at 524 Short Street.

This kid had a future with the Greenfield Police Department for as long as he was Chief, and it was sure to be something special.

As Chief Fitzsimons tilts his head back to get the last few drops of Smithwicks, he realizes it truly had been a solid three days of stress-free police work. It was mainly due to him spending those days at McCormick Place and attending the IACP Annual Convention.

The fact he lived no more than 20 minutes from McCormick Place helped immensely, which allowed him to catch up on his sleep, which was something he definitely had been lacking these past few months.

Secondly, he had attended two workshops, which could be beneficial to the members of the Greenfield Police Department.

The workshop yesterday was from Wolf.com on the use of body cameras.

He thought the representative from this company did a nice job explaining the product to the audience. The actual product was reasonably priced as well.

He never thought when he got promoted years ago, someday his personnel would be wearing body cameras, but with the way things were going, it would be as common for all street cops as the gun and handcuffs they currently carry.

The workshop this morning was from the king of bulletproof vests, Point Blank.

He especially liked some of the newer versions for his women officers, which they had on display. He had enough information from both of those workshops to give to Deputy Chief Gyondski when he returned to work on Monday.

As an added bonus, his cell phone hadn't rung these past three days from Sandy Elloy, which meant there wasn't any brush fires for him to have to handle.

Leaving his empty beer bottle on the kitchen counter, he opens beer number two and heads back toward the family room to watch the end of the Cubs game.

It's still too early to start thinking about dinner.

Speaking of which, he will have to call after the game and make a reservation at his favorite steakhouse, Chicago Cut Steakhouse, at 300 N. La Salle Street, for dinner tomorrow night with his son, Russell.

His mouth starts watering just thinking about the possibilities for a delightful dinner and catching up with Russell.

Chief Fitzsimons' professional life is very good right now, and the fact that the Cubs are on fire only helps make life even better. It is hard for him to believe just how good the Cubs are this year as they sit all alone at first place in their division. Tom Ricketts is the real deal, and he has turned into the new Rocky Wirtz in this town.

When Ricketts purchased the team, every Cub fan had doubts about how devoted he would be in making the Cubs into a contender.

Those doubts were erased when Ricketts hired Theo Epstein to be the president of baseball operations, on October 25th, 2011.

Epstein made it clear to Cubs fans it would take some time to get this mess straightened out and granted the first few years under his control, the team was as bad as any Chief Fitzsimons had ever seen.

His Chicago Cubs went through some lean years but, gradually, the team started to get better and a ray of hope shined on Cub nation when Joe Maddon accepted the managerial job.

The days of Bruce Kim, Kelly Lacheman and of course, Lee Elia were over.

The Cubs had finally landed a real manager.

Granted the Mets swept the Cubs in 2015, but it was easy to see they were well on their way to a potential World Series in 2016.

Now, with the arrival of Aroldis Chapman to close games, Chief Fitzsimons was confident he would be watching his Cubbies have the best year ever.

He can't begin to fathom how Cub fans, who had waited 108 years for a World Series, will handle one this year. Pat Hughes is talking about Anthony Rizzo, who is at the plate, but as Chief Fitzsimons enters the family room, he ignores the television and walks over to one of his floor-to-ceiling windows, to look out at Lake Michigan.

The 17th floor view is majestic, as well as unobstructed.

He's in awe of the boaters, roller bladders, joggers, and bicyclists all enjoying a beautiful Thursday in Chicago.

He realizes if catching up on sleep is his number one priority, then exercising is a close second.

He catches a brief reflection of his body off one of the windows and it's not a pleasant site.

He can't remember with all of the shit going on with his Police Department, the last time he broke a sweat exercising.

The stress of everything had caused him to do what other people do under these circumstances—eat and drink more than was needed.

He had tried to combat it by walking up the stairs whenever he got the opportunity at the Police Station.

Unfortunately, the fact there were so many lunch meetings

and functions to attend as the Greenfield Police Chief, didn't help matters at all.

Plus, he's experienced a few chest pains recently, with the stress of Officer Chambers' death, which he hadn't experienced with the other Greenfield Officers murders.

Maybe he will hold off on dinner for a while and grab the Trek mountain bike he stores in the basement cage, next to his department car.

Life could be so cruel in so many different ways, it was hard to fathom. The energetic, hard driving man he was when he took over the Greenfield Police Department had now become an out of shape, old man in a matter of months.

In reality, when Alice died early last year of cancer, things hadn't been the same. Alice had been a great wife for over thirty-two years of marriage and had given him five children, who in turn, had given them three grandchildren. God, he loved being a grandfather.

All his friends who had grandkids were right when they told him how much he would enjoy it.

But he rarely, if ever, saw his children or grandchildren.

If ever a song was a parody of his life, then the old Harry Chapin song, *Cats In The Cradle* was it.

If Russell did make it to dinner tomorrow night, it would be the first time seeing his father in close to three months.

He was confident Russell would find some excuse to cancel at the last minute, and once again he would be eating dinner alone at the bar.

None of his children ever called him, but then again, he never called them either.

The job had definitely taken a toll on his relationship with both Alice and the children when they were growing up. The missed soccer games, homecoming dances and family dinners had added up. It took a special woman to be a cop's wife, and Alice had done a magnificent job in basically raising the children all by herself.

Slowly, Chief Fitzsimons walks over and sits on the couch as Javier Baez steps in to the batter's box.

"Strike one to Baez on a fastball from David Robertson," Pat Hughes says.

The pain Chief Fitzsimons had experienced in his chin earlier suddenly reappears, only this time, its stronger.

"Baez steps out of the batter's box to adjust his batting gloves," Pat Hughes calmly says.

He moves his left hand up to rub his chin while holding the Smithwicks in his right hand.

Suddenly, Chief Fitzsimons starts to experience pain in the entire area of his left chest.

"Baez steps back into the batter's box," Hughes says.

For the first time since he's been home and sitting on the couch, he starts to sweat profusely, even though the thermostat in his condo is set at a very comfortable 69 degrees.

"Here's the pitch from Robertson, and it's inside, high and tight, causing Baez to hit the dirt," Pat Hughes says.

"Purposeful pitch Pat, Robertson isn't happy about something Baez is doing, possibly stepping in and out of the batter's box so often," says color analyst Ron Coomer.

Chief Fitzsimons realizes something is terribly wrong as the pressure in his chest becomes so intense, he's finding it difficult to breathe.

"Baez is back on his feet and in the batter's box and appears to be having words with the White Sox Catcher Dioner Navarro Ron," Pat Hughes says as his voice starts to rise.

Chief Fitzsimons' sweating has increased and both armpits, on his Polo dress shirt are stained.

The Smithwicks slips out of his right hand and rolls off the leather couch onto the beige carpet.

"Navarro just stood up and is raising his catcher's mask fans, and he's really jawing at Baez," Hughes says and the excitement in his voice has risen to the loudest it's been all day.

Chief Fitzsimons is having a heart attack and he starts to realize it.

His lack of any kind of major exercise, reliance on a diet of red meat high in sodium, stress level at an all-time high and a history of high blood pressure, has all led to this impending illness.

Unknown to him, his arteries are 99% blocked, preventing critical blood flow to his heart.

"Baez has just thrown a punch at Navarro's face fans. It's A.J. Pirerzynski against Michael Barrett all over again, and here come players from both benches on to the field," Hughes says.

Chief Fitzsimons hears Hughes yelling, but isn't paying attention to any of it as he fights for his life. Lying on the marble table are his Greenfield Police Department phone and his lifeline to a Chicago Fire Department ambulance.

"It's 2006 all over again and the bullpen players are running toward home plate to join their teammates," Pat Hughes says and the excitement level in his voice is still on the rise.

Chief Fitzsimons fights to get to his feet, in an effort to get to his telephone, but it's a valiant effort which is unfortunately, too late.

Once he gets to his feet, he passes out from a combination of pain and lack of oxygen.

"THIS IS INCREDIBLE AS BOTH BAEZ AND NAVARRO ARE THROWING BLOWS AT EACH OTHER AS IF THEY WERE ALI VS FRAZER," Hughes screams.

DOWN GOES BAEZ WITH A BLOW TO THE RIGHT SIDE OF HIS FACE," Hughes yells.

Down goes Fitzsimons, face first into a corner of the marble coffee table.

"This is unreal as now fights have broken out in different parts of the stands between White Sox and Cub fans, which this reporter has never witnessed before," Hughes says. You can tell he is having a hard time broadcasting all of this by his shortness of breath.

It doesn't matter to Chief Fitzsimons, who lies dead on top of his empty bottle of Smithwicks beer.

Indirectly and in a strange, peculiar way, Tyler Hale can add another name to his list of victims from his Greenfield Police Department rampage.

The question though, will Chief Fitzsimons be the last name on this list?

CHAPTER 41

"**R**eally wasn't much of a funeral service if you ask me," Beth Gyondski says as she steers her Audi A4 down Skokie Boulevard.

"Considering the Irish are known for having big funerals and tons of drinking, I have to agree with you. It was more than a little let down," Frank Gyondski says.

Beth knows her husband has matters of much more importance on his mind, but she's trying to play the good wife and get his mind off those matters as quickly as possible.

"I think the fact it wasn't a police line of duty death played a big role in all of this," says Frank, plus none of his children or for that matter, grandchildren seemed all too disturbed by his death, which also contributed to what we just participated in tonight."

"Did he ever talk about his kids at work?" Beth asks.

"Never," Frank answers. "I don't ever recall seeing a picture of any of them in his office," Frank says as he gazes out the side window, from his front passenger seat.

Slowly, they pull up to the traffic signal at Lake Avenue in Wilmette.

Both of them in completely different worlds, alone with their thoughts.

Frank Gyondski hasn't ridden in his wife's car for the past three months and is impressed with how low the engine is idling at.

"Somebody at the service said he laid in his condo for two days before being found, is that true?" Beth asks.

"No," Frank answers. "Maybe 30 to 32 hours at the most, until his son Russell showed up late for dinner on Friday night and couldn't reach the Chief. I mean, his father."

"Did he have a key or did the Chicago Police Department force the door?" Beth asks.

"Neither, apparently, they had to call the Chicago Fire Department to come over and spread the door—that's what they call forcing the door," Frank answers. "I'm sure when they got in and saw his crushed skull and all the blood, they probably thought they had a homicide or suicide involving a gun."

"Amazing," is all Beth is able to say as the traffic signal shows a green turn arrow for her left-hand turn.

She presses the accelerator and heads westbound on to Lake Avenue, towards home.

"Yeah, you were out grocery shopping when I got a call from the Watch Commander of, I think he said 18th District, some guy named Ryan, giving me a step-by-step play of what they had done when they realized they were dealing with a Chief of Police, as opposed to some lawyer or doctor," Frank says.

Beth doesn't say a word but is ecstatic she's able to get her husband to talk about something, instead of counting the minutes to the phone call.

"You could tell Ryan probably spent his whole life growing up and working in Chicago because he had the whole accent thing down really well," Frank says.

Then, he turns towards Beth with a slight grin on his face.

"A real 'these and those' type guy, you're telling me," Beth says.

Beth turns her head momentarily, taking her eyes off the road to glance at her husband.

"Exactly," Frank responds and his smile broadens. "One of those 'over by their' types."

Beth turns back to watch the road, especially as she's nearing the point where westbound traffic is coming off the Eden's and they are attempting to merge with her.

"Ever been to Donnellan's funeral home before?" Beth asks casually.

"Yeah, one of my records clerks, Hope Bell's father passed away, and he was waked there. They were friendly then and just as friendly tonight," says Frank.

As they pass Loyola Academy High School, Beth asks, "Dairy Queen or Meier's Tavern? Either one would work for me right now."

Frank is back to looking out the window. He doesn't even turn his head when he answers, "Neither, we've got a ton of Haagen-Dazs in the freezer back home, and I just restocked the basement bar with a trip to Binny's the other day, but thanks for the offer, my dear."

"You would think he would ask me a question about my day," Beth thinks. Once again, they drive along in silence.

Suddenly, a whole new topic of conversation pops into her mind and she asks, "So, what's the latest with the new police station plans?"

Frank turns away from looking out the passenger window and offers his left hand to his wife, as he softly says, "I'm on to you Beth Gyondski, and I love you immensely for trying to take my mind off it. But it's going to be all right, whichever way the trustees vote."

Beth grabs his left hand with her right hand.

She holds the leather steering wheel with her left hand, and is fine, due to traffic at this time of night being sparse on Lake Avenue.

Beth knows her husband is lying through his teeth right now and putting up a brave front for her.

"Any idea how the Village President or Village Manager feel about you?" Beth asks.

"Not a clue," Frank answers. "Although both seemed impressed with the plans for the new station. They had sent emails to Fitzsimons about it, which he had forwarded to me."

Frank, looks at his watch before saying, "They should be out of their executive session meeting anytime now so we won't have to wait much longer."

The word longer had just come out of his mouth when his Motorola, Greenfield Police Department phone rings in the cup holder, for his side of the car.

Instinctively, he looks at Beth, who is staring a hole in him.

"Good luck Babe," she says and then turns her attention back to the road.

He looks at the display on the phone and lets out a brief sigh because he doesn't believe the caller has good news for him.

"Hello Trustee Coconato," Frank says casually into his phone.

"Frankie, how you doing this evening?" Coconato asks.

But before Frank can say a word Coconato is back on the phone.

"First off, I want to offer my deepest condolence on the loss of your Police Chief, my friend."

"Thank You," Frank answers shortly and crisply in an effort to get to the point of this phone call.

"Now, having said that I can't be a hypocrite and tell you I was a fan of the big mick in any way, shape, or form," Coconato says with a tone like he was holding a press conference instead of just speaking on the phone.

"Oh God help me," Frank says so softly he doesn't believe it's heard by anyone other than himself.

"Now enough about the dead. Let's get to the reason for my phone call. As you know we met tonight after a rather quick Village Board Meeting in executive session to discuss a temporary replacement for Fitzsimons," Trustee Coconato pauses to catch his breath.

Frank grabs Beth's hand tighter and slowly starts saying a Hail Mary prayer, mostly to himself.

For some unknown reason, Trustee Coconato sets the stage for who was involved in the process of picking the Acting Chief, throwing out in no particular order the name of the Village President, Village Manager and every Village Trustee who attended this meeting and voted.

Frank hears what he's saying but isn't listening.

Like a number of other professionals in blue- or white-collar jobs, he's developed selective hearing and is able to drown out the dribble and noise until the speaker is saying something which directly impacts him.

So far, all of the shit coming out of this pompous asshole's mouth, means nothing to him.

Finally, he hears the words, "so the vote between you and Deputy Chief Bart wasn't even close my friend."

Frank closes his eyes and presses his head back as hard as he can into the headrest of the Audi.

"Deputy Chief Bart, effective immediately, will be the Acting Chief of the Greenfield Police Department and I wish I had better news for you buddy," Trustee Coconato says.

Frank doesn't move his head from the headrest.

While the phone never leaves his left ear, his eyes slowly fill with tears.

He has nothing left to say and a combination of anger and shock comes over him.

After a full minute of silence between the two of them, Trustee Coconato asks "Frankie you still there...?"

"Yes, Trustee Coconato I heard you," Frank says before asking "Can you do me a huge favor?"

"Why of course, anything for you Frankie," Trustee Coconato answers.

"GO FUCK YOURSELVE ASSHOLE," Frank yells into the phone so loud it makes Beth jump in her seat.

Fortunately, the Audi A4 is stopped for a red light at the corner of West Lake and Milwaukee Avenue.

Beth is a brilliant business woman and smart wife.

She knows nothing she can say will ease the pain her husband is going through right now, so she doesn't say a word and puts both hands back on the steering wheel.

"Johnny's Kitchen and Tap is over on the left and I need a drink," Frank says as he wipes the tears from his eyes.

Once the light turns green, Beth hits the accelerator and passes the Dunkin Donuts quickly before making a left turn into the strip mall parking lot for Johnny's Kitchen and Tap.

Being 8:45 pm, on a Thursday night, makes finding a spot somewhat easy, in this huge parking lot.

After she pulls into the nearest parking space she can find, she turns off her car.

With the car keys still in her right hand and her head turned toward her husband, she's confident she finally has something of relevance to say to ease his pain.

"Got any security guard openings at your business, boss lady?" Frank asks with a slight grin on his face.

"Nope," she answers and then follows up with "But I do have a few sick days to use which might require me to stay in bed all day, seeking some form of comfort from my husband."

Beth leans over and gently kisses Frank on the lips.

Instinctively, Frank reaches over and takes the car keys from her right hand and places them back in the ignition.

"We've got booze at home," he says. "I need to comfort someone as quick as possible so hit it, Gal Pal," Frank says.

"Fasten your seat belt, Mr. Gyondski, you're in for the ride of your life," Beth answers as they laugh all the way home, to Arlington Heights and ecstasy.

CHAPTER 42

"**G**reenfield 327 and 329," Susie Patz broadcasts from the dispatch center of the Greenfield Police Department.

"327," Officer Matt O'Neil acknowledges over the Norcom radio from his squad car.

"329," Officer Marc Dombrowski answers off his portable radio, apparently out of his squad car at some unknown location.

"Respond to 524 Short Street for a suspicious person with more to follow," Patz says.

She then gets back on her telephone with the caller, who is reporting the suspicious person.

"10-4," Matt answers.

"10-4," Marc Dombrowski answers and the way he is breathing into his shoulder microphone indicates he's walking to his squad car.

Matt starts driving to 524 Short Street and begins to reminisce about the day which changed his life, as well as his career forever.

He sees T.C. Chambers' body with part of his face partially blown off, Kurt Thompson coming over the hill with his gun drawn, and the dead body of Tyler Hale.

Matt says the name repeatedly over and over, "Tyler fucking Hale."

"Greenfield 327 and 329, additional information," Susie Patz says as she gets back on the radio.

"327," Matt says rather calmly, considering where he is headed.

"329," Marc says and it's easy to tell from his transmission he's back inside his Ford Interceptor.

"The refused complainant is reporting a male, white, 40 to 45 years old, walking around the house dressed in blue jeans and a red t-shirt. His vehicle is a silver, Ford pick-up of some unknown type, parked in the driveway of the residence," Patz is able to get out in one breath.

"327, 10-4," Matt answers.

"329, is also 10-4," Marc calmly says.

Matt almost rear ends a black Range Rover at the intersection of Harlem Avenue and Greenfield Road because he's so caught up in the moment and not paying attention to the road.

"Shit," he yells out as he brings his squad car to a screeching halt, at the last possible moment.

"329, is 23 Greenfield and copy a plate for me,' Marc says.

"Go with the plate 329," Patz responds.

"Illinois plate of Tom Henry George 4562 Boy Truck plate," Marc says, "I'll be out of the car here."

"10-4 329," Patz responds and is on her terminal running the license plate Marc has just given her.

"I'm also 10-4 on all of that Greenfield," Matt acknowledges over his radio while he's also running the license plate off the mobile data terminal in his squad car.

"GREENFIELD 329," Patz yells into her radio with a tone Matt has never heard before.

"329," Marc answers with an inquisitive tone in his voice.

"Use caution 329, the complainant just called back and said the person walking around the house has something black in his hands and believes it might be.some kind of a handgun," Patz says.

"329 is 10-4," Marc answers with a noticeable scared tone in his voice.

Matt immediately activates all the overhead squad car lights and the siren.

A silver colored, BMW, ahead of him, instantly pulls over to its right, which allows Matt easy access through the street.

"I'm not going to lose another classmate today, so help me God," Matt says out loud and is ready to get on the radio, when he is suddenly interrupted.

"Greenfield 317 is also going from Post 27," Sgt. Barton says forcefully, thinking the same exact thing as Matt.

Post 27 is the car wash located in Morton Grove, which a number of local police departments use to clean their squads.

"Greenfield 317 to 329," Sgt. Barton says.

"Go Sarge," Marc answers.

"Marc, grab some cover, I'm only a few blocks away," Sgt. Barton says.

"10-4, Boss," Marc says and you could tell he's walking back to his squad car while answering Sgt. Barton.

"317 GREENFIELD," Patz is back to yelling in her radio, which has set a record in Matt's mind as he has never heard her yell this much on one call.

"Go ahead Greenfield," Sgt. Barton answers in the same monotone voice he's been using from the first day Matt and the rest of the Greenfield group have been working for him.

"Registered owner of the Ford is a Chase Branding out of Woodridge," Patz says. "Be advised, he does have a carry conceal permit, and he's clear and valid with no criminal history or 99s."

"10-4, Greenfield and thank you for the update," Sgt. Barton says.

Since the car wash is considerably closer than where Matt is coming from, he eases off the accelerator a bit; confident Marc is going to be in good hands soon.

"317 is also out at 524 Short Street," Sgt. Barton says.

"10-4," Patz answers, "No additional information from the refused complainant. Use caution."

"10-4, Greenfield," Sgt. Barton replies.

"All Greenfield units hold the air for 317 and 329," Patz says in the most forceful voice she can muster. "Emergency traffic only."

Seconds passed but they seemed like minutes to Matt and everyone else who is monitoring the radio frequency.

"We're out with him Greenfield, at the rear of the house," Marc says calmly into his microphone.

In the background, Sgt. Barton is yelling "Put your hands in the air, and don't turn around until I tell you to."

Matt's heart actually skips a beat.

In all the time he had worked for Sgt. Barton, not once has he ever heard him yell at someone.

"Greenfield 327 is 23," Matt says calmly into his radio, hoping to try and deescalate the situation.

"Greenfield 317," Sgt. Barton calls, slightly irritated.

"Go ahead 317," Patz replies, sounding thrilled to hear his voice again.

"Anyone else coming here can disregard because the black object the refused complainant was referring to is a Minolta camera" Sgt. Barton says with a disgusted tone in his voice.

"Camera, 10-4," Patz says and then quickly adds, "Greenfield units, you can resume normal radio traffic."

Matt quickly exits his squad and moves his right hand so it covers his Glock but keeps it in his level three holster.

"Greenfield 329, a 27, 29 by file," Marc says into his radio with a much calmer voice than before.

As Matt comes around the rear of the house, Sgt. Barton has his back to him with the before mentioned camera on the ground, next to his right leg.

Marc is now facing Matt and looks up from the individual's driver's license to smile at him.

The suspect is standing and facing Sgt. Barton, with his head down and is shuffling from leg to leg, as if he needs to piss.

This individual must have heard Matt coming, because he looks up and when he sees him and starts screaming, "He's here, he's here," pointing directly at Matt with his left hand.

"What are you talking about?" Sgt. Barton asks.

"The hero is here, the one who saved Officer O'Brien. I read all about it in the *Chicago Tribune,* and saw him on the Channel 9 Morning News. Hey, is Erin as hot in real life as she appears on TV?"

Matt starts to blush, as both Sgt. Barton and Marc are looking at him, with sarcastic smirks on their faces.

The individual pointing at Matt is indeed the registered owner of the truck, Chase Branding.

He's correct in one aspect; Matt is a hero in a number of people's eyes.

In the span of the last five days, Matt's been notified he's up for Officer of the Year awards by both the American Legion and more impressively, the International Association Chiefs of Police, all due to his appearance on WGN television.

Matt had appeared on the Channel 9 Morning News, to talk about the shootout.

Chase Branding is correct, Erin is indeed hot, but so is Robin, who was also especially nice to him during the interview.

Marc walks over to where Sgt Barton and Matt are standing and says, "Sarge, he's clear." Marc proceeds to hand Branding his Illinois Driver's License back and then gives him a death stare.

"Alright Mr. Branding, you're free to leave," Sgt. Barton says. "By all means, don't come back here."

"Thanks, Sarge and I was wondering if there was a chance I could have you take a picture of Officer O'Neil and me in front of the house, to prove to my friends?"

"Get the hell out of here now and don't come back, is that understood?" Sgt. Barton spits out as he watches Branding practically run to his truck.

The three officers then walk to the front of 524 Short Street, to make sure Branding has gotten into his vehicle and is leaving.

Branding does leave and almost backs into Matt's squad car in the process.

"Unfreaking believable," Matt says while shaking his head.

"Easy hero boy, your fan club is getting out of control," Sgt. Barton says and then he starts to laugh.

"This is our third time responding over here this month and I can't believe someone would actually drive all the way down from Belleville, Michigan last week, to see this stupid house, after hearing about the shootout," Sgt Barton says in a fit of disgust.

"Greenfield from 329," Marc says softly into his radio.

"Go 329," Susie Patz answers in a calmer voice, much to the relief of everyone.

"We'll be 10-24 for now, go with a 4 Edward," says Marc. "I'll add some additional information to the Cad Ticket, when I get back to my squad."

"10-4, 329," Susie Patz says "I have another assignment for you to copy when you're ready." It's clear she's back to being her old self again, on this second transmission.

"Go ahead with the new assignment, Greenfield," Marc answers.

"Cook County is handling a 10-50PI," Patz says. "They are asking for assistance with traffic control on Golf Road at James Court and requesting only one car at this time, due to the Fire Department being on scene and messing everything up."

"10-4 Greenfield, I'll be responding," Marc answers.

He taps Matt on his left shoulder as he passes him on the walk to his squad car.

"Hey Sarge, regarding the problems this house is causing," Matt says, understanding he is slightly to blame for it.

"Greenfield 317 from 302," the transmission from Acting Chief Bart comes loud and clear over their radios.

"Go for 317," Sgt. Barton responds.

"Reggie, call me immediately regarding 524 Short Street," Bart says.

"10-4 Boss," Sgt. Barton replies.

In a matter of seconds, he has dialed Bart's phone number and has the phone next to his right ear.

Bart answers it after only the second ring and does all the talking for the next two minutes, as Sgt. Barton listens with a stoic look on his face.

Since he was 10-8 and still wanting to talk to Sgt. Barton about the predicament, regarding 524 Short Street, Matt hangs around.

Knowing the phone call could last for more than a couple of minutes, Matt puts both of his hands in their respective Blauer work pants pockets.

He takes a few steps forward until he is standing in the street where he found T.C. Chambers' body, exactly two months earlier.

Squatting straight down over the spot where T.C. Chambers had been lying, he whispers so Sgt. Barton doesn't hear him, "God, I miss you bud and if you see Chris up there, tell him hi, for me," Matt says.

He is going to say a quick prayer for both of them, but he sees Sgt. Barton walking over to him.

Matt stands up just in time as Sgt. Barton reaches him.

"Going into the station, apparently Bart has lined up a meeting with a Greenfield Building Department representative and Realtor Jerry Doetsch, of Berkshire Hathaway, who is now listing this place. We're going to see if they can do something about this situation," Sgt. Barton says, pointing at the realtor sign on the front lawn.

"10-4 Boss," Matt acknowledges.

While Sgt. Barton is walking to his squad car, Matt walks to the back of the residence, where Branding had been standing, to make sure he's taken his camera with him, when he left.

Upon reaching the back of the house and not seeing the camera, Matt continues walking, until he's standing where the Ford Bronco had been.

He decides to see what Tyler Hale had been looking at on that dreadful day.

Consequently, Matt walks over to what he believes is the exact spot where Tyler Hale had been standing, when he shot at him.

LTJG Ben Zimmerman had been contacted through a series of elaborate steps with the Navy and was told how his vehicle played a major role in the death of a Greenfield Police Officer.

A very apologetic Zimmerman said he had already collected the insurance money on it and didn't want it anymore.

He was currently at an undisclosed location and wouldn't be back into the United States for another 62 days.

The Greenfield Police Department rumor mill was spreading that Deputy Chief Gyondski had sent Zimmerman documentation regarding where his vehicle was located and now it was his responsibility to get it off the Village of Greenfield's property.

Consequently, the Ford Bronco now sat in the back row of the Greenfield Police Station parking lot, next to a beautiful, BMW X5.

A week earlier, Officer Larry Driash made a traffic stop on the driver of the BMW for the possibility of DUI.

During the course of the traffic stop, probable cause was found for drugs inside this vehicle.

Two ounces of cocaine were found by Officer Driash.

Under the Illinois Asset Forfeiture Procedure Act, Driash took custody of the vehicle. This case would be pending for months, but chances were pretty positive, the Cook County Courts would award this vehicle to the Greenfield Police Department for the purpose of being auctioned off in the future.

Matt stands there for two or three minutes, reliving the shootout in his mind.

Next, he walks a few feet forward towards the house and turns to the right, heading to where Megan O'Brien had been lying when she almost bled to death.

The minute he stepped on it; he knew exactly what it was because he had done so other times on the police range.

While still standing, Matt is able to pick up his left foot and rest it across his right knee.

The fact he'd purchased new work boots, only a couple of days ago, makes it tough to bend his foot, due to the boot's stiffness.

Yet, the pattern on the bottom of the boot is so new, it holds the object perfectly in place.

Matt reaches down with his right hand and grabs it from his boot, holding it close to his face in an effort to identify it.

The sun hits its gold-colored casing and bounces off it into his eyes.

Matt turns it over, and the markings on the bottom of it convince him.

He knows exactly what he is holding—a fired 40 caliber Greenfield Police Department round, shell casing.

CHAPTER 43

M att O'Neil doesn't know what is spinning faster, the 40-caliber shell casing in his right hand, or the different theories as to how the casing happened to be in the backyard of 524 Short Street.

Repeatedly, he turns and twists the shell casing.

He looks at the bottom of it, which reads Speer on its top rim and 40 S&W on its bottom rim.

"Slow down kid, take a deep breath, and let's concentrate for a minute," he says out loud, since he's the only person there.

Just to prove to himself it is a Greenfield Police Department round; he removes a magazine from one of the pockets on his bullet proof vest, holding it next to the bullet casing, he just found.

The shell casing matches perfectly.

But now a new element enters his mind.

Matt estimates 20 to 25 different law enforcement personnel had spent time, walking around this yard, on the day of the shooting.

Firemen and paramedics were on scene from Greenfield, Gilles, and Morton Grove

All of these people were walking around and moving gurneys, defibrillators and drug boxes, in the wet grass and mud, while wearing some type of boot.

Not one of these people had looked down, in all probability, as they were focused on their assignment and getting it done.

Every one of the law enforcement personnel, had probably walked over to see either the Ford Bronco, or the spot where Megan O'Brien had been lying, before she was taken away.

The reason wasn't very complex at all and known by cops everywhere.

A good police officer is noisy, curious, and suspicious of every type of crime scene, or individual type of person.

Kelly stopped asking a couple of months after they were married, why Matt needed to look at the driver of every car stopped next to them at a red light, when they were out.

Or why he seemed to read the license plate number of every car he was stopped behind on the road. Any girlfriend of Kelly's who was dating a new guy, got the third degree from Matt.

After 7 to 8 minutes of questioning, one guy turned to his girlfriend and asked, "Do I need an attorney?"

Curiosity could be a great thing in police work.

Unfortunately, it had also ruined countless cases over the years, by police personnel walking through a crime scene, for no apparent reason.

Yet, for some reason, Matt is convinced the shell casing he holds in his hand is from his own Police Department.

He starts sweating profusely; thinking about what his next move should and would be.

He turns to his left, so he is now facing the rear of 524 Short Street.

Now a completely different thought comes to him, "Where did the round come from which nearly killed me?"

Slowly and in a bit of shock, he walks back to the exact spot where he was standing the afternoon he shot and killed Tyler Hale.

Matt knows this is substantiated by both a Cook County Medical Examiner's Report and a thorough investigation by a solid NORTAF Team.

Turning his body slightly to the left, he looks directly at the spot where Megan had been lying and says out loud, "Could the shot have come from her?"

Then, he turns so he is facing where Tyler Hale had been standing, saying again to himself, "This is where the shot came from, I think."

Finally, Matt thinks of Kurt Thompson's involvement in all of this and rules him out for now.

Matt realizes there is a possible solution to all of this waiting directly behind him.

Turning around, he walks to the rear of the house and takes out his Terra Lux flashlight.

He shines it on the siding of the house, looking for one simple thing.

The bullet hole showing where the round went after it passed the left side of Matt's head.

Matt figures the angle of the hole could possibly indicate the direction of where the shot came from.

Being a relatively small house makes it easy, and it doesn't take him long to find the hole.

What should have answered Matt's question only makes the situation more complex.

The hole is barely visible due to being filled with some type of caulking material. Whoever had filled the hole, never even bothered painting over it, figuring no one in the world would ever come and check on it.

Matt stands there, looking at the hole and trying to figure out what the hell is going on.

"Greenfield 327, a parking complaint," Susie Patz says.

Matt doesn't answer his radio as he continues looking at the hole in disbelief.

He needs answers to a multitude of questions about this entire situation.

He needs to check the background on some of the individuals involved in this mess.

He needs to see all of the reports on this incident and figure out what he's dealing with and why.

Only one person can help him accomplish this.

The burning question is, "Would this person be willing to lose a career over helping Matt?"

CHAPTER 44

"How the hell could there be this much stuff for one single police shooting?" Matt O'Neil thinks.

He's looking at the stack of files neatly situated on the table in front of him.

There are more boxes on the floor below the table.

Sgt. Barton had been a man of his word and came through for Matt once again.

Sitting alone in the armory section of the Greenfield Police Department, Matt takes a moment to reflect on this whole situation, which had taken on the personality of a *Mission Impossible* movie.

Last Tuesday night around 7:00 Pm, they sat in the farthest booth from the Shermer Road entrance of the Land Mark Inn, located in Northbrook.

It was the perfect location for what Matt had in mind when he picked the place.

Dimly lit, small booths, and tables filled with customers involved in conversation on a weeknight, took away any possible suspicions of the two guys eating their Monte Cristo burgers and having a couple of Bud Lights, while engrossed in conversation.

This was exactly the way he had planned it.

Matt was surprisingly blunt in explaining the entire situation to Sgt. Barton, who mostly sat in silence and took it all in.

Holding a French fry full of ketchup in his right hand, Sgt. Barton finally asked, "Yes or No, are you telling me Tyler Hale had help in the killing of Greenfield Police Officers?"

Knowing this would be huge in getting Sgt. Barton firmly on his side, Matt paused a few seconds and finished the last of his Bud

Light. Placing the bottle back on the table, he leaned forward in the booth and looked directly into Sgt. Barton's eyes.

Matt said in a matter-of-fact tone, "I'm 100% sure he didn't' act alone, which is why I need your help proving it."

Matt sat back in his booth but kept both of his hands on the table in an open position, signaling he was looking for both help and ideas.

Matt hated himself for doing it, but he was lying through his teeth.

Sure, he had a hunch, but he couldn't throw one piece of concrete evidence on the table, if Sgt. Barton pushed him as to why he thought Tyler Hale had an accomplice.

Matt didn't have long to wait.

"I agree with you, O'Neil and every person I've spoken with, even Chief Fitzsimons before his passing, told me they'd seen all of the reports and evidence, which tends to agree with you also. They just weren't sure which way to turn next," Sgt. Barton says forcefully.

Matt let out a long breath, realizing he wasn't't the only person on the Greenfield Police Department, thinking this way.

"Then you'll help me?" Matt asked, as he took his hands off the table and moved forward in the booth.

"Yes, you looking at the case can only help," Sgt. Barton said and then reached for his bottle of Bud Light.

"It has to be done in secret, doesn't it?" Matt asked, just to make sure, but he was pretty confident he knew the answer to his question before he asked it.

Sgt. Barton lowered the beer bottle from his lips.

For a large man, he was surprisingly gentle as he placed the bottle slowly back down on the table.

This time it was Sgt. Barton's turn to lean forward in the booth so his face was only inches away from Matt's when he said, "You know you were a prime suspect after Officer Ortego's death, don't you?"

Matt was surprised how the word, suspect, stunned him the minute it came out of Sgt. Barton's mouth, especially after the way

Detective Golden acted toward him during the interview at the Northland Police Department.

"O'Neil, are you still with me?" Sgt. Barton asked.

The way Sgt. Barton said it, pushed Matt back in time, when he was sitting in the rear seat of a Greenfield squad car, covered in Chris Mill's blood.

"Okay, I'm in," Sgt. Barton said.

"Here's the best way I see us pulling this thing off." Sgt. Barton said, while pushing his empty beer bottle aside and pulling out a small note pad and Bic pen, from his blue jean jacket.

For the next thirty minutes, Sgt. Barton spoke and Matt listened intently, only occasionally nodding his head in agreement, to show he was paying attention.

This coming Sunday night was chosen as the day Sgt. Barton could conceivably get the case files from Lt. Alderman's office. This would work out great, since Matt's regularly scheduled day off would be the next day.

If anyone ran into Sgt. Barton after he was done placing the files back in Lt. Alderman's office, he would just lie and say he came in early to work out, before heading to Northwestern University Center for Public Safety. Sgt. Barton was enrolled in the prestigious School of Police Staff and Command, and Monday would be his first day of the ten-week course.

Acting Chief Bart was a big fan of Sgt. Barton and sending him to this school only guaranteed it to every member of the Greenfield Police Department,

The armory would be Matt's viewing station, since no one ever used this room unless there was a range qualification scheduled. Since the entire department had qualified last month, this wouldn't be an issue.

The only issue would be just how much time Matt would have available for him to get through the endless streams of reports.

Sgt. Barton decided on a start time of 0130 since the shift working should all be on the street, and in some cases, resting comfortably in their squad cars.

But the ending time would be 0500, and not a minute past for Matt, which would safely allow Sgt. Barton to get all of the case files and boxes back into Lt. Alderman's office.

It was decided Matt would only glance at the killing of T.C. Chambers and Secretary of State Investigator Petrov.

With time being of the essence, he would concentrate mostly on the facts of the backyard at 524 Short Street.

Matt would be forced to lie to Kelly for the first time in their marriage.

Matt would tell her he needed to go back to work for a surveillance, because he would be attempting to find a group responsible for stealing cars not only in Greenfield but the entire North Shore for the past six months.

The part about the group stealing cars wasn't a lie, since Greenfield had sixteen cars stolen in their town alone.

The M.O. for each of the stolen cars was the same in each case.

Doors to the cars were left unlocked and the keys for the vehicle were left somewhere in the car. Thus, allowing the owner of the car to never have to worry about where they left them, the last time they used their car.

It was even more appalling to the Greenfield cop who handled the last stolen car report, when the owner told him, there was a 9mm Smith and Wesson M&P Shield, fully loaded, with a 9-round magazine, in the glove box, of their missing Nissan Sentra.

Matt wasn't happy he needed to lie to his wife, but it was for a worthwhile cause.

Plus, in the past month, it seemed like the pregnancy had caused some minor memory losses for Kelly.

She had been misplacing her cell phone or car keys, so Matt had a back-up plan at his ready.

Being their first baby, Matt was so concerned about the memory issue, he brought it to the attention of Kelly's obstetrician at Lutheran Family Center Hospital, at one of their scheduled visits.

After a thorough examination of Kelly, Dr. Lewis said the memory issue was normal and not a concern at this time, much to the relief of Matt.

Since his Camaro was so noticeable, Sgt. Barton decided Matt should drive Kelly's Honda Accord, and park it near a construction trailer the village had already put at the site of the new police station.

This trailer was roughly a little over a half mile from the current Greenfield Police Station and nothing more than a brisk walk for Matt.

The plan was in place and had gone to perfection. As a sign of respect by Sgt. Barton, Matt came upon the box marked T.C. Chambers death, which was sitting on his chair, when he first entered the armory.

Quickly, Matt took the lid off the box and pulled out the detailed NORTAF report, which explained precisely how Matt's best friend was ambushed and killed.

Matt thought it would be one of the hardest reports to review.

He was correct and it was tough as hell.

Call it simply love for one of his best friends, but Matt spent more time looking into the reports on T.C. Chambers and Investigator Petrov, than he had planned. He found nothing out of the ordinary with the NORTAF report, but never expected to. Matt can't figure out why the Lord Jesus Christ would take another great friend of his, at such a young age, when he had so much yet to offer.

Matt never bothers to look at any pictures of Investigator Petrov's death, instead he focuses mainly on a picture of T.C. Chambers' face, profoundly disfigured after being blown off.

"Fucking Tyler Hale," Matt says over and over for a full minute, whispering to himself when in reality he wants to scream it out loud.

Slowly and carefully, he puts T.C. Chambers' photo back in the file among the DVD of other pictures of this particular crime scene and then puts the lid back on the box. When finished, he takes the box and puts it on the floor and out of sight.

He is ready to focus more on his next concern.

He thumbs through a box and numerous files, until he finds exactly what he is looking for, Tyler Hale's autopsy report.

Matt starts to realize he has become obsessed with finding out everything he can about this prick.

Apparently not wanting to take any chances, the Chief Medical Examiner for Cook County, did Hale's autopsy and did a very thorough job.

It actually scares Matt how much enjoyment he's getting in slowly reading, word for word, the manner in which Tyler Hale had died.

Tyler Hale was a substance abuser as track marks were found during the autopsy on both arms.

"Heroin, if I was to make a guess," Matt thinks.

Matt's attention is fully raised when he finds in the report the sentence containing the words, "Human Papilloma Virus found on lower extremities of Hale."

Matt has never heard of this illness, and he makes a mental note to look into it in the future.

In a separate file is the Toxicology Report for Tyler Hale.

Heroin was the correct guess from earlier, but it wasn't enough because Tyler Hale's B.A.C. was .142.

Matt's eyes grow wide while reading the report, seeing the different amounts of drugs that were found inside Hale's body. He is familiar with the anti-depressants, and the pain medications, but there must have been at least seven to eight other medications found on the toxicology report completed on Tyler Hale, on the day of his death.

Setellmorie, is mentioned prominently in this report.

Matt has no idea what some of these drugs are, or what their purpose was.

This is taking too much time, yet could be an important piece of the puzzle down the road.

Matt pulls out his iPhone and carefully takes pictures of the entire toxicology report, before placing the report back in its proper file.

Matt glances at his watch, which shows 0245 hours. He is relieved, because he has plenty of time left to read the main reports on the shooting in the backyard of 524 Short Street.

Matt finds the box containing all of this information after moving every other box on the floor near his feet·

Strangely, it is the only box marked with red dry marker on its lid reading, "Rear residence shootout at 524 Short Street." Matt takes off the lid and drops it to the floor, on the right side of his body·

He is particularly interested in viewing the pictures first. The original digital photos had been burned onto a DVD and inventoried as evidence. There is a copy of this DVD in the case file and, luckily, a set of index prints, printed four to a sheet. Hopefully, he would be able to see the details he was looking for on the smaller printed images and not have to resort to viewing the photos via the DVD on a computer.

There is a department computer in the range control booth, roughly 10 to 12 steps from his present position in the armory. But Matt would have some explaining to do if anyone found he had been logged onto it at 0300 hours, on his day off.

Since the files are well organized, it doesn't take long to find the ones he is looking for. The reconstructions of this shooting incident are separate from all the other crime scene photos and reports.

He finally finds the photos of the back of 524 Short Street and looks at the sequence of photos of the bullet hole.

Even though he knows what he is looking at, he really doesn't understand it.

Matt reads the written report, which explains the photographs as well as the investigative findings. Matt doesn't' like at all what he is reading and needs to carefully read it again, to make sure he has the outcome correct·

The report explains the forensic team couldn't locate a second bullet hole to determine the bullet's path after it went through the outside wall. This wall was a single layer of World War Two era steel with no insulation on the inside. The forensics team searched for the bullet but was only led to "numerous bullet fragments." Basically, the bullet disintegrated when it hit the steel wall.

The report goes on to say, "Although the precise origin of the fired round could not be confirmed by angle measurements, the findings are consistent with the statement of Officer O'Neil that the origin of the shot was from the passenger area of the Ford Bronco."

"Damn those guys are good, but they're not helping confirm my suspicions," Matt says softly to himself, even though he is confident there's not another working Greenfield cop in the police station.

Matt sits back in his chair, report still in his right hand. He worries this entire thing is a waste of both Sgt. Barton and his time. But after thinking about what he has read, Matt sits straight up in his chair, realizing their findings don't eliminate the possibility that his suspicions may be correct. The forensics team was reporting what they had found or didn't find, which is what they were supposed to do.

Matt keeps reading, looking at the photos as well as the CAD drawings. The locations of all the evidence items were documented on the drawing of the house and backyard areas. Each little dot had a letter next to it, which corresponded to a table at the bottom of the sheet of paper. Next to each letter in the table was the description of the item. There were also photographs of the item with their letter tent marker, that had been used to mark their location at the crime scene.

The hairs on Matt's neck seem to rise when he sees a dot with the letter, "A," next to it, which is where he had fallen after firing the single round that struck and killed Tyler Hale. In the table was the letter, "A," next to the description that read, "Federal .223 shell casing."

Matt's eyes continue scanning the drawing, and he sees a dot with the letter, "D," located near the passenger side of the Ford Bronco. The description in the table reads "D-Speer .40 caliber shell casing."

"Wait, was this the same shell casing? Why didn't the team collect it?" Matt thinks.

Matt's mind at 0315 hours is trying to understand it all and then he notices it. The dot for item, "D," is right next to the Bronco. That was the ejected casing from Megan's struggle with Tyler Hale when he shot her while attempting to take away her gun. The Glock 22 Gen 4 ejects the fired casing back and to the right, like most semi-automatics, and that shell casing location would be consistent with the Glock firing while pointed away from the Bronco. This definitely was the round, which struck Megan.

But that wasn't the exact area where Matt had picked up the shell casing in his boot, which was further away from the Bronco and closer to the house. Matt places one finger on the approximate spot where he picked up the shell casing and thinks, "If this casing landed back and to the right of where the gun was pointing, it means whoever fired the shot was doing so from the driver's s side of the Bronco, where Megan had been.

"Megan tried to kill me and not Tyler Hale?" Matt says softly to himself in shock.

Matt has mixed feelings about this realization confirming his suspicions.

Yet, he wants more proof and realizes he is racing against the clock, which shows 0322 hours.

Matt feels he needs to go back to 524 Short Street and look around inside the house, because none of this is seeming to make sense right now.

As he has done previously, he carefully repacks the box containing all the reports.

This time, he leaves it on the chair for Sgt. Barton, instead of on the floor for the Armory.

Slowly and carefully, he opens every door he comes to, in an attempt to get out of the Greenfield Police Department, without encountering one of his fellow police officers.

Luckily, he's successful and in record time is headed toward 524 Short Street in Kelly's car.

The shock of Megan somehow being the one firing at him is mind boggling.

Could it have been Hale, who ran for cover by the passenger's side door of the Bronco after firing?

Matt is so caught up in speculation, he doesn't' even realize he has gone through the intersection of Moody and First Street, for a good five seconds.

Looking up through the glass in the Honda Accord's roof, he says, "C'mon Chris, you started this mess now help me figure this shit out."

Before Matt knows it, he has parked Kelly's Honda in Lakeview Park and is headed eastbound toward the rear of 524 Short Street.

The morning air is crisp for August, and helps to revive him slightly, as he starts to formulate a plan for what he will do once he gets to the back door of the residence.

Up and over the cyclone fence, as well as the railroad tracks, and he's standing at the old back door of 524 Short Street.

Matt finds himself face to face with a yellow, 5x7 sticker, with an official Cook County Seal, located on the left side of the door stating, "This home is the site of an ongoing police investigation and entrance inside this residence is strictly forbidden by order of law unless part of the team handling this investigation."

Matt pauses for a moment to try to figure out if almost getting killed on this property and then helping solve this investigation made him part of the team.

Matt pulls his Spyderco Delica knife, which was clipped onto his left pants pocket and begins to open it but stops, thinking to himself, "I wonder how many laws and Greenfield Police Department procedures I've broken this morning?"

This thought brings a slight smirk to his face.

The door is locked but the lock isn't a good one and there was no deadbolt.

Using the knife blade to push back the doorknob latch, he's able to push the door open with relative ease.

He quickly enters the residence and not wanting to take any chances by turning the lights on and arousing suspicion with neighbors, he leaves them off.

Yet, he needs to see where he's going, so he pulls out his Terra Lux flashlight from the front pocket of his favorite Chicago Cubs sweatshirt.

He carefully turns it on, but keeps the beam aimed toward the floor, for now.

The photographs are off the wall and have been removed as evidence, but everything else is the same as it was when they were clearing this house after the shooting.

The first place Matt goes to is the metal wall to look for the hole, he finds it still filled with the putty compound.

The NORTAF guys were right.

Not much on the inside could be used to determine direction of the bullet.

Matt looks around using the flashlight and thinks about his hunch.

If the round had been fired from Megan's side of the Bronco, it would take a path leading it closer to the corner of the opposite wall.

He looks in that area and finds nothing.

Matt walks back to the door and thinks about what to do next.

As he prepares to leave, Matt shines his flashlight back into the room.

He slowly scans from left to right.

What he's looking for, he doesn't even know.

There is absolutely nothing there.

He is so frustrated, he doesn't care who sees the light of his flashlight, coming from the residence.

As the beam reaches the right wall, he sees a slight glimmer, in the window curtains.

It's up high, where the curtains are threaded on the curtain rod.

At first, he dismisses it, but then changes his mind and slowly walks to see what was reflecting.

As he is standing next to the curtain, he can't see anything unusual.

Matt reaches out and gives the curtains a gentle shake, which dislodges a piece of shiny copper, that falls to the floor.

Matt bends down to pick it up and begins smiling.

For Matt now holds in his right hand, the mangled and distorted copper jacket, from a bullet fired, if he is correct, from the driver's side of the Ford Bronco.

CHAPTER 45

Matt O'Neil can't take the smile off his face, as he makes a right hand turn in Kelly's Honda out of the parking lot of Lakeview Park.

From the second he picked up the copper jacket of the fired bullet he found; it's remained in his right hand for safekeeping.

He knows this isn't enough to bring Megan in for questioning, but it's a start and he'll leave the rest up to Sgt. Barton, after he speaks with him later today.

Matt stops at the traffic light at Golf Road and Harlem Avenue and it suddenly dawns on him, "Did I secure the back door of 524 Short Street?"

"I believe I did," Matt thinks and, in his mind, he tries to remember his actions of what he did after finding his dream item on the floor.

The problem is he can't do anything correctly right now.

He's so tired, mainly from the stress of today, more than his physical actions.

Matt jumps a bit in his car seat as the air horn on a Laidlaw garbage truck sounds behind him.

He realizes the traffic signal had turned green for both of them, but he never' moved.

Roughly two minutes later, he's pulling into the driveway of his Morton Grove home.

For the last time this morning, Matt looks at the item in his right hand and realizes he can't walk into the house carrying it by the slight chance Kelly is awake.

Instead, he looks around her immaculately kept car for

something to put it in when he finds unexpectedly a Chipotle bag laying on the floor of the car, on the passenger side.

Matt remembers Kelly telling him, roughly a month into her pregnancy, about her daily cravings for these wonderful salty little treats.

Looking inside the bag, he checks to make sure its empty.

It is and he drops the fragmented copper jacket of the bullet inside it.

Before he gets out of the car, he hits the garage door opener on the sun visor. Slowly, the garage door rises and shows his beautiful, freshly washed and waxed Camaro.

Getting out of Kelly's car, he walks over to his car and opens the passenger side door.

Matt hits a small button on the glove box, which opens it immediately.

For some strange reason, he actually kisses the Chipotle bag before placing it gently inside the glove box. Then, he covers the bag with four to five brown, McDonald's napkins.

Matt closes the overhead garage door as he goes out a side door of the garage. Pulling a house key from his blue jeans pocket, he slowly opens the side door to the house and walks in, taking off his New Balance gym shoes in the process.

He's a bit surprised to find the love of his life sitting at the kitchen table, reading a novel and sipping a cup of hot tea, already in her hospital scrubs.

"How did the stakeout go babe?" Kelly asks.

"Boring as all hell," he answers, "Honey, I'm exhausted and really just want to go to bed."

Matt walks to a position directly behind her.

Before Kelly can say a word, he bends over so both of his arms are now down around Kelly's waist. Matt finds himself staring straight down and is pleased at the beautiful sight in front of him.

Kelly's breasts have grown considerably in the past ten days, as well as her belly, which holds their future.

He can't wait to become a father and had finished the nursery ahead of schedule, four days ago.

"I totally understand sweetie because quite frankly you look exhausted," Kelly replies.

"Thanks," Matt says and gently kisses the right side of Kelly's neck.

"Dinner out tonight wherever you want and we can catch up on each other's lives as well Kelly," Matt says.

"Deal, Mr. Smooth Talker," Kelly answers as Matt releases his arms from around her body and heads upstairs to their bedroom.

In record time, Matt has the Colt Commander out of his pancake holster and empty's the weapon, with the slide in the open position. Ever so gently he places it on top of the armoire in their bedroom and puts the magazine for the weapon right next to it, along with the pancake holster.

All of his clothes, except for his Fruit of the Loom briefs, are dropped on the floor in a neat pile on his side of the bed. In one swift, rolling move, Matt slides into a somewhat warm bed, left this way by his wife and has the covers over his head in a matter of mere seconds.

Matt believes he will fall asleep the minute his head hits his pillow and is looking forward to a solid six to seven hours of deep sleep, satisfied with his recent accomplishments.

He falls asleep, but in record time his eyes open.

He looks at his clock, on the night stand next to his side of the bed, which reads 10:15 am.

Instinctively, he grabs Kelly's pillow and places it over his head, trying to get at least one, if not two more hours of sleep.

Rolling back onto his side, the pillow fits naturally on his head and partially covers his face.

He lays there thinking of any other possibilities to help him fall back asleep, especially when today will be one of the biggest days of his life.

Nothing comes to mind and looking again at the clock, it reads 10:25am.

Matt realizes his efforts are fruitless.

Slowly, he drags himself out of bed and takes roughly four to five minutes to make the bed nice and neat.

Kelly only has a few rules around the house, but making their bed is at the top of her list.

Matt turns on his iPhone and checks for messages but finds nothing. Next, he opens his ESPN app and, to his delight, the Cubs beat the Dodgers, in Los Angeles last night.

Matt has a strong feeling this will be the Cubbies opponent, in the NLCS, and any win or psychological advantage his baseball team can get before they face them in the playoffs, is only a good thing.

Last, Matt checks the weather forecast on his phone which calls for a high of 92 later today with possible thunderstorms rolling into the area around 7:00 pm tonight.

He picks up his Cubs sweatshirt and socks, takes of his underwear and drops all of these items inside the laundry hamper, which is located just outside their bedroom.

Walking over to the bedroom dresser, he pulls out the second drawer and grabs two fresh pair of underwear. He puts one of the pairs of underwear on and with the other pair still in his right hand, he walks over to the bedroom closet, turning on the light before entering it.

He finds his green colored Nike workout bag immediately, since it's been in the same spot, day after day, when he's not using it.

Quickly, he puts the underwear inside the bag after first checking to make sure he has all the workout clothes he's going to need, and one extra item as well.

Although tired, he's convinced all the items are in place.

While picking up his bag with his left hand, he grabs the first clean t-shirt, in a pile on the shelf to his immediate right.

He laughs a bit when he realizes the shirt, he grabbed off the pile is his favorite yellow Nike t-shirt, with the company's traditional swoosh below the lettering on the front.

His laughter quickly stops, and he's slightly upset about how long this process is taking him with so much to do today, before taking Kelly out for a lovely dinner.

Quickly, he leaves the bedroom closet and walks back to his side of the bed, to put on his favorite pair of blue jeans, which he'd worn just hours ago.

Down the stairs he heads to the refrigerator in the kitchen.

Opening the refrigerator door, Matt grabs a 12-ounce can of Coca-Cola, as well as a 1-liter plastic bottle of Smart Water.

He puts the can of Coca-Cola inside his Nike workout bag, and then swings this bag over his right shoulder.

Walking directly to the food pantry, he finds his favorite apple pie Larabar on a bottom shelf, and puts two into his right pants pocket.

It's much easier to do without carrying his off-duty weapon, but where he's headed, he can't bring it inside.

He knows if he left his weapon in the Camaro, he wouldn't get anything done due to being so worried about the gun, as well as his car being stolen.

Matt needs to get some energy and clear his mind as best as possible.

He heads to Lifetime Fitness in Skokie, off Old Orchard Road, in an attempt to accomplish this.

By the time he pulls into one of the primo parking spots near the front door of the gym, all the food and can of coca cola have been consumed.

Matt also has finished half of the smart water, which is sloshing around his stomach.

An hour of swimming laps fails to get the job done.

He winds up spending a good 20 minutes in the whirlpool, alone, tending to his slightly sore muscles.

A quick shower and after gathering his things, he heads out to his Camaro to call Sgt. Barton and give him an update. Once inside the Camaro, with his Nike workout bag in the trunk, he checks his phone for any messages he may have missed.

Of course, the only phone call he missed while working out is from Sgt. Barton.

Checking his watch, it reads 12:43 Pm, and Matt realizes Sgt. Barton is either back in, or headed to class at the Northwestern Traffic Institute.

Matt decides to phone him around 4:45 Pm, when he's convinced Sgt. Barton will be out of class for the day.

Still hurting energy wise, Matt heads for the Starbucks, located in the 5000 Block of Dempster Street, in Morton Grove.

Matt believes it should only be blocks away from his third and final stop of the day.

With most people back at work after their lunch break, he gets to the Starbucks in a matter of minutes.

With no one in the drive through lane, he's ordered and is handed his Iced Coffee Grande, with two shots of espresso, in record time.

Matt has never been to stop number three, so he puts the address for it in his phone, 6140 N. Lincoln Avenue, Morton Grove, Illinois 60053.

In a matter of seconds, his iPhone shows he's exactly two miles from stop number three.

"Finally, something right," he says to himself before gently placing the iced coffee in the cup holder nearest to him.

In less than five minutes, he pulls up to the front of 6140 N. Lincoln Avenue and sits in his Camaro, staring at it.

He's amazed how small the Morton Grove Library looks from the outside.

If you didn't know better, you would swear it was a bank or something else.

Grabbing what is left of his ice coffee from its holder and the notebook lying on the front passenger seat, Matt locks his Camaro and heads inside.

He walks practically to the back of it, before finding a table he's comfortable at.

Pulling his iPhone from his front left pants pocket, he holds down the switch located on top it, to turn it off, so as not to be disturbed.

Then, he places the phone on the table he's sitting at and precedes to open the notebook laying on the table in front of him to its first page.

In large, red ink he sees the notes he has made on this page, which is his reason for being in the library.

Find out everything about the drug Setellmorie and why it was in Tyler Hale's body.

What is the effect of two other drugs which were found in Tyler hales body, if he has time today.

Determine a possible motive Megan O'Brien or Kurt Thompson may have for killing me.

Could Tyler Hale have shot at me from the driver's side of the Bronco and then made it back in time to the passenger's side, where I killed him?

Put together a quick report for Sgt. Barton on what he found at 524 Short Street.

Matt isn't sure why, but a tidal wave of exhaustion suddenly comes over him.

Apparently, the ice coffee hadn't kicked in yet, combined with lack of sleep, along with general exhaustion is kicking his ass.

Grabbing the phone, he puts it on top of the now closed notebook.

Then, he folds his arms on the notebook and puts his head straight down into his arms.

Matt figures it's roughly 1:30 Pm and he can grab a fifteen-minute nap before digging into his work.

Matt's snoring is so loud the librarian taps him on his right shoulder to wake him up.

Immediately, Matt sits straight up and begins rubbing his eyes with both of his fists.

Matt looks at this employee's name tag which reads Jamie, before saying, "So sorry, Mister..."

"Marquez, Jamie Marquez, I'm the head librarian here Sir," he responds with the sternest look Matt's seen in quite some time.

Matt finishes rubbing his eyes and asks Mr. Marquez, "What time is it?"

Looking directly over Matt at a clock mounted on the wall he answers, "Three fifty-five in the afternoon."

Matt wants to scream "Holy shit!" and jump up.

Instead, he answers in a very calm and polite voice, "Thank you very much and could you please point me in the direction of the library's information desk?"

"Why certainly," Mr. Marquez replies. "My shift at the information desk starts at 4:00 Pm so if you want to just gather your belongings, you can follow me."

Matt doesn't need to be asked twice.

In record time, his phone is back in his pants pocket and notebook in his left hand, as he finds himself trying to keep up with Mr. Marquez, who seems like he doesn't want to be late for his fellow employee he will be relieving.

Matt manages to catch up to Mr. Marquez as he's taking his seat behind the information desk, and typing his name into a computer terminal he's seated behind.

When finished, he looks up at Matt and asks him, "So what do you need information about?"

"Everything you have on the drug, Setellmorie, please" Matt replies.

Without saying another word, Mr. Marquez begins typing feverishly on his keyboard.

When finished, he waits roughly 30 seconds before a smile appears on his face and he points at the computer screen in front of Matt, who needs to sit down on a small couch to read it.

"It's from the American Medical Association," Mr. Marquez says. "In a nutshell, it says the individual using this drug will remain conscious, but only have some semblance of muscle control, while slowly breathing. But the key point you need to know is they will be immobile and totally unresponsive to pain," Mr. Marquez says so clearly, he must have been reading it off his screen as well.

"Wow," Matt is only able to say, before sitting back in shock with this new information.

"Second person to ask me about this drug in the past three months, which is a bit peculiar," Mr. Marquez says.

"Excuse me?" Matt mumbles as he's still trying to digest all the information on the screen in front of him about Sentellmorie.

"Roughly three months ago, a woman came in like you saying she needed any and all information on the drug Sentellmorie, for a class project she was working on at Loyola University," Mr. Marquez says.

"What specifically did she want?" Matt asks, as his attention is no longer on the computer screen but instead Mr. Marquez.

"She wanted confirmation about Sentellmorie impacting someone's motor functions," Mr. Marquez replies.

"Can you describe her by chance?" Matt asks.

"Sure, beautiful red hair, blue eyes in pretty good shape, with really long legs, although she seemed a bit old to be a student at Loyola University," Mr. Marquez says.

"Did she happen to have freckles?" Matt asks then holds his breath, afraid of what Mr. Marquez might answer.

"Wow!" he says. "Now that you mention it, she did."

"Megan," Matt mumbles and springs off the mini couch.

If he could have run to his Camaro and not caused a scene, Matt would have.

Instead, he strides confidently, knowing he now has more than enough to tell Sgt. Barton when he speaks to him in a few minutes.

Matt doesn't even wait to get to his car to turn on his phone, instead turning it on as he's walking to his car.

Once activated, he checks his phone messages and finds only one—a voice mail from Mark Dugan.

Getting inside the Camaro, he hits play for his voicemail and throws the notebook on the front passenger seat of his car.

"Matt, where the hell are you. I have big news and then I have even bigger news buddy. Call me immediately when you get this and you will owe me, pal, trust me."

Matt turns on his Camaro and pulls out of his parking spot, heading for home.

He figures he will call Sgt. Barton from home, before dinner with Kelly.

Matt hates being a hypocrite and loves writing tickets for 12-610.2, but this is an emergency.

Matt will take all of the side streets to get home and hopefully, not see a Morton Grove cop on the way.

He stops at a stop sign in the parking lot of the library and hits the "call back" button on his phone so he can find out Dugan's big news.

Dugan's phone rings only once before he picks it up yelling, "Jesus Christ, O'Neil, I've got huge news here in Green Bay Packerland! Where the hell have you been?" he asks.

"Sorry buddy, but I was in the Morton Grove library and needed to turn my phone off so I didn't bother anybody," Matt says before continuing, "But I got some unbelievable news which should help with the investigation into my shooting at 524 Short Street."

"Well, I'm happy for you buddy, but believe it or not my information could possibly top yours," Mark Dugan says.

"I doubt it, but bring it my friend," Matt answers.

"Sooooooo let's start with the smaller stuff first, such as Kurt Thompson went to high school with Tyler Hale," Dugan says rather nonchalantly.

Matt jerks his Camaro, making a hard right on the side street he's currently on, nearly striking the rear of a U.S. postal truck, delivering mail.

"Talk to me Mark, because this is incredible," Matt says, slightly out of breath due to the fact he had stopped breathing 30 seconds earlier.

"Yeah, I won't bore you with how I found this out but if you go to the website, Classmates.com, and type in Stoughton High School, year 2012, then search for the Varsity Football picture, you will find them in their purple and white Vikings uniforms. Hale was the team punter and Thompson center and linebacker on defense," Dugan says rather proudly in his effort to one up Matt.

"Holy shit," is all Matt can mumble.

Between this information and what he just received from Mr. Marquez; Matt can't get his head to stop spinning.

Matt realizes he also needs to try and figure out how this new information plays a role in the big picture of 524 Short Street.

"Yeah, thought you would get a kick out of that information, but it's really small shit compared to what I have next," Dugan says.

"You have something even bigger?" Matt asks, as he's just catching his breath again.

"Of course, I do," he says boldly, apparently, a Wisconsin State Trooper has to solve all of your cases down there."

He can envision Dugan talking into his cell phone and sticking his chest out.

Matt figures nothing else Dugan has information wise can possibly top what he's just given him, so he checks his side view mirror and convinced the street is safe, turns left, to get back on the side street and head for home.

"Well, I started dating this smoking hot Irish chick named Maggie, from don't laugh, Green Bay roughly a month ago," Dugan says with a tone in his voice like a proud father, whose kid had accomplished something great.

"Happy for you," is all Matt can get out of his mouth, before Dugan starts up again.

"Yeah, she's a technician with a private lab up here called, DNA Today." I met her when she came to testify for the defense, on a Criminal Sexual Assault case I was working, which of course I got a guilty verdict," Dugan says.

Matt knows better than to interrupt Dugan when he's rolling like this.

"Not sure how she did it, but she got my personal cell phone number and called me a week after the verdict saying she needed some help getting an Order of Protection against her ex-boyfriend. She wanted to make sure he was served with it, which I did personally," Dugan says proudly, while Matt listens on his cell phone while driving.

"Well, she also told me if there was anything, I needed from her, not to hesitate and ask. I was thinking, with her professional expertise and me being able to get all of the wine glasses and beer bottles from Detective Kenbridge's car from our class reunion and this really not being a criminal matter," Dugan's voice trailed off at the end.

Matt has to admit his curiosity is increasing by the second in this story.

"So, Mark, what did Ms. Maggie find out?" Matt asks, while stopped in front of his home, and waiting to turn left into his driveway.

"Brace yourself Matt," Dugan replies with a curious tone in his voice.

"I'm about as braced as I will ever be," Matt answers as his Camaro starts its left turn.

"Tyler Hale and Megan O'Brien are cousins, on her father's side," Dugan says.

Matt hits the brakes so hard on the word, "cousins", he almost flies over the steering wheel, due to not having his seatbelt on.

Apparently, Dugan is waiting for Matt to respond to this news so he doesn't say a word.

However, Matt can't talk because his heart has stopped.

Dugan must have gotten scared after a good half minute of silence as he says, "Matt, you still there? Talk to me, O'Neil."

Matt finally comes back on the line and asks, "Mark, do you have any documentation on this."

"Absolutely buddy, Maggie got me a copy of the report dated yesterday and the whole thing is legit," Dugan says and continues with, you want to know how we got Hale's DNA?

"Not right now, but we'll be in touch very soon, I'm home now and have to check on Kelly," Matt says as he slams the driver's side door shut after exiting it and runs toward the side door to his home.

"Understood," Dugan replies "and give her my best."

Once inside his house, Matt turns of his phone and repeatedly yells, "Kelly, Kelly," but gets no answer.

Pulling his iPhone from his pants pocket, he quickly goes to his list of favorites.

Quickly, Matt finds Kelly's phone number and dials it.

Patiently, he waits for her to answer.

Instead, her phone's distinctive ring tone of Adele's *Hello* plays from their second-floor bedroom.

Matt bounds up the stairs to their bedroom with his own cell phone in his right hand, repeatedly yelling, "Kelly, Kelly!"

Adele's sweet voice is just ending, but it still allows Matt to see the location of Kelly's phone, which is on the nightstand next to her side of their bed.

Kelly apparently had left it behind when she went off to work.

Matt turns and runs back down the stairs to the exact spot he was at in the kitchen less than a minute ago.

With their crazy schedules, Kelly had put an answering machine in the kitchen for them to keep track of each other's activities.

Matt looks carefully at it, seeing a red number one slowly flashing, indicating a message is waiting for him.

With his right index finger, he hits the play button and hears a stoic female voice advising him, "You have one message," before Kelly's sweet voice comes on.

"Hi babe, apparently baby brain kicked in again and whether you know it or not, I left my phone at home, which is why I'm leaving you this message instead of calling you. Anyway, I can't do dinner due to completely forgetting tonight is baby shower planning night. I would have completely forgotten if I didn't get a phone call at work reminding me this afternoon. Hey, I have to go since Megan's standing next to me in her kitchen and wants to get started. Love you, Sweetie."

"Megan's place?" Matt says slowly to himself.

CHAPTER 46

"Fucking, fucking woman," Kurt Thompson says out loud repeatedly.

"Why in God's name, does she have so many freaking issues, Max?" He finds himself suddenly screaming at apparently the only friend he has left in the world, his German Shepard puppy.

Apparently, Max has had enough and quickly runs into the family room, with his tail between his legs.

"Great, now apparently I'm pissing off four-legged friends also," Kurt says, totally pissed.

All of this frustration could be traced to his on again-off again relationship with Megan O'Brien hitting the skids.

Kurt was under the impression, like her injury, their relationship was on the mend, since he had been nursing her back to health after her gunshot wound.

Obviously not, as she had clumsily packed the few belongings she had at his place and went back to her place, while he was working in Gilles today.

Roughly 15 to 20 minutes ago, he had arrived home to find a brief note on the kitchen table, which read:

Kurt,

Things have changed in the way I feel about you. I'm really not sure where our relationship is going at this time so I believe it's best for me to go back home and try and get my head together.

Thank you for the great treatment you gave me after my injury. I will never forget you.

Your Friend
Megan

The last thing he wants right now is a female friend.

Kurt has a ton of male and a few female friends from his days at SIU and now he also has Max, who was looking at him like he was crazy, while hiding under a coffee table.

Kurt isn't totally caught off guard by this latest development, because he started to see her personality change the minute the Greenfield Police brass ordered her to go to therapy, due to her being injured in the shooting.

Megan hated going, which caught Kurt by surprise.

Even he had encouraged her to go, seeing nothing but benefits from attending.

"Honey, you're ahead of schedule on healing physically, so what would be the harm with your mind being in the same place as your shoulder?" He asked her the night before her first session with the Greenfield Police Department assigned psychologist, while giving her a gentle back massage.

"Wow, did that idea backfire," he thinks now to himself.

Their very limited sex life also seemed to hit the skids, soon after's Megan's first therapy session

More questions by Kurt only led to the infamous, "Everything is fine," sarcastic response from her.

He knew everything wasn't fine, but couldn't put his finger on why.

Not only was her personality changing, but her body as well. He started to notice it when she was staying at his place recovering, but thought nothing of it due to her physical injury.

But it really hit him when he was sitting across from her, at the ILETC reunion, in the Rockford VFW Hall.

Her skin tone had turned into a slight ghostly white.

Plus, deep bags had developed under both eyes and were purplish with tints of red also. A couple of times, Kurt caught Megan putting eyes drops in her bloodshot eyes, first thing in the morning, which made no sense to him because she was sleeping great.

Even though he was serving her an occasional Steak and Shake strawberry milk shake, which he would pick up on his way home from work, she had easily dropped four to five pounds and her clothes now fit loosely.

But being totally objective, Kurt was starting to realize she wasn't the only one whose body was starting to change for the worse.

He'd developed a sudden shortness of breath when he was jogging, a persistent cough and a general feeling of tiredness, which he couldn't understand.

Then, just like that, Megan was out of his mind and Jackie Stone was in her place.

Kurt never realized what a prick tease she would be, after how she acted during their initial meeting at the front counter, on his first day back from his suspension.

They had gone out twice since then and Kurt unfortunately, had been only able to get to first base with her.

"Even kissing her isn't as good as kissing Megan," Kurt yelled at Max, who apparently had enough and ran from under the coffee table, up the stairs, into a different room on the second floor.

However, Jackie Stone did tell him on their first date, "I'm being completely honest with you when I tell you I'm still a virgin and saving myself for the right man and our very special wedding night."

The perfect challenge in Kurt Thompson's mind.

But so far, his efforts had really been a waste of time.

It was time for him to use his go to line, "Jackie, I just came out of a really bad relationship, so I'm a bit vulnerable right now and not sure I can have my heart broken again."

This line worked twice at SIU and he was confident it might work on Ms. Stone, as long as he used the proper facial expressions when he said it to her.

Kurt couldn't get over all of the issues he had experienced, in his relatively young life, when it came to woman.

To be born into a family with a bipolar mother, was just the start. Then to go through his teenage years without a steady girlfriend, forcing him to be the only player on his football team to miss his senior prom, upset him more than he thought it would.

Finally, in the past 12 months to be dating a nymphomaniac in Francesca, an ice queen in Megan and finally a prima donna in Jackie, was more than most men could handle.

First, he needed to finally get closure with someone once and for all, before he gets to work on romancing Jackie Stone.

Looking at his watch, it reads 4:47 Pm, which he figures should give him plenty of time to accomplish what needs to get done and still get home in time for work tomorrow.

Max had already been walked since Kurt had come home from work, so his evening was free.

Kurt walks out of his residence and into his garage, turning on his home alarm in the process.

Getting into his car, he hits the ignition button.

Hearing the roar of his beast only gives him an extra boost of confidence.

"Coming for you Megan," he says softly to himself, never realizing Antioch, Illinois will never be the same.

CHAPTER 47

Matt O'Neil sprinted back upstairs at the completion of Kelly's message on their answering machine.

Upon reaching the second floor, he went straight to their bedroom and knew exactly what he was looking for since he had left it there earlier this morning.

Grabbing it off the Armoire he put the magazine into it, hit the slide release button and was set.

Carefully, he put the Colt Commander inside its pancake holster, which he had already put on his pants belt.

Running back down the steps, he went out the side door of his house, locking it after exiting it.

Once outside, he stopped for a brief second to collect his thoughts and make sure he had everything he needed.

Confident he did, Matt grabbed his iPhone from his left pants pocket, which was easier to do standing up, as opposed to sitting down.

Even though he had never been there, Megan's address of 1234 Love Rd. in Antioch, had been the subject of a ton of joking, mostly by her FTO'S and always behind her back.

Consequently, Matt had no trouble remembering her street and put it in his Maps-App on his phone.

Directions to Megan's house appeared to be simple, two left hand turns and two right hands turns would be all it would take.

From his home in Morton Grove, it showed straight up Dempster St. to I-94, which he would take west to Exit 176, for Rosecrans Rd.

Then he would travel south on Rt. 176 to her street, which was in the New Haven Complex.

The distance was 43.6 miles but Matt would be fighting rush hour traffic, which would add to his time of 55 minutes.

He backed out of his driveway and turned left upon reaching Dempster St.

Once on Dempster St. he headed west, swerving around traffic and heading for I-94. Every intersection he came to forced him to come to a stop due to a red light.

'Fuck me," he yelled when he came to his fourth consecutive one at the intersection of Dempster St. and Ballard Rd.

While sitting at the red-light Matt realized he still needed to telephone Sgt. Barton, but not before he collected his thoughts on what he knew to be true, not rumors or speculation.

The facts Matt had were Megan kept the information she was related to Tyler Hale a secret.

Tyler Hale was responsible for the deaths of Javier Ortego, Chris Mills, as well as T.C. Chambers, but there appeared to be no way of ever linking him to the death of Ron Thomas.

In regards to speculation, the minute he learned from Dugan about the Tyler, Megan connection, Matt believed they were working together in the killing of everyone.

Matt wondered what reaction Sgt. Barton would have to all of this, when he spoke with him.

Secondly, would Sgt. Barton come out to Antioch and confront Megan with him, especially now with all of this new information he would give him?

Matt grabbed his phone and proceeded to call Sgt. Barton's cell phone, but after five rings, only got his voicemail.

"Boss you need to call me the minute you get this message, due to just receiving some troubling information regarding Megan and Tyler Hale being related. Sir, it's not speculation but factual, since we have the physical evidence to prove it. I'm heading out to Megan's now so I will be waiting for your call."

At the completion of the phone call, for what was probably the fourth time today, Matt dropped his cell phone on the passenger seat of the Camaro and concentrated on his driving.

Traffic was congested at points but he was still able to dart through most of it and was making pretty good time.

He was so focused on his driving and getting to Kelly, he forgot he would be seeing it, until he was right next to it.

Great America's Goliath roller coaster, sitting at 165 feet in height and seemed to fill the sky.

It had been advertised as the tallest, fastest and longest roller coaster in the world.

Matt had hung out of a HH60 Pave Hawk attack helicopter, on a raid in Afghanistan and killed a man in hand-to-hand combat, yet he had one fear in his life.

Roller coasters, which dropped out of the sky at both record speeds and from record heights.

As he passed Great America, Matt again picked up his phone and hit the button on the bottom front of it.

Instantly, the home page for his cell phone came on, showing a picture of T.C. Chambers, Chris Mills, Kelly and him, on the Goliath roller coaster, roughly a year ago.

The look on Matt's face of sheer terror, brought back memories of a fantastic day among great friends. Granted, it meant three minutes of fear in his life, which almost made him change his underwear that day.

The smile on his face quickly changed to a frown as he realized in a strange, peculiar way, he had played a small role in the death of both Chris Mills and T.C. Chambers.

While lying in his hospital bed at Landstuhl, Germany, is when it first occurred to him.

A career in the military wasn't going to be in his future.

Nothing in the Navy Seals had caught him by surprise and he actually enjoyed most aspects of it, except for the part about getting blown up and nearly dying.

What had changed his mind, career wise, was how much his love for Kelly had grown.

Kelly was his future and he believed she wanted to start a family as much as he did.

Granted Coronado, California, where his Navy Seal Team was based was beautiful, but neither Kelly nor he were California people and the price of everything there just blew them away.

If only he could incorporate his career, with living in a small town such as Morton Grove, Illinois, as opposed to Chicago, where he grew up, he would be a very happy man.

Every chance he got; Matt would extol the virtues of what a wonderful life on the North Shore could hold for his Seal Team.

He couldn't wait to tell anyone who listened, about the fantastic schools, low crime, proximity to both downtown Chicago and State of Wisconsin and areas of some affordable housing.

When asked about jobs, Matt's answer would always be the same, "careers in law enforcement."

Apparently, his message was so powerful it convinced both Chris and T.C. to follow him.

Granted neither of them had lived in Morton Grove, but each became Police Officers for the Greenfield, Illinois, Police Department.

Now because of him, both were dead.

Matt couldn't think about it anymore as his phone said to him "Rosecrans Rd. exit one mile ahead."

Since he was doing close to 85 mph, Matt was off I-94 and on this exit, in practically no time.

As the Camaro rolled to a stop in traffic, he couldn't help but wonder "Why the hell would anyone live this far from work?"

He couldn't imagine what the commute must be like in the wintertime, after a long midnight shift, with truckers and snow on the roads.

From Matt's front door, to the parking lot of the Greenfield Police Station, on a bad day, was ten minutes.

To make matters even stranger, there were currently two members of his Police Department, living in Kenosha, Wisconsin.

When Matt asked them about it, both had the same story, "Bigger house for the money and lower property taxes."

Matt recalled asking Megan one time about the drive, when he heard she lived so far from work and she answered, "Every morning I stop at the B.P. Amoco on Rt.173 for my morning cup and if that place ever moves or burns down, I'm screwed."

As Matt approached this gas station at the intersection of Rt. 173 and Rt.45, his whole body tightened up, as he knew he was close to Megan's home.

In less than a minute, he was at the New Haven complex.

Making a right hand turn on to Savage Rd. he slowly drove down it, as it curled around the complex.

Love Rd. was the third street in and he pulled on to it.

The first thing he saw was Kelly's Honda, parked in a driveway.

Matt assumed this was Megan's place when he saw Kelly's car parked in her driveway, but he was shocked to see Marc Dombrowski's Ford Escape, parked there also.

Matt quickly backed his Camaro up; afraid Megan would recognize it the minute she saw it.

Grabbing his cell phone off the passenger seat, he placed it inside his left front pants pocket and next checked to make sure his Colt Commander was covered by his Under Amour sweatshirt, as he got out of his car.

He wanted to sprint to the front porch of Megan's house, but knew it would raise immediate suspicion by her neighbors, so instead, he slowly walked with his head partially down, towards the sidewalk.

With every step Matt took, his anxiety level went up, causing his breathing to become shorter.

It seemed like an eternity to walk from his car, to Megan's driveway.

In reality, it was only two minutes and upon reaching it, he quickly walked up it, between Kelly's and Marc's parked cars.

Instead of standing by her front door and attempting to hear something, he positioned himself immediately by a living room window.

Quickly he looked in and what he saw, nearly dropped him to his knees.

Kelly was seated facing him, in a brown colored, wooden kitchen chair.

She couldn't move, due to her arms and legs being flex cuffed to different portions of this chair.

Another chair was positioned directly behind hers, but facing the opposite way.

Seated in this chair was a figure believed to be Marc, due to his distinctive crew cut and physical build.

Matt could see Marc also couldn't move, due to also being flex cuffed to his chair.

Megan was standing with her back to Matt, holding her department issued Glock 22 Gen 4 near Kelly's face.

She was yelling and swearing at Kelly, but Matt really couldn't make out what Megan was saying.

Matt suddenly had a difficult time breathing and knew he needed to come up with a plan.

For a brief second, Kelly looked away from Megan and made eye contact with Matt.

Kelly looked at him longer than she probably should have, but she was in deep shit and needed her Navy Seal right now to save her.

Kelly then turned her focus back to Megan, who was still yelling at her and had moved the Glock from the face area, now to Kelly's forehead.

Matt's emotions were overruled by his training and he quickly moved pass the front door of the house, around the right side of the house, finally stopping by the rear door.

He was helped by the fact Megan didn't own a dog, thus no need for any type of fence in the rear of her property.

Upon reaching the home's back door, Matt was surprised to see it standing partially open.

He wasn't' worried about the screen door since with its flimsy lock he could just rip it open in a second or two.

Slowly he removed the Colt Commander from its holster, while trying the screen door with his left hand.

The screen door was also unlocked and slowly he started to open it. Carefully moving the Colt Commander to eye level, with his head tilted at a forty-five-degree angle to the right, he had a clear and accurate view of his target, through his combat sights.

In one quick motion he opened the screen door and quickly kicked the wooden house door, with his right foot, as he entered Megan's place, with two quick steps.

Matt was now facing Marc Dombrowski, who yelled from the living room," Look out!"

This would be the last thing Matt would remember for a while, as a blow from the butt of a Glock, to the left side of his head, knocks him unconscious and to the floor of Megan's kitchen.

CHAPTER 48

Matt O'Neil wakes up on the floor of Megan's living room. His head is exploding from the wound he has just suffered, on the left side of it.

Blood is slowly trickling down the left side of his face and occasionally, he shakes his head violently from side to side, to rid himself of it.

Only now does he blink his eyes to try to clear his vision, of what is in front of him.

What he sees is the love of his life, with a peculiar look on her face.

Instantly, Matt moves forward to kiss Kelly, only to be jerked back by the flex-cuffs, binding his wrists together, behind his back.

Instead, he moves his head slowly, until his lips and Kelly's are touching.

As he finishes kissing her, he notices instead of being soft and moist, her lips are slightly hard and cold.

He moves his head back a few inches and looks at Kelly's face.

Her expression hadn't changed from the time he had opened his eyes and found her directly in front of him.

Its only then he sees it, directly over her left breast.

A bullet hole, which is difficult to make out, since the wound is covered in blood.

It was the perfect kill shot, since it went directly into her heart, killing Kelly instantly.

"Jesus Christ, Sleeping Beauty, it's about time you woke up and joined us," Megan says, while standing over Kelly's body.

With difficulty, he looks straight up at a smiling Megan, who is holding Matt's Colt Commander in her right hand and his iPhone in her left.

"Man O'Neil, you really look like you got your ass kicked and can you believe it, by a girl?" Megan says and begins to slowly laugh.

With his head now raised and in a new position, Matt sees him. This individual's head is directly behind Kelly's.

Looking carefully, Matt sees both this person and Kelly's hands had been flex-cuffed together, again behind their backs.

"Marc Dombrowski, but his goofy haircut should have given it away," Megan says, with a huge grin on her face. "Speaking of giving it away, what in the hell took you so long to figure this entire thing out, Matt? I went out of my way to lead you here, with a bread crumb trail after I asked the kid in the Morton Grove library, Jamie Marquez, about the drug Setellmorie," Megan says.

When finished, she raises both of her hands in the air, as if she is a football referee signaling a touchdown. Matt isn't looking at, or listening to Megan anymore. For some reason, he is fixated on Marc and the bullet hole on the left side of his head, which obviously killed him.

"Yes, Matt he's dead and in a few minutes, you will be too. But, unlike him and the rest of the dead assholes from our shift, you may have a shot at joining your lovely bride and baby in heaven," Megan says.

Instantly, Matt looks back down at Kelly's face and then her stomach.

When he sees it, both his breathing and heart stop.

A same sized bullet hole, as the one over Kelly's left breast, is in the middle of her belly.

"NOOOOOOOOOOO!" Matt screams, as his eyes immediately fill with tears and a rage fills his body, unlike any other time in his life.

Instinctively, he attempts to get up off the family room floor, but the combination of flex-cuffs and Megan placing her left foot on his back, forces him back to the ground.

"WHYYYYYYYYYY?" he screams out of frustration and in the hopes a neighbor on either side of her, will hear him and call the Antioch Police Department.

Through tear-filled eyes, he looks up at Megan, all the while twisting and bending the flex-cuffs in hopes he can loosen at least one of them, which will allow him to stand up and strangle the bitch who has taken away his life.

Matt's a bit surprised to find the boastful, cocky, Megan had backed up during his rant, fearful of him.

Slowly, she begins inching her way back towards him.

Once she reaches him, she bends down and presses the Colt Commander against his forehead.

"Well Matt since I'm going to be pretty busy in a few minutes cleaning up dead bodies around here, including yours, I'll give you the condensed version. It's all I have time for and what you deserve," she says.

Matt looks directly into Megan's eyes for the first time, while twisting and bending his wrists, trying to loosen the flex-cuffs.

"Remember the night before graduation practice? The entire class, except you and I went to P.J.'s Sports Bar?" Megan asks.

Matt says nothing and continues looking directly into Megan's eyes.

"Well, it was around 11:00 Pm and my roommate Cynthia was off with her new boy toy. I was getting ready for bed when there was a knock on my dorm room door, which I foolishly answered," she says.

As Matt looks at Megan, she pauses for a few moments, both collecting her thoughts and suddenly breathing a bit heavier than only minutes before.

"It was Chris Mills and he asked to speak to me privately about an issue he was having. He asked me to open my door, which I did and it changed my life forever," Megan says.

"How so?" Matt asks quickly.

"Once inside, Mills was followed by the rest of the Greenfield Officers, with Marc Dombrowski being the last one. Marc immediately locked my door and stood against it," Megan says. She pauses again and suddenly starts crying hysterically.

With tears running down her cheeks, she suddenly stands up and walks over to where Marc Dombrowski's body lay.

Upon reaching it, she kneels down and presses Matt's Colt Commander to Dombrowski's chest.

Without a bit of hesitation, she fires one round directly into his heart, causing his body to jerk back quickly.

Standing back up, through a bit of smoke from the fired round, Megan walks back over to Matt.

Standing roughly an arm's length from him, she points his Colt Commander directly at his face and screams, "SAY WHAT THEY DID TO ME MATT!"

As calmly as he can, Matt slowly answers, "They Criminally Sexually Assaulted you."

"NOOOOOOOOOOOOOOO!" Megan screams and says, "I DON'T WANT THE CLEAN STATE STATUE FOR IT, MATT! I WANT THE STREET VERSION OF IT. SAY IT NOW OR SO HELP ME GOD I'LL KILL YOU."

"They raped the shit out of you," Matt says again as calmly as possible, in hopes of deescalating a situation, which is getting worse by the second.

"Like a lamb being chased by a pack of wolves, they fucked me. Each and every one of those pricks," she says, as her crying becomes worse.

For a moment, she lowers the Colt Commander, so it's no longer pointed directly at Matt's face.

Instinctively, Matt pulled with every ounce of energy he has left on the flex-cuffs, seeing this as maybe his last opportunity to survive.

The one on his right wrist starts to loosen a bit, while the one on his left wrist doesn't budge at all.

"I WAS A VIRGIN UNTIL THAT NIGHT," Megan begins screaming once again, "I HAD ONLY KISSED TWO BOYS MY ENTIRE LIFE," Megan yells.

Suddenly, she begins coughing and is barely able to catch her breath.

For over a minute, Megan continues coughing so violently, she walks towards the kitchen, needing to put both Matt's gun and cell phone down on the kitchen counter.

Then, she goes inside her purse on the counter and grabs some type of inhaler.

Matt continues pulling violently on his flex-cuffs.

Now, the left one starts to loosen, as well as the right one.

With her cough apparently under control, Megan walks back into the living room.

This time, she is only holding Matt's gun, leaving his cell phone in the kitchen.

When she stops, about a foot away from him, Matt calmly asks, "So you decided to kill each and every one of them, didn't you?"

"Of course, I did," Megan responds.

"Chris Mills?" Matt asks nonchalantly.

"Tyler said he was a piece of cake, the big fat asshole," Megan says "And he never saw the Bronco, until he was lying in the street, after it struck him. It was the perfect plan when I found the house at 524 Short Street to hide the Bronco."

Matt knows better than to say anything to Megan about Chris at this time, with the fragile mental state she's in.

"Ron, it truly was a pleasure killing, that gigolo fucking asshole. It was so easy in his drunken condition; he practically fell out of the canoe. Well, maybe I pushed him a tad," Megan says with a wicked look on her face.

"Javier, my little Latin lover, was the worst who fucked me. He actually begged for his life, before Tyler shot him," Megan says and then follows up with, "I had seen enough of his tickets and reports at work, to copy his writing style, for the suicide note."

"You needed to show Tyler where the key was hidden, didn't you? Matt asks.

"That was part of the reason, but I wanted to look in his and every other face of those motherfuckers who raped me," Megan answers.

"Tyler brought the shotgun but didn't shoot T.C. Chambers and Inspector Petrov, did he?" Matt asks, fearful of Megan's response, but needing to know the truth.

"Of course, not you fucking idiot. I almost got both with one round but man, they went down so fast and it's so amazing the damage a Benelli shotgun round can do," she calmly replies.

Matt is seething, but needs to stay as calm as possible and keep Megan talking to buy time.

He asks, "Wouldn't have been difficult to hit Tyler with a hypodermic after you killed the two in the front of the house?"

"Not a problem at all, for my drug using cousin, who would kill for me as long as I kept the drugs, weed and cocaine coming his way," Megan answers.

Matt continues looking at Megan and she realizes she hasn't answered his question, so she quickly says, "We were walking toward the backyard when I gave him the shotgun, to guarantee his fingerprints would be on it. He was smoking a joint, so it was easy to hit him with the hypodermic full of Setellmorie," Megan smiles broadly as she's proud of her accomplishment.

"Let me guess, by doing so, it would immobilize him behind the passenger door and then you buried the hypodermic quickly under a tire of the Bronco," Matt says.

"Not bad O'Neil, sooooooo take it the rest of the way," Megan says, with a weird grin on her face.

"This way he couldn't move and was an easy target for me to kill, but from the ground you also shot at me didn't you"? Matt finishes up with.

"Bravo Matt, but I fucking missed you due to being in so much pain from my self-inflicted gunshot wound to my left shoulder," Megan says rather softly.

"WHY KILL KELLY, WHO HAD NOTHING TO DO WITH ANY OF THIS?" Matt yells, realizing it's too late, in all probability, to save himself, since he's making no new progress with the flex-cuffs and can't get to his phone.

"My life is over Matt and soon yours will be also. I needed to get both Kelly and Marc up here for the murder suicide lover's triangle angle, I will be pushing to the NORTAF team. They will be handling this mess later today," Megan says and actually begins giggling, to the amazement of Matt.

Matt is very confused, but thankful at least now he has something new to work with, to keep him alive a bit longer.

"Juanita and you as lovers Matt, you think we didn't hear the rumors about this throughout the police department, when the NORTAF Investigators questioned you about it?" Megan asks.

Matt knows where Megan is going with this, but he wants her to spell it all out for him and buy more time, so he remains quiet.

"Kelly found out about this and decided to get even with you by seducing someone who you would never suspect. Consequently, she picked the wimp, Marc Dombrowski. It was her idea to use my house for this romance, which you found out about and took matters into your own hands with your Colt Commander." Megan smiles proudly of the way she has just spelled out her plan.

Once again, Matt remains quiet, trying to come up with some type of idea to save his life.

"Just a couple of small details I omitted," Megan continues. "I will tell Investigators your lovely bride asked to borrow a spare key to this place. I will tell them, she needed to set it up for a baby shower, I would be throwing for her, when in reality it was to meet her lover. Secondly, you will be killing yourself by placing this Colt Commander under your chin. Once your dead, I will make sure your fingerprints, covered in your own blood are on it. Finally, both Marc and Kelly were killed with your gun, so thanks for bringing it today, but I knew you would asshole."

When finished, Megan actually takes a bow, as if she is performing in a Broadway play, which has just ended. Apparently, the combination of speaking so long, combined with the bow, had been too much for her.

Once again, a coughing spell comes upon her.

This time, it is twice as severe as the first one.

For a full two minutes, Megan continues coughing and is totally distracted from what Matt is doing.

The right flex-cuff has been reduced to only covering fifty percent, of his right wrist.

Unfortunately, he's making no progress with the left one.

Instinctively, he begins softly praying for some type of miracle to save his life and end Megan's. Matt is shocked when seeing a slight trace of blood on her left hand, makes him realize something from what she had just said.

"Why did you say your life is over a few minutes ago Megan?" Matt asks.

"Because basically it is," Megan says and has already removed a few Kleenexes from her right front blue jean pocket, and is slowly wiping the corners of her mouth.

Matt realizes he has some extra time to play with, and decides to keep his mouth shut.

"I was an honest to god, good person Matt, when I went to the Illinois law Enforcement Training Center. All I wanted to do was be a good cop, meet someone and raise a family with four to five kids, before these assholes took it all away from me," Megan says, before quickly continuing

"My doctor tells me I have a very rare form of Mycoplasma Genitalium, and the only way you can acquire this disease is through sexual contact. Because I was a virgin entering ILETC, and didn't have sex with anyone until I was raped, I had a pretty good clue how I obtained it," Megan says in a matter of fact tone this time, instead of yelling.

Matt sees an opening to buy even more time and replies simply, "Tell me about the disease".

"Nice try Matt, but all you need to know is the fact it's a sexually transmitted disease and one of the side effects of it, is the fact it causes tubal infertility" Megan says and again in an amazingly calm voice.

"They took away your ability to have children, didn't they"? Matt asks, in the most caring voice he can muster, considering the circumstances.

"Yes, "Megan replies softly and she suddenly walks over to where Matt is and kneels down, directly in front of him.

"Exactly and since I can never have children, why should you have one, your kid wouldn't have any parents to love and care for them anyway?" Megan says.

Matt immediately closes his eyes both in anger, but also not wanting to see what's going to happen to him next.

"Since I only had an idea of who gave it to me but wasn't sure, I needed to kill each and every one of them. Trust me, Kurt Thompson, is next on my hit list," Megan says and begins inching forward on her knees to kill Matt.

The sound of breaking glass from the middle of the back door and Kurt Thompson's voice yelling, "REALLY," causes Megan to stop and turn, partially raising Matt's gun toward the door.

The target area for Kurt's rounds has increased drastically, with this reaction by Megan, who never had a chance.

The three rounds from Kurt's off duty, Glock 17, hits the left side of her chest, killing her instantly.

CHAPTER 49

One man stands at a gravesite located at St. Adalbert's catholic cemetery in Gilles.

Three miles down Milwaukee Avenue, another man stands over a gravesite, at Mary Hill cemetery.

What these two men have in common is the gravesites they stand by, hold the bodies of women they once loved.

Yet, the difference between the two men is, one gravesite holds the body of a woman who was the love of his life and the future mother of their child.

The other gravesite holds a former friend, who he killed in a rare situation, to save the life of someone he really doesn't care for.

"God, I miss you babe," Matt O'Neil says softly, as he stands now all alone, on the left side of Kelly's gravesite, on the same ground where one day, he will be buried next to her.

It's been eight days since he lost his wife to the hands of Megan O'Brien.

Unlike all of the other Greenfield Officers' deaths, Megan's death barely makes the newspapers and there is no wake.

Kelly's death, on the other hand, was handled as a festival of life, with her father using Simpkins Funeral Home in Morton Grove to hold her wake and spared no expense. A Lady of Guadalupe casket, white in color, held Kelly's damaged body.

Her casket was surrounded by rows and rows of flowers, holding cards from all who sent them.

Megan's body was released to the only individual who claimed it.

He used a simple pine wood casket to place her body in.

The turnout for Kelly's wake was big, but nothing like her funeral.

Out of respect for Matt, over seventy percent of the Greenfield Police Department had attended, led by Acting Chief of Police, Andrew Bart.

The mass was held at St. John Brebeuf and Pastor Ray Barlog gave the sermon of his life, touching nerves of every person who attended.

One lone hearse, followed by a single vehicle, Ford Cobra, was the entire funeral procession for Megan O' Brien.

Since both the church and cemetery for Kelly are in Gilles, Matt expected the trip would have been uneventful for Kelly's thirty-five car funeral procession.

Instead, Gilles Police Officers and auxiliary police officers blocked every intersection for traffic control, which didn't go unnoticed by Greenfield police personnel.

Megan O'Brien's casket sat, while two employees of Mary Hill cemetery worked feverishly to finish her gravesite.

After a series of prayers, Kelly O'Neil's casket was slowly lowered into the ground as tears flowed from the 65 people gathered around her gravesite.

Finally finished, Megan's wooden casket was also slowly lowered into the ground, as Kurt Thompson stood by it, all alone

Today, the sun starts to set in the west and clouds start to form over both gravesites.

The small bundle, wrapped completely in pink, starts to wiggle in Matt's arms and he looks carefully at it, but can only see her face.

"Thanks mom," Matt says out loud, even though they're all alone. Since his mom slowly and carefully wrapped her as she was being released from Ann and Robert Lurie's Hospital in Chicago, three hours ago, for the first time.

"She's been through so much, yet she's beautiful Kelly," Matt says, as he continues to rock her back and forth, slowly in his arms.

Suddenly Matt stops moving her and instead slowly transfers her into his hands, in such a fashion the baby is now directly over

Kelly's gravesite and looking directly down at her deceased mother's coffin.

With tears streaming down his face and falling on Kelly's grave, Matt can barely speak and it takes him a minute to try and compose himself.

Matt can't, but somehow in a mumbled tone he spits out the words "Kelly meet your daughter for the very first time, Maeve Rose O'Neil" and he bends over, lowering their daughter, so she's only inches above the grave.

Embarrassed by his crying, Matt suddenly moves Maeve, so now she's only inches from his face.

"You're a miracle, no you're our miracle," Matt says softly to his baby daughter, as his tears slowly fall on Maeve's face.

Almost on cue, as a tear falls on Maeve's closed eyelids, her eyes open in a dazzling display of blue, like her late mother's.

Matt wasn't exaggerating on the miracle part, since he had so many people whom he still needed to thank, for allowing Maeve to be alive and in his arms.

The list started with paramedic Phil Xavier, of the Antioch Fire Department, who was the first fire official on the scene, at Megan's house.

Acting quickly, he somehow found a slight pulse on Kelly and got her to Kendell Medical Center, in Libertyville.

Kelly was pronounced dead at this center, but then a team of doctors and nurses worked desperately, trying to save the baby she was carrying.

Matt's phone call to his father-in-law, Seamus Walsh, telling him of his daughter's death, was the hardest phone call he'd ever had to make.

Knowing time was critical, Walsh telephoned his former mentor at Engine Company 71 in Chicago, Captain Tommy Lyons, who had retired and now ran Shamrock Ambulance service, out of all places, Libertyville, Illinois,

Within 12 minutes of getting Seamus' phone call, Lyons was pulling up to the emergency room doors, in an ambulance, at

Kendell Medical Center. Quickly, the medical team had Matt and the baby in this ambulance and was headed to Lurie Children's Hospital, in Chicago.

Finally, to the entire nursing staff and team of doctors at Lurie, who were able, after two operations, to give Maeve a chance at life.

Almost simultaneously, although only five miles apart, both Kurt and Matt kneel down today, at their respective gravesites, but have great difficulty in doing so.

Kurt unaware, due to a sexual virus, which is slowly killing him.

Matt due to having suffered both a concussion, as well as head wound and holding his pride and joy, now back in his arms.

Five miles apart, yet Kurt and Matt having injuries and illnesses caused by the same person, Megan O'Brien.

Each man, while still kneeling, takes a red rose they had for this occasion, kisses it and watches as they drop it on the respective gravesites, they're at.

Nothing in common, yet everything in common, when death is the final answer.

CPSIA information can be obtained
at www.ICGtesting.com
Printed in the USA
LVHW082032220621
690724LV00010B/85